BLOWBACK '07

BLOWBACK '07

When the Only Way Forward Is Back

FOR JEN,
THERE'S FEW HORSES
IN THIS STORY,
BUT IT'S A GOOD RIDE!

Brian Meehl

B Meehl

MCP Books | Minneapolis

MCP Books
322 1st Ave North, 5th Floor
Minneapolis, MN 55401
612.455.2293
www.mcpbooks.com

Summary: Clashing teenage twins, Arky and Iris, uncover a family secret
that triggers a battle spanning three centuries. It begins when Iris sends
Arky's troubled friend and star quarterback, Matt, back to 1907 and the
Carlisle Indian School. While Matt is forced to play football on the Indian
team that will change football forever, Arky and Iris make a discover that
might bring him back and lead to the ultimate rescue: their mother, who
vanished a year before.

ISBN-13: 978-1-63505-186-5
LCCN: 2016912060

Distributed by Itasca Books

Edited by Gerri Brioso
Cover Design by Elizabeth Mihaltse Lindy
Typeset by M.K. Ross

Printed in the United States of America

First Edition

For my friends in sport,
on and off the field.

blowback

when things travel in a direction opposite of the usual one:
unintended consequences

PART I

ENSEMBLE

1.

TWO-AND-A-HALF MUSKETEERS

Arky Jongler-Jinks ran along the trail winding through the woods. His gold shorts and singlet rippled in the cool air. As his running shoes sprang off the ground, his brain fired questions. *If I'm running 13 miles per hour and the earth spins at 800 mph, does that mean I'm running backwards at 787 mph? If I'm running backwards at 787 mph, shouldn't I be dumped on my ass and turned into a skid mark?* Arky concocted brainteasers when he raced to keep his mind off his aching legs and burning lungs.

As he closed the gap on a red-suited runner, he fired the answer. *Galilean relativity: the law of uniform motion in an isolated system. Just as people in a moving car keep uniform motion, the earth is a giant tour bus spinning at 800 mph.* He passed the City High runner. *And I'm jumpin' to the front of the bus!*

The City High kid fired the only thing he had left that might catch Arky: spit. The white glob fell in the poison ivy lining the trail.

"Sorry, dude!" Arky shouted as he churned into his 500-meter kick. "Gravity hates a spitter!"

A year earlier, such thoughts had not tumbled through Arky's mind as he ran cross-country, nor did he have the times he had been clocking this season. The previous year he had been a back-of-the-pack tenth grader. Coach Skeller's assessment had been blunt: "Arky, if you could run off with your legs the way you run off with your mouth, you might be a runner." Now a junior, Arky had something no coach could instill: an obsessive desire to kick everyone's ass.

What had transformed Arky from tortoise to hare wasn't a

growth spurt; he was still short and only tipped the scales at 130. What had made him a good runner was one event. A year before, the Monday after Thanksgiving, his mother had vanished.

Whether Dr. Octavia Jongler had abandoned her family or been abducted by some psychopath was unknown. In the months that followed her disappearance, the lack of a ransom note or the discovery of a body pointed to abandonment; she had left her husband, Howard Jinks, and deserted their teenage twins, Arky and Iris Jongler-Jinks.

By the time the next Thanksgiving had come and gone, Arky had lost hope that their mother would ever be found, dead or alive. He had steeled his heart and moved on. Part of that moving on was running like a fox being chased by hounds. And not only in 5Ks; he had a personal marathon to run. It began with escaping the idiocy of high school and getting out of Belleplain. He would get into Harvard or Yale, become a Rhodes Scholar and conquer the world.

Arky churned past two more runners and crossed the finish line. He had placed third overall, been the first North High Cyclone to cross the line, and clocked a new personal best.

After pulling on his warm-up suit, Arky jogged across the athletic field toward North High's stadium. Large grandstands rose from both sides of the football field. The school had about 1,200 students and, like many places in the Midwest, football was king.

Arky moved down the rows of bench seats, picked one, and swung a leg up to stretch his hamstring. The stands held a sprinkling of students who had come to watch the Cyclones in their last practice before the big game. The next night the Cyclones were playing in the semifinals of the state championship. The winner would advance to play for the ultimate boast: state champs.

Arky's best buds were seniors and top jocks at North. Matt

Grinnell was the Cyclones quarterback who lived up to his number: 10. Matt was on track for a Division 1 scholarship and maybe the NFL. Danny Bender, the ace pitcher on the baseball team, also played football. While Danny had the lanky build of a wide receiver, he excelled as a defensive back. No one expected a guy built like a spider to hit like a train blasting a car off the tracks.

Arky watched Matt take a snap, drop back and launch a bomb. The football spiraled true as a bullet against the blue sky. The ball descended toward Tripp Olson, Matt's go-to receiver. Tripp gathered it in and got hit by Danny Bender. The ball popped out like a loogie from a llama.

A whistle split the air. "Bender!" the head coach shouted. "It's no-contact! What is it about no-contact you don't get?"

Danny raised his long arms in an *Oops* gesture. "Sorry, Coach, thinkin' tomorrow night."

"Hey, Danno," Matt yelled downfield. "Rewind it twenty-four before you hurt someone."

"Check!" Danny spun his hands down and grabbed his crotch. "Got my hands on the joystick."

The team cracked up.

A voice bullhorned from the stands. "What's it gonna be, boys, state champs or slapdicks?"

The field went quiet. While the players often talked over Coach Watson, they shut up for the man with the bullhorn, Gunner Grinnell. Gunner was a former Div 1 quarterback who had taken his Big Ten team to three bowl games and been a first-round draft pick in the NFL. His dream ended halfway through his rookie season when Gunner dumped his motorcycle and destroyed a knee.

Gunner continued through his bullhorn. "Coach, how 'bout we see the same air-out to the strong side?"

Watson shrilled a whistle blast. "Let's do it!" The coach

resented Gunner's intrusions but endured them. After all, Gunner knew the game inside out and his meddling was almost over. Friday night, college recruiters would be watching Matt's every move. If he could lead the Cyclones over the Lakeside Spartans, it would be a win-win: Watson would take his first team to the state finals and Gunner Grinnell would be one game away from shutting up and going back to selling cars and trucks at his Ford dealership.

Arky watched the team run the play to the right. As Matt lofted another soaring spiral, Arky felt a pang of envy. He had always wanted to play football but he lacked the stats. Matt was six two, 210 pounds of muscle; Danny was six three, 180. Arky was five six and skinny as a thumb drive. For Arky, football and cross-country were opposites. Cross-country was running through the woods like a Roman messenger. Football was stepping into the Coliseum and fighting like a gladiator. It wasn't Arky's fault he was a gladiator trapped in a messenger's body. He blamed his twin sister; sharing a womb had been a size restrictor.

As practice broke up, Matt walked toward the fence where his dad was waiting. Pulling off his helmet, Matt's long black hair fell over his shoulder pads. His hair was a compromise Matt had made with his dad: he could grow his hair to his knees as long as it stayed under his helmet. No son of Gunner Grinnell's was going to be a "showboat."

Matt approached the fence and braced for the list of dos and don'ts his father delivered after every practice and game. Years ago, Matt had resigned himself to being half of a sports cliché—the father's dashed dream would be made real by the son. Matt would win the trifecta Gunner had lost: All-State, All-American, All-Pro.

To Matt's surprise, his father greeted him with a smile. "You looked good out there."

A compliment was even rarer. Matt rolled with it. "Arm feels good; I just hope Tripp holds onto the ball tomorrow."

"Which is what I wanna talk about."

Matt wasn't sure where this was going. "Got a new play you haven't told me about?"

"Not a new play," Gunner said. "A new look."

A warning bell sounded in Matt's head. "What do you mean? A formation?"

"Yeah." Gunner pointed at Matt's mane of hair. "The formation around your head."

Matt frowned. "Dad, we've got a deal."

Gunner raised a hand. "Just hear me out. Tomorrow's semi is a big game. There are gonna be mega scouts watching your every move. You gotta show 'em 100 percent football, not 90 percent football and 10 percent attitude. The hair, the renegade thing, I get it. You gotta be different. But scouts can smell it a mile away. Every other player can go renegade, but not a QB starting out. They wanna see a leader."

Matt was steamed by his dad wanting to rip up their deal. "Tomorrow night, I'll show 'em so much football, they won't care if I'm wearing pigtails. If my hair makes me look like a shitty leader, that's their problem, not mine!"

Matt, Danny and Arky headed for Matt's F-150 in the school parking lot. All three wore black-and-gold letter jackets displaying the Cyclones' C. Despite the late autumn chill, Matt and Danny sported their off-the-field uniform: cargo shorts and flip-flops. Defying the weather was part superstition until the football season was over and part maintaining their tough-jock look until the first snow. Arky wore jeans and sneakers. Besides wanting to be warm, he didn't need girls snickering at his chalk-stick legs.

Around school the trio was known as "the two-and-a-half musketeers." Arky only tolerated the dig because he was the musketeer with the rapier wit. Under his mop of brown hair were sharp features, eyes that rarely missed a thing, and a tongue that could cut you to ribbons.

Even in shorts and flip-flops, Matt's flowing hair, olive skin and broad shoulders gave him the look of a swashbuckler. He had mastered the balance between cocky and cool that every quarterback needs.

Danny might have equaled Matt's heartthrob looks except for one flaw. His chiseled features and blond hair, shaved to a buzz cut, were compromised by jug-handle ears. The buzz cut signaled his own dream of escaping Belleplain. He planned to go boots-on-the-ground as a soldier, or cleats-on-the-mound in the Major Leagues. While the Majors were a long shot, becoming a warrior was not. He had dreamed about it ever since opening his first *Captain America* comic book. He *was* Steve Rogers: the skinny kid waiting to bust into manhood.

Matt drove his black-and-gold-trimmed pickup; Arky rode shotgun. Danny was sprawled in the backseat of the extended cab. By the time they left the parking lot, Danny had his hand-held PlayStation out and was racking up kills.

Arky turned to the virtual shooting. "Lemme guess, you got bored with 'Call of Duty' and you're playing 'Die Zombie Gamers.'"

Danny ignored him as Matt asked, "'Die Zombie Gamers,' is that a new one?"

"Yeah," Arky quipped, "it's about putting zombie gamers out of their misery after their thumbs fall off from too much gaming."

Danny didn't look up. "Hey, little man, you take AP courses, I train to be a Navy SEAL."

"That's not training to be a SEAL," Arky retorted. "That's training to sit in a trailer in Vegas and fly drones in the Middle East."

Danny shrugged amidst a flurry of shooting. "If that's how it works out, my first drone strike will be to smoke your ass."

Matt laughed at Danny's surprising zinger.

Arky fired back. "I'd respond to that, Thumbelina, but I don't wanna turn you into a quivering noodle before tomorrow's game."

"Speaking of tomorrow," Matt interjected, "the party's still on, right?"

"Of course," Arky answered. "As long as my dad goes out of town and you big sticks beat the Spartans."

Matt arched an eyebrow. "Are you saying the party's off if we lose?"

Arky shrugged. "Just keeping the pressure on."

Matt replied with a dismissive huff. "Back in Roman times, Spartans wore skirts, right?"

"Spartans would be *Greek* times," Arky corrected. "But yeah, Spartans wore skirts."

"So tomorrow night they're gonna get rocked on their heels and throw up their skirts."

Arky grinned. "Just like the girls at the party?"

Matt slid him an assured look. "Your party, you make the rules."

The pickup pulled into a semicircular drive fronting a two-story colonial. Arky jumped out.

Danny, still working his handheld, emerged from the back to get in the front. Matt cut the engine and got out. Danny looked up. "Where you goin'?"

"Gotta pay a visit to Doctor TD," Matt answered.

"You're a day early for juju."

Following Arky, Matt tossed back, "Never too early for juju."

Danny folded himself into the passenger seat and dove back into Game World.

2.

MUSIC GEEK

Matt had a thing for Arky's house. It was so unlike the Grinnell house, with its picture-perfect furniture surrounded by shelves and walls displaying the sports heroics of father and son, Gunner and Matt. The difference wasn't surprising given their contrasting parents. Matt's dad sold cars; his mom sold houses. Arky's parents sold knowledge. Howard Jinks was a history professor at Belleplain University; Dr. Octavia Jongler, before she had disappeared, had been an astrophysicist at the university.

Coming through the front door, Arky went into the kitchen and dumped his backpack on the center island.

Matt moved through the entrance hall into the living room. It reminded him of a museum that had run out of space. The room was crammed with Mr. Jinks's and Dr. Jongler's two obsessions, history and science. Howard's passion for the American Civil War and Octavia's fascination with "spacetime" had sparked a turf battle throughout the house. Displays of muskets, pistols, sabers and tattered flags crowded the walls. His decorative wall-grabs had been answered with her collections of time and space. The musket hanging over the fireplace was partially obscured by a statue of Father Time on the mantle with his hourglass and scythe. A table made from a sundial was cluttered with real hourglasses and ancient clocks. The stone wheel of a Mayan calendar hung on one wall. In the center of the wheel, a scary, tongue-lolling face glared across the room at a print of a wildhaired physicist juggling the planets in their spherical orbits. The only thing the clashing collections of war and spacetime had in common was a layer of dust.

While Matt delighted in the eccentricity of it all, one object had triggered his imagination more than any other.

Matt crossed the living room to a bay window looking out on a deck. Next to the window was a marble pedestal. Standing on the pedestal was a wooden figure, about a foot high, of an ancient Egyptian. The man had a headpiece like King Tut. Above the Egyptian's head, like horns, human arms lifted in the sign of a touchdown. Even though a plaque at the bottom of the statue identified the figure as KA, Matt was convinced it was a case of mistaken identity. Anyone with a set of arms on top of his head signaling a touchdown had to be Dr. TD.

The first time Matt had spotted the statue, before a big game in the previous season, he had jokingly dropped to his knees, sworn allegiance to "Dr. Touchdown" and asked the statue to rack up the score in the game. Dr. Touchdown delivered, and the Cyclones won the game. The week after, when Matt failed to visit the Egyptian statue, the Cyclones suffered a humiliating defeat. Since then, Matt had never missed a pregame visit to his football god. It was as much a part of his ritual as having his mother make him a five-egg omelet containing a four-leaf clover.

Matt's devotion to Dr. TD had not escaped Arky, who thought all superstitions were bogus. He was certain everything boiled down to science: sports, life, even getting girls. Which explained why Arky had never had a girlfriend. But he didn't challenge Matt's superstitious rituals. A gladiator had to do what a gladiator had to do.

Matt knelt before the statue and raised his arms, mimicking Ka. "Doctor TD, tomorrow night, the semis. Okay, I just found out that our enemy, the Spartans, wear skirts. So I'm hoping you'll help us stomp their girlie butts. I'm asking you, Doctor TD, to use your awesome mutant powers to shower us with touchdowns and give us the W. If you do, we will go to State and bring home the trophy."

He lowered his voice so Arky couldn't hear him from the kitchen. "One more thing, TD. I've been having some twisted thoughts. You know, the kind of stuff you don't take into a game. So, if you could just zap 'em outta my head, I promise you this"— he resumed in full voice—"when we bring home the trophy, I'll fill it with brew and we'll drink to the mind-blowing awesomeness of the great god of football! Two, three, break!" Matt clapped his hands and jumped to his feet.

Unbeknownst to Matt, his beseeching of Dr. TD had been witnessed by Arky's twin sister, Iris. Standing on the other side of the room and holding a black oboe case, she took him in with the bemused expression of *Really?*

Iris shared her brother's slight build and dark hair. The resemblance ended there. While Arky's face was edges and planes, Iris's was softened with baby fat. She was pretty but did a good job hiding it. Bangs covered her forehead and her medium-length hair was tucked behind her ears. Her eyes peered through black-framed glasses. The only jewelry she wore were earrings, always unmatched, usually some kind of big feather in her left ear and a smaller array of earrings in her triple-pierced right. These included simple studs combined with hanging earrings of her own making. These "found-object fobs" could be anything from an antique safety pin to a presidential campaign button from a past century. She was a music geek in retro skin.

When Matt turned and saw Iris, he shook off his embarrassment with give-it-up honesty. "Whoa, busted." He flashed a grin that had launched a thousand crushes. He jerked a thumb at the statue. "Getting in my juju huddle with Doctor TD a day early." He flipped his hair and the subject. "How's it going, Iris?"

Even though she knew about Matt's pregame supplications to Ka, Iris wasn't done watching him squirm. "'Twisted thoughts'? What was that about?"

Matt felt his cheeks flush and tried to cover it with bravado. "Hey, that's confidential between me and the doc."

"Okay, but when you're playing in college, will you still be needing your football shrink? Will you be coming back before every game to see Doctor TD?"

"Nah." Matt waved a hand. "I figured I'd buy it from you and take—" He froze, realizing his misstep.

"It belongs to my mom," Iris said flatly. She never referred to her mother in the past tense. Every day, Iris woke up with the same thought. *This is the day Mom's going to walk through the door.* She was unflinching in her faith that Octavia Jongler was out there, somewhere.

"Right." Matt whacked his head. "Duh." He tried to think of something that would smooth the knit in Iris's brow. "When I'm playing Div One, we could FaceTime. You know, you, me and Doctor TD."

Arky entered from the kitchen with a soda and a sandwich. "The day you two FaceTime, I become a cyber terrorist and crash social media to the Stone Age."

"How do you know we're not FaceTiming already?" Iris jibed as she headed to the kitchen.

Before needling his sister for wishful thinking, Arky reminded himself to be nice. If he was going to pull off Friday's after-game party without their dad finding out, he needed his sister's cooperation. "Hey," he called after her, "I'm just trying to protect my sis from the paws of football thugs."

"We're not animals," Matt protested, following Iris into the kitchen.

"Yeah, right," she mumbled. Iris began assembling a sandwich from the cold cuts Arky had left out.

Looming over her, Matt held up his large hands. "Maybe I got paws, but they wanna do more than throw a football."

She chuckled. "I'm sure they do. But isn't that a line for your girlfriend, what's-her-name?"

Joining them, Arky supplied the answer, "Kelly," then whacked Matt in the arm. "Remember her, Tarzan?"

Matt put on a befuddled look. "Now Tarzan confused. Is my girl Kelly or Jane?" Encouraged by a chuckle from Iris, Matt grabbed three oranges from a bowl. "All I'm saying, Iris, is that I've always wanted to juggle. Since you know how, how 'bout throwing me a lesson?"

She glanced up with mock concern. "But juggling is a nerd sport. It would destroy your jock cred."

"Juggling isn't a sport." Arky took the oranges from Matt and returned them to the bowl. "It's clown skills."

Iris continued making her sandwich. "Whatever. Fact is, it takes more balls to juggle than play football."

Matt laughed as a horn beeped outside.

Arky seized the moment to end their banter. "Captain America's waiting." He pushed Matt toward the front door. "And you've got a game to focus on. You gotta be thinking three-step drop and release, not flinging fruit."

"Okay, okay," Matt acknowledged. "Iris, rain check on a juggle huddle?"

"A juggle huddle!" Iris echoed after him. "You're on!"

After getting Matt out the door, Arky scowled at his sister. "What are you doing?"

"Relax, I'm just messing with you." She cut her sandwich in two. "It must be tough being the second-born. You're always a step behind." She bit into her sandwich.

"Hey, I could've been first," Arky protested. "But even then I was a gentleman. I held the door for you."

Iris cringed. "Okay, okay, you win by gross-out."

3.

DODGING BULLETS

The door leading to the garage opened and the twins' father entered. In addition to looking like a rumpled professor, Howard Jinks had the frayed look of a man who no longer had a wife to tamp down his loose ends. He stopped and eyed his children with surprise. "My tempestuous twins in the same place at the same time? What's this about?" He held up a hand. "Let me guess. You've changed your minds and are fighting over which one of you is going with me to the reenactment this weekend." He swung his briefcase onto the island. "So, who's the lucky kid?"

Arky and Iris pointed at each other.

Howard enjoyed a laugh. "See, there's twinness in you yet! I wish your mother could've seen that."

Arky and Iris held their breath. They never knew how mention of their mom might affect their dad. He could let it slide or go into a funk for hours.

Howard glanced at the wall clock. "The Civil War Express leaves in an hour and seventeen minutes. If one of you is going, you'd better get packing."

They breathed a sigh of relief as Howard pulled a glass from the cupboard. The funk had been dodged.

"Got orchestra rehearsal all weekend," Iris explained.

"Got the big semifinal for State," Arky added.

"Right," Howard said as he filled the glass at the sink. "Who's got some good news?"

"I ran a personal best in the 5K," Arky announced.

"Awesome!" Howard offered a high-five. "Next year the

state record." Arky slapped his hand and Howard turned to his daughter. "And you?"

Iris cracked a smile. "I made a date with Matt Grinnell."

Her father blinked in surprise. "Really?"

She tossed up her hands. "Why does that seem so farfetched?"

He backpedaled. "That's not what I meant."

Arky jumped in. "It's okay, Dad. She's still clueless about the difference between an alpha male, like a quarterback, and the little omegas, like music geeks, who scurry around Matt's feet."

With half of her sandwich in one hand, Iris grabbed her oboe case off the island. "If Matt Grinnell's the alpha male, that makes you the boil on his baboon ass."

As she pushed open the door to the garage, Arky threw a parting shot. "I'll be sure to tell Matt you've been thinking about his boootocks!"

Iris resisted the urge to throw back the ammo she had on Arky and his jock friend: that the Cyclones' QB1 was having "twisted thoughts" going into the big game. She could always use it later, but for now, it was her secret. And Iris knew how to keep a secret. She let the door bang on her way out.

Howard forced a smile. "It's so good to be home."

"Look on the bright side, Dad"—Arky checked the clock— "the Civil War Express leaves in an hour and fifteen."

Howard pulled out a stool and sat. "From what I just heard, I'm thinking about canceling the trip."

Arky's gut knotted with alarm. "Why would you do that?"

"It's something your mother taught me: the *now* of family is more important than the *then* of history."

"Dad," Arky reassured him, "you don't have to worry about us. We're just a couple of snarky twins working out stuff that didn't get settled prenatal. We're just lobbing darts. You deserve a vacation from us. That's why you've gotta go and lob some

15

minié balls at—who are you this time, Union or Confederate?"

"Union, and we don't lob minié balls, we shoot blanks," Howard corrected.

"Even better, you'll come home without a scratch!" Arky's feigned enthusiasm couldn't check his smart-ass instincts. "And I'll make sure Iris doesn't have her friends over and keep the neighbors up all night blasting Mozart sonatas."

Howard gave his son a dubious look. "That's not at the top of my worry list."

Arky confronted his father's suspicion head-on. "Dad, if the Cyclones win tomorrow and there's a party at someone's house, believe me, it won't be here. Most of the players think our house is kinda creepy."

Howard tilted his head. "Really? How so?"

Arky regretted moving the conversation down a dark alley. He had to pull his dad back from thinking "creepy" was a reference to Octavia's disappearance. "I mean, the place is so crammed with old stuff it's like we're a bunch of hoarders living in a storage unit."

His father's brow creased. "That's how your friends see us?"

"Yeah, we're the Addams Family."

Howard glanced out the window and stared. "Minus one."

Arky pulled out a stool and sat next to his father. He had to stop him from sliding into the dark place that could sabotage everything. Arky played his most unused card: sincerity. "Yeah, Dad, minus one. There are only three of us now. It's been over a year and we've done everything we can. There's nothing else we can do. That's why you need to go to your first reenactment since last fall—to take a vacation from *all* of it, to enjoy a weekend shooting at a bunch of guys and come home in one piece. Don't you think that's what Mom would've wanted you to do?"

Howard took Arky in with watery eyes. "You're right." He chuckled. "You know, whenever I came home from reenactments, I always had to check and see if Mom had replaced some of my Civil War stuff with her stuff. She was sneaky that way." He stood up. "Maybe if I go away, she'll come back"—he spread his arms wide—"and take it *alllll* down!" With a hopeful laugh, Howard disappeared into the garage to pack the car with his tent and battle gear.

Arky breathed an uneasy sigh. He felt bad about invoking the memory of his mom to keep his dad on track for the weekend. But he had done what had to be done to save Friday night's party. That's what alpha males did.

4.

DOUBT BOMB

Friday at North High didn't feel like a school day. Schoolwork was eclipsed by the excitement of the semifinal game that night. The fan fever spiked at a pep rally in the gym that ringed the football team. The gym shook from boards to I beams. Matt and the players seated at midcourt were stone-faced and silent. The cheering kids and teachers knew what their heroes were up to: going Cyclone.

A Cyclone didn't just put on a game face; a Cyclone retreated into a vortex of violence that slowly turned inside him, building power and speed the closer he got to game time. At the first whistle, the churning vortex inside each warrior would explode into a massive cyclone that would blow and tear at their enemy until the last horn sounded.

After the pep rally, Arky hooked up with a buddy from his AP Physics class to catch a ride home. On game days, Matt drove home alone unless Danny's pickup was on the disabled list, which it often was; then Matt would give him a ride. But Danny was on the team, and part of Matt's pregame routine was to avoid "civilians."

As Arky and his buddy walked through the parking lot, Arky was surprised to see Matt's pickup ease up beside them. "C'mon." Matt motioned to Arky. "Give you a lift."

Arky looked puzzled. "I don't wanna mess with your juju."

"Since when did you start believing in juju?" Matt motioned again. "C'mon."

Arky waved to his physics buddy and got in the truck.

They rode in silence. Arky wasn't about to weaken Matt's inner cyclone with chitchat.

Matt finally spoke. "Party still on?"

"Yeah," Arky said. "My dad left a note before he left last night saying that when he was 'in Union blue and bivouacked,' his cell phone would be locked in the car. So if Iris freaks and busts us, the worst she can do is leave a message."

Matt shot him a look. "You haven't told her yet?"

"I've got my timing. You take care of the Spartans, I'll take care of my sister."

Matt's focus returned to the road. "Yeah," he said quietly, "but who's gonna take care of the thirteenth man?"

Arky's face pinched, thrown by the question. "The thirteenth man? Who's that?"

"Guess."

Arky sensed something in Matt's mood that was more than a Cyclone spooling up for battle. "Okay, eleven guys on the field make the *twelfth* man the crowd, cheering on their team. Every fan knows that. So the thirteenth man's gotta be Coach Watson."

Matt let out a derisive chuckle. "Not even close."

"Then it's gotta be your football god at my house, Dr. TD."

Matt frowned. "Wrong house."

Arky got it. "The thirteenth man's your dad?"

Matt nodded.

"You said someone's gotta 'take care of him.' What do you mean?"

Matt wrestled with the thoughts that had been hounding him. "For the first time ever, I wish my dad wasn't comin' to the game. I wish he'd never come to one again."

Arky stared at his friend. "Ah, that's not possible."

"Yeah, it is."

"Unless he gets hit by a truck," Arky pointed out, "I don't think so."

Matt slid him a sardonic look. "C'mon, Ark, I thought you

were the smartest kid at North. What's the way to guarantee Gunner never sees me play football again?"

"What's with the weird questions?" Arky countered. "You should be visualizing your three-play packages for the game, not fogging your brain with riddles."

Matt gazed ahead, but his eyes didn't seem focused on the road. "He can't see me if I don't play."

Arky blinked. "What the hell are you talking about?"

"Tonight might be my last game."

"No way," Arky protested. "The Cyclones are gonna kick ass, we're going to the finals, then you're gonna do what you've always wanted: Division One, Heisman Trophy, NFL."

"There's one problem with that."

"Okay," Arky conceded, "if you don't win the Heisman, it's not the end of the world."

Matt returned the quip with a tight smile. "It's skills and will, buddy. I've always had both. I'm not sure I've got the second anymore."

Arky stared at him. "You're jerking my chain, right?"

"I wish I was." Matt released a breath. "More and more I feel like it's all about the thirteenth man. Like I'm Gunner Grinnell 2.0. I can't shake the question: Am I chasing *my* dream or zombie-walkin' through his? And sometimes when I walk on the field, I get the creepy feeling that I'm not Matt."

Arky had never heard Matt talk like this. He wasn't sure where to begin. "Bud, this is *not* where you wanna be before a huge game."

"I know," Matt acknowledged with a shrug. "I just had to drop the doubt bomb on someone. You know, someone who wasn't on the team. I figured you could handle it."

"Handle it? I feel like I've been hit with hazardous waste. I need a decontamination shower."

Matt chuckled as he steered the pickup into the driveway fronting Arky's house. "You make me laugh."

"You make me crazy!"

The truck stopped and Matt put it in park. "I also figured you might give me some advice."

Arky returned his friend's gaze. "Look, I get it. Your dad's under your skin and it's making you think crazy shit like quitting football. You have to get him outta there. So why don't you come inside, confess to Doctor TD, and get him to do a Gunner exorcism?" He opened the passenger door. "I'm serious. C'mon."

Matt didn't move. The open door had filled the cab with sound: an oboe playing classical music. Matt leaned over the wheel and traced the music to an open window in the second story of Arky's house. "Is that Iris, playing her . . . whatever it is?"

"Oboe," Arky filled in, "but 'playing' is generous."

"Shhh," Matt hushed. He was captivated by the rise and fall of the plaintive music.

Matt's increasingly weird behavior compounded Arky's worries. First, he talked about quitting football, now he was hypnotized by oboe music. "Are you coming in to see Doctor TD or what?"

Matt listened for another moment, then pushed back in his seat. "No need." He flashed Arky a smile. "Iris and her oboe just knocked the thirteenth man outta my head."

Dumbfounded, Arky stared at him. "You're kidding."

"Nope." Matt kept grinning. "All is good."

Arky wasn't convinced. And it wasn't the only thing bugging him. "You're not having weird thoughts about my sister, are you?"

Matt chuckled. "Now who's having twisted thoughts? Don't worry, Ark, in Girls 101, Iris is a type."

"Girls 101?" Arky echoed. Matt's zigzags were getting hard to follow. "You've never mentioned Girls 101."

"Never had reason to," Matt explained. "But now that you're freakin' about me and Iris, it's time."

Arky answered with a *Bring it* gesture.

"There are three types of girls, Ark. A Vertical, a Horizontal and a Vertizontal."

Arky looked incredulous. "You're bullshitting, right?"

"Shut up and listen. A Vertical is a girl like Iris. I like talking to her, and now"—he waved a hand up to her bedroom—"hearing her music. But that's the end of it. A Horizontal is a girl who may start Vertical, out of necessity, but she becomes a Horizontal."

"Kelly's a Horizontal."

Matt wagged his head. "Pretty much. And the reason you have Verticals that become Horizontals is the ultimate test: to see if she's a Vertizontal."

"The ultimate girl?" Arky guessed.

"Exactly." Matt grinned. "The one who's the perfect balance between Vertical and Horizontal."

Nonplused, Arky fixed on him for a moment. "That is the stupidest, most simplistic, caveman way of looking at girls I've ever heard."

Matt shrugged. "It may be stupid, simple and caveman but it works. You should try it, bud." Matt put the truck in gear. "Now, I gotta go scarf down a five-egg omelet."

As Arky watched the pickup pull away, he looked anxious. Yeah, Matt's Girls 101 was a sign QB1 had reclaimed his grip on cocky and cool. Yeah, the omelet was a sign Matt was back to his pregame ritual. But oboe music defusing Matt's doubt bomb? Arky didn't think so.

Arky shelved his worries. There was no time. He had a ton of party stuff to buy. And Iris was home with the car the twins shared.

5.

SECRETS

In her bedroom, Iris was playing Francis Poulenc's "Sonata for Oboe and Piano." In February, it would be her audition piece for getting into a summer program at a top music school: Juilliard in New York or the Oberlin Conservatory in Ohio. Doing a summer program after her junior year would give her a leg up for acceptance into one of the schools for college.

Glancing outside her window, Iris saw Arky back their mother's Subaru wagon out of the driveway. She stopped playing. When the house went empty and quiet, Iris's insides were pulled in two directions: to recoil or rejoice at the silence. The silence was the sound of the void her mother had left, and an invitation to find her in the emptiness.

Iris reached under her bed and pulled out an old music case. The wooden case, scratched and darkened with age, was bigger than her oboe case. She put it on the bed, opened it and lifted out two dark wooden pieces belonging to a cor anglais, more commonly known as the English horn, the largest instrument in the oboe family. Unlike a modern English horn, which is straight, the pieces of this antique cor anglais were curved.

Whenever Iris twisted the instrument's long pieces into its bow-like arc, her insides twisted along with them. Its tarnished keys aligned along with the ivory inlay on the back of the woodwind. The inlay depicted a net or web. She lifted the pear-shaped bell from the case and twisted it onto the bottom end of the cor anglais. Removing her hand revealed another decoration. Carved on the wooden bell, in high relief, was a large black spider. She lifted a looped strap from the case, dropped the loop over her head and attached it to the cor anglais.

Iris never assembled the ancient cor anglais when anyone was home. It was her secret, and the greatest mystery surrounding the disappearance of Octavia Jongler.

A year earlier, Iris had been the first to discover their mother was missing. Iris had come home from school, seen her mother's Subaru wagon in the driveway, and gone into the house to find her. When she found the first floor empty, Iris went to the second floor and climbed a narrow stairway to the attic office where Octavia Jongler had been spending most of her time during the sabbatical she was taking from the university.

As Iris climbed the stairs, she sensed something was wrong. The door to the attic office was open; her mother always closed the door when she was up there. Finding the room empty, Iris started back down the stairs.

On the second floor, Iris noticed something odd. Her bedroom door was shut. Iris usually left her door open, except when she wanted privacy or was practicing. Going into her room, Iris was shocked to see on her bed a wind instrument she had never seen before: a curved cor anglais with a spider rising from the bell. On her desk was an old wooden music case, open and lined with purple velvet. Her most shocking discovery, also on the bed, was a crinkled note, as if it had been handled several times. It read:

Dearest Iris,

If you are reading this, I have gone on a journey: a "crossing" I am only beginning to understand.

The old cor anglais I have left behind has been in the

Jongler family for hundreds of years. I can't write any more about it. This will seem an absurd request, but I beg you not to show this note or the Jongler cor anglais to anyone, not even your father and brother.

It claws my heart to burden you with such a secret, but I *know* you have the strength to endure it. You are a Jongler with special powers. One day, your fortitude and patience will be rewarded with a full understanding of why I have taken this seemingly cruel leave from my beloved family. *Tempus omnia revelat.*

Timeless Love,

Mom

P.S. Don't be afraid to play the old cor anglais up in my office, in secret. It may reveal a thing or two.

Iris had immediately looked up the Latin expression. *Tempus omnia revelat:* Time reveals all things.

Obeying the request to keep the "Jongler cor anglais" and her mother's note a secret from her father and brother was the hardest thing Iris had ever done. With each passing month, as the aching void of her mother's absence grew, it only became more difficult. The one thing that eased Iris's anguish over keeping such vital clues hidden was the music that came from the old wind instrument when she had the chance to play it.

Iris climbed the narrow stairs to the attic. She held a double reed in her mouth and carried the curved cor anglais in front of her.

During the summer and fall before their mother had vanished, the attic office had been Octavia's "woman cave."

She had had the room soundproofed because of the unusual nature of her sabbatical. Octavia had purchased a modern cor anglais—most likely to shield the existence of the Jongler cor anglais—and claimed to be writing a book about a middle-aged astrophysicist dropping the world of science and taking up the challenge of mastering a difficult instrument. The challenge was eased by the fact that Octavia, like her daughter, had played the oboe when she was young. The book she told everyone she was working on was titled *A Year of Magical Playing: An Astrophysicist Explores Inner Space through Music.*

After Octavia went missing, the office was scoured by the police and forensics experts. Her computer yielded a log of her lessons on the modern cor anglais, a history of the instrument, and notes on the trips she had taken to Poland, where she researched the origins of the English horn, and to Africa, where she learned about the wood the finest woodwinds are made of. The only clue in the office pointing to Octavia's abduction or domestic desertion was a boxy antique safe, which had been left open and emptied. The police had speculated that Dr. Octavia Jongler had left, voluntarily or not, with a large amount of cash.

Iris knew better. The safe had been the hiding place for the ancient cor anglais, which, for some reason, her mother had always hidden from the family. That is, until she left it to Iris.

Iris opened the door at the top of the narrow stairs and entered the office. Because Howard wished the office to stay exactly as his wife had left it, nothing had been changed. The house's gable roof created two sloping walls, opposite each other, with a dormered window in each. The end walls were A-framed by the roof. One of the end walls was dominated by Octavia's desk and practice area. The opposite wall, painted midnight blue, held a display. Unlike her more thematic collections on the lower floors, the attic assemblage, her last, was a peculiar fusion.

Hanging on the deep-blue wall was an uneven circle of

large photos displaying galaxies and supernovas gyrating and exploding in colorful brilliance. In the center of this wheel of cosmic events was a black "sun" housed in a Plexiglas case. The foot-wide black disk was the cross-section of a tree trunk. It was African Blackwood, known as grenadilla, which was used to make fine wind instruments. Octavia had brought the cross-section back from her trip to Africa. Laid over this odd planetary system was what made the assemblage even stranger. Octavia had driven dark nails into the wall and, using white silk fiber, had created a giant spiderweb, with expanding radials and taut spirals. Her orbiting cosmos seemed to be caught in the web with the black disk of wood resting at the center like a silent, motionless spider.

Several weeks before their mother disappeared, when Octavia had been erecting this bizarre assemblage, the twins had asked her about it. The only explanation she ever gave was cryptic. "To be a scientist," she told them, "is to contemplate realms where reason does not apply."

At the time, Arky wondered if pushing air through the reed of an English horn for hours every day was beginning to scramble their mother's brain. Having watched her leave science in the dust in pursuit of music, he feared their mother was doing more than *contemplating* reasonless realms; she was mind-warping into madness.

Iris, as she had watched the attic display come together, had also worried about their mom's mental state. But weeks later, after finding the Jongler cor anglais, Iris realized there had to be a connection between the cosmic events caught in a spiderweb and the spidery decoration on the curved cor anglais. She didn't tell her brother about it, though. The secret of the Jongler cor anglais was still hers and hers alone.

The creepy feelings the spidery wall and woodwind gave her always disappeared when Iris sat in her mother's practice chair. She breathed in the silence for a moment, then secured the reed in the bocal, the bent crook at the top of the old cor anglais. She lifted the instrument, curving toward her hip, and sounded a note. Lower than the oboe, the cor anglais sounded haunted and forlorn. Iris played, filling the room with lamenting music.

Having mastered the simpler yet demanding fingering on the old cor anglais, Iris was always struck by how much easier it was to play than her oboe, and how beautiful the music sounded. Playing it felt effortless, as if the ancient woodwind was an extension of her body and soul. But there was something else the cor anglais gave her, something her mother called "special powers."

As well as sharing the secret of the instrument, Iris and Octavia both had a neurological disorder called synesthesia. People with synesthesia experience a cross-wiring of the senses. A synesthete might *see* music, or *hear* colors, or *taste* words. When Octavia and Iris played music, sometimes they *saw* it. Their music-induced visions were mostly geometrics or shapes, but sometimes they were more complex. In the past year, as Iris had secretly played the curved cor anglais, her episodes of synesthesia had grown more vivid and frequent. Every time a vision came to her, she hoped it would provide a clue as to her mother's fate, and a sign she was alive and well.

As Iris continued to play, a new vision did come. White strands floated across her visual field. At first she thought the silk fibers on the opposite wall were playing tricks on her. But the white strands drifted into a ribbon, like a musical staff. Brightly colored leaves began to appear and stick on the wavering staff. The leaves matched the notes she played. Mesmerized, she watched the leaf-notes grow brown and wither. Then they fell from the staff and drifted lifelessly to the floor.

Iris yanked the reed from her mouth. The vision was a rude slap. It's what her oboe teacher had been telling her about the

Poulenc sonata. "I hear the notes, not the *music*. There's no air under the wings. It doesn't soar!"

Iris sucked in a breath. Her auditions for the summer programs would be a disaster if the music from her oboe didn't soar from her soul.

6.

SEMIFINAL

After Iris returned the cor anglais to its hiding place under her bed, she went downstairs for a snack. She suspected Arky was plotting something when he walked in from the garage with two large bags of groceries, then went back to the car for several more. When she asked why all the food, he told her a few players were coming over postgame.

She eyed the overflowing bags. "That's enough to feed the team."

"After a game," Arky explained, "they can eat a mastodon."

"If it turns into a party, I'm calling Dad."

"Don't worry," Arky said as he carried the bags down the stairwell to the basement den. "It's just a few guys."

She called after him. "So keep 'em downstairs."

Because of the thousands of fans who wanted to see the semi-final game between the North High Cyclones and the Lakeside Spartans, the game was being played in the big stadium at Belle-plain University.

It was a perfect night for football. The air was crisp, and a gibbous moon hovered high above the oval stadium. The stadium lights turned the arena into a bowl of daylight. Twenty thousand fans had shown up, as well as a press contingent and more than a dozen college recruiters. The bands from the schools were already "locking horns" as they threw brassy versions of pop songs back and forth.

In the Cyclones' locker room, Coach Watson was finishing

up his pregame pep talk, a jumble of platitudes that always ended with, "This game is yours to win."

Matt had stopped listening and was immersed in his favorite ritual before a game: his pregame numb-out. He always took a minute or two to drain his body and mind of any and everything, to reduce himself to nothing but breath. Then he put his mind on free-range: whatever thoughts or visuals that visited him were free to come and go. He let them flow. As he felt his chest rise and fall, no thoughts or visuals came. But sound did: slow, lyrical oboe music, the same he had heard coming from Iris's window. The music curled back into the silence of his breath.

When the Cyclones burst through the veil of paper held by North's pep squad, the band was drowned out by the roar of 15,000 fans on the Cyclones' side of the field. It was a harbinger for the night. After the Cyclones exploded onto the field, they were soon ripping the Spartans to tatters. As a radio announcer put it, "The Cyclones look like a dog pack bringin' down a feral hog." By halftime, Matt had led his team to a 27-3 lead.

During the game, as the Cyclones racked up touchdowns, Matt noticed the occasional play call he knew his father had texted to Coach Watson from the stands. As irksome as it was, Matt couldn't complain; the game was a rout, and the recruiters in the stands had to be impressed by the Cyclones' QB. He was executing the game plan by the numbers and finding every hole in the Spartans' defense.

As Arky watched from the stands, his anxiety over Matt's mind-set had evaporated. He couldn't help but take a little credit for it. After all, lending Matt a sympathetic ear that afternoon had helped get QB1 back on track.

At the end of the Cyclones' 38-10 victory, Arky skipped the celebration on the field and hurried to his car. He had details to attend to before the party. First on the list was calling his dad's cell phone on the way home. As expected, Arky got Howard's voicemail. He was probably sacked out in his Civil War tent. Arky left a detailed description of the game—so detailed that the voicemail kept cutting him off. After several calls of his continuous play-by-play, a disembodied voice informed him that the message box was full. Mission accomplished.

When Arky got home, he called up to Iris in her room. He told her if she wanted to avoid the hassle of a few guys coming over, the car was hers to take to a friend's.

She appeared at the top of the stairs. "You're having a party, aren't you."

"Hey," he protested, "I was trying to be nice."

"You didn't answer the question."

"If it gets out of hand, just grab a rifle off the wall and shoot me."

"Unfortunately, the guns are wired to the walls and not loaded."

Arky snapped his fingers, feigning recall. "Right." He scooped up the basket of Hacky Sack balls Iris kept by the couch for juggling. "You can Hacky Sack me to death."

"Or," she warned, "I can call Dad."

He jabbed a finger. "Right you are. That's why we're gonna be on our best behavior."

After Iris retreated to her room, Arky went to work. The basement had already been set up with snacks and soda. The players were bringing the beer. Knowing the party would swell to the first floor, Arky did a sweep of the living room. He removed everything on tables and shelves that, if broken, would lead to the death penalty.

7.

PARTY

The basement den quickly filled with kids. The cheerleaders arrived with the keg Matt and Danny had procured midweek with their fake IDs. When the players showed up, the party, like the rising river of music, noise and revelers Arky had predicted, pushed upstairs to the first floor.

Responding to the encroaching threat, Iris came down from her bedroom. She found Arky in the living room, which had become a dance floor of gyrating bodies. She pulled him into the hall. His first defense was that his gathering had been crashed. She shot it down. Trying to gain some credit, he pointed out how he had anticipated party crashers and had moved all the breakables to the garage.

Iris didn't buy it. She pulled out her cell and called their father. When a voice told her his mailbox was full, her eyes narrowed. "I can't believe you did that."

Arky played clueless. "Did what?"

"Filled his mailbox!"

He feigned innocence. "It was probably all his Civil War buds calling him to go AWOL for a brew."

Realizing she was dealing with a pathological liar, Iris thumped up the stairs, delivering an ultimatum. "If anyone comes up here, I'm calling the police."

Arky got stools from the kitchen and set them at the bottom of the stairs. It wasn't much of a barricade, but he hoped everyone got the hint.

"Hey, Arky!" someone yelled.

Arky turned to find Matt holding a big cup of beer. He was

in his flip-flops and cargo shorts but his t-shirt was new. It was black with gold letters declaring STATE. All the players were wearing them.

Matt jerked a thumb toward the living room. "Wanted to see Doctor TD and thank his Egyptian ass, but he's gone."

Arky ignored the slur in Matt's words. He had played a great game; he had earned his beer buzz. And his quitting-football demons seemed pacified. "Doctor TD doesn't like loud parties," Arky explained.

For the next hour, Arky did his partying on the ground floor to make sure no one jumped the stool-fence and crossed Iris's line in the sand. No one did.

When Arky made it back down to the den, he found it crowded with football players and cheerleaders, along with other big-stick jocks and their girlfriends.

Matt's girlfriend, Kelly, sat on his lap. She was in her cheerleader uniform and wearing the white-and-gold button-down letter sweater she had earned playing soccer. Matt now looked more than buzzed.

Kelly tried to penetrate his boozy bubble. She leaned in with an elongated "Hel-lo," transforming it from a greeting to a demand for attention.

As Arky refilled his cup at the keg, he watched Matt grab Kelly's shoulders and turn her torso to the room. "Here it is, my Cyclone brothers," he proclaimed. "The reason we war up Friday nights!"

Arky tried to ignore how hot Kelly looked in her sweater, especially with Matt's hands gathering bunches of material and tightening the sweater across her boobs. Arky waited for the roar of approval to die down. "Wow," he deadpanned to the room, "I never knew anyone who went to war for a button-down." He got his laugh.

Kelly weighed in on being objectified. "No, *this* is why you war up." She planted a wet kiss on Matt and the room went frat house.

As the noise subsided, the sliding door opened and Danny Bender entered from the darkness of the backyard. He had been at the party most of the night but had slipped out. He held up a DVD in a paper sleeve. "Got it!"

"Got what?" Matt asked.

Danny waggled the DVD. "Game film of the other semifinal and the dogfaces we're playing for State."

The girls in the room shouted protests. Kelly led the effort as she turned to Matt. "Tomorrow the team does game film of the semi, *then* you do film for State."

Matt flopped an arm at Danny and the DVD. "No harm in takin' a peek at the last speed bump in the road."

Kelly grabbed Matt's chin and found his eyes. "Matty, you've said it a hundred times. There's an order to when you do what you do. When you get outta sequence, you get outta rhythm; when you get outta rhythm, bad stuff happens."

Matt gave her a rubbery grin. "I'm not outta rhythm." He bumped her up and down. "I got rhythm to spare."

The room erupted again in hoots and catcalls as Kelly gave Matt a whack on the head. He was the stud duck of the team, the school and her life. There was no saying no.

Matt waved a hand at Tripp Olson, who was sitting near the flat-screen TV. "Shoot me the remote."

Tripp pulled a remote off the media cabinet and tossed it to Matt. He bumbled the catch but gathered it in.

As Danny worked the DVD player and dropped the disc in the tray, everyone shifted for a view of the big screen.

Tripp asked the question that had slipped everyone's beer-fogged minds. "Who we playin', Danno? Wolverines or Raptors?"

"Wolverines," Danny answered, then slapped a hand to his mouth. "Oops," he muffled, "forgot the spoiler alert."

"Nuthin to spoil," Matt announced. "Iz all good." He hit the play button on the remote.

A picture flashed on the screen. It wasn't football, but a clip of two girls in a backyard pool, swimming toward the camera. One was Kelly, the other was Becca, Tripp's girlfriend.

Matt squinted at the screen. "Is it jus' me, or is the field really wet?"

Kelly and Becca, who was standing behind Tripp, were too beer-challenged to recall the video right off.

On the screen, Kelly and Becca reached the shallow end of the pool and stood in the waist-high water, as a voice behind the camera sounded, "C'mon, ladies, show us your tan lines." The voice was Matt's.

Recognition dawned for Kelly and Becca. "Shit!" they blurted.

On the screen, the same girls shared a laugh and simultaneously lifted their swim tops.

The boys in the den roared their approval. Most of the girls hooted and laughed at the Mardi Gras moment, except for Kelly, Becca and their allies.

"Turn it off!" Kelly snapped as she grabbed for the remote in Matt's hand.

He held it high, snatching it away from her grasp. "Grinnell to Olson!" Matt yelled, and tossed the remote.

Tripp made a one-handed catch, adding another reception to the night.

Kelly vaulted off Matt's lap after the remote. As Becca held Tripp's arms, Kelly captured the device. She punched a button— the wrong one—and the picture on the screen froze. The humiliation and raucous noise continued.

Kelly found the stop button and killed the picture. Groans of disappointment followed as she punched the DVD player's eject button and snatched up the disc. She spun on Danny. "Where'd you get this?"

Danny held up innocent hands. "Matt told me to bring it and say it was the Raptors-Wolverines game. I swear, I didn't know I was holding your boobs."

The room cracked up as Kelly's flushed face darkened with rage. "You didn't ask what it was?"

Danny stood ramrod straight and snapped a salute. "Captain America only gives his name, rank and serial number."

Kelly turned on Matt. "You're such a prick!"

"C'mon, Kell," he beseeched, "iz a joke."

She snapped the DVD in half on the edge of the media cabinet and hurled the pieces at Matt like ninja stars. "*You're* the joke!"

He barely got his hands up to deflect the DVD pieces. "Hey, watch the eyes."

Kelly turned to ice. "If the season was over, I'd rip 'em out." She turned and headed for the sliding door.

"Where you goin'?" Matt asked, looking startled. "You're my des'nated driver."

She didn't bother turning back. "Crawl home."

Becca turned on Tripp. "Did you know about this?"

Tripp answered with a helpless gesture. "QB One calls the plays. Receiver One runs the routes."

Becca spun and followed Kelly out the sliding door. The rest of the cheerleaders followed. When the homecoming queen leaves the ball, her entourage is sure to follow. The last girl to hustle out left the sliding door open. A cold draft joined the pall filling the room. You could hear a beer cup drop.

Arky stared at Matt. "Great joke. And the punch line is ...?"

Matt, looking sheepish, answered the best he could. "More beer for everyone?"

The nervous laughter that followed was punctured by a crash from upstairs.

Arky hustled to the stairs, taking them two at a time.

8.

CATCHING THE MOON

Iris didn't hear the crash. She wasn't in her room. The party noise had driven her up to her mother's attic office. Even though Iris was breaking one of her rules—only play the Jongler cor anglais with the house empty—she had taken the old instrument with her. No one could hear her playing, and the beautiful sound was soothing her anger over Arky hijacking the house for a drunken bash.

When Arky found the source of the crash in the living room, it wasn't as bad as he had feared. Someone had knocked a cheap lamp off a table. It could be replaced, and his father might never notice. Arky used the excuse of the broken lamp to herd the upstairs partygoers down to the basement where there was now room to spare.

As the party wound down and kids drifted into the night, Arky finally had a chance to talk to Matt. He was stretched out in a Barcalounger with his hair fanned out on the headrest. Arky pulled up a chair and sat next to him. "Are you gonna tell me?"

Matt lifted his eyelids enough to identify Arky. "What?" he mumbled, reclosing his eyes.

"Why you'd make such a stupid move and piss Kelly off."

"C'mon, Ark"—Matt managed a sleepy smile—"you know you've always wanted to see her boobs."

Arky frowned. "That's not the point. What if we saw more than that? What if we saw you two break up?"

"She'll get over it," Matt muttered.

"Lucky for you if she does." Arky kept pressing. "I don't get it. You were looking at a perfect night: a win, a buzz and Kelly.

Why blow it? Does this have anything to do with what you were saying this afternoon?"

Matt played dumb. "What'd I say?"

"Oh, just some crazy shit about the thirteenth man, and quitting football to flip off your dad, not to mention Girls 101. Does your big plan to reboot your life include dumping Kelly, your main Horizontal?"

Matt opened his eyes and found focus on the ceiling. "Maybe you're right."

"Right about what?"

He turned to Arky. "It's skills and will, bud."

"What are you talking about?"

Matt's gaze returned to the ceiling. "Football playbook, girl playbook, they have one thing in common: skills and will. Kelly and me have some sweet skills, no doubt there," he added with a sated smile. "But the will, it's fadin'. Football's no different. If you got skills without will, you're just a dumb jock. If you got will without skills, you're just a dreamer. You gotta have both. If you don't, you're just wastin' time."

Arky waited to make sure he was done. "Lemme get this straight. You're saying because you're leakin' will with Kelly, and because you're leakin' will with football, you wanna quit both? Just throw 'em away?"

Matt let out a laugh and pushed the Barcalounger upright. "I'm half-drunk, dude. I dunno what I'm saying. I just know that tonight"—he slapped a hand on Arky's shoulder—"thanks to some brew, I washed my dad outta my head." He worked an imaginary handle and made a flushing sound. "Pshhhhhh. Goodbye, Gunner. Pshhhhhh!" He leaned over the chair and looked into his imaginary toilet. "Oops, flushed my designated driver too."

Arky nodded. "Ye-ah."

Matt struggled to his feet. "Looks like I'll havta walk." He started for the sliding door. "See ya, Ark."

"Danny can give you a ride."

"Nah." Matt exaggerated his unsteady walk. "I'm practicin' my dodgin' and weavin' for the wolf pack." He slid open the glass door, made like it was a slice of daylight between Wolverines, and darted out into the darkness.

Still pretending to dodge imaginary players, Matt moved around the house to the front yard. The cold night air was having a sobering effect. By the time he reached the sidewalk, he felt wide awake. Awake enough to realize that going wide with Kelly's and Becca's boob flash had been a stupid move, as stupid as throwing an interception.

He shook off his regret, took a deep breath and stared up at the gibbous moon. It looked like an overinflated football. He struck a pose like a wide receiver reaching for a pass and waited for the moon to drop in his arms. After a moment, he fell off balance and tossed up to the moon, "'Kay, catch ya nuther night."

His eyes slid to the roof of Arky's house. A dormer window glowed with light. Matt had never noticed the dormer before. He wondered who was up there. *It can't be Arky's dad,* he thought. *He's gone for the weekend.*

The light in the attic went out, followed by Danny's voice in the backyard. He was saying goodbye to Arky. Other voices joined in, leaving as well.

Matt didn't want to see anyone and didn't want to be offered a ride. He wanted to walk home, alone. He ran and hid behind the tall bushes in front of the house. Wedged between arborvitae and the siding, he watched Danny and the last party stragglers pile into two cars and drive away.

In the basement, Arky filled a large cup at the keg, chugged it, let out a belch and filled the cup again. He sat on the couch and raised his beer. He knew it had been a good party because he had once read that a party is only great if it produces a scandal.

No doubt about it, Matt and Kelly had done that. He raised his beer. "To scandal."

Matt hadn't moved from his hiding place behind the shrubbery. He couldn't stop thinking about the light in the attic. His speculations had run the gamut, from the Jongler-Jinkses having a secret maid they were too embarrassed to tell anyone about, to the possibility that Mrs. Jongler had never disappeared; she had gone crazy and the family had her locked in the attic. Then he entertained his wildest guess. *Arky moved Dr. TD to the attic for safekeeping. But because Dr. TD comes to life at night, he was the one who turned out the light and is now back in the living room.*

As ludicrous as the idea was, Matt was overcome by an urge to see if Dr. TD was back in his place. If so, the football god had to be thanked for helping the Cyclones make it to State.

9.

BLOWN AWAY

Matt went to the front door and slipped inside. Going stealth, he stepped out of his flip-flops and shoved them in the side pockets of his cargo shorts. In the living room, he found the lights dimmed. Party detritus littered the place. He moved to the marble pedestal where the Egyptian statue usually resided. Dr. TD had not returned to his perch. It didn't stop Matt from addressing his absent god.

"Okay, TD, you're not here," he whispered, "but I know you can hear me. Thanks for the win tonight. When it comes to the next game, the showdown for State—which may be my last . . ." He shook his head and waved a hand. "Gonna save that for when we're face-to-face. Anyway, got a special request for State. Can you keep the thirteenth man out of it? We all got our assignments and coverages, and that's yours. You da man, you da god, and you're gonna take thirteen down."

Matt froze at the sound of someone on the stairs. He quickly retreated to the shadows. Iris came down in pink pajamas and moved into the kitchen. He listened as she opened and shut a cupboard, filled a glass with water, and came back through the living room. This time Matt recognized her pajamas: Hello Kitty. He bit his lip to hold in a laugh and noted a small triumph. Now they were even. She had him on confessing twisted thoughts to Dr. TD; he had her on Hello Kitty.

He waited for Iris's upstairs bedroom door to shut. As he moved across the living room toward the front hall, another distraction caught his eye. A patch of moonlight next to the couch illuminated a basket filled with Hacky Sack balls. Even though Matt was sobering up, he was still infused with enough happy juice and victory swagger to have his craziest idea yet.

Iris was about to disassemble the Jongler cor anglais when she heard a gentle knock on her door. She flipped the bedspread over the wooden case and set the old cor anglais on the floor beside her bed so her brother wouldn't see it if he opened the door. "You had your party. Go away," she ordered.

"It's me," the voice sounded through the door. "Matt."

Iris eye-rolled. "I told Arky if anyone came upstairs, I'd call the cops."

"Don't call 'em," Matt implored. "I just wanna thank you."

"Thank me for what?"

"Can I open the door?"

"No!"

"I heard you playing this afternoon. The oboe, right?" He waited for her answer. She didn't give one. "Anyway, it was really nice. It put me in the right head for the game."

She was flattered he liked her playing, but that was as far as it went. "I'm glad a music geek did something for the Cyclones, but aren't you supposed to be off celebrating with Kelly?"

"She's all pissed at me."

Iris frowned. "So you're bugging me?"

"I'm not trying to bug you. I just wanted to see you for a sec."

She didn't like where this was going. For all she knew, the "twisted thoughts" she'd heard him mention to Dr. TD the day before had something to do with her. "Matt, you have the wrong idea. The only reason I mix it up with you is to annoy my brother. That's it. We have nothing in common."

The door suddenly cracked open and Matt's face appeared, followed by a wave of dark hair. "But we do."

She threw up her hands. "Do you mind?"

He lifted a Hacky Sack ball. "I'm just saying we both like juggling, and you said you'd give me a lesson. I thought maybe you'd throw me one now. We could go downstairs or out in the yard."

Iris had heard enough. "Arky!" she shouted. "Get up here and remove your friend from my room!"

Arky didn't hear her. Having made a sizable and speedy dent in the keg, he had passed out down in the den.

Matt waved the ball. "Okay, okay, no juggling lesson. I promise to go if you just do one thing."

"What?" she asked, not hiding her exasperation.

"Play your oboe again?"

The strangeness of his request threw her. "You've gotta be kidding."

"No, really," he pleaded. "Just a note or two. That's all I need."

She shook her head in dismay. "You don't give up, do you?"

He flashed a smile. "That's why we're going to State."

She calculated that if Arky had heard her shout, he would be coming up the stairs by now. She answered Matt with hard eyes. "You absolutely promise to go if I play?"

He pushed the door open enough to raise his other hand. "I swear on the altar of Doctor TD."

"Okay, a minute," she conceded, "then you go."

"Promise."

Iris started around the foot of the bed toward the dresser and her oboe case. "Do you always get everything you want?"

Matt grabbed the chance to enter and moved toward a chair in the corner. "I'll just sit over here."

She tried to stop him. "No, that's—" But he was already across the room to a straight-backed chair.

As he sat down and stroked back his hair, he noticed the woodwind instrument on the floor beside her bed. He pointed at it. "Weird place to put your oboe."

Iris had to do some fast mental juggling. If she took her oboe case off the dresser and assembled her oboe, she might have to explain the *second* instrument on the floor. If she did that, Matt might blow her secret to Arky. If she pretended the Jongler cor anglais was her oboe, Matt might never know the difference. But if she played the cor anglais and her brother finally appeared, she'd be busted and he would insist on knowing where it came from.

As Iris circled back to the cor anglais on the floor, she shut the door against the chance of Arky showing up. She pointed at Matt. "Don't take that the wrong way. The acoustics are better when the door's shut."

Matt grinned. "You're the expert."

She picked up the old cor anglais and sat in the swivel chair at her desk. "One minute, then you go."

Matt stared at the curved woodwind in her hands. "I don't remember oboes being bent."

Iris's stomach tightened. "Some are, some aren't. When was the last time you saw an oboe?"

"Like, almost never," he replied. "I promise, one minute and I'm gone. Two minutes, and Tarzan will be tamed."

Even though her stomach unclenched, she resented that her mother's secret was being violated by a beer-soaked jock. Nonetheless, she figured if she played a few measures, she would be rid of him and the long night would finally end. She wetted the reed, took a breath and began to play.

Matt was struck by how the tune sounded lower and sadder than when he had heard it that afternoon. *Booze effect,* he told himself, and let the music captivate him.

As she played, Iris hoped her synesthesia wouldn't kick in and give her some weird vision. The sight of Matt in her room, gaping at her like a lost puppy, was weird enough.

Along with the soulful music, Matt was transfixed by her

fingers dancing on the keys. He couldn't believe such beautiful music could come from a long bow of black wood. Then he noticed something. Carved on the ballooned-out end of the instrument was a spider.

Iris fingered a phrase that would take her to a pause in the melody that would make a good stopping point. A strange thing happened on the way. Her fingers began to feel light. The lightness grew stranger. The keys seemed to press against her fingertips. She thought it might be a new misfiring of her senses: instead of *seeing* sound, she was *feeling* sound. The sensation increased. Her fingers weren't doing the playing; it felt like the keys were playing her fingers. Her breath even felt controlled by the instrument, forcing her lungs to feed the cor anglais.

The music shifted to a style she had rarely played or heard. Cascading trills and strange notes spilled out in a jerking, jarring train of sounds. It sounded like a fusion of Middle Eastern and madness.

Matt gaped at the sight of Iris and her instrument locked in some kind of struggle. He didn't know if his beery fatigue was messing with his eyes, or if Iris was messing with him. Whatever he was witnessing grew wilder. A thread of mist snaked from the end of the instrument. He shook it off as a hallucination, but it didn't go away. The mist curled into a tendril that continued to coil from the wildly playing woodwind. When he found Iris's eyes to confirm whether he was seeing things, it didn't help. Her face was ashen, her eyes wide with fear. She didn't control the instrument; it controlled her. The Hacky Sack balls dropped from his hands.

More strands of mist serpentined from the instrument toward him. Matt jumped from the chair and tried to shout. Nothing came out; he felt trapped in a vice. His only escape was backwards. He thumped into the wall, knocking into an old hook board for hanging keys that now held dozens of earrings. The board slid down the wall and disappeared behind a low book-shelf with a crash. Matt stared in terror as the twisting strands thickened and curled around him. Trying to scream, his mouth only stretched open.

Iris desperately tried to stop playing. She was powerless against the surreal grip the cor anglais had on her, and the instrument's will to disgorge music and mist. The coiling ribbons streamed from the bell until Matt was bound in a luminous cocoon of white.

The cor anglais sounded a rising trill that seemed from another world. The white cocoon began to pulse. As the frenzied music reached an unbearable pitch, Matt reappeared inside the cocoon. But he was transparent, dissipating like mist.

The sound scaled to an air-shattering shriek. The cocoon exploded in a cloud of radiance.

Iris ducked against the blast, tearing the reed from her mouth. She gasped for air. For a moment she looked dazed, thunderstruck. Her eyes darted around the room. She couldn't find Matt. Wherever the insane music and enveloping mists had gone, Matt had gone with them.

Iris tried to grapple with the inconceivable. It was too much. Her eyes rolled back as she blacked out, her body slumping in the chair.

10.

PRANK

Matt Grinnell perceived inky blackness. When he tried to open his eyes, he realized they *were* open. His insides bolted with the fear that he had gone blind. Flickering pinpoints of light flashed in the blackness. The pinpoints stretched into wavering lines. The lines danced into geometric patterns. The patterns gyrated into shapes and emerged into recognizable forms: a bedpost, chair legs, a small wooden barrel. The fear pounding in his chest eased. He realized what had happened: he had passed out, or had had some kind of seizure, and Iris's room was reappearing.

Matt rolled on his back expecting to find an EMT or Iris or Arky. All he saw was a wooden ceiling of beadboard. He scooched onto his elbows. It wasn't Iris's room. He sat up and brushed back a fall of hair. The room was stark, with simple wooden furniture and windows on three sides. It was a cabin or one-room house. His confusion was compounded by a rooster's crow.

He jumped up and winced as a pain shot through his head. *Wicked hangover*, he thought before noticing his bare feet. He knew he still had some brain cells left because he remembered where he'd put his flip-flops. He yanked them from the pockets of his cargo shorts and toed into them. It was the first time he noticed how cold his feet were. In fact, the room was like a refrigerator. He spotted a colorfully striped blanket on the foot of the bed. He unfurled it, tossed it around his shoulders and pulled his hair out from under his improvised robe.

When he stepped out of the one-room house into the morning light, he grimaced against another knife of pain. *Gotta stop drinking so much.*

As the flaring light shuttered down, Matt took in a barnyard. On the far side was a wagon with a double team of horses. Behind that was some old-looking farm equipment. *Great,* he thought, *I passed out, Arky got the guys to come back, and they hauled me to an Amish farm in the country and dumped me. Ha ha, very funny, you pricks.*

An old farmer in overalls, a beat-up coat and an old-fashioned hat came around a shed. Seeing the young man with long hair wrapped in a blanket, the white-bearded farmer moved toward him.

Matt waited for the farmer to recognize him. Just about everyone within forty miles of Belleplain knew Matt Grinnell, the star QB of the Cyclones.

The farmer stopped and gave Matt a onceover, from long locks to odd shoes. "Had some strange ones through here," he said in a worn voice, "but never a blanket Indian."

Matt got out half a laugh before it was strangled by another brain pain. "I'm not an Indian. I'm Matt Grinnell."

"Well," the farmer said with a nod, "least ya got a Christian name. I'm not one to book-judge by the cover."

Realizing the old man hadn't heard of him reinforced Matt's suspicion that the farmer was Amish and not one to watch the sports news. "Look, I had a rough night," Matt explained, "and I ended up in your"—he waved back at the one-room house—"shack. Hope you don't mind."

"Not a bit," the farmer said. "You're like a homing pigeon."

Matt blinked. "A what?"

The farmer's weathered face crinkled with a slight smile as he pointed at the one-room house. "That's your bunkhouse for the next few months."

"Very funny, pops. But maybe you didn't hear, the Cyclones are going to . . ." Matt opened the blanket and displayed his black t-shirt with STATE in gold letters.

The farmer squinted—"State"—then shot Matt a look. "If you're from the State Lunatic Hospital, there's been a helluva mix-up."

"It's the state *football championship!*" Matt boasted. "Don't you Amish follow anything?"

"Amish? Not around here," the farmer said, then spit. "I'd say it's time we got sumthin straight. Yer here for the outing, isn't that right?"

"Outing?" Matt echoed. "What *outing?*"

"Yers, of course."

A laugh jumped from Matt. "Do I look *gay?*"

The farmer stroked his beard. "Nope, but it looks like ya hitched yer wagon to gay last night."

Matt's growing confusion was punctured by a loud backfire that made them both jump.

An antique car, juddering along and spewing smoke, drove into the barnyard. With its big spoke wheels, brassy styling, and canopy over the top, the Model S Ford Runabout looked more like a motorized buggy than any car Matt had seen. The farmer took in the motorcar and the two men in the front seat, then slid Matt a quizzical look.

The vehicle jerked to a stop and the engine cut out with an airy gasp. The two men swung their legs onto the running boards and stepped out. The driver was a slight man with wire-framed glasses; he wore a dark three-piece suit and a stylish hat. The other man was young, not much older than twenty, also wearing a suit. Matt noticed his dark skin and parted black hair as the young man pulled a suitcase from the backseat.

"I'll be damned," the farmer chortled as he turned to Matt. "Yer not my boy, are ya?"

"I'm nobody's boy," Matt snapped.

The farmer greeted the approaching men and addressed the man with glasses. "Sure glad ya showed up with my Indian, 'cause I think this-un"—he jabbed a finger at Matt—"is one-a yer runaways, Mr. Jongler."

Matt wasn't sure he had heard right. *Jongler?* He stared at the slight man. "Your name is Jongler?"

"That's right," the man said. As he took Matt in, his eyes lingered on Matt's strange footwear. "Alfred Jongler."

Matt didn't know Arky and Iris had any relatives around Belleplain. But maybe Arky had a reason to keep this weird-looking dude under the radar.

The farmer crossed to the young man with the suitcase and shook his hand. "Welcome to my place, son. C'mon," he motioned. "I'll introduce ya to the missus."

As they moved toward the farmhouse, Matt stared at Alfred. Despite the man's slicked-down hair and retro suit, Matt was struck by how much he resembled Arky. He had the same sharp, pointed features as his friend.

"What's your name?" Alfred asked.

Not being recognized by anyone was beginning to bite. "Is everyone off the grid around here? I'm Matt Grinnell. I just won a huge game and the Cyclones are going to State." He opened his blanket again, displaying his t-shirt with its gold-letter pronouncement. "State!"

Alfred stared. He didn't want to believe it, but he couldn't deny the growing evidence: a young man wearing a strange undershirt and foreign-looking shoes, speaking in alien phrases. Alfred had been warned of such things. He felt himself shake with fear or excitement or both. He took a breath and reminded himself that if this was indeed what he thought, precautions were necessary. *Don't tip your hand,* he reminded himself. *The process of discovery should be incremental.*

Alfred offered Matt a slight smile. "Perhaps, Matthew, this 'game' you speak of has yet to be played."

Matt huffed with disdain. "Well, duh, yeah, we're going to State."

Alfred's face knitted. "So what is it exactly that you and your undershirt wish to state?"

Matt flailed his arms, knocking the blanket to the ground. "I'm talkin' the state football championship!"

"Oh, that kind of 'state,'" Alfred exclaimed with the satisfaction of gathering a clue: Matt was a footballist of some sort. "I thought . . . never mind. I understand. And what you need to know, Matthew, is that you don't belong here, on this farm. That is, at this time." Alfred paused to regroup and take control of the situation he had often wished would never arise.

"You got that right, mister"—Matt swept a hand at his strange surroundings—"wrong place, wrong time. I'm supposed to be at our Saturday morning game-film meeting."

Alfred didn't know what "game film" was but seized the chance to move things along. "Can I take you there?"

Matt gestured to the motorcar. "In that?"

"Yes, my beautiful Runabout."

"Let's do it." Matt started for the motorcar. "I've had enough of this friggin' prank." Drawing closer, he noticed the name stamped in the gleaming brass capping the car's radiator: FORD. "My dad sells Fords." He stopped at the windowless door and took in the minimal dash and open space under it. "But they're a lot more tricked out."

Alfred picked up the blanket Matt had thrown to the ground, and hung it over a hitching rail. "I don't know about 'tricked out,' but it sure beats a horse and buggy."

The remark made Matt wonder more about this under-the-radar Jongler. "So you know Arky and Iris?"

"Arky and Iris who?" Before he finished Alfred realized his mistake.

Matt's eyes narrowed. "Jongler-Jinks, of course. Aren't they related to you?"

"Of course, yes, of course." Alfred laughed off his miscue and took note of the interesting fact that married names would evolve into hyphenates. "They're close kin," he explained, "but I rarely see them. Our holiday calendars never seem to mesh." Alfred moved to the front end of the Runabout, and feigned a recollection. "And one of them, is it Arky or Iris, who plays a wind instrument?"

Matt suddenly recalled the wild vision he had had before passing out in Iris's room. She had been playing an oboe with a spider carved on it when strands of mist started snaking out of the thing and winding around him. He shook off the drunken hallucination. "Iris," he answered. "Yeah, her playing can make you see stuff."

Alfred pushed his glasses to the bridge of his nose. "Excellent. Music is at its best when it transports the listener." Bending down in front of the Runabout, he smiled at his clever remark. He grabbed the crank protruding from the radiator and gave it a vigorous turn. The engine chugged back to life.

11.

VOYAGER

With Matt in the passenger seat, Alfred drove the Ford Runabout down a dirt lane. As the motorcar's pistons fired under the bonnet, Alfred's mind fired with another reminder: *Show, don't tell. Let normal reveal the abnormal.* He began as normal as it gets. "It's nice to meet you, Matthew."

The low windshield didn't stop the wind from catching Matt's hair. "It's Matt," he corrected.

"Matt it is." Alfred removed his hand from the wooden steering wheel and offered it.

Shaking the man's warm hand reminded Matt how cold his own were. It's not like the Runabout had a heater. He rubbed his hands together and blew on them.

Alfred gestured over his shoulder. "There are blankets in the back."

Matt turned and saw a pile of folded red blankets on the bench seat behind them. "Why all the blankets?"

Alfred chortled. "You never know when you're going to meet an underdressed stranger."

The creepiness of his answer deepened Matt's chill. *Maybe Arky never mentioned this uncle, or whoever he is, because he's some kind of pervert.* Matt grabbed the top blanket and draped the scratchy wool over his legs. Noticing the gold C in the blanket's field of red, he figured some booster had gotten cute with the Cyclones colors, black and gold. "So you *are* a Cyclones fan and you're messing with me."

"No," Alfred replied. "I'm a Carlisle fan."

Matt had never heard of it. "What's Carlisle?"

"A school."

"What kind of school?"

"Like no other."

Matt frowned. "Okay, how 'bout we drop the chatter? I'm being pranked, right?"

"Pranked?" Alfred echoed. "I didn't know it was a verb."

Matt scowled at Alfred. "I get it, okay? The team got together with the booster club and this is a big joke. But don't you think you should've waited till after we win the championship?"

While Alfred drove, he kept nudging his traveler toward full comprehension. "Maybe this football championship you speak of isn't the only game in town."

"What's that supposed to mean?" Matt demanded.

Alfred speculated that it was too early to broach the *why* of Matt's predicament. While Alfred was working with a severely limited guidebook, he did have common sense, and common sense suggested that his traveler needed to discover the where and when before the more ticklish why. A Jongler family saying popped into Alfred's head. "*Tempus omnia revelat,*" he announced.

Matt scowled. "What's that?"

"Latin. It means 'Time reveals all things.'"

Matt's brewing anger over the little man's confounding answers was sidetracked by an approaching scene. Where the dirt lane ended in a T-intersection was an old store with a wooden sign: DEEDS' CORNER MARKET. A horse-drawn buggy and a horse-drawn wagon were parked in front. It contradicted what the farmer had told him about no Amish being nearby. "I knew it," he said. "This is Amish land."

Alfred braked the Runabout to a stop at the intersection and pointed to the store. "That's not Amish."

Before Matt could disagree, another antique motorcar churned down the gravel road they were about to turn on. The car's gleaming novelty was tarnished by a sick feeling in Matt's stomach; it wasn't right. As it chugged by, he grasped for an explanation. "There some kinda car show around here?"

Alfred worked the stick shift back into first. "These days, every motorcar is a show in itself."

Matt's eye caught something in the distance that was equally shocking. Mountains. There were no mountains around Belleplain. "Where the hell am I?"

Alfred maneuvered the Runabout into the intersection. Pleased by his subtle steering of his voyager from normal to abnormal, Alfred felt he had earned the right to drop a hint. "*Where* is important, but not as important as *when*."

Matt's insides roiled with dread. He wasn't being pranked, he was being kidnapped by a psychopath.

He threw off the blanket and jumped from the moving motorcar. He lost one of his flip-flops and hissed in pain from the road's sharp gravel. A quick check revealed Alfred had stopped the old car but was still behind the wheel, watching him. Matt limped to his flip-flop, jammed back into it, and flop-jogged toward the store on the corner.

Inside Deeds' Corner Market, the owner behind the counter wore a long apron. He was ringing up a purchase on a brass cash register for a customer.

Matt barged through the door and stopped. He waited for his eyes to adjust to the dim light. The store bloomed into view. It looked like he had stepped into a general store from a bygone era, where everything you ever needed was under one roof. But this was no Wal-Mart.

The owner and the customer stared at the wild-looking young man with long black hair; he seemed to be wearing nothing but an undershirt and what looked more like bloomers than short pants. "If you're lookin' for a warm coat," the owner announced, "they're against the back wall." His hand reached under the counter. "You know my motto," he added with an easy smile, "'Here at Deeds', we meet your needs.'"

Matt spotted something on the wall behind the counter and rushed toward it.

The owner pulled up a revolver and pointed it at the charging young man.

"Whoa!" Matt jerked to a stop, throwing his hands in the air.

"If you want trouble, sonny," the owner warned, "I got that too."

Hands still up, Matt waggled a finger at what had caught his eye behind the counter. "I just wanna know, what's with the old calendar?"

The owner cut a look to the feed company calendar on the wall. The top banner read SEPTEMBER 1907. The days were crossed out through the 28th, a Saturday. The man's eyes slid back to Matt. "You got a point, sonny. I forgot to cross out Sunday. I'll fix it after you take your business elsewhere."

Matt started backing out. Whatever hangover still lingered was flooded by bewilderment. If the calendar was right, it wasn't only the wrong *day*, it was the wrong *century*.

Outside, the Runabout waited near the buggy. Alfred smoked a cigarette as he leaned against the motorcar's front fender. When he saw Matt's stunned expression and ashen face, Alfred realized that his traveler had caught his first glimpse of a new "country." Matt's expression also helped Alfred realize a crucial next step: to ensure that Matt's voyage didn't end before it began by crashing on the rocks of madness.

Alfred decided to begin with the facts he had come to believe were the case. "You are not being 'pranked.' You have been sent here by a Jongler, which is most likely a descendent of mine named Iris Jongler-Jinks. And a Jongler, myself, has found you." He dropped his cigarette and crushed it with his shoe. "I

think it would be best if you stick with the only clue you have"—
he splayed a hand on his chest—"me."

Matt glared defiantly. "Why?"

Alfred met his angry gaze. Even though his voyager didn't
look ready, it was time for the penny to drop. "You have discovered a country called Tempi Passati."

Matt lunged forward, collared Alfred and bent him over
the Runabout's bonnet. "Knock off the foreign shit and tell me
where I am!"

Alfred's lips quavered. He wondered if any Jonglers had
been killed by their time voyagers. "*Tempi passati*," he repeated
in a quaking voice. "Time past."

Matt jerked up and released him. "Bullshit!"

As Alfred tried to calm his racing heart, he raised his hands
in submission. "I am simply your pilot in this particular bay of
time." He gestured to the open road. "If you insist on sailing off
on your own, I can't stop you."

Matt glared at the infuriating man. He was right about one
thing: this was way too elaborate to be a prank. But it could be
a nightmare, or some kind of psychotic episode brought on by
alcohol and Iris's weird music.

The Cyclones' QB sucked in a breath and gave himself a pep
talk.

*Whatever I'm lookin' at from behind center, I've seen forma-
tions more threatening than this. Sometimes the only way to find
their weak spot is to let 'em come at you with what they've got.*

12.

MORNING AFTER

During Iris's fitful night of sleep, she slipped in and out of a terrible nightmare that included Matt and the Jongler cor anglais.

As dawn grayed her windows, she escaped the nightmare and opened her eyes. Still in her pajamas, Iris lay on top of her bed. She shuddered as she recalled the part in the dream where the Jongler cor anglais possessed her with wild music, mists slithering from the instrument's bell.

To escape the freaky image she turned her head. She came face-to-face with the spider carved on the cor anglais. She gasped and launched off the bed. More details confirmed she was still caught in the nightmare's web. A corner of the wooden music case poked from under the bedcover where she had hidden it. Three Hacky Sack balls lay on the floor where Matt had dropped them. But she felt wide awake, not at all like she was dreaming. Clinging to the hope that her synesthesia was triggering a powerful vision unaided by music, Iris rushed from the room.

She threw open the door to Arky's bedroom, hoping to find her brother. Even better would have been the sight of Matt sleeping on the floor. The floor was empty. The bed hadn't been slept in.

She hurried downstairs. She hardly noticed the mess in the living room as she checked the couch. Matt wasn't there either. She thumped down the stairs to the basement den.

When she found Arky sprawled on the couch, she shook him awake. He groaned in protest. "Arky," she implored, "wake up. I think"—she couldn't bring herself to blurt her worst fear—"something freaky happened."

His eyes barely unstuck. "You missed a great party. That's not freaky, it's normal."

"I think I made Matt"—she didn't know how to put it—"go away!"

Despite his grogginess, Arky went for the dig. "You'd make anyone go away." He groaned and turtled under a pillow. "Now leave me alone or I'm coming out blowing gorilla breath."

Iris stood bolt upright. She had forgotten the one thing that would prove it had all been a bad dream.

She ran back up the two flights of stairs, rushed into her room and moved to the straight-backed chair where Matt had been sitting the night before. Behind it was the wall he had bumped into while trying to escape. The wall was bare. Her eyes dropped to the slice of darkness behind the low bookshelf. She reached down and pulled up the old hook board holding her earrings.

She stared at it, dumbfounded. Her mind reeled. Nightmares didn't knock things off walls. Visions flooded her mind: strands of mist coiling out of the cor anglais—snaking toward Matt—his terrified look—the cocoon of pulsing fog exploding—Matt gone. It wasn't a nightmare, or some mega-episode of synesthesia. She wasn't crazy. Something terrifying and bizarre had happened.

Her eyes darted to the old cor anglais lying on the bed. She flipped the bedcover off the wooden music case and opened it. She snatched the note from the purple velvet lining the case and reread her mother's last paragraph for the hundredth time.

It claws my heart to burden you with such a secret, but I *know* you have the strength to endure it. You are a Jongler with special powers. One day, your fortitude and patience will be rewarded with a full understanding of why I have taken this seemingly cruel leave from my beloved family.

The fear gripping Iris gave way to thrumming excitement. Clutching the note, she rushed from the room.

Arky had settled into a rhythmic snore when Iris thundered down the stairs. She shook her brother's shoulder and dodged the pillow he hurled at her. "Ahhhhhhhh," he exhaled like a dragon, trying to fell her with his breath.

Iris ignored his air assault and read the note in her quivering hand. She read the entire note out loud, ending with "'*Tempus omnia revelat.*'"

Arky was fully awake. "What is that?"

"It means 'Time reveals all things.'"

He sat up and winced at the sharp reminder of a hangover. "Not the Latin, the note."

Iris swallowed and blurted her secret. "Mom left it the day she disappeared."

"Sure she did," Arky said with a pinched frown, "and told you to never show it to me or Dad."

"Yeah," she replied tersely. "And I didn't for a year, along with something else."

In her room, Iris held up the antique cor anglais. "She also left this."

Arky squinted at the wind instrument with its crescent-like curve and the spider carved on its bell. "Creepy. Who bent it?"

"It's how they were made hundreds of years ago."

Iris explained how she had found the old cor anglais on her bed the day their mother had vanished. She told him how she had played it in secret over the last year, and how it had amped up her synesthesia. Then she revealed how Matt had come to her room and refused to leave until she played for him.

Arky sat in the straight-backed chair and listened to her story without interrupting. His eyes shifted back and forth from Iris to their mother's note in his hand. It wasn't clear if he had been rendered mute by his hangover or if he was actually letting his sister finish a story.

As difficult as it was for Iris to get through the shocking details of what had happened to Matt and her part in it, she managed to relate every detail because of the silver lining in the black cloud of his disappearance. "If Matt could vanish like that, so could Mom," she told Arky. "Maybe that's what happened. Mom played the cor anglais and disappeared too. That's why I found the instrument on my bed with the note. Maybe they even disappeared to the same place, but they went *somewhere* and we have to find them." She sucked in a breath and waited for her brother to spark with the same exhilarating hope.

Arky nodded pensively. "Wow, that's—"

"I know," she blurted. "It's scary and crazy and it changes everything!"

He continued. "I mean, if you wanted to get back at me for having a party, wouldn't it be easier to just tell Dad?"

She tightened against his dismissal of everything she had told him. "It's got nothing to do with the party. It's what I saw. It happened!"

"Right." Standing, Arky's hangover sent a razorblade-like reminder. He winced. "Great joke, sis, but it's really kinda sick bringing Mom into it."

"It's not a joke!" She grabbed the Jongler cor anglais. "This has something to do with Mom leaving!"

He gestured to the instrument. "I don't know where you got that"—he lifted the note—"or how you got good at Mom's handwriting." He tossed the note onto the bed. "But it doesn't even sound like her. Mom may have veered off the scientific path, but she'd never write 'You're a Jongler with special powers.' Only you'd write crap like that."

As he started for the door and the cup of coffee he craved, she fired back. "You really think I'd waste time and money hunting down an ancient cor anglais and forging Mom's hand-writing just to jerk you around?"

He turned at the door. "If I knew how your mind works we'd be identical twins. Lucky for me, we're not."

"I'm not making it up!"

Moving down the hall, Arky went into science-speak. "Observables: Brother's brain needs coffee; sister's brain is firing crazy gene. Brother posits sister had her own little party last night with Colorado pot candy."

The chime of a doorbell stopped him at the top of the stairs. Through the side windows flanking the front door, he spotted two men: a policeman and someone else. Arky's stomach lurched. Someone must have ratted him out for the party.

Iris brushed past him. "I'll handle this." She clutched a robe over her Hello Kitty pajamas.

After opening the door, Iris welcomed the policeman and Gunner Grinnell and invited them in. She didn't care if they saw the evidence of the party as she led them into the kitchen.

Iris and Arky soon learned that an underage drinking party wasn't their visitors' concern. Matt Grinnell had not come home the previous night, Gunner had reported him missing, and they wanted to know if the Jongler-Jinks twins knew anything about it.

As Arky shifted a look to Iris and hoped she wouldn't spout her whacko story of Matt going poof in the night, he tried to come up with an explanation of why Matt had gone AWOL. However, Arky's usual lightning-fast mind was dulled by the lingering effects of alcohol.

Iris was clearheaded enough to bottle her emotions and answer their visitors' queries. When the party was breaking up, Matt had come up to Iris's bedroom and tried to get a juggling lesson. She got Matt to leave by convincing him that she would give him a lesson after he won the state championship. He said he was going to walk home and left. That was the last time she saw him.

Arky finally spoke up. "Have you tried his cell phone?"

"Yes," Gunner answered. "He left it in his bedroom, like he always does on game days."

"Right," Arky added with a nod. "It's one of his superstitions."

The cop and Mr. Grinnell asked the twins to report anything they might hear or see regarding Matt's whereabouts and left.

When the door closed, Iris turned to her brother. "Now do you believe me?"

"Yeah," he said with a frown. "I believe what you told them. Matt's probably off somewhere doing what I should be doing, sleeping off a hangover."

"I saw what I saw," she said firmly. "He was in my room and then he was gone."

Arky heaved a beleaguered sigh. "Iris, people and things, configurations of matter, don't go *poof*. If they did, I would've poofed you years ago."

Iris ignored the dart. She grabbed the coffee pot and went to the sink. "I'll make coffee. You're gonna need it."

13.

OVERTURE

The Ford Runabout transporting Alfred and Matt puttered along a gravel road cutting through a patchwork of cornfields and pasture.

Suspecting that his passenger was either in a state of shock or denial, Alfred drove in silence. He thought it best given that Matt's process of discovery was at a fragile stage. Like an infant going from milk to solid food, it was about taking baby steps.

Matt glowered at a passing field. A team of horses pulled a reaper cutting hay. Equally unsettling were the wooded mountains, dappled with autumn colors, obscuring the horizon. But the greatest assault on Matt's senses was the disturbing feeling that he was not in some nightmare. There was nothing threatening or terrifying about it; it was a panorama of normal and bland. Despite his churning anxiety, he stuck with his game plan: play along to get along until he figured out what was going on.

He turned to Alfred. "Where are we?"

Alfred kept his eyes on the road. "Just outside Carlisle."

"Carlisle where?"

Alfred dutifully answered. "Pennsylvania."

"Pennsylvania?" Matt laughed in disbelief. "That's a couple hundred miles away."

Alfred censored the urge to ask Matt where he hailed from. Where and when a voyager came from was probably less important than helping the traveler acclimate to his new location. "Look on the bright side," Alfred offered, "you could have gone to the North Pole. The way you're dressed, you'd be dead by now."

Matt's brow furrowed. "So you're saying if that guy back in the store had shot me, I'd be dead?"

The thought of losing his voyager so soon made Alfred shudder. He certainly didn't want to be remembered as the Jongler who'd lost his first voyager within an hour. "I can tell you this," he said. "This is not a dream. All the rules of life apply here."

Matt chuffed. "And one of 'em is that Iris Jongler-Jinks can play a weird oboe and blow me to Pennsylvania?"

"Yes," Alfred replied, "to another space *and* time; 1907, to be exact."

"Yeah, yeah," Matt grumbled. "I'd say 'It's so last century,' but I'm not in the mood."

Alfred repressed a smile. His voyager had just signaled his century of origin, the twenty-first. It made him want to return the favor. "So what is the date of this state championship that is so important?"

"December third," Matt answered.

"It's only September thirtieth here." Alfred brightened. "On the monthly calendar, you've got plenty of time."

Matt smirked. "If you're telling me I'm stuck here for two months, forget about it."

Alfred peered over his glasses with a somber look. "It might be longer if you don't play your cards right."

"What 'cards'?"

Alfred contemplated his answer. Now that Matt seemed to be accepting bits and pieces of his where and when, he needed a hint of *why*. Alfred took a breath and plunged in. "I can't see the hand you've been dealt, Matt. I don't know *what* you're coming from. But for some reason you've been sent to me, Alfred Jongler, in the fall of 1907. Some families exchange gifts through the mail. We Jonglers exchange people through time."

Matt shook his head. "That's impossible."

Rather than disagree, Alfred nodded. "Okay, it's impossible.

Now, you tell me something from the future that I would never believe in my wildest dreams."

Matt thought for a moment. "We landed a man on the moon."

Alfred arched an eyebrow. "Really? 'That's impossible.'" While Matt frowned at the little man's trick, Alfred forgave himself for stealing a diamond of truth from the future. "You see, impossible is in the eye of the beholder." He gestured to the surrounding countryside. "And what you're beholding is not only possible, it's real."

Matt blew a sigh. "Okay, let's say it is. But why me? Why 1907?"

Alfred smiled. "Why you and why here are mysteries we will have to solve before we can send you home."

"Mysteries?" Matt echoed. "What mysteries?"

"I don't know. That's the nature of mysteries."

Matt pulled back. "Are you saying you don't know *how* to send me back?"

Alfred didn't dare answer truthfully. Not only was Matt his first voyager from the future, but Alfred's exposure to the time-travel guidebook had been minimal. It wasn't his fault. Alfred wasn't supposed to have the Jongler cor anglais and the responsibilities that came with it. His older brother James had inherited it. And before James died in Paris in 1894, he only conveyed to Alfred a few basics about the cor anglais and its powers. Which was why, thirteen years later, Alfred Jongler was flying by the seat of his pants.

"Of course I know how," Alfred answered with propped-up confidence. "I'm simply saying that in the same way it took a storm of circumstances to blow you off course to my coordinates of space and time, it will take a certain storm of circumstances to blow you back to your 'hometime.'"

Matt tried to follow. "Like a perfect storm?"

Alfred smiled at another term gleaned from the future. "Yes," he replied. "A perfect storm that might be called *tempus omnia sanat*."

Matt's jaw clenched. "Which means?"

"Time heals all."

As they passed a WELCOME TO CARLISLE sign, Matt gave up on getting big answers from his evasive driver and went for a small one. "What's in Carlisle?"

"The Carlisle Indian Industrial School."

"Never heard of it. What's Indian about it?"

"It's America's finest school for Indians," Alfred replied. "It's where I teach, and where I'm going to enroll you."

Matt gaped. "You're shittin' me."

Alfred realized not all terms from the future were delightful. "No, I am not."

"I'm not an Indian!"

"How do you know? It's 1907; you haven't been born yet."

Matt exploded. "Then why the hell am I here?"

Alfred cringed at Matt's outburst and instantly regretted his quip. Even though he didn't have the Jongler family guidebook, Alfred suspected that making fun of a voyager's predicament was inexcusable. "I apologize for the bad joke. It was below the belt."

Matt glared at the quaint houses lining the road with their groomed yards and white picket fences. A trolley car moved down the center of the street. The strangest sight was how the horse-drawn wagons and buggies outnumbered the motorcars. He felt like he was driving into a postcard. But postcards didn't smell like horse manure.

Alfred chided himself for not preparing Matt for the approaching hurdles. He made one last attempt, employing what came to him naturally: humility. "Matt, I don't have all the answers. As a music teacher, I only know that the overture is a prelude to the main composition. I suspect the same rule applies to time: the past is an overture to the future. For some reason, you've been sent back to this time and place"—he waved a hand at their surroundings—"this *overture*, which could affect the composition of your future. So keep your ears open. There's music here that you might want to listen to."

Matt's only response was a grunt as the perfect houses gave way to a tall white fence stretching a hundred yards. Alfred turned the car onto a lane flanked by the white fence and a row of leafy elms beginning to change color. As Matt wondered what was on the other side of the fence, he heard real music drifting over it. "Okay, I hear the music," he snarled. "Can I go home now?"

Alfred chuckled. "I was speaking metaphorically. What you hear is the Carlisle marching band."

"What do a bunch of Indians need a marching band for?"

"Their football team."

Matt blinked. "This place has a football team?"

"One of the best in the country," Alfred announced cheerfully. "The Carlisle Indians."

14.

MAKING HER CASE

Iris was on a mission. After the cop and Mr. Grinnell had confirmed that Matt was missing, whatever doubts she harbored about what had happened in her room the night before had vanished. And, as traumatic as blowing someone into oblivion should have been, the PTSD that might have consumed Iris had been trumped by the significance of the event: Matt's expulsion from her room had thrown open a window to their mother's fate. If their mother had disappeared just like Matt . . . But Iris was getting ahead of herself. The first vital step of her mission was simple. She had to make Arky a believer.

She started by making her brother a pot of coffee and brewing herself some tea. She had already forgiven him for not believing a word of her account. She would have done the same if she had not witnessed it firsthand. And she knew who she was up against: Mr. Science.

Armed with coffee and tea, Iris asked Arky to go with her to their mother's attic office. After quipping that her tale about Matt was more entertaining than his hangover, Arky agreed. He had to drink his coffee somewhere.

On the way to the attic, she collected the Jongler cor anglais from her room. When she grabbed it, she had a scary flashback of Matt being imprisoned by the snaking mists and the exploding cocoon that, for all she knew, might have killed him. She shuddered at the thought of being a murderer.

In the attic office, Iris steadied her insides and presented her case to Arky. She pointed out the modern cor anglais in its black plastic case that their mother had supposedly been learning to play during her sabbatical, while she had been secretly playing the curved and far older cor anglais. After reminding Arky of the safe their mom had left open the day she had disappeared, Iris corrected the assumption made by the police. Octavia had not left with a secret hoard of cash; she had removed the Jongler cor anglais from the safe and taken it to Iris's room, where she had played it and disappeared in the same way Matt had.

"Big assumption," Arky interjected. "We only have two observables. Mom's been missing for a year and Matt is *allegedly* missing. I still think he's off somewhere sleeping off the party."

"Okay," Iris conceded, "you have your observables, I have mine. In fact, I have a couple more for you." She lifted the curved cor anglais so Arky could see the ivory inlay of a spiderweb on the back of the instrument. "The cor anglais is decorated with a web and a spider." She pointed at the midnight blue wall with Octavia's assembly of galaxies and supernovas orbiting around a black disk of wood, all of it caught in a silky spiderweb. "I didn't put the web up there, Mom did."

"Right," Arky conceded, "but you knowing about it made renting a cor anglais with a spider on it a clever choice."

"Really?" She held up the spidery instrument. "How many of these do you think are out there?"

Arky took a sip of coffee. "That would take some research."

She dug into the pocket of her robe. "Oh, look, another observable." She held up the note Octavia had left on Iris's bed.

He recognized it. "I've seen it."

"You didn't turn it over." She flipped the note and read aloud what their mother had written on the back.

Wind in the wood
Tips on the keys
Add drifting souls
With silent pleas

Makes the music
A Jongler sees

She looked up for his reaction.

He silently kicked himself for being so brain-challenged that he hadn't looked at the other side. "Okay, sis, 'cause I haven't finished my coffee, I'll play along. Let me see your forgery."

She handed him the note.

He scanned the poem. "I get the first two lines. 'Wind' is breath, 'tips' are fingers. But, 'Add drifting souls / With silent pleas'? Gimme a clue."

She brushed aside his indifferent tone; at least he was listening. "I didn't know what 'Drifting souls / With silent pleas' meant either"—she pointed to the computer on their mother's desk—"until I read her research on the book she was writing, *A Year of Magical Playing*. "People think 'cor anglais' means 'English horn.' But that's not what it originally meant. In the early seventeen hundreds, in the part of Eastern Europe where the instrument was first made, 'cor anglais' actually meant 'horn of angels.'"

"If you ask me," Arky interjected, "no 'horn of angels' would have a spider and a web on it. Maybe it's a horn of demons."

"There's no such thing as a *cor diablo*."

"That's 'devil,'" he corrected. "You meant '*demonio*.'"

Her mouth tightened. "You know what I mean."

"Actually, I don't. I have no idea what some 'horn of angels' has to do with 'drifting souls' and 'silent pleas.'"

Iris got back on track. "In Bible lore and in other religions, what do angels do? They help people who have gone astray and are in need of help. Maybe that's what 'Add drifting souls / With silent pleas' means. Maybe Matt has problems we don't know about. I mean, I heard him talking to Doctor TD the day before the game about 'twisted thoughts' he didn't want to take into the game."

The revelation caught Arky off guard but he didn't show it. "He told me about his twisted thoughts Friday afternoon. He's got some issues with his dad; so does everybody. That doesn't make him a 'drifting soul.'"

"What if it's more than that?" Iris asked. "Maybe he's got bigger problems and that's why the cor anglais blew him away." She took the note from her brother, flipped it over and quoted from it. "'You are a Jongler with special powers.' That's what Mom wrote to me. Mom knew it because she has special powers too. That's what she was messing with before she vanished."

Arky massaged his face. "Lemme see if I've got this straight. Matt is a drifting soul, so he got blown away by you, Miss Special Powers, and the 'horn of angels.' And Mom, *Mrs.* Special Powers, was cleaning her angel horn, had a little accident, and blew herself away."

Iris knew that penetrating her brother's armor of cynicism was a long shot, but she didn't have a choice. Matt's disappearance was the key to finding their mother. "Look, Arky, I don't believe in angels strumming harps in the clouds any more than you do. But maybe the *idea* of angels, which is thousands of years old, came from something that western science doesn't know about, like some invisible force that humans ended up accessorizing with white robes and wings and harps."

Arky's eyes widened. "Are you saying angels are the original Mr. Potato Head?"

Iris clamped down on a chuckle and pressed on. "The point is, I don't know what pushed the mists out of the cor anglais that wrapped up Matt and probably Mom and blew them away. But I do know what Mom taught us about quantum physics: that every body, chunk and speck of matter in the universe boils down to *energy;* that science has always looked at the treasure of the universe through a keyhole. Mom told us the actual universe is more varied than any universe we can imagine." Iris tossed a hand at the display on the dark blue wall. "What if there *is* some energy or force hidden in the matter that the Jongler cor anglais is made of? What if Mom woke up that energy and I woke up the same energy with Matt?"

Arky stared at her, impressed by her heartfelt appeal. "Sis, that was beautiful. And I accept that music can take you places *emotionally*. But there's no way music can take you places *physically*. I believe in the hard science of cause and effect, not the squishy art of science fiction. There's no way oboes can blow smoke and make people vanish."

"I didn't think so either," Iris said, trying to match his calm logic. "But don't you think it's weird that Mom, the astrophysicist, who's married to the scientific method as much as she is to Dad, was up here in the attic taking a wild ride into *unscientific* stuff?"

Arky put on a befuddled look. "Are you saying Mom was having an affair with an astrologist?"

Iris lifted the note and tried another tack. "Do you at least understand the last two lines? 'Makes the music / A Jongler sees.' Do you get it?"

Arky shrugged. "I'm all ears."

"It's about the visions me and Mom have because of synesthesia, *and* the mists that made Matt disappear."

Having finished his coffee, Arky stood up. "Right, and I've got a party mess to disappear."

As he reached the door, Iris cast her last line. "You used to play the oboe too, and you still listen to music. Have you ever had a vision, even the tiniest one?"

"Not a glimmer," he said, starting down the stairs.

She rose and called after him. "How 'bout I play the cor anglais and let's see if you do?"

"No, thanks."

"What's the matter? Think I'll blow you away?"

"Not a chance."

As he reached the second-floor hallway, Iris set her hook. "If you're so sure it's all a crock, why not give it a try? Or has my brother, the guy who waited to be born second, been a chicken from day one?"

15.

ORIENTATION

The Model S Runabout reached an open gate attached to a low stone building with a tin roof. Alfred drove through the gate and stopped the motorcar. "We need to register at the Guardhouse," he told Matt. "Let me do the talking."

Matt stepped out of the Runabout. "What kind of school needs a guardhouse?"

"The Indian Wars may be over, but there's still plenty of fight in the Indians," Alfred said before stepping through a low doorway.

Matt had to stoop to follow him in.

Inside, sitting behind a wooden table, was a smartly dressed soldier in what looked like a cavalry uniform from an old western. He looked up as Alfred and Matt entered.

Matt found the sight of the western-looking soldier reassuring. Finally something looked totally out of whack, like in a dream.

"I've got a new student, Sergeant," Alfred announced.

The sergeant lifted a hand. "Entrance papers?"

"They were lost in transit," Alfred explained. "I'll handle that with the major."

The sergeant took Matt in, from his long black hair to his strange shorts with big pockets. His eyes settled on Matt's dusty bare feet and flip-flops. "There's a first," the sergeant said, "open-air moccasins."

"Flip-flops," Matt corrected.

The sergeant's eyes shot up. "Rule number one: no speaking Indian here. You speak English."

Matt raised his right hand like a Hollywood Indian and uttered the one phrase he could think of that sounded Indian. "Hakuna matata."

The sergeant stood, scraping his chair on the plank floor. "Go ahead, boy. Say that again and see what happens."

Before Matt could oblige, Alfred jumped in. "That's his Indian name, Hakuna Matata. His English name is Matt Grinnell."

A voice sounded from one end of the building. "Carlisle no good road! Carlisle make red apples!"

The sergeant scowled. "Rule number two"—he fixed on Matt—"insubordination is not tolerated. Excuse me for a moment." As the sergeant went through a side door, he grabbed a ring of heavy keys off a hook.

The voice shouted again. "Long Knives kill past! Me bleed white, not red!"

Matt was doubly perplexed: Where was the voice coming from and why did it sound like the stilted Indian-speak he had just mimicked? He turned to Alfred. "Who's that?"

"The Guardhouse has a holding cell where we lock up incorrigible students and runaways," Alfred replied.

"What's a 'red apple'?"

"Indian on the outside, white on the inside. It's why Carlisle was founded: to kill the savage but save the man."

"I'm not a savage," Matt huffed. "And I don't have a drop of Indian blood."

Alfred gave him a wry smile. "Neither did a few black Irish who went to school here. You've got the hair and the complexion. That's all it takes."

They heard the clack of a lock being opened and the creak of a heavy door. Then came the whizzing crack of a whip or crop, followed by loud yelps. As the yelps turned to whimpers, they listened to the door creak shut and the metallic snap of the lock.

Alfred exhaled with disapproval and continued Matt's orientation. "If the sergeant asks, you're from the Mandan tribe of North Dakota."

"Why Mandan?"

"They tend to be light-skinned, and there are no Mandans in the school right now to ask questions about your kith and kin back on the reservation."

The sergeant returned; his face was flushed from exertion. He treated Matt to a sadistic smile as he sat down. "We've still got some wild in that redskin, but he'll come around when he gets a hankering for more than bread and water."

Matt turned to Alfred. "Is this a school or a prison?"

Pleased to hear Matt's English, the sergeant answered. "A little of both, which accounts for our success. There are only two ways out of Carlisle: with a diploma in one hand and a trade in the other, or with your hands crossed over your chest. That's how it works here, Mr. Grinnell."

Matt's comeback was stifled by hearing "Mr. Grinnell." It was a name he only associated with his father.

Alfred and Matt got back into the Runabout. They turned onto a loop road and passed in front of a long, two-story building with porticos stretching the length of both floors. The wooden building was one of many elegant buildings, all painted white, that surrounded a vast quadrangle of grass. Along with great elms showing autumn colors, a bandstand rose from the quad.

Matt felt like he was in a postcard again, but there was no smell of manure this time tainting the view. He couldn't help but be impressed. If none of this was a mega-twisted dream, if he really had been zapped to someplace in the past, he had to admit it looked kind of cool, like a boarding school for kids of the rich and famous.

Alfred stopped the motorcar at the end of the long building.

He killed the engine and asked Matt to wait in the Runabout for a few minutes until he came back. Matt answered with a shrug.

As he continued taking in the picturesque scene, Matt saw a parade coming along the road toward him. A horse-drawn wagon with a covered bed in dark wood led two columns of Indian children. The horse's clopping hooves and the hymn the children were singing grew louder. The bronze-skinned little boys in the parade were dressed in dark suits; the little girls wore long black dresses. There were only a few adults; some were Indian, some white. As the wagon passed by, Matt realized it was a funeral. The wagon was a hearse, carrying a small, black coffin.

Matt stared. Some of the boys and girls, singing mournfully, stared back. Matt shuddered at a chilling thought. If this was 1907, not only was there a dead kid in the coffin, but all of them, kids and adults, would be dead in a hundred years. They were ghosts burying a ghost.

While the procession moved on, Matt's attention was pulled to the building Alfred had gone into. The sound of violins playing scales wafted through an open window. It triggered a memory of being outside Arky's house and listening to Iris's oboe music coming from the second floor. Even though it was only yesterday, it felt long ago.

As the scale-scratching violins continued, Matt remembered something Alfred had said earlier. *He's a music teacher. This is the music building. And if he's a music teacher*—Matt hustled toward the building entrance.

Inside, Matt moved toward the sound of the violins. He threw open a door and found a classroom of teenage Indian girls, all playing violins.

The sight of the hulking boy in his bizarre clothing brought the student musicians to a squawking stop. They erupted in giggling laughter. Matt ignored them and turned to Alfred, who was writing exercises on a blackboard.

"I figured you wouldn't stay put," Alfred said. "I needed to make sure my class had their lesson."

"I gotta talk to you," Matt declared.

His rude demand shocked the girls into silence.

Alfred finished his instructions, directed an older student to take over the class, and ushered Matt into the hall.

After shutting the door against a chorus of scales, Alfred got in the first word. "I'm sorry about the funeral. It's not much of a welcome. Many students arrive here in a weakened state or bring diseases from their reservation: typhoid fever, tuberculosis—"

Matt cut him off. "I don't wanna talk about what kills you here. I wanna talk about getting back to my home turf, or whatever you called it."

"Hometime."

"Right. If Iris sent me here, and you Jonglers have some sick habit of blowing people around in time, I figure you must have another oboe that can blow me home."

Alfred had been wondering how long it would take Matt to figure this out. Rather than hiding the fact, Alfred took the opportunity to continue his voyager's orientation. "Actually, it's the same oboe Iris has in the future. It's called a cor anglais."

"I don't care if it's called a cor ugly," Matt retorted. "I want you to blow me back."

"It takes more than just playing it."

"I know. It takes blowing into the thing, getting shrink-wrapped in fog"—he armed a long pass—"and bombed to another century."

Alfred's pulse quickened. Over the years, as he had played the cor anglais and experienced the visions that the music sometimes induced, he had seen strands of mist dance in the air and wrap around the things and people in his visions. But he had never known what the mist signified. His dying brother hadn't shared such details. Alfred wanted to ask Matt what he meant by "shrink-wrapped in fog" but he stopped himself. If a Jongler had to ask his voyager how things work, it might throw the voyager into a panic.

Matt plunged a hand into a pocket of his shorts, extracted his wallet, and pulled the bills from it. "If you want money, here." He thrust the bills at Alfred. "There's almost eighty bucks. I bet that goes a long way here."

Alfred eyed the bills and was struck by how little U.S. paper money would change in the next century. "Put your money away before someone arrests you for being the worst counterfeiter to ever roll ink."

"It's real money!"

"Not if it's got the year twenty-something on it." As much as Alfred was curious about every item in Matt's wallet, he got back on task. "If you'll put that away, I'll make you a deal. I will try to play you back—"

"Great!" Matt exclaimed, jamming the wallet back in his pocket. "You blow, I go, and I'll be back in time for State. Where do we do this?"

Alfred resumed his bargain. "However, if the cor anglais fails to deliver, you will go with me to the superintendent's office and enroll in the school."

Matt just wanted to get to the cor anglais and be done with 1907. "Fine, deal."

Moments later, in Alfred's office, Matt watched with anticipation as Alfred stepped into a supply closet and emerged with a wooden music case. He set it on his desk, undid its leather straps, opened it, and lifted the pieces of an old woodwind from the velvet lining. As Alfred assembled the long, curved instrument with tarnished keys, Matt had no doubt it was the same one Iris had played. A black spider, carved in high-relief, rose from the fat bell of the cor anglais.

Alfred lifted a glass vial from the case, extracted a reed and inserted it in the cor anglais's bocal. He wet the reed and began playing a classical tune.

Matt watched and waited for the music to get weird, for the strands of mist to curl from the bottom of the woodwind. As Alfred played, the melody did get lively and playful, but nothing emerged from the instrument but music. Matt sensed Alfred was mocking him. "You're playing it wrong," he protested. "It's supposed to get weird."

Alfred extracted the reed from his mouth. His eyes danced with curiosity. "Is it?"

"That's not what Iris played," Matt insisted.

"I'm not surprised."

"Then play the right tune," Matt ordered.

Alfred sighed. He was disappointed himself. He wanted to see the cor anglais come to life and work its magic too. "I don't know what the right tune is," he confessed. "I don't think any Jongler does. Only the cor anglais knows."

Matt scoffed. "Gimme a break. It's just a bent tube of wood with metal keys."

Alfred raised the cor anglais and presented it to Matt. Even though he lacked full knowledge of how the ancient instrument unleashed its powers, Alfred's visions while playing it had provided hints. "If it's only a bent tube of wood with metal keys, would it have sent you here? I suspect it has a will of its own. And when the 'perfect storm' awakens it, I would guess it is not the Jongler who plays the cor anglais, but the cor anglais that plays the Jongler."

16.

MAJOR MERCER AND THE DELILAH BRIGADE

Alfred and Matt walked along a path leading across the grassy quad surrounded by buildings with long porches.

"Where are we going?" Matt asked.

"You're on Carlisle ground but you're not enrolled in the school yet," Alfred replied.

"What am I gonna do, take Rain Dancing, Smoke Signals and Casino Management?"

Alfred chuckled at Matt's sarcasm and censored the urge to ask what he meant by "Casino Management." Like Matt's wallet, there was baggage a voyager brought from the future that was best left unexamined. "It's time to meet the superintendent."

They moved onto the porch of a large white house and entered. Alfred asked Matt to wait in the foyer, then proceeded to Major Mercer's office.

As Matt checked out the framed photos on the walls, he could overhear the conversation in the office. A gruff, forceful voice answered Alfred's greeting. "We're not expecting a new student." Matt figured the voice belonged to Major Mercer.

"Yes, I know, but—"

"We're up to our eyeballs in Indians as it is," Mercer interjected. "Why do you think we're sending more students on outings to surrounding farms?"

"I was just thinking, since we lost Albert Jackson—"

"His spot was filled yesterday," the major declared tersely.

"I see." There was a pause before Alfred spoke again.

"Perhaps this young Indian, Matt Grinnell, might help us with a couple of problems I've been hearing about."

"What *problems* are you referring to, Mr. Jongler?" Mercer demanded with growing ire.

"It's just a rumor," Alfred began casually, "but I heard the school is being investigated for receiving government checks for students who don't exist."

"That's completely false!" Mercer boomed.

"I'm relieved to hear that," Alfred acknowledged. "So there would be no point in wanting a flesh-and-blood student to fill the shoes of one of these phantom students, because the fact is Carlisle has *no* phantom students and the government investigation will prove fruitless."

Mercer grunted. "Exactly. But you said this student might solve *two* problems. What's the other?"

Matt didn't hear the answer; he was fascinated by a picture on the wall. It was a black-and-white photo of a team. If there hadn't been a player holding a fat-looking football with '94 painted on it, Matt wouldn't have guessed it was a football team. They didn't have helmets, they weren't wearing pads, their uniforms resembled fencing outfits, and they all looked scrawny and underweight.

"Matt." The voice pulled him away from the photo. He turned to find Alfred in the doorway. "Major Mercer wants to see you."

Matt went into the office. The major was a solid man with a bushy moustache. Dressed in a military uniform, he was seated behind a huge wooden desk. Matt was taken by the similarity between the major and the man in the picture on the wall behind him: President Theodore Roosevelt.

Mercer eyeballed Matt. "You're one big Indian."

"Yes," Alfred said before Matt could jump in. "Isn't that the kind of material Pop is looking for?"

"You ever seen a football?" Mercer asked.

Matt smirked. "I had one in my crib."

Alfred led Matt along a path skirting the quad. "Congratulations," Alfred announced. "You're a Carlisle Indian."

"Hardly," Matt retorted.

"Okay, you're not the first white to sneak under the teepee," Alfred conceded before breaking into a smile. "But you're the first to come from the tribe of the future."

"So is that why I'm here?" Matt asked. "To show these scrawny Indians how to play football?"

Alfred chortled at Matt's presumption. "Maybe, or perhaps they'll show *you*. But first we've got to get you cleaned up and into some proper clothes."

"That's okay," Matt said. "I'll be fine in these."

A bell clanged and students began to pour from the long building with a double portico. The girls wore long white dresses while the boys were in uniforms, a simpler version of what the sergeant had been wearing: stiff-collared blue jackets with brass buttons and pants with a stripe down each leg. For Matt, the weird part was seeing cavalry uniforms topped with Indian faces. "Are they dressed up 'cause of the dead kid?"

"No, that's the school uniform."

Matt scowled. "So it's a military academy."

"Absolutely," Alfred said. "It's part of their transformation from savage to civilized."

Three young boys came briskly toward them. The boys were used to seeing new arrivals at Carlisle who had yet to shed their Indian look, but Matt looked like a breed of Indian they had never seen. As they passed, one of them pointed at Matt's strange cargo shorts and spoke in imperfect English. "Don't know tribe, but know his name."

"What?" one of the boys asked.

"Wears Own Saddlebags."

The laughing boys scampered on.

Matt's urge to hurl a comeback was muted by the contrast of prim little schoolboys spouting Indian-speak. The students pouring from the Academic Building only added to his confusion. "What's with all the short hair? They're Indians, right?"

"A few go back to long hair after they graduate," Alfred explained. "But here you get a Carlisle cut."

"Not me," Matt snorted. "No one touches my locks."

"I understand the reluctance," Alfred sympathized. "For many Indians, long hair is a symbol of rain, of fertility. A haircut can be the equivalent of castration."

Matt flipped his hair. "This isn't a symbol of shit. It's just hair, and I make the call on how long it is."

"Whatever you say, Samson." Alfred glanced behind them. "You can take that up with the Delilah Brigade."

Matt turned to see four big Indians in uniforms bearing down on them. "Who are they?"

"We call them assistant barbers."

The four guys pounced on Matt. Despite his skill at scrambling, he was surprised how fast they had his arms pinned as they whisked him toward a building at the end of the path. He thrashed and struggled but was outmuscled. The foursome hauled him into the building and threw him into a barber chair.

"Settle down, hotshot," one of the Indians said as the others lashed Matt into the chair with ropes. "If we have to scalp you, it's an extra charge."

Hearing an Indian speak normal English didn't stop Matt's retort. "You assholes are gonna pay—" A gag splitting his mouth did.

The Indians stepped away from their bound and muted captive. The one with the strongest Indian features spoke with clipped precision. "Your protests and profane language do not offend our ears. But it reminds us of the time one of our brothers wailed over the prospect of losing his hair. It roused the entire school, and soon all of Carlisle was wailing along with him. Today, such loud and disruptive grief would not be right since we are grieving for a brother who is being buried. Your hair is about to return to Mother Earth. Rejoice, my brother, that your body is not doing the same."

Matt wanted to ask him if his name was Speaks So Pretty, but all he could do was growl. A moment later, he felt a tug on his hair and heard the slice of scissors.

Just because Matt's long hair had been shorn didn't mean he had lost his macho. When the Delilah Brigade untied him, he lunged at Speaks So Pretty. To his surprise, Speaks So Pretty also swung so pretty. The undercut caught Matt on the chin and lifted him in the air. By the time he was reunited with his long black strands littering the floor, Matt was out cold.

17.

DISCOVERY

On the second floor of the Jongler-Jinks house, Arky stood in the doorway of Iris's bedroom. After getting a second mug of coffee, he had answered his sister's taunt about being a chicken and had accepted her challenge. By listening to her play the Jongler cor anglais, he would kill two birds with one stone. He would prove he wasn't afraid of the spidery old instrument, and it would satisfy his crazy sister so he could begin cleaning up the party mess before their dad got home Sunday.

As to Matt's disappearance, Arky had his own theories. If Matt wasn't off somewhere sleeping off a hangover, he had probably gone missing to freak out his father and reinforce his bad-boy jock reputation. His vanishing act might even be his opening gambit in the weeklong run-up to the state championship: he was feeding the rumor mill. *Did you hear about the Cyclones' QB? He's a total psycho. Yeah, I hear he's a hit man and had to disappear for a couple days to whack a guy.*

Arky took a sip of coffee as Iris lifted the cor anglais. "As I play, just relax and listen." She sat in the swivel chair at her desk. "It might be better if you sit." She gestured to the straight-backed chair near the bathroom door. "The more relaxed you are, the more receptive you'll be to a vision from the music."

Arky glanced at the chair. "I'm not sitting in the chair you claim was Matt's ejection seat to the Land of Drifting Souls."

Iris half smiled. "Since when did you start getting superstitious?"

"Never. It's called playing the odds."

"Whatever, Matt was standing when he vanished."

"In that case, I'll sit." Arky pointed at her desk chair. "But I wanna sit where you're sitting."

"Why?"

"I want the swivel chair so when you play your spider crook and my head starts spinning, my body will spin with it."

Iris frowned. "If you're not going to take this seriously there's no point. You have to keep an open mind."

"Sis, studies have shown that ninety percent of open minds are empty minds."

Iris laid the cor anglais across the chair arms. "You know, before Mom disappeared, your sarcasm was funny. Now it's just mean. There's no reason to give up. There are people who were kidnapped for a decade and were finally found. Mom's only been gone a year. She might be alive, somewhere, in some place or some reality we don't know about. But if you're such a genius in your own mind, if you know how the world works down to every grain of silica in every microchip in the motherboard of the universe, then you tell me, where did Mom go? Where did Matt go?"

Arky set his coffee mug down and leaped on her bed, just missing the old wooden music case. He rolled onto his back. "Okay, Doctor Special Powers, gimme the treatment. Play a tune that'll cure me of my delusional attachment to reality."

"Thank you," Iris said curtly, and raised the cor anglais to her mouth.

Arky shot up a hand. "Wait a sec. If you really did make Matt disappear, aren't you scared of doing the same to me?"

"Yes, I am," she said quietly. She was terrified that that was exactly what might happen. But she also knew she had played the cor anglais countless times without incident. She was fairly sure the cor anglais had its own hidden logic as to what it did and when, and that Arky was not in danger. "If the horn of angels only comes to life to help a 'drifting soul' with 'silent pleas,'" she explained, "I think you're safe. There's nothing *drifting* about you, and you wouldn't ask for help if you were sinking in quicksand."

Arky laughed. "Guilty as charged."

"I have a bigger fear than blowing you away," she added.

"What?"

"You not believing me."

The sincerity in her voice gave Arky pause. If this whole thing was a prank, she was going for an Oscar. "You know what they say," he said, "seeing is believing."

Choosing the Poulenc sonata she was working on for her auditions, Iris began to play.

Lying on the bed, Arky let the beautiful music sweep over him. He was immediately struck by how much better Iris sounded playing the piece on the old cor anglais rather than her oboe. He stared at the ceiling, waiting for the music to trigger a vision. Nothing. He rolled on his side and faced Iris, still playing. As much as he wanted to compliment her, he didn't want to fuel her weird obsession with the even weirder instrument. "All I hear is music," he said. "All I see is my sister, whom I cherish even more now that I know she'll spend the rest of her life in a loony bin."

Iris barely heard him. She had been swept into the music. The instrument was not pushing on her fingers, taking over her hands like the last time she had played it. It was a different sensation. It was the sense that she, the cor anglais, and the music were one and the same, inseparable, a harmonious being of flesh, wood and sound.

As she played she saw a vision, fuzzy at first: the torso of a young man, on his back. She thought it might be Arky, lying on the bed. The figure grew clearer. It was a solid-looking young man, someone she knew. It was Matt. But his long black hair had been cut. His eyes were shut. She could see the flutter of movement under his eyelids and the lifting and falling of his black t-shirt as he breathed. There was something splattered on the gold letters declaring STATE. It was red. *Maybe blood,* she thought as two hands reached into the vision, grabbed the bottom of Matt's t-shirt and pulled up, exposing his chest. The hands continued to pull the shirt up, raising Matt's limp arms until the shirt was over his head, covering his face.

Iris blinked and the vision was gone, replaced by her room. She pulled the reed from her mouth. She turned and found Arky staring at her with a placid expression.

"What?" he asked. "Forget the next measure?"

She began describing her vision of Matt.

Arky interrupted. "If you've got the special-powers juju going, pick up your horn and bring Matt back to the chair you launched him from."

She took up the cor anglais and resumed playing. It wasn't the same; she couldn't recapture the effortless playing. She stopped. Her frustration was tempered with resignation. "I think that was it," she said. "That's all the cor anglais wants to give us now."

Arky sat up with a mocking expression. "'All the cor anglais wants to give us now?' Like this is foreplay? Like the spider crook is holding out on us? Like it's not going to bring Matt or Mom back till we both fall under its spell?" He got up and headed for the door. "Go cuckoo all you want, sis, but I'm not going to Planet Freak along with everyone else in the family."

Iris stood up. "Arky, I'm not crazy. Last night, I saw Matt disappear in a heartbeat, and I just saw him in a vision that felt totally real."

He turned at the door. "Okay, Iris, let's say you did. And I haven't brought this up till now—I'm not a total shit—but tell me this. Have you gone off your meds for synesthesia or PMS or whatever you take 'em for?"

Her body braced against the scream she wanted to unleash.

She refused to give him the satisfaction. "It's got nothing to do with that."

"So if you're not jerking my chain and it's not your meds"— he thrust out a hand—"then give me the instrument."

She clutched the cor anglais. "Why?"

"'Cause I've heard enough of this crap." His voice rose along with his mounting anger. "'Cause I'm sick of the bullshit story you've concocted! I don't give a rat's ass where you found the spider crook, but here's what I wanna do with it!" He grabbed the wooden music case off the bed.

"Don't!" Iris yelled.

He hurled it. The case sailed across the room like a spinning butterfly with wooden wings. It hit the straight-backed chair with a splintering crash.

The twins' eyes blazed with the hatred siblings can share when confined to the same house and gene pool. The only thing that stopped Iris from swinging the cor anglais at her brother's head was something she spied in the damaged music case.

Having seen it too, Arky moved to the case on the floor. A patch of red peeked from between the broken slats of the case's outer shell. He pushed aside the slats and pulled out a leather-bound journal. It had been hidden between the wood and the inner layer of purple velvet.

By the time he turned the journal over, Iris was at his side. In unison, they read the title imprinted in the red leather: *The Book of Twins.*

18.

THE GRIDIRON

Matt regained consciousness. He was no longer on the floor of the barbershop, but lying on a bed. He jerked up, hoping to finally wake from his long nightmare. What he saw made his heart sink. He was in a small room with two metal-frame beds. The room was sparsely furnished with old-looking stuff. Above the wainscoting, the walls displayed old pictures, pennants and a bamboo cane.

Feeling the stiffness of his clothing, Matt looked down. He was wearing one of Carlisle's military uniforms. There was a note on his chest secured with a safety pin. He ripped it off and read it. It was from Alfred, explaining that after Matt had been cold-cocked, he had been given new clothes, assigned a dorm room, and left there to recover until he was ready to begin his schooling at Carlisle. Matt crumpled the note and hurled it across the room. Being trapped in 1907 was a train wreck that wouldn't end.

Remembering something, he stood up and patted his pockets. His wallet was gone. "Great," he grumbled. "I've been robbed of time *and* money."

He went to the mirror over a washbasin. His reflection grimaced. "Shit." His hair had been shorn to a few inches and slicked down with a hard part to one side. Not only did he look like a nerd, he resembled his dad. He tried to muss it up, but the choirboy's cut sprang back into place. For the first time he found a positive. *If I'm marooned in 1907, at least I'll have time to grow my hair back.*

Matt strode across the quad. He no longer turned heads but blended in with the Indian students. The only thing that set him apart was his size. He asked a kid where the football field was; the kid pointed to a gap between dorms with multi-tier porches. Matt headed for the gap. After passing through it, he heard the familiar sound of a coach berating his players.

As he came around a brick building, a playing field appeared. It was marked in a strange way. The yardage lines were every five yards instead of ten, and the white lines ran the width *and* length of the field, making it look like a checkerboard. It was truly a *grid*iron.

Taking in the throng of guys scrimmaging in the middle of it, Matt wondered if he had been directed to the wrong field. The way the clumps of players slammed into each other and pushed and shoved, it looked more like a mosh pit at a concert. The pileup untangled, and a man in a long coat stabbed a cigarette at them, barking orders.

As Matt moved toward a man standing on the sideline, he noticed the players hardly wore pads. A few had leather headgear; some were bareheaded. Matt stopped next to the slight, fit-looking man. He wore a suit and looked more like a light-skinned black than an Indian. Matt figured he was a curious spectator.

"What are they playing?" Matt asked. "Rugby?"

The man gave Matt a friendly smile. "No, it's football, Pop Warner style."

Matt watched as the surprisingly small players lined up for a play. "Yeah," he quipped, "they look about the right size for Pop Warner."

The man gave Matt a curious look. "What do you mean?"

"They're a bunch of peewees."

"Those 'peewees,'" the man said with a chuckle, "just beat Villanova. People are saying we've got the material to go undefeated this year."

Matt jogged his head toward the players. "Those shrimps are *college* players?"

"Carlisle isn't a college," the man replied. "But we play all the best: Harvard, Yale, Princeton, Penn State, you name it." He extended his hand to Matt. "I'm Jimmie Johnson. Who are you?"

Matt gave him a quick shake. "Matt Grinnell."

"Do you play football?"

"Like all my life."

"Where?" Jimmie asked.

"Belleplain Cyclones."

"Sorry to say I haven't heard of them."

Matt shrugged with a half smile. "They're the team of the future."

"Interesting. That's what they call us." Jimmie gave Matt a once-over. "How much do you weigh?"

"Two-ten."

"We're always looking for heavy material up front."

"I'm a quarterback."

Jimmie cocked an eyebrow. "You look more like a snap-back."

"Look, I don't know your code," Matt asserted. "I just wanna know who I gotta see to suit up."

Jimmie gestured toward the field. "You could go right to the top. The man in the coat is Pop Warner."

The claim threw Matt. He'd grown up playing Pop Warner football, but he'd assumed it was just a brand name. "Pop Warner is a real guy?"

Jimmie laughed. "Some sportswriters would have you believe Pop's only a legend, but we've got the Old Fox back here this year in the flesh. Now, if you want to try out for the team, you don't have to talk to Coach Warner. You've talked to me, Jimmie Johnson, Assistant Coach." He waved toward the brick building at the end of the field. "Go to the Cage, tell Caleb Phillips I sent you, and he'll get you squared away."

After entering the Cage, Matt moved past a weight room and found what seemed to be the locker room. It was missing one thing: lockers. It was more like a hook room. Surrounding benches and a couple of tables were three walls of hooks holding the players' school uniforms. Matt noticed an entrance to an open shower room. Then his nose caught the dank plume of souring sweat coming from a doorway like a BO-breathing dragon. *Some things never change,* he thought, *especially the stench of the equipment drying room.*

A scrawny kid emerged from the dragon's mouth. Barely over five feet, Caleb Phillips had a bright face with lively eyes that took Matt in. "You must be the head-on material Coach has been looking for."

Matt resisted telling the squirt that he was about to blow away the Carlisle Indians with his QB skills. "Jimmie sent me to suit up."

Caleb frowned. "Jimmie?"

"Yeah, the assistant coach."

"You mean Mr. Johnson."

Matt shrugged. "Johnson, Jimmie, JJ, J-Jo, whatever."

Caleb answered his flippancy with a serious look. "You know he was an All-American."

Matt blew a laugh. "All-American what, midget?"

Caleb came back with a wry smile. "I hope your game's got the same ginger as your mouth." Then he waved Matt into the odor-choked lair from which he had emerged.

Caleb pulled pieces of uniform off drying lines. He handed Matt a white t-shirt, a lumpy jersey and the strangest pair of football pants Matt had ever seen. He held them up. They were made of stiff canvas and had some kind of kneepads, but the thigh protection was truly weird. It looked like each thigh was a vertical washboard. "What's in these things? Chopsticks?"

"Cane," Caleb said, exposing a snaggletooth grin. "Get

banged up and bruised enough and they give you zebra legs."

"Speaking of banged up," Matt said, holding up the jersey and feeling one of the lumps in the shoulder, "is this all you get for pads?"

"It's the finest horsehair in Cumberland County," Caleb bragged. "And it's prevented many a broken clavicle."

Matt stared at the flimsy uniform. "So you guys play football with chopsticks and horsehair for protection?"

Caleb held up a jockstrap. "We also protect the family jewels." He flipped it to Matt. "Go change in the dressing room and I'll bring your other armor."

Matt turned, shaking his head over "dressing room."

After Matt struggled into the stiff pants and the horse-hair-lumpy jersey, Caleb appeared with a pair of high-top clod-hoppers and leather headgear that looked like an old flying helmet.

Matt took the shoes and almost dropped them. "Are these cleats or cement shoes?"

Caleb offered the headgear. "This is optional, but you're better off without it. You need someone to knock some sense into you."

19.

WRONG-WAY PANTS

Once Matt was suited up, he and Caleb exited the Cage. The weight lost from thin pads and a leather hat was made up for by the shoes. They felt like ankle weights. Matt headed toward the field where he had talked to Jimmie.

"Where are you going?" Caleb asked.

Matt thrust an arm at the players still scrimmaging at midfield. "To show those squirts how to play the game."

"You won't be showing the Varsity anything." Caleb pointed toward a grassy ridge. "You start with the Hotshots and reserves on the lower practice field."

"What are the Hotshots?"

"The second-string team."

Matt scoffed without changing direction. "Been there done that, kid. I can handle Varsity."

He clump-jogged to Jimmie on the sideline and told him he was ready. Jimmie looked down the field at Caleb, who answered with an *I-did-my-best* shrug.

Jimmie took Matt onto the field and interrupted practice. "I've got some new meat here, Pop. His name is Matt Grinnell. He says he's got some football in him."

Pop Warner was a square-built man in body and head. As he took in the new prospect, his blue eyes shimmered with intensity. "We're not in the habit of letting anyone leapfrog to Varsity," he said. "But we like pluck and we like pounds. How's your pass?"

Matt held back a smile. "Like a cannon."

Pop pointed to a football on the ground at the line of scrimmage. "Get on the ball and let's see it."

Matt moved to the ball, picked it up and set like he was taking a snap. The ball was bulbous and overinflated, like old-fashioned footballs he had seen before, but as long as it had stitches, he figured he could throw it. He yelled "Hut, hut," and quickstepped back.

"Wait!" Pop interrupted. "What are you doing?"

"Showing you my pass."

The players snickered as Pop waggled a finger. "The only pass I wanna see is your snapback. Now let's see it."

Matt knew football had gone through a lot of "backs," including "nickel" and "dime," but this one stumped him. "What's a snapback, like a quick lateral?"

The players chuckled as Pop treated Matt to a stern gaze. "I thought you knew the game."

"I do," Matt insisted.

"All right then," Pop said, granting him the benefit of the doubt. "Maybe you need some reminding." He pointed to a squat player built like a bullfrog and just as ugly. "Shouchuk, show 'im what I want."

Shouchuk, an Alaskan Eskimo, hardly had to bend down to get over the ball and snap it between his legs to a skinny kid with a boyish face.

Realizing the confusion, Matt turned to Pop. "I'm not a center, I'm a quarterback."

The players exploded with laughter.

Matt's cheeks flushed.

"Son, we've got three quarterbacks." Pop jabbed his cigarette at the player who had taken the snap and two others. "Mount Pleasant, Island, and Pikey."

"Yeah, but do you have one that can throw?" Matt asked as he turned to the Eskimo. "Shoochuckie, hike me the ball, and someone run a post pattern."

No one moved. They didn't take orders from anyone but Pop and their captain.

Matt grabbed the ball from Mount Pleasant, gripped it, faked a snap and hurled the ball downfield. It turned end over end for about twenty yards and bounced off the turf.

"It could've been slick," Pop said as he gestured to his smallest quarterback to throw the ball he was holding. Island flicked a perfect spiral at Matt.

Matt took a quick drop as he gripped the bulbous ball and tried to launch a bomb. It was another dud, a drunken spiral that flew twenty-five yards. Next, he threw his excuse. "What's with the overinflated balls?"

Pop chuckled as he rolled a fresh cigarette. "Just to be fair, Mr. Grinnell, let's assume your paws are having a bad day. Let's see if your peds are feeling better."

"Peds?" Matt asked. "What's that?"

Pop nodded to his starting quarterback. "Mounty."

Mount Pleasant moved back with a ball in his hands, took a stride and dropkicked the ball through the goalposts.

Although impressed, Matt's confusion kept growing. "I'm not a kicker, I'm a QB."

Pop lit his cigarette and addressed the team. "Boys, I don't think I've ever seen a greener redskin try for the team. First, he forgets to roll out five yards left or right to throw a forward pass."

"Since when do you havta do that?" Matt demanded.

"Since last year," Mount Pleasant answered.

Pop continued his assessment. "Second, his forward pass looks like a dying quail, and third, if you can't kick, you've got no business in the backfield. There's a reason they call it 'football,' son. Which brings me to my last point. We do have some over-inflated balls around here, and they're in your trousers." As the team cracked up, Pop waved at Matt. "Now, run along and join the other boys learning the game and someday you might make a decent guard or tackle."

Jimmie beckoned to Matt. "C'mon. You had your shot."

Matt spun and started away. He didn't get two steps before one of the tallest players swung in front of him. "Mr. Grinnell," he announced, "it would be unkind to not acknowledge and reward your chesty effort. The least we can do is give you a proper name. Your demonstration has reminded me of the first Indian boys who came to Carlisle in 1879. When they traded in their buckskins for button-up pants, they didn't know if the buttons went in the front or the back, so many of them put their pants on backwards. Since you know as much about football, we shall call you Wrong-Way Pants."

As the team laughed and applauded, Matt clenched a fist. He checked his rage with a realization. *What's the point? These guys are just a bunch of long-dead losers.* He stepped around the player and headed for the lower field.

20.

THE BOOK OF TWINS

After Arky pulled the red leather journal from the damaged music case, he and Iris made a startling discovery. *The Book of Twins* was their mother's journal. On the first page, she had written a subtitle: *Sphere of Music.* Another page revealed it to be a diary their mother had begun on the first day of her sabbatical from Belleplain University.

Seated at Iris's desk, they hovered over the journal as Iris read Octavia's opening entry out loud.

> Plato said astronomy and music are "twinned" studies of sensual recognition: astronomy pleases the eye, music pleases the ear. While astronomy is the science of looking out, music is the art of listening in.

> For over two decades I've lived my life in the sphere of astrophysics. I now shift to the sphere of music. I enter the musical sphere with a question: Is there any truth to the Jongler family legend?

> While my father warned me to never put the legend in writing, my scientific self defies superstition and urges me to begin this account with the crux of the legend. We Jonglers possess an instrument that opens the fourth dimension, the Sphere of Time, and delivers humans to the past.

"That's where she went," Iris exclaimed. "To the past!"

Arky answered her near-levitating excitement with a dubious look. "Yeah, and I'm Albert Einstein."

She ignored the remark. "That's where Matt is too, in the past."

"Right, like he's a time-traveling bounty hunter chasing after Mom." Even though Arky remained skeptical, this new discovery was troubling. It was highly improbable his sister had the pranking chops to forge a journal, hide it in a music case, and goad him into busting it to find the thing. Rather than dwell on this disquieting observable, he turned to the next page. "Stop speculating and read."

Iris returned to Octavia's first entry and continued reading aloud.

> What little I've just written of the Jongler family legend probably has my father spinning in his grave. For that reason I will resume being a true Jongler and obey the directive he gave me along with the Jongler cor anglais: "The family legend shall never be written. It shall be passed from generation to generation by sound alone: by human voice or the music-induced visions of the cor anglais."

Arky slid Iris a look. "You and Mom are the only synesthetes in the family. Has the 'Jongler family legend' ever come to your mental movieplex?"

"No. Now shush." She kept reading.

> It has always been my plan to put off experimentation with the cor anglais until the twins went to college. But in recent months, my episodes of synesthesia have increased in intensity and duration. At first, I thought these preternatural visions were being triggered by the stress of teaching, research, raising twin teenagers and

assuring my husband that he still has a wife. However, as the visions magnified, I realized they were not the result of *external* pressures. They were coming from within; they were the flickering lights of a road not taken, a road that needed to be taken sooner rather than later.

Because this path is a radical departure, and because I do not wish to alarm my family or have them think I'm mentally unstable, I will disguise my true work by doing what many professors do on sabbatical: write an inconsequential book that no one will read.

Iris glanced up. "We were right. Learning to play the modern cor anglais and writing *A Year of Magical Playing* were a cover for experimenting with the Jongler cor anglais."

Arky nodded. "And it's the sanest thing she's said yet. Books about oboes don't make bestsellers. Keep going."

Iris read on.

This journal, *The Book of Twins: Sphere of Music*, will be the diary of my playing the Jongler cor anglais, a record of the visions it produces and, if there is any truth to the legend, a leap into the unknown.

It doesn't mean I'm abandoning scientific ways; a leopardess cannot change her spots. But this book is not the place for hard science. My parallel research—into the second law of temporal dynamics and the principle of the spacetime web—is being kept in another volume: *The Book of Twins: Sphere of Science*.

Iris shot a question to Arky. "Are those real laws?"

He shook his head. "Never heard of 'em." Such bizarre concepts reinforced Arky's worry that their mother had begun her drift away from sanity well before she had vanished.

Arky's pensive expression was a relief to Iris. His cynicism had been derailed, at least for a moment. "Did she ever mention those laws to you?" she asked.

"Never. And when I went through Mom's computer in the attic, there wasn't any mention of *The Book of Twins: Sphere of Science*. Her computer only has research and notes on her book about learning to play the modern cor anglais."

"That's all I found too," Iris said. "But why '*The Book of Twins*'? Does this have something to do with us?"

Arky scoffed. "Doubtful. If it was about us, why would she walk out on us?"

Iris's eyes widened. "Wait a sec, the police went through Mom's computer first. Maybe they stole *The Book of Twins: Sphere of Science*."

"If we're going to go conspiracy theory," Arky said, "maybe she did an Edward Snowden; maybe she took her *Sphere of Science* files with her. Maybe she's working on them right now in a Starbucks somewhere."

"Yeah," Iris came back with a smile, "maybe in the *first* Starbucks back in the twentieth century."

He let her have the last word and took up reading aloud where she had left off.

While I use my sabbatical to immerse myself in these twin endeavors, I'm not blind to the dangers. Just as all explorers and scientists risk being bitten by what they discover, as Marie Curie discovered radiation only to die from exposure to it, I accept the risk of exploring the frontier of the past.

I have no choice. I am a Jongler, and Jonglers must eventually answer the call of *tempus ludendi:* a time for playing. My time for playing is now.

Octavia Jongler
June 8

"That proves it," Iris declared. "Mom tapped into the powers of the old cor anglais just like I did when Matt disappeared. For a year she's been lost in the past!"

Unmoved by her excitement, Arky turned the page. "June 9" was written at the top. He scanned a few lines. It was an account of Octavia's first practice session with the old cor anglais. He pushed himself to his feet.

"We have to keep reading," Iris protested. "I've been waiting forever to find something like this!"

"First off," he said flatly, "you gotta get a grip."

She jumped up, waving the journal. "This is our map to finding Mom and Matt!"

"That's what you *want* to believe."

"What do *you* believe?"

"I believe in the God tangle."

Iris pulled back. "What?"

"No one can prove God exists," he explained, "and no one can prove He *doesn't* exist. You can't prove Mom and Matt got relocated to the past, and I can't prove they didn't. But for the hell of it, let's take a trip to Planet Whacko and assume everything you saw last night with Matt, and everything Mom wrote in this journal, is true."

"I didn't make it up and neither did Mom."

He raised a hand. "*If* it's all true, then two things are certain. One, Mom wasn't abducted, she abandoned us."

"How?"

He thrust an arm at the cor anglais lying on the bed. "By playing Russian roulette with a friggin' oboe! By doing a gonzo experiment and leaving us with the mess!"

While his outburst startled Iris, she took it as a good sign. It meant her brother's heart was beginning to entertain what his mind refused to accept.

Arky reclaimed his cool. As much as the growing pile of observables was shaking his bedrock of science, he refused to admit it, especially to Iris. "The second thing is that *if* there's some bizarre truth to any of this, then we can't say a word to anyone till we figure it out."

"What about Dad?"

"Especially not Dad," Arky stressed. "If he thinks you can go century-surfing, he'll want you to blow him back to the Civil War and then we'll be orphans."

Iris conceded a smile. "Right."

"And until we figure out what's going on," Arky continued, "we have to act like nothing happened. We have to act normal." His eyes slid to the clock on her desk. "Which means not being late for your orchestra rehearsal."

"There's no way I'm going to rehearsal"—she lifted the journal—"when I've got this. I'm gonna call in sick." She started for her cell phone on her desk. Arky grabbed her wrist. His move shocked her. They hadn't had a physical fight since they were ten.

Equally surprised by his impulsive move, Arky let her go. "Iris, the police have already come sniffing around here once. If you don't show up for rehearsal, it could raise suspicions. We have to act totally normal."

"But Arky, this is a new normal."

"You may think so, but I need more than Mom's diary and her claim of going Daniel Boone to the 'frontier of the past.' I need Mom's other book, *Sphere of Science*, if it even exists. For all I know, Mom could've mind-warped into madness. And you, like Mom talked about in her journal, might be ramping up your own synesthesia. You could have hallucinated the whole thing. For all I know, Matt jumped on a train to New Orleans and is on a Bourbon Street bender. I can't prove anything. And until we can, we have to act normal. You've got to go to rehearsal and I've got to start cleaning up the house. Are you with me?"

Iris understood her brother's stubborn skepticism; he hadn't seen what she had. Besides, he had a point. If you were the one who blew Matt Grinnell to another time, avoiding suspicion was smart. "Okay, I'm with you." She raised the journal. "But I'm not leaving till you promise you won't do anything to Mom's diary or the cor anglais."

"Believe me, sis, if—and it's a big if—the only thing that'll get Matt and Mom back is that spider crook and some secret in this journal, they're both safe."

21.

SHOCKS

Caleb walked alongside Matt as they headed to the lower field where the Hotshots and reserves were practicing.

Bouncing along, Caleb reinforced Matt's realization that the "silent Indian" was a stereotype. "That was Antonio 'the Wolf' Lubo who gave you the nickname," Caleb explained. "He's our captain. I bet you're wondering about the Indian names when we're supposed to use English all day. We're not even allowed to dream in our native tongue." He shot Matt a look. "That was a joke."

"Not in the mood," Matt groused.

His surliness didn't deter Caleb. "Pop likes us to use Indian names on the field. The names have power, and it reminds all the palefaces we play who we are. Some college boys get jittery playing against Indians, and Pop will do *anything* to get an edge. That's why he's the Old Fox."

Reaching one end of the lower field, they watched a play unfold downfield in another scrimmage. The up-the-middle play collapsed in a heap of bodies while a player standing nearby urged them on. As the pile untangled, Matt was struck by how the Hotshots and scrubs were even smaller than the Varsity, not averaging 150 pounds a man.

"That's Newashe," Caleb said, pointing to the Indian running the practice and moving with a limp. "He's the player-coach of the Hotshots. Right now he's banged up. I'll introduce you."

Matt watched the team run another play. He didn't want to meet anyone; he just wanted to bust some heads. A running back suddenly broke through a hole in the line with a burst of acceleration. Besides his speed, Matt was struck by something he had never seen a small running back do. Instead of relying on his quickness to dodge the secondary moving up to tackle him, the back ran at the tacklers so he could run over them. It was like watching a bowling ball with a mind of its own, seeking pins and leveling them.

After leaving a trail of players sprawled behind him, the ball carrier ran straight at Matt and Caleb, daring one of them to stop him. They dodged out of the way as the kid leaped in the air and touched the ball to the ground across the goal line. And there was no end zone, Matt noticed. The wooden goalposts were planted right on the goal line.

The runner bounded over to Matt and Caleb. He was built like a weed but had a broad jaw and an infectious smile. His skin, like Matt's, was lighter than the other Indians'. He hardly breathed, like he had only jumped up a couple of steps. "Hi," he said, not offering his hand. He didn't need to. The way he stood in front of Matt reminded him of a dog that had returned a ball and eagerly awaited the next throw. "I'm Jim Thorpe."

"Yeah, right," Matt scoffed, "and I'm Peyton Manning."

The kid offered his hand. "Nice to meet you, Peyton."

"I'm not Peyton!" Matt snapped.

The kid's grin widened. "Well, when you remember who you are, let Jim know." He spun away and kicked the football on the ground into the air toward the goalpost. The ball bounced off the upright, he caught it, and ran back to midfield as effortlessly as a leaf in the wind.

Matt stared after him, dumbfounded. What little he knew about Jim Thorpe his father had told him. Thorpe had won two gold medals in the 1912 Olympics, but had been stripped of the medals when officials found out he had played semipro baseball and wasn't an amateur during the Olympics. But there was no way this scrawny kid could be an Olympian. "That's *not* Jim Thorpe," Matt declared.

Caleb eyed Matt. "Do you know another Jim Thorpe?"

Matt realized his answer might blow his from-the-future secret. "Actually, I do." He pointed toward Thorpe. "But *that* Jim Thorpe, he goes here?"

"He's got to go somewhere."

Meeting Jim Thorpe took some of the sting out of Matt's humiliation in front of the Varsity. Getting tossed to the second-string wasn't so bad when you got to share the field with the kid who, in a few years, would be called "the greatest athlete in the world."

Matt jogged toward the throng of players, introduced himself to Newashe, the player-coach, and didn't say a word about being a QB. In fact, he told Newashe that he knew squat about football. Newashe told him the best place for a big fellow like Matt to start was at guard, because a guard had the least amount of turf to cover and the least to learn. "When your side has the ball, don't let 'em come through you and spoil the play," Newashe instructed. "When the other side has the ball, knock the tar out of your man and tackle the runner."

That's what Matt tried to do. Unfortunately, having not practiced blocking or tackling since junior high, Matt looked like the rank beginner they thought he was. Newashe berated him for not staying low, and for charging too high while blocking or tackling. "You look like a chick in a nest reaching for a worm," he scolded. "Now get down, stay down, and show me a hog rootin' in the dirt."

Matt's poor lineman skills weren't his biggest surprise. In the first series, after his team had run three plays, he lined up for fourth down. But the opposing center was over the ball, ready to hike it. Matt figured it must be one of their weird scrimmage rules. After a couple more three-down series, he asked the tackle next to him, "What happened to fourth down?"

The tackle, Asa Sweetcorn, gave him a funny look and

answered in stilted English. "Any team need four downs to make ten yards play like squaw. Three plenty."

Matt chuckled at his answer and the notion of being in a time and place where saying "squaw" was still okay. He made an addition to the 1907 football rulebook he had begun compiling in his head: *Three downs, not four. No more three and out, it was two and out.*

For the rest of the scrimmage, what Matt lacked in skills and knowledge of the 1907 game he made up for with the forty pounds he had on every player. But even though he was used to taking the occasional hit as a QB, getting hit every play was a shock. After dozens of collisions with the Indian opposite him, or with Jim running into him like rolling steel, Matt was tapped out and wobbly-legged.

As the sun began to set, Newashe called for one last play. Matt was on defense and relieved when the offense sent Jim on an end run around the other side. But then Jim, not liking what he saw, reversed field. Matt was the only one who hadn't chased the play, which left him the only one between Jim and open field. Matt was going to let him go, but Jim, being Jim, ran straight at Matt. Matt's only choice was to tackle him in self-defense.

Jim put his head down and ran into Matt like a bullet train. For Matt it was a bullet train going into a tunnel: everything went black.

The next thing Matt felt was stinging in his nostrils. He sputtered, sneezed and opened his eyes. He was staring up at an oval of blurry heads, all Indians. As their bronze faces swam into focus, along with Caleb holding a bottle of smelling salts, Jim's face rubbered into a grin. "Next time Jim runs at you, get out of his way."

"Won't be a next time," Matt grumbled. It was the second time he had been knocked out in a matter of hours. As he struggled to his feet, a couple players tried to help him but he brushed them off. He touched the lump protruding from his forehead. "Don't you guys know about concussions? Head trauma? Dementia?" They stared at him like he was speaking Chinese. "You need harder helmets and rules about shots to the head."

"Harder helmets would hurt more," Newashe pointed out.

"Not if everyone was wearing them!" Matt shouted. He paid for it with a stab of pain in his head. "This isn't football, it's cage fighting. I'm outta here." He pushed through the circle of players and headed off the field.

Caleb followed. "I think you just broke a Carlisle record: the shortest football career ever. One hour and—" He pulled a pocket watch from his vest.

"Leave me alone," Matt snapped.

"I can't."

"Yeah, you can. It's easy. Stop following me, shorty."

The insult stopped Caleb. He let Matt go.

22.

SPHERE OF MUSIC

In the Jongler-Jinks kitchen, Arky sat at the counter with his coffee mug and the leather journal he and Iris had found in the wooden music case. *The Book of Twins: Sphere of Music* was what Octavia had described : a diary of her practice sessions with the old Jongler cor anglais when her husband was at work and her kids were at school.

Arky was looking for clues or the smoking gun that would prove their mother had lost her marbles or had walked out on her family for a specific reason. Such evidence would support Arky's belief that the disappearance of Octavia Jongler and Matt Grinnell were not linked. It would also shred Iris's conviction that the Jongler cor anglais was a "horn of angels" with paranormal powers.

As he read, he sometimes heard his mother's voice and the way her clinical tone became infected with enthusiasm. When this happened he had to shake her voice out of his head. Reading her descriptions of musically-induced visions was one thing, but *hearing* her voice gnawed at his doubts. It's hard to hear your mother and think, *Liar.*

According to the entries, just about every time she played the curved cor anglais with the spider on it, her synesthesia kicked in and the music provoked a vision. As her entries progressed, so did the intensity of her hallucinations. Some described patterns and geometrics that built into an eruption, like a geometry book exploding into fireworks. Others were cinematic visions of people, places and things, but they appeared in a jumble of circumstances, out of time, out of place, straight out of the no-rhyme-nor-reason world of dreams.

From what Arky had read so far, there was no clue Octavia was about to launch herself into the past. The evidence pointed to their mother using her sabbatical to play the old cor anglais while doing hallucinogenic drugs or simply using the time to divorce herself from reality.

As much as he leaned toward those probabilities, a few details in *Sphere of Music* contradicted them. There were hints that Octavia was still employing logic, and still had a hand and her mind in *The Book of Twins: Sphere of Science*. There were two entries titled "Wroclaw, Poland," and "Africa." Arky was certain these didn't refer to visions. In the months before Octavia had disappeared, while she was allegedly working on her book, she had taken two trips. One was to Wroclaw, the city in Poland where the wind instrument that became the cor anglais was first made in the early 1700s. The other was to Tanzania, where Octavia had visited a forest of grenadilla trees, the most desirable wood for wind instruments. It was from this trip that she had returned with the cross-section of a grenadilla tree that now hung in her attic office.

For Arky, the baffling thing about these entries was that, with the exception of the page listing the place and dates of each trip, the accounts had been ripped out. *Why rip them out but leave the first page?* he wondered. *Were they too scientific for the* Sphere of Music? *Had they been moved to the* Sphere of Science? *If so, where was this second volume?*

Reading the journal, Arky didn't hear the pickup in the driveway. It wasn't until the front door opened that he looked up and saw Danny Bender coming inside. Arky swept the journal off the countertop and plunked it on the stool next to him. He tried to look casual as he took another sip of coffee.

Danny was too upset to notice. "Matt never showed for

game film," he declared. "Gunner and the police showed up and said Matt's missing. I called his cell but all I got was his voicemail. What the hell's going on?"

Arky offered his versions of what he believed had happened: Matt had gone AWOL for the weekend to rattle his dad's cage or was off somewhere sleeping off a hangover.

"So let's go look for him," Danny urged. "I know a few places he might be holed up."

"I'd love to join you for a rescue op, Captain America, but I'm on KP." Arky gestured at the mess still littering the kitchen. "I gotta de-partify the house."

"If we find him, we'll help you clean up," Danny offered.

Arky dug for another excuse. "You guys are in training for State. There's no way I'm risking one of you getting injured"—he spread his arms—"in a superfund cleanup site. Trust me, Cap, Matt hasn't left the troposphere."

Danny shot him a hard look. "And you never leave the bullshit-sphere." He banged out the front door. "When I find 'im, we're gonna come back and kick your ass!"

As Danny peeled out of the driveway, Arky lifted the journal back onto the counter and read more entries of music-triggered visions. Another nagging detail began to appear that defied the notion that his astrophysicist mom had discovered Planet Crazy. Scattered through the entries were notations, like "C-3" and "F-12." Arky figured they were cross-reference notations to the missing cache, *Sphere of Science*.

To be sure this record had not been overlooked, Arky went up to the attic office, fired up Octavia's computer, and scoured it again for any signs of her scientific research on the cor anglais and time travel. Nothing.

As he came back downstairs, the alphanumeric notations in *Sphere of Music* kept plaguing him. Cross-referencing was the kind of thing a *scientist* did. The notations pointed to a method to her madness. And that's what worried him the most: if there was a method, maybe the disappearances of Octavia and Matt *were* connected. Maybe Matt wouldn't be in school on Monday. Maybe he might even miss the state championship.

23.

THE PLAN

Matt lay on the bed in his dorm room. He knew enough about concussions to know he shouldn't fall asleep. But he was totally wiped from a day that wouldn't end. Every time he felt sleepy, he poked himself with the safety pin Alfred had left on his jacket. Between pokes, he considered his next move.

There was no reason to stay at Carlisle with a bunch of Indians. The only thing keeping him there was the cor anglais, which was supposedly his ticket back to the present. A game plan formed in his head. He would go with the program till late that night. He would sneak out of the dorm, find the cor anglais in Alfred's office, take it, and find another Jongler who knew how to play it right. He knew it wasn't the best game plan he'd ever drawn up; in fact, it sounded stupid. But given the bizarre circumstances, it was the best he could think of.

His eyes were growing heavy when the door opened. Caleb Phillips stepped into the room. "I told you to stop following me," Matt growled.

"I heard you the first time," Caleb said, looking hurt. "I live here."

Matt stared. "You're my roommate?"

"Looks like it." Caleb sat at a small table strewn with books. "You know, as much as I was hoping you would be on the team, you probably made the right decision."

Matt's head dropped back on his pillow. "Duh."

Caleb's face tweaked with curiosity. "What's that mean?"

"It means duh."

"Okay," Caleb said without taking offense. "I'll look it up in the dictionary later." He glanced at his pocket watch. "It's almost time for dinner. Are you hungry?"

Matt rose up on his elbows. "I could eat a horse."

"Sorry," Caleb replied, "we only get that on special occasions."

Matt didn't know if he was kidding. It didn't matter. In a few hours, he would be gone.

As they walked to the dining hall, Caleb was chatty. "Don't feel bad about what happened on the field today."

"It is what it is," Matt said. "I crashed and burned in front of the Varsity, and I got run over and knocked out by a bantamweight nutcase."

"You talk funny."

"You talk too much."

Caleb laughed. "Touché." He went silent for a few steps. "I'm just saying that you're not the only one adjusting to a new game."

"New game?" Matt echoed. "What's new about it?"

"There were big changes to the rules of football last year. The days of flying wedges and battering rams of bodies slamming into each other are gone."

Matt touched the knot on his forehead. "Coulda fooled me."

"Oh, it used to be worse," Caleb announced with excited eyes. "In 1903, twenty-five college players were killed during the football season."

"From what?"

"Playing football, of course. In the 1905 season, eighteen men died. Then one broken nose changed the whole thing."

Matt slid him a skeptical look. "All these guys are dying and all it took was a broken nose?"

"Yes, but not *any* broken nose. President Roosevelt's son was playing for Harvard, and Teddy Junior got his face smashed up so bad the president said, 'Change the rules of football or I'm going to ban the game.' So a committee got together and changed the rules."

"What were the big changes?"

Caleb rattled them off. "Six men have to line up on the line of scrimmage. No more locking arms. No more hurling players over the pile. No more running starts before the center snaps the ball so a runner hits the line like a freight train. And they legalized the forward pass."

Matt blinked. "The forward pass was illegal?"

"Until last season any pass over ten yards was illegal. But the air attack is still risky. If a forward pass isn't caught, it's a fifteen-yard penalty from where the ball was thrown. And if a pass hits the ground before it's touched by a player on the passing team, it's a turnover to the enemy."

Matt shook his head in disbelief. "With those kinds of rules, who would wanna pass?"

"That's the idea. Old-time footballists hate the forward pass."

Matt's curiosity eclipsed his urge to laugh at *footballists*. "Why do they hate it?"

"Football is supposed to be hand-to-hand combat that turns men into warriors," Caleb explained. "If you start throwing the ball too much, it'll turn football into basketball and men into sissies."

Matt let out a scornful laugh. "You believe that?"

"No, but I read it in the newspapers."

"Well, the long pass isn't going anywhere as long as you play with a ball the size of a watermelon."

Caleb brightened. "Wait till you see Mounty throw it!"

"Who's Mounty?"

"Mount Pleasant, our quarterback. Everyone calls him Mounty, and he can launch the ball a mile!"

"Good for him." Matt lowered his voice as students joined them moving toward the dining hall. "But I'm not sticking around to see it. I'm outta here."

Caleb's eyes widened. "Where are you going? Back to your reservation?"

"Something like that, yeah."

"But it's a new century, a whole new road for the Indian," Caleb urged. "Don't you want to live in the twentieth century?"

Matt chuckled. "I'd rather live in the twenty-first."

Caleb shook his head. "That's a long way off."

Matt nodded. "Tell me about it."

In the dining hall, they sat at a long table. Matt went silent as Caleb talked and joked with his friends.

Matt was amused that all the girls were seated on one side of the hall, all the boys on the other. It made checking out the local talent easier. The girls' full white dresses accentuated their bronze complexions and mounds of pinned-up black hair. Matt chortled over how Kelly would look among them: a shining blond in a sea of dark. He wondered how she was handling his disappearance from Belleplain. *Probably saying, "He got what he deserved,"* he thought, *or balling her eyes out.* He dismissed his thoughts of Kelly and returned to the Indian girls. A few wore skinny black ties over their dresses. He wondered if it was the 1907 equivalent of women's lib. *Or,* he considered, *the ties were the last to go on a girl's way to naked.*

Matt's horny musing was interrupted by little Indian boys serving beans, rice, gravy ladled from a bucket, and bread without a pat of butter in sight. Having not eaten in twenty-four hours, Matt wiped his plate clean and finished Caleb's leftovers.

During the meal, Matt looked for the football players he had practiced with that afternoon. He only saw a few of the scrubs.

Walking back to their quarters through the dusk, Matt asked Caleb, "Where do the football players eat?"

"They have their own dining room and their own dorm," Caleb answered wistfully. "They get milk, beef, potatoes and all the butter they want."

Matt was struck by the lack of resentment in his voice. "Kinda unfair, don't you think?"

Caleb shook his head. "They're football players. They have to be strong to show the white man that we're still great warriors, even if only on a football field."

As Matt thought about Caleb's answer, Jim Thorpe bounded up to them. "How's your head?" he asked Matt.

"Still on my shoulders."

"That's debatable," Caleb told Jim. "He says he wants to live in the twenty-first century."

"I've run away to lots of places," Jim said with twinkling eyes, "but never another century. Jim thought his runaway days were over, but if you decide to spring for the next century, let me know. I'll go with you."

Matt had to smile. "Thanks, I'll keep it in mind."

Later, while Caleb studied and Matt lay on the bed, Matt asked the question that kept popping into his head. "Why did Jim say his runaway days were over?"

Caleb looked up from his book. "The only place he'd be running to is the graveyard."

"What do you mean?"

"All of his folks are dead. He's a Carlisle man now."

Matt wanted to say that none of his folks had been born yet, but Caleb probably thought he was loony enough.

Retreating into silence, Matt thought about Belleplain again. He wondered if time was still ticking away there . . . if everyone was freaking out about him going missing . . . if the Cyclones were drawing up a new game plan for State without Matt at the helm.

24.

PANIC

Arky had yet to begin the after-party cleanup. He was in the kitchen, making more coffee. As he waited for the coffeemaker to beep, he stared out the window. His brain was in a knot. The signs in his mother's journal of her still being scientifically minded were eating at him. *The cross-reference notations in the journal have to refer to another body of evidence,* he told himself, *her* Sphere of Science. *And what did she mean by "the second law of temporal dynamics and the principle of the spacetime web?"*

Temporal, of course, means time, Arky told himself. From his AP Physics class, he also knew the law sounded like a real one, the second law of *thermo*dynamics. It proves there's disorder in any system, including the universe, making it susceptible to randomness and collapse. *What was she proposing?* he wondered. *That just as the universe is prone to randomness and collapse, time itself is prone to randomness and collapse?*

And her "principle of the spacetime web," what was that? Does it relate to the web of galaxies and supernovas on the wall in her office, and the spider on the Jongler cor anglais? Does she believe we're caught in a "spacetime web" but can break free? His thoughts kept tumbling. *The idea of a spacetime web isn't totally alien. It's like a theory in physics: the "block universe." It claims that the four dimensions—three of space, one of time—have created a cosmic "loaf of bread" that can be sliced in any direction, the cosmic equivalent of tectonic plates that can shift and open fissures to the past or future.*

The *beep!* of the coffeemaker seemed to explode, shocking Arky from his reverie.

After filling his mug, he returned to his mother's journal. He came to an entry that was different from her daily report of playing the Jongler cor anglais. In the entry, Octavia was contemplating one of the paradoxes of time travel.

> If, as the legend has it, time travel to the past is possible, and has been going on for the four centuries the JCA has been in existence . . .

Arky recognized "JCA" as the acronym for the Jongler cor anglais and was surprised that it might be four hundred years old.

> . . . why don't time travelers who make a voyage to the past and return to their present speak of their extraordinary travels? Perhaps in past centuries, voyagers who spoke of traveling through time were thrown into madhouses and asylums. Perhaps people of today who believe they've had "past lives" are actually remembering bits and pieces of time travel and confusing it with a "past life."

His mother's ruminations sent a bolt of fear through Arky. *If Mom hasn't gone mad scientist, if she and Iris are right and Matt is off in some past, what if he comes back and starts blabbing about time travel? What if he remembers how he was blown into the past and accuses Iris of being the blower? What if our house gets surrounded by a media circus? What if we become a freak show?*

Arky shook away his ballooning paranoia. *Time travel is totally theoretical,* he assured himself, *the stuff of fiction and bad movies.*

He returned to the journal. The words swam in front of him. He couldn't escape his fears. "Ah!" he shouted. A door banged open, doubling his outburst. "Ahhh!"

Iris barged in from the garage. She stopped at the sight of her brother's ashen face. "What happened?"

"Nothing!" he blurted.

"So why are you shouting?"

"I'm not shouting." He threw the attention back on her. "What are you doing here? Rehearsal can't be over."

"It's not." She put her oboe case on the island. "I couldn't focus and my playing sucked. I told 'em I was sick. I couldn't stop thinking about Dad."

Having almost regained his color, Arky's face scrunched. "What about him?"

"When he gets home, I think we should tell him."

"Tell him what?"

"Everything."

Arky stared in disbelief. "You're insane."

"I'm serious. Dad should know about the cor anglais, about the journal and where Mom is."

"Iris, there are tons of reasons not to tell him."

"Really?" she threw back. "Name one."

"How 'bout two." Arky finger-counted. "One, we don't actually know *where* Mom is. Two, if we told Dad that she's lost in the past, it would fill him with hope. And that would be cruel."

Iris was heartened by the concern she heard in his voice. "Gee, Arky"—she pointed at the journal on the counter—"that must be really good. I hear a crack in your armor."

"Not even close," he declared.

"Then why do you look scared?"

"That's your observable," he shot back, "here's mine. Time travel may be *theoretically* possible, but even if that spider crook could blow someone away at the speed of light, their body would never survive the g-forces. They'd be blown to smithereens."

She studied him. "You keep thinking the cor anglais is malicious and evil. You keep thinking only bad stuff is going to happen. I think something incredibly good is going to come from this."

"Really?" he answered. "Is it *good* that even if your demon stick blew Mom to another quadrant in spacetime she might be dead? Is it *good* that it might have disappeared Matt a week before the state championship? Is it *good* that if either of them shows up blabbing about time travel, it'll blow up in our face and we'll be branded as freaks? Is it *good* that having the first working time-travel machine would have the CIA or some black-op military cell all over us?"

Iris answered his serial paranoia with a serene smile. "For all we know, the CIA has already confiscated a time machine or two, and when they seize ours, they'll put us in the time-travel witness protection program."

Arky glowered. "Not funny."

"There's one way to shut me up."

He exhaled loudly. "Bring it."

"My turn to read the journal."

25.

A SOLDIER RETURNS

Arky had made major headway in cleaning up the house from the party. All incriminating evidence from the kitchen and den had been bagged, and he was now working on the living room. In the meantime, Iris had retreated to her room with their mother's journal, *Sphere of Music*.

Arky dumped pieces of the broken lamp in a full garbage bag, spun the bag shut, and carried it to the kitchen. What he couldn't bag were his ongoing worries about Matt's disappearance. Worst-case scenarios kept haunting him. *Wherever Matt is, what if he doesn't get back till after State? What if he misses the football game of his life, points the finger at Iris and the cor anglais, and Gunner Grinnell accuses us of kidnapping? I mean, if Iris is right about what happened, it's what she and the cor anglais did: kidnap Matt and hide him in the past.*

In the kitchen, he put the bulging bag next to another full bag by the door to the garage.

Iris thumped down the stairs. She entered the kitchen carrying the open journal and waving it at him. "Did you rip out the entries on Poland and Africa?"

Arky wrinkled his face. "Why would I do that?"

"To hide something from me."

"Trust me, sis, I only hide normal stuff"—he gestured to the evidence at his feet—"like a party from Dad." He grabbed one of the wire ties on the island countertop. "It's you and Mom who hide crazy stuff, like creepy oboes and secret notes and diaries. I have no idea why she ripped out the entries on Wroclaw and Tanzania."

Before Iris could respond, they heard a car race into the driveway and *screech* to a stop. Their eyes darted to the window. "Oh, shit!" Arky exclaimed.

He grabbed the journal from Iris, quickly opened the bag he had brought from the living room, dropped the journal in it, re-spun the bag shut and twisted the wire tie.

He barely got out of the way as Howard Jinks charged in from the garage and almost tripped over the garbage bags. As Howard vented his wrath, he looked oddly comical in the blue uniform of a Union soldier.

"I go away for the first weekend in a year, a weekend I've been planning for months, and halfway through it a state trooper tracks me down on the battlefield and tells me I need to contact the Belleplain Police as soon as possible!" He kicked the garbage bag with the journal in it toward Arky. "I then learn you threw a wild party in the house that ended with Matt Grinnell going missing!"

Despite their father resembling a walk-around in a Civil War theme park who had lost it, Arky felt the brunt of his words. Whatever satisfaction Iris might have enjoyed at her brother getting busted was overwhelmed by a temptation. She wanted to rip open the garbage bag and show the journal to their father.

When Howard demanded an explanation, Arky stepped up and delivered his pitch. He took full responsibility for the party, then repeated the story Iris had told the police early that morning: Matt had last been seen when he had gone up to Iris's room to ask for a juggling lesson. He'd then disappeared into the night, on foot and alone.

It wasn't the first time Howard had heard his son cherry-pick the facts, throw them into the blender of his conniving mind and deliver a half-truth smoothie. But more troubling was Iris's silent compliance. She was usually the first to provide the missing facts. "Iris, is that true?"

"Yeah," she said with a nod, "that's what happened."

Howard wasn't satisfied. In an attempt to divide and conquer, he delivered his edict. "You're both grounded for a week except for school activities."

"But, Dad," Iris protested. "I didn't have anything to do with the party. I was in my room the whole time."

"You're twins!" Howard roared. "What goes for one goes for both!"

He kicked the garbage bag again and glared at Arky. "Now get this crap out of the house before I get my muzzle-loader and put you in front of a firing squad." Howard slammed back out the door to unpack his gear.

The twins stood for a moment, letting their father's wrath dissipate in the silence. Arky's curiosity kicked in. "I thought you wanted to tell him everything."

"Right now, he's so pissed off I think you're right," she explained. "If he knew what the cor anglais can do, he'd want to go to the Civil War . . . or wherever Mom is."

Hearing their father noisily unpack in the garage, Arky reopened the garbage bag and pulled out the journal.

Iris stepped toward him. "I'll hide it in my room."

He stuffed the journal in the back of his jeans and hid it with his shirt. "I'm gonna finish it first."

She offered a compromise. "Why don't we read it together?"

Arky chuckled. "If Dad saw us doing anything together, he'd know something was up. I'll give it to you tonight. Promise."

26.

ESCAPE

At 9 pm, a bugle sounding taps drifted across the Carlisle campus.

Lying in his dorm-room bed, Matt watched the lights flicker off in the Small Boys' Quarters across the quad. He had gathered the coat he'd been issued, a blanket roll, some bread he'd stuffed in a pocket during dinner, a candle and some matches. He had his plan and was ready to roll.

Caleb doused the light and got into bed. After a moment, he spoke. "Here's what you should know about running away. If they don't catch you and bring you back, you can come back on your own. That's what Jim did, and he's on the right path now. That's what his Indian name means: Bright Path. There's power in that name. For your sake, I hope your path takes you where you need to go."

Matt laughed. "For my sake, I hope there's no power in my name: Wrong Way."

"That's not your real Indian name," Caleb insisted. "And you don't have to tell it to me. Sometimes the most powerful name is the one never spoken."

"Thanks, Caleb," Matt said softly. "If I don't come back, it was good knowing you."

"That's how I feel too."

An hour later, the buildings were all dark; the campus was quiet. All Matt heard was the steady breathing of Caleb sleeping and the rhythmic hoot of an owl calling to its own kind in the nearby woods. It was the sign Matt was waiting for. It was time to go back to his own kind.

Matt walked swiftly through the dark toward the Academic Building. A bulging half moon lit his way. His blood raced with adrenalin and the excitement of his escape.

Inside the building, he lit the candle and headed for Alfred's office. Finding it, he went inside. Matt was surprised to find the wooden music case on an upper shelf in a closet, where he had seen Alfred leave it before. While he was puzzled that the music teacher had made no effort to hide it, Matt wasn't going to look a gift horse in the mouth. He pulled down the case and left the office.

As he made his candlelit way back to the building's entrance, he reviewed his plan. He would go into town, find a phonebook, if such things existed yet, and see if there were other Jonglers around. If not, he'd go hobo and jump trains to Belleplain. He was hoping Arky and Iris's ancestors had been in Belleplain for a few generations, which might put a Jongler there in 1907. Besides, if he had to sit on the bench and rot in the twentieth century, he figured he'd rather do it in his hometown.

Leaving the building, he blew out the candle and tossed it in the grass. Halfway across the quad an odd feeling struck him. The wooden case felt light for something holding an extra-long oboe. In the moonlight, the bandstand loomed in front of him. He stepped up and under its circular roof. He moved to a patch of moonlight on the railing, set the case on it, and undid its leather straps.

He lifted the lid and stared in shock. The sections of the cor anglais were missing. They had been replaced by rolled-up clothing, a leather wallet and a pair of flip-flops. Before he could mutter an obscenity, the creak of a floorboard spun him around.

On the other side of the bandstand stood a slight man in a long nightshirt: Alfred Jongler. He was holding the curved cor anglais. "Looking for this?"

Matt flung a hand at the music case. "What do you think?"

He wanted to lunge forward and grab the cor anglais but a noisy struggle would only wake the whole school. "How'd you know I was leaving?"

"When I heard that you quit the football team, I played the cor anglais again. I had a vision"—he gestured to their surroundings—"and this is what I saw."

"Oh, yeah?" Matt bristled. "How does it end?"

Alfred smiled. "My vision ended when you spun around and found me. You'll have to show me what's next."

Matt didn't know if Alfred was lying. It didn't matter; he needed to scramble. "Look, Mr. Jongler, for whatever reason your family blows people around in time, I got the message. I'm a spoiled jock who needed his ass kicked. I've eaten dirt and been knocked out twice. I get the point. I'm ready to go home and man up."

Alfred couldn't contain his curiosity. "Man up?"

"Yeah, it means"—Matt tried to think of an equivalent he had heard in 1907—"taking the right path. The path of respect and humility. I'm there, okay? So play that thing and blow me home."

"It would wake everyone up," Alfred cautioned. "Imagine the impression it would make if you disappeared with hundreds of witnesses."

Matt grabbed his stuff out of the music case and slid the case across the floorboards. "Then put the oboe back."

"Good idea." Alfred knelt and began to disassemble the cor anglais. "What's the plan?"

"Since it takes a Jongler to play that thing right," Matt declared, "I'm gonna find one who does."

"Where will you find a Jongler?"

"You tell me."

"I wish I could," Alfred said, looking up with a sigh. "But I'm the last one."

"Bullshit."

Alfred placed the last piece in the case and closed the lid. "Unfortunately, it's true. I'm sorry for that."

Matt prickled. "You should be sorry for being a crappy oboe player."

Alfred secured the leather straps. "No, I'm sorry for being a 'crappy' Jongler. I've tried to help you understand why you are here and I've failed." He stood up. "I can't tell you what to do." He gestured to the music case. "Take it if you want and look for a Jongler who's a better oboe player. I can't stop you."

In the silence that followed, Matt wrestled with his decision. To escape Alfred's unblinking gaze, he glanced up. What he found in the night sky forced a bitter laugh.

"What's so amusing?" Alfred asked.

Matt jabbed a finger at the gibbous moon. "It's the same moon as the night I got blown back here."

"It certainly is," Alfred said with a nod. "It's as inescapable as the earth we stand on. We can't quit the moon, we can't quit the earth, and we can't quit our own skin."

The strange talk puzzled Matt. "What's that supposed to mean?"

Alfred answered pensively. "I can't quit being Alfred Jongler. Sometimes I wish I could. Sometimes I wish I had never inherited this unusual instrument and the burden that comes with it. Sometimes I wish Iris Jongler-Jinks had never played this thing and sent you here. But here you are, forcing me to be who I am."

Alfred's quiet confession released a tremor in Matt, awakening his own doubts. "I get what you're saying. But what if football isn't part of who *I* am?"

"Maybe it isn't. Maybe that's what you're here to find out."

Matt's face, a knit of distress and confusion, prompted Alfred to cut to the chase. "I talked with Major Mercer and Pop Warner. Pop said you have two things no coach can give a player:

size and moxie. They're giving you a second chance to attend Carlisle and play football." Alfred lifted a foot and shoved the music case back to Matt. "It's your call, Matthew. Take it, and find another Jongler. Or stay, and see which way the ball bounces."

PART II

SOLO

1.

ATTIC VISION

It was the middle of the night, long after Iris and the twins' father had gone to bed. Arky made his way silently down the hall to his sister's room. He pushed opened the door and went to her bedside without turning on the light.

"Iris," he murmured, poking her shoulder. "Wake up."

She opened her eyes and groaned. "Go away."

Arky held up their mother's journal.

Iris was instantly awake. She reached for it but Arky pulled it away. "You can have it after you get the cor anglais and go with me to the attic."

"Now?"

He nodded.

"Why?"

"I'll explain in Mom's office."

The twins climbed the narrow stairs. Iris held the cor anglais, fully assembled. They were careful to walk softly. A noise on the stairs might wake their father in the master bedroom on the ground floor. But they would not be heard once they reached the soundproofed attic.

After locking the door, Arky asked Iris to sit in their mother's practice chair. He moved the desk chair and sat across from his sister. "Remember when you played the cor anglais and you got a vision of Matt having his t-shirt pulled over his head?"

Iris didn't know whether to trust Arky's serious tone. She wondered if something in the journal had finally convinced him.

"Of course," she answered. "He was unconscious. I saw blood on his shirt before it was pulled over his head."

Arky opened the journal to a page he had dog-eared. He read a passage aloud.

> This is not the first time I have played the cor anglais and had a vision of someone who seemed out of place in the past. Their dress, their manner, their speech all make them "strangers in a strange land." The land they have traveled to is an era in which they don't belong. The persons I see in these visions fit the same pattern: they are voyagers who have traveled from the future. They are exploring a new frontier known as Tempi Passati.

Arky looked up and translated. "'Time past.'"

Iris felt her heart pounding. It was racing for two reasons. Hearing her mother's words made her feel like their mom was in the room—living, breathing, speaking—but hearing her brother read them without an edge made Iris want to jump up and hug him. Of course she didn't. She just echoed her mother. "Tempi Passati, I like that."

"In all of your visions," Arky asked, "have you ever seen Mom as one of these voyagers in the past?"

"I wish I have. But no, never."

Arky returned to the journal and continued.

> Given the frequency of these visions of time voyagers, my playing sessions are becoming like musical séances. The cor anglais is the medium giving me access to time travelers. Just as mediums, witches and shamans have spirit guides, the cor anglais seems to be my *object* guide to the past. The paranormal crowd also believes

that objects give off "emanations." Those emanations grow stronger in the presence of the people associated with the object. In fact, with the right people surrounding the object, a tipping point can be reached that releases the object's power.

Arky glanced up at Iris. She could hardly sit on her excitement over his change of attitude. She didn't say a word; she just wanted him to read on. He did.

This makes me want to call Howard and the twins to the attic, shut the door, fire up the cor anglais, and see what happens. I can't, of course. If my visions are more than visions, if the Jongler family legend is more than a legend, who knows what would happen.

Arky closed the journal and fixed on Iris. "We're 'associated' with the cor anglais. And if there's any truth to objects 'emanating' stuff"—he waved at the journal—"this is emanating Mom. Since the cor anglais is surrounded by the right people, maybe it's ready for a 'tipping point.' Maybe it's ready to show us a clue about Mom."

Iris beamed.

Arky took it the wrong way. "What's so funny?"

She wanted to say nothing was funny. She wanted to tell him the room was filled with more than emanations, it was filled with the power of belief. But she wasn't about to rain on his abnormal parade of hope. She simply lifted the cor anglais and said, "I'm just happy to play."

She began playing the Poulenc sonata. Within a few measures, her fingers filled with a sensation she had experienced only once before. They felt incredibly light, like they were barely touching the keys. At the same time, her synesthesia kicked in; she started to see dots and lines dancing along with the music. The music was changing too, from lyrical to lively, almost burlesque, as the keys, pressing on her fingers, guided the melody. Along with the wild sensation of a living instrument in her hands, the geometrics dancing in her vision began to transform into shapes, forms, objects.

The memory of the last time the cor anglais had possessed her unnerved Iris. The music swiftly turned harsh and atonal. She wrestled the reed from her mouth.

"Why'd you stop?" Arky asked.

She caught her breath. "When this happened before, Matt disappeared."

"I don't care if one or both of us go poof," Arky declared. "You're onto something. Keep playing."

Her wide eyes held on him. She was scared.

"C'mon," he urged, "don't let the moment pass."

She took in a breath and resumed playing. It was surprising how quickly the cor anglais took over again, like when you wake from a dream, then fall back into it. The melody revisited the wild version of a dance hall cancan, then shifted into a soulful last section of the Poulenc sonata. Iris was relieved by the familiar music as the random images swimming in front of her melded into a scene. There was a small wooden stage, lit by footlights rising from the front edge. A woman stood on the stage in a long black dress. She too was playing a curved cor anglais, and playing the same haunting tune as Iris. They were a duet.

At first, Iris didn't recognize the woman, but the vision pushed closer. The woman's trim figure and face became recognizable. It was their mother, Octavia Jongler. The shock would have made Iris stop if she was in control of the cor anglais, but she wasn't. Even more surprising, as Octavia drew closer, was the instrument she played: the same ancient curved cor anglais with the spider on the bell.

Seeing her mother for the first time in over a year, albeit in a vision, flooded Iris with joy. And it didn't feel one-sided. Octavia also seemed to see Iris, greeting her daughter with shining eyes.

The surprises kept coming. At the end of a measure, Octavia lowered her instrument, granting Iris and her cor anglais the solo. Octavia drew closer, her mouth set in a loving smile. Octavia's eyes then shifted, as if taking in a larger room. She spread her arms and dipped her head in a slight bow. Then, without warning, two black curtains sliced in front of her with the speed of a guillotine.

The shock yanked the cor anglais from Iris's mouth.

Arky jumped. He had been mesmerized by the music and his sister's soulful playing. "What happened?"

Iris's insides roiled. The joy of finally seeing her mother, the rapture of sharing a moment together, had been swept away by the closing curtain. Iris choked out a sob.

"What is it?" Arky implored. "What did you see?"

Between tearful starts and stops, she shared the vision. She barely got out the part about the closing curtain. Then she sobbed, "I think Mom's dead!"

2.

OUT-OF-BOUNDS

Matt's escape from Carlisle had taken him no farther than the bandstand. He had decided, as Alfred had put it, to see which way the ball bounced.

He spent the next morning taking placement tests and being assigned to one of the shops where his industrial training would begin. He was put in Room 11, and would be spending his mornings taking classes in Literature, Advanced Mathematics, Biology and Government. They tried to put him in History but he opted out; he didn't want to become like Nostradamus and tell everyone what would happen in the next hundred years. He convinced them that his weird way of speaking meant he needed a grammar class. After lunch, he was told to report to the Printery where he would learn the printing trade and help print everything from the school newspaper, *The Arrow*, to forms for the U.S. Government. The rest of his afternoons were to be spent on the football field.

The biggest surprise came at lunch when Newashe caught up with Matt before he entered the dining hall. "You don't eat that slop anymore." Newashe steered him toward another building. "You're on the football team. You chow down in the Football Quarters."

"Do I live there too?" Matt asked.

Newashe chortled at his presumption. "You're not that high on the totem pole, chief. You have to make the Varsity before you bunk with the Carlisle eleven."

The Football Quarters was a two-story building with double-tiered porches. The training table for the players was a different world from the dining hall. Matt sat at the table of Hotshots and stuffed his face with beef, potatoes, bread and butter and fruit, washing it down with huge glasses of milk. The Hotshots gave him some ribbing for coming back on the team and eating like a "savage." He took the teasing with a mouth too stuffed to respond. It was the first good meal he'd had since coming to Carlisle. His stomach told him he had made the right decision.

He checked out the Varsity players he recognized from the day before. They sat at the head table. None of them looked his way. He knew the routine. He was invisible: a lowly scrub or third-string Hotshot, he wasn't sure which. He planned on sorting that out in practice.

When Matt reported to the Printery, it was another time warp. It reminded him of when his family had visited a living history museum, and they had watched people in aprons putting together a jigsaw puzzle of lead pieces until it finally printed a newspaper. But now he was no longer watching; he was one of the puzzle makers. He suppressed the urge to blow away his coworkers by telling them that one day the entire Printery would fit in a computer and a printer the size of a shoebox. It was one of the rules he had decided to impose on himself: *No talk of the future: it will only make me more of a freak than I already am.*

As he quickly learned to set type on a composing stick, he found a certain comfort in it. It reminded him of the quiet pleasure he had always gotten from marking X's and O's in a notebook as he diagrammed football plays.

After he finished his work at the Printery, Matt had ten minutes before he was due at the Cage to suit up for practice. But he had to do something first.

That afternoon, he had made a vow. If Alfred was right, and playing football for the Carlisle Indians was somehow connected to getting him back to his hometime, then he had to learn the rules of the 1907 game. Since nobody had given him a rulebook, and he couldn't exactly Google one, he hoped to borrow a notepad from Caleb, tuck it in his uniform, and every time he learned one of their whacko rules, he'd write it down.

As he moved along the path skirting the quad, he looked across the expanse of grass to the Girls' Quarters. A dozen girls in white dresses were spinning fancy umbrellas in unison. Matt had once seen a Marine color guard working rifles in perfect unison, but never an all-girl squad spinning parasols. He had to check it out.

He started across the grass. The closer he got to the line of girls, the more distracted they became. Some broke from the routine, giggling, with their hands over their faces, or stepped back in shock.

"I just wanna watch," Matt informed them.

It made them giggle louder, except for one girl. She continued her parasol-spinning, ignoring the intruder. What also made her stand out was her very dark skin, and the black tie she wore over her white dress, bowed by the contour of her chest.

Wanting to see the full routine, Matt focused on the dark-skinned girl wearing the tie. Not only was he impressed by the smooth rhythm of her movements and the riveted focus of her black eyes—she was pretty. She had a soft face with a strong jaw that accentuated her full lips. The contrast between her locked-on eyes and the sereneness of her expression held him. It was a look Matt knew well; she was "in the zone." She finished with a flourish by spinning the parasol into a blur, then stopped it dead still, all except the silky fringe rocking gently.

Matt's applause was interrupted by a shout. "Hey there!"

He turned to see half a dozen guys running toward him. At first he feared it was another Delilah Brigade about to jump him and cut his hair even shorter, but he recognized them: football players, led by Jim Thorpe.

"Hey," Matt shouted back.

Jim was the first to step up to the girls with parasols. Other girls had appeared on the dorm's porches. Some of them were pointing and laughing. Jim put on a pompous voice and addressed them with sweeping gestures. "Ladies, our deepest apologies. This member of our football tribe has once again earned his name, Wrong-Way Pants, and run out-of-bounds. But fear not, we will save you from his offense and set Wrong Way right."

Jim and his friends grabbed Matt and hustled him across the quad away from the Girls' Quarters.

Matt was clueless. "What did I do?"

As Jim laughed, the Hotshots QB, Yankee Joe, explained. "You're on the girls' ground. We're not allowed there except on special occasions and with a chaperone."

Jim jumped back in with the Indian-speak he put on. "Better ways to get on girl ground if you're heap sneaky Indian. Some night, Jim show you," he added with a wink. "Right now, we have game to win."

"There's a game today?" Matt asked.

"Yes," Yankee Joe said. "The Carlisle Hotshots take on the Soldiers' Orphans School. It'll be your first battle as a Redman."

3.

HORIZON EVENT

The twins were still in the attic office. Iris's vision of their mother being swallowed by a curtain, and its fatal implication, still had her upset.

Arky tried to comfort her as he flipped through their mother's journal. "It's not what you think. The vision's not about death." He found the passage he was looking for and read it aloud.

> There is another pattern in my reoccurring visions of time voyagers to be noted. After I have seen the same one a few times, my last sighting of him or her ends in a distinct way. The voyager may disappear around a corner, or climb a ladder out of view, or close a door, or draw a shade, or be obscured by a passing vehicle. After this last glimpse, I never see them again. But there's no sense they are gone for good. They have just disappeared from my view, like a ship disappearing over the horizon. I call these last glimpses of voyagers "horizon events."
>
> I've considered many reasons why the cor anglais shows me horizon events, including the possibility of the observer effect.

Even though Iris had only seen the "horizon events" of Matt and her mother, she wiped her tear-stained cheeks and asked, "What's the observer effect?"

"In science," Arky explained, "the presence of an observer can affect an experiment."

"How?"

"If scientists have to subject an experiment to light so they can see it, the light itself can change the outcome of the experiment."

She gave it some thought. "It's like practicing in your room is one thing, performing for an audience is another."

Arky quirked a half smile. "I've never thought of it that way, but yeah, that's the observer effect too." He returned to the journal and read on.

Why do horizon events occur? I can only speculate. Perhaps there comes a time in a voyager's journey to the past when they must "go solo," when they must disappear to even a Jongler's visionary consciousness. For some reason, whatever they are seeking in the past, they must find it without us looking over their shoulder. While a Jongler can use the cor anglais to send a troubled soul to the past, at some point, the voyager must discover what's needed from the past on their own. In that discovery, I suspect, is the healing that allows the voyager to come home.

Iris couldn't stop thinking about the moment in her vision when their mother had stopped playing the cor anglais and let Iris play on by herself. *It wasn't me who went solo,* she thought, *it was Mom.*

Arky closed the journal. "If what she's saying is true, Mom's not dead."

"Yeah." Iris's eyes shone with hope. "What I saw was her 'horizon event.' She's gone solo."

Arky nodded. "And when you saw the t-shirt lift over Matt's head, hiding his face, that was probably his horizon event. He may have gone solo too, and we've been locked out of the experiment. If it's true, all we can do is wait."

"And hope he gets back in time for the state championship," Iris added.

Arky appreciated the thought. He handed the journal to her.

She took it. "But if Mom's in the past because she's a 'troubled soul,' what do you think *she* was sent to find?"

Arky stared at the cosmic and spidery assemblage on the opposite wall. "I don't have a clue." He turned to Iris and bugged out his eyes with a hint of mockery. "Maybe she disappeared to make us work together."

4.

SAVAGES

Matt never got the chance to fetch a notepad from his room. The Hotshots took him directly to the Cage, where they suited up for their game against the Soldiers' Orphans School. Jogging onto Indian Field, Matt noticed Caleb working the sideline as the water boy. He thought about asking to borrow the notepad Caleb usually carried with him. But what Matt saw while riding the bench was more than memorable.

The first surprise was the opening kickoff being from the 50-yard line. After Carlisle grounded and pounded downfield, with Jim doing most of the running, he crossed the goal line for a touchdown. Then came another eye-opener. The referee didn't call it a touchdown until Jim touched the ball to the ground. Matt suddenly realized that touching the ball to the ground wasn't some quirk of Jim's when he scored; a "touchdown" was done literally: a *touch down* of the ball.

The surprises kept coming. The kid working the wooden scoreboard on the side of the field only gave Carlisle five points for the TD instead of six. And the extra point, called a "conversion kick," wasn't kicked in front of the goalposts. It was kicked from the side and straight back from the point where Jim had crossed the goal line. Matt made a mental note of the weird-angle extra-point kick. After the kick sailed through the uprights, Matt was relieved to see it was worth one point. *Finally,* he thought, *the old-timers got something right.*

After the Soldiers' Orphans received the kickoff, they were as pathetic as their name. Their two running plays were stuffed and they had to punt. Carlisle went back on offense and things got wackier. They tried a short pass. When the receiver dropped the ball and it came back to the ref, the ref started walking yards off against the Indians.

"What's the penalty?" Matt asked Sweetcorn.

"Uncomplete pass."

Matt ignored his odd word choice. "You get penalized for dropping a pass?"

Sweetcorn nodded. "Fifteen yard from where pass fly."

Matt recalled what Caleb had told him about the newly legal forward pass and the penalties against it. "And if none of the pass receivers get a hand on the ball, it's a turnover, right?"

Sweetcorn nodded again. "Heap big turnover. Also turnover if passer throw ball out-of-bounds."

"C'mon," Matt said as he tried to imagine not being able to throw out-of-bounds to avoid a sack. "You're yankin' my chain, right?"

Sweetcorn, not knowing the expression, gave him a wan smile. "My English bad. Your rules more bad."

Despite the mental exertion of tracking the rule changes, watching the game hit Matt in another way. He kept flashing back to a trip he'd taken with the North High Cyclones to the Pro Football Hall of Fame in Canton, Ohio. There, he'd seen grainy black-and-white footage of football being played in the 1920s and '30s. Now, sitting on the bench in 1907, he marveled at the fact that the old-style football games he'd seen on film had yet to be played. He couldn't resist feeling the awesome weirdness that he wasn't just riding the bench, he was front and center in a living history museum of football.

When the game's second half began, the Carlisle Hotshots were crushing the Soldiers' Orphans 34-0. Matt didn't know if these "orphans" had really lost their parents, but they were sure losing their tempers. During the inside runs, fists had begun to fly. Strangely, the Indians never hit back.

The Hotshots kept racking up points, including some by their player-coach Newashe, who booted a field goal through the uprights. Matt noticed a field goal wasn't the same either. It was worth *four* points.

Newashe trotted to the sideline with a couple of other Hotshots and called for substitutes, including Sweetcorn. Caleb came over and sat next to Matt. "You better get ready. You might be going in soon."

"I can't," Matt said. "I'm flat-out dizzy from the weird rules."

Caleb ignored his verbal oddity and went with the basics. "Just block on offense, tackle on defense, and remember our most important rule: no punching."

"Why not? The Orphans are throwing 'em right and left."

"We don't stoop to the white man's game," Caleb said sternly. "It's our way of proving who the savages are."

During the next few series, Newashe sent more subs in but didn't tap Matt. He was thinking he would ride out the game on the bench when a bell began clanging from the road on the other side of the school's high wooden fence. One of the Redmen on the field sprinted toward the Guardhouse gate as the clanging bell traveled down the road.

Newashe threw up his hands. "There goes Twoguns!"

Matt turned to Jim, who had joined him on the bench. "Is that another rule?" he asked sardonically. "A clanging bell means the home team loses a player?"

Jim laughed. "No, Twoguns loves fire wagons. He wants to be a football player, but he wants to be a fireman more."

"Grinnell, in for Twoguns," Newashe barked. "Left guard."

Matt stood and jogged onto the field. *Block and tackle,* he told himself, *and forget the crazy rules.*

He faced off against an Orphan that was almost a foot shorter but probably weighed as much. He was so squat and fat, his face bulged wider than his headgear. Matt figured he could handle him no problem. And he did, except the kid used his shortness in a unique way. During each play, if he wasn't throwing body punches into Matt, he was throwing dirt in his face. The ref never saw it or didn't care. Matt put up with it as the replacement Hotshots drove the hapless Orphans down the field.

After another combo to his stomach, Matt pushed the Orphan away. "One more time, fatso, and you're goin' down."

The kid leered up at him with rotten teeth.

When they lined up for the next play, Fatso growled, "I'm gonna queer you."

Matt straightened up. "What'd you say?"

Fatso stood up and shouted it louder. "I'm gonna queer you!"

Matt punched Fatso in the stomach, doubling him over. Then he locked his hands and brought them down on the kid's back. Fatso did a face-plant and lay still.

The ref ejected Matt from the game. As Matt trotted off the field, Newashe glared at him. "Keep on going, to the Cage."

Walking down the cinder track circling the field, Matt moved past groups of students and teachers watching the game. The last pair of eyes in the gauntlet belonged to Alfred Jongler. He was smoking a cigarette. "What was that about?" Alfred asked.

Matt kept walking. "He said he was gonna queer me. Nobody calls me a queer."

Alfred swung alongside Matt. "I didn't know it was a noun, but I do know that if you keep picking fights you're going to *queer* yourself."

Matt wheeled on Alfred. "Say that again—"

"You're going to *ruin* yourself," Alfred interjected. "That's what *queer* means: to ruin."

As it sunk in, Matt kept glaring. "Great. Now I need a rulebook and a *dictionary*." He broke into a jog toward the Cage.

While Alfred watched him go, his face pinched. As relieved as he was that Matt had not run away with the cor anglais, Alfred worried about what damage Matt might do during his time at Carlisle. He wondered if the first voyager for all Jonglers was always so difficult.

5.

PACIFISTS

Back in his quarters and after a shower, Matt stretched out on his bed. Remembering the piece of chalk he had lifted from one of the classrooms earlier that day, he pulled it from his pocket. He turned to the wall and did a quick calculation. He had been in Carlisle for two days even though it felt like forever. He chalked two marks on the wall, then tucked the chalk under his mattress. He shook his head over the weirdness of it all. He was counting days that had come and gone over a century ago. He wondered how many days he would mark on the wall before he escaped *Prison 1907*.

When Caleb got back to the room, Matt asked if he had been kicked off the team. Caleb told him he was still a Hotshot, but Newashe had a request. For the Varsity home game on Wednesday against Susquehanna University, normally all the Hotshots and scrubs sat on the bench. But Newashe wanted Matt to cool his heels and sit in the stands so he would have a better view of how football was played.

As much as Matt wanted to tell Caleb that it was the Indians who didn't know jack about football, he kept his mouth shut.

He did the same when he showed up for dinner in the Football Quarters. It's not like he had a choice. None of the other players sat near him or said a word to him. He figured he was being shunned, which was fine by him. It's not like the silent treatment was going to "queer" him.

After dinner Matt headed back to his quarters. He went around the corner of a building and ran into a half a dozen Hotshots, including Jim. They surrounded him. A short stocky player, Jordan, spoke first. "We want to make sure you get the message: we don't hit palefaces."

Two players grabbed Matt, and Jordan delivered a blow to his abs. Matt doubled over but was lifted back up by an uppercut from another player. They each landed a punch until it was Jim's turn.

"Let him go," Jim said. "Jim wants a fair fight."

Matt straightened up, wiped his bloody mouth and squared off as Jim grinned. Matt couldn't wait to knock the smile off his face and shut up the weird way Jim used his own name. Matt had barely finished the thought when he saw a blur and felt like he had walked into a wrecking ball. He went down but not out. He shook off the wheeling stars and yelled at them. "You guys are pacifists!"

They burst out laughing. "How can we be pacifists?" Jordan asked between guffaws. "We just beat you up!"

Matt struggled to his feet. "Okay, I get it. I get my ass kicked by my team for kicking ass on the other team. Anything else I need to know about your insane rules?"

Jim nodded. "Heap big reward for taking a beating." He signaled to two players. "You get to bunk in the hospital." The players reached behind a row of bushes and pulled up a stretcher. "We even give you a ride."

Matt stared at the stretcher. "You're kidding."

Jim went stone-faced. "Jim never kid."

"What's so special about a night in the hospital?"

"You'll see," Jim replied with a wink.

At the school hospital, Jim and the players made a big deal to the admitting nurse about how Matt had taken a turn for the worse after the pounding he had gotten in the game, and that they were worried about internal bleeding.

The nurse admitted Matt and had him examined by a doctor. While the doctor found nothing more serious than bruises, contusions, minor cuts, a bloodied nose and the knot on his forehead, he thought it best to keep Matt overnight for observation.

As Matt lay in the dark of the empty ground-floor ward, he listened to the coughing and hacking of patients in the ward overhead. *Great,* he thought, *it wasn't enough they beat the crap out of me, now they're gonna finish me off by infecting me with pneumonia, typhoid, or whatever deadly germs are raining down.*

Matt escaped into sleep for several hours before he was visited by a dream.

He was driving his Ford F-150 through the countryside around Belleplain. He sped along a straight road that dipped and rose through fields of high corn. His windows were open. His long hair blew wildly around him, sometimes obscuring his vision. It didn't matter; he knew the road by heart. His eyes shifted to the rearview mirror. For the first time he noticed something in the pickup's bed. He turned for a closer look. The object stretched the length of the bed. Then came recognition. It was a man-sized version of Dr. TD, the wooden statue of the Egyptian god with touchdown-arms jutting above his head. Dr. TD suddenly sat bolt upright, scaring Matt to death. He screamed and heard a blaring horn. Matt whipped back around as a huge truck sped toward him. He barely swerved his pickup out of the way as the screaming horn turned into a blaring bugle.

Matt jolted awake. The bugle continued, but farther away. In the darkness, he recognized the sound of reveille being played at 5:30 am. The nightmare wasn't as bad as the rude awakening that he was still in Carlisle. He heaved a breath and looked at the upside: he was in the hospital and could go back to sleep. Rolling on his side, an array of pains reminded him of the beating he had taken the night before. He thought about his dream. *Was it a sign that Dr. TD had something to do with this? I mean, it was kinda his fault. If I hadn't gone back in Arky's house to see Dr. TD, I wouldn't have seen Iris. If I hadn't seen Iris, I wouldn't have wanted a juggling lesson. If I hadn't gone to her room, she never would've picked up the cor anglais and blown me away.* He made a mental note: *If I survive 1907 and get back to Belleplain, they're gonna pay. I'll get the cor anglais, bust Dr. TD in two with one swing, then break the cor anglais over my knee.*

Matt's vengeful thoughts faded back into sleep.

6.

TAWNY OWL

An hour later he woke again as first light filled the ward. Someone sat in a chair near the bed. It was a girl in a nurse's uniform, with her long black hair pinned under a white cap. She was working a pencil on a sketchpad in her lap. When she looked up, Matt recognized her. It was the pretty girl from the parasol routine, the girl with intense dark eyes and a serene face.

She went back to her drawing and said, "Good morning."

"What are *you* doing here?" he asked.

She glanced back up. "It's my turn to watch you."

"You're a nurse?"

"I'm training to be one."

He pointed at her sketchpad. "What's that?"

"Homework for Drawing class," she replied.

"Can I see it?"

She held it up, revealing her finely rendered pencil drawing. It was of Matt sleeping in the bed.

"That's really good."

"Miss De Cora is a good teacher." She stood up, putting the sketchpad and pencil in a big pocket in her uniform, and took a dish off a nearby table. "I'm going to apply this poultice to that bump."

While she used a wooden depressor to spread the moist material on the knot on his forehead, he cruised her long eyelashes, brown skin and full lips. His eyes drifted south. Her white uniform couldn't conceal her curves. A thought bent his lips into a smile. *Of all the things Alfred said I can't quit—the moon, the earth, my own skin—does it include girls?*

As she taped some cotton over his contusion, he asked, "Is that an Indian cure you put on it?"

"We don't use Indian ways here," she corrected. "We only practice the white man's medicine."

"Wow," Matt said, straightening up. "You're almost a doctor, you're an artist, and you spin a wicked umbrella. You're a triple-threat."

Her mouth pushed into a frown. "That doesn't sound nice."

Realizing he'd probably stumbled into future-speak, he tried again. "I meant it as a compliment."

She sat in the chair. "We shouldn't be talking about me. We should be talking about you. How do you feel?"

"Well, in the last forty-eight hours I've been knocked out twice and beat up once. If I can make it through today without getting hit by a train I'll be the luckiest Indian on the reservation." The hint of a smile he got from her felt like a conquest. "What's your name?"

"Tawny Owl."

"That's a name?"

"Yes. So is Wrong-Way Pants."

He eye-rolled. "Geez, does everyone know that?"

She pulled a newspaper from under her chair, a copy of *The Arrow*. "Everyone follows the football team, and you made the school paper."

"I was just printing them the other day. I didn't see anything on me."

She opened the paper and read from the bottom of the back page. "It's in a little item called *From the Ball Bin*. It says, 'Coach Newashe adds new player to the Hotshots: Matt Grinnell, from Room 11. Pigskin.'"

"What's Pigskin?"

"That's who wrote it. He's a reporter for the paper."

"Pigskin? What kind of name is that?"

"It's a pseudo-name—I mean, a pseudo*nym*," she said, correcting herself. "No one knows who he is."

Matt didn't care about some stealth reporter, but he liked talking to her. "Why doesn't Pigsty use his real name?"

Her mouth pursed. "It's Pig*skin*. And I don't know. Maybe so he can criticize the team or Pop Warner without getting in trouble."

"Makes sense. Can I ask you something, Tawny?"

She stiffened. "Please, 'Miss Owl.'"

"Okay, Miss Owl. Can I take you to the Susquehanna game this afternoon?"

She looked shocked. "No, Mr. Grinnell, you may not."

"Why not?"

"For one, I'm already going."

"Oh, so you have a boyfriend."

"Whether I have a boyfriend is not important," she said curtly. "I'm in the band."

Matt grinned. "In the band, huh?"

"Yes."

His head cocked. "Do you play the oboe?"

She stifled a smile. "There are no oboes in the band, Mr. Grinnell."

They were interrupted as a man entered the ward. It was the assistant football coach, Jimmie Johnson.

Tawny stood up and kept her eyes directed at the floor. "Good morning, Mr. Johnson."

As Jimmie exchanged pleasantries with Tawny, Matt noticed she never looked at Jimmie, the former All-American. She looked like she was blushing. It was a good sign: maybe she had a thing for football players. When the coach asked if he could speak to Matt alone, she left.

"On behalf of the team," Jimmie told Matt, "I would like to apologize for the hazing you received last night."

Matt shrugged it off. "They were making a point: don't return a punch."

"Yes, but that point shouldn't be made with a punch."

"That's what I told 'em. But we're cool."

Jimmie's brow wrinkled. "So, you accept the apology?"

"Sure, but I'd rather trade it for a favor."

"And that would be?" Jimmie asked, looking skeptical.

"I get the feeling Coach Warner can wave a wand and get stuff done around here."

"It depends on the request."

"Do you think I could get transferred from one of my classes into Miss De Cora's Drawing class?"

Jimmie lifted an eyebrow. "Why the sudden interest in drawing?"

Matt thought fast on his feet. "I've got some ideas for how to improve our football uniforms and I want to be able to draw 'em up."

"I'll see what I can do," Jimmie replied. "Now roll out. We're getting you out of here before you get hit with something worse than one of Jim Thorpe's stunts."

7.

SUSQUEHANNA

The next day, after the bell ended Government class, the teacher handed Matt a note instructing him to transfer to Miss De Cora's Drawing class the day after. He smiled as he turned the note over. On the back it read, "At the game today, watch and learn. Someone will help you. Coach Johnson."

At lunch Matt learned who that "someone" was. Lone Star Dietz, a Varsity player who had been injured in the Villanova game, introduced himself and told Matt to join him in the stands that afternoon. Lone Star impressed Matt. He was bigger than most of the players, around 175, and instead of a military uniform he wore a snappy three-piece suit, which matched his formal manner and put a polish on his rugged good looks. Lone Star also looked older than the other players.

When Matt reached Indian Field for the game against Susquehanna, it looked like a hybrid of a football game and a car show. The hill overlooking the field was dotted with antique motorcars. Some had been parked and left empty; others provided more comfortable seats than the backless wooden bleachers. He was amused by a realization: the original luxury boxes in stadiums were cars.

Another surprise was how everyone, including the students, was dressed as if they were going to church. The boys wore their best suit or sharpest uniform. The girls wore fancy white dresses with big hats as wide as pizza platters that were decorated with big bows or feathers. Matt chuckled at how different it looked from a stadium with painted torsos and cheeseheads.

Matt found Lone Star and joined him in the bleachers.

The Carlisle band had already filled a section. Matt scanned the uniformed members of the band until he found Tawny. When the Susquehanna Crusaders ran onto the field, Alfred raised his baton and the band launched into a song. Tawny played the flute. The crowd reacted to the music with cheers and laughter.

"What's so funny?" Matt asked Lone Star.

"It's a joke we play on our white visitors. They're playing 'Great Big Indian Chief Loved a Kickapoo Maiden.'"

"Right," Matt deadpanned. "Hysterical."

The Carlisle Varsity trotted onto the field. They were greeted by waving handkerchiefs and rousing cheers.

As the two teams warmed up, Lone Star informed Matt that no opposing team had scored a touchdown against the Redmen on Indian Field in six years. When he noticed that Matt was more interested in the band than the players on the field, Lone Star said, "I thought you were learning how to play guard, not tackle."

"I am," Matt said. "What makes you think I'm a tackle?"

"From the way you keep eyeballing the band, it looks like you want to tackle one of them."

Matt gave him a courtesy laugh. "Okay, busted. I met one of the flute players yesterday."

"Who?"

"Tawny Owl."

Lone Star nodded. "She's in my Drawing class."

Matt grinned. "I'll be in it tomorrow."

Lone Star gave him a dubious look. "So how about keeping your eyes on football today, and wearing them out on her tomorrow?"

Matt pulled out the notepad he had borrowed from Caleb. "I'm all over it."

The Redmen took the opening kickoff, marched down the field with a no-huddle offense and scored. After the Susquehanna Crusaders got the kickoff, they went no-huddle as well. Between practice, the Hotshots game, and this one, Matt hadn't seen a huddle yet. His curiosity kicked in. "Does everyone run a hurry-up offense these days?"

Lone Star came back with his own question. "What's hurry-up about it?"

"I mean, don't you ever huddle"—Matt rephrased in case "huddle" was future-speak—"you know, group up behind the line and call a play in secret?"

Lone Star nodded. "Sure, but huddles are only for indoor games when it's so noisy you can't hear the play at the line. Huddles are for the deaf and the lazy."

In the Crusaders' first possession, their opening running play got stuffed. On second down, they tried a forward pass. Matt watched the Crusaders' QB roll right as the end ran a ten-and-out to the same side. The QB threw a wobbly pass; before the ball got to the receiver, two Redmen knocked him flat. The Carlisle rooters cheered.

Matt waited for a ref to throw a flag. None came. He turned to Lone Star. "What was that?"

"It's called a mugging."

"Yeah, and pass interference."

"No, that was a *lack* of pass interference," Lone Star corrected.

"Huh?"

Lone Star told Matt to keep watching, that the Indians would soon demonstrate proper "pass interference."

As Lone Star predicted, after the Redmen took over at midfield and executed a few running plays, they tried a pass. Mounty dropped back as the two ends, Gardner and Exendine, and the fullback, Pete Hauser, sprinted downfield. Mounty launched a Hail Mary pass and Matt took in the startling sight of Hauser and Exendine knocking the defensive backs on their butts. Gardner, who was uncovered, hauled in the pass and ran several yards before getting tackled.

As the Carlisle side cheered, Lone Star pointed to the obvious. "You see, it's up to our downfield players to run pass interference for whoever's going to catch it."

All Matt could manage was "Who knew?" as he scribbled in his notebook: *Downfield, every man for himself.*

During the first half, it appeared that Carlisle's six-year record of not allowing anyone across their goal was going to stand.

Matt's amazement over the 1907 rules didn't let up. Every time he saw a Carlisle receiver subject a Susquehanna defensive back to "pass interference," he imagined how Danny Bender would love this kind of free-for-all. Thinking of Danny made him wonder how his team, the Cyclones, was doing as they ramped up for the State finals. Then a weird thing happened: he couldn't remember who the Cyclones were playing. He finally recalled it: *The Wolverines, of course!* He shook off the brain lapse and gave himself a warning. *Don't let this place get to you.*

In the second half, as the Indians racked up touchdowns and field goals, another mystery stumped Matt. He pointed to Pop Warner down on the sideline. "Why does the Old Fox just stand there smoking cigarettes? Why isn't he sending in plays or yelling at his players?"

Lone Star answered with a quizzical look. "You really don't know anything about football, do you?"

"Not the kind you play."

"Coaches aren't allowed to send in plays. The game is run by the captain and the players."

Matt laughed at the memory of his dad texting plays to Coach Watson. He lifted his hands to heaven. "Finally, a rule I like."

In the end, the Indians prevailed 91-0.

8.

HANDPRINTS

Matt looked forward to art class. Whatever qualms he had about liking a girl in 1907 when he had a girlfriend in the next century were complicated by unknowns. For all he knew, Arky was right and Kelly had dumped him. And there were bigger questions. *Even if Kelly's still my girlfriend,* he wondered, *does it count as cheating on her if Kelly hasn't been born yet?* Just as puzzling was the age difference. *Is it totally sick to go after girls who were born around 1890?* But that's what he liked about Tawny Owl. Looking at her made him forget what century he was in.

When he entered the Leupp Art Studio, he was surprised by all the Indian art on the walls, including paintings and weavings. The huge chalkboards displayed geometric Indian patterns and a chalk drawing of an Indian on a horse.

Matt reminded himself he wasn't there for the art; he was there to get hang time with Tawny. He scanned several groups of girls in the room. In their long white dresses and black hair, they looked pretty much alike. A laugh pulled him to three girls standing by the window. The girl with her back to him had her hair in a braid that hung down her back. She seemed to be tossing something in her hands.

As the teacher called for everyone to take their seats, the girl turned. It was Tawny; she was casually spiraling a football from hand to hand. Matt started toward her. It was the perfect chance to score some points with Tawny by showing off his own football twirling skills. Sure, he couldn't throw the fat football yet, but twirling was a no-brainer. Tawny put the football on a shelf with some old sports equipment and followed the girls toward a big circle of chairs with a small display table in the center. Matt changed directions, hoping to grab a seat next to her.

As he entered the circle, Tawny recognized him with a smile. She pointed across the circle. "Boys on that side."

"Come on, Wrong Way," Matt heard someone call. It was Lone Star waving him to the boys' side of the circle. "It's Drawing class, not a social."

As students laughed, Matt shrugged off his brazenness and sat next to Lone Star. At least he had a good view of Tawny. Again, she wore a black tie over her white dress.

The teacher blocked his view as she made adjustments to a still life of squashes and a sunflower on the central table. Angel De Cora was an Indian in her thirties with a serious manner. Satisfied with the still life, she pulled a sketchpad and pencil from her art smock and handed it to Matt. "Welcome to our drawing circle, Mr. Grinnell."

"Thank you, Miss De Cora," he answered. "Glad to be here." He flashed Tawny a smile. She looked down and opened her sketchpad.

For the next half hour, Matt tried to make his still-life drawing not look like rotting vegetables. When he saw how good Lone Star's was, he gave up looking at the real thing and tried to copy Lone Star's sketch. His hand was beginning to cramp when Miss De Cora announced a five-minute break.

The break gave Matt a chance to talk to Tawny. She was standing in front of one of the chalkboards, copying a geometric pattern into her sketchpad.

Joining her, he served up his opening volley. "I can draw a football better than a squash."

"That's nice," she said, not looking up from her sketch. "But can you throw a football?"

Matt wondered if she had heard about his disastrous tryout for quarterback. He played the humble card. "I'm working on it.

Before class I saw you flipping some pretty good spirals. Maybe you could give me a lesson."

Tawny shot him a glancing smile. "I'd be happy to teach you how to twirl a parasol."

"That'd be great," he said with a chuckle. "Then everyone would think Wrong Way went both ways."

Her brow arched. "I don't follow."

Matt checked his future-speak. "Not important, just a dumb joke." Running another play, he gestured to the room. "What's with all the Indian art? I thought this school was about learning nothing but the white way."

Tawny continued sketching. "When Miss De Cora came here she said that if the way of the white man is to make money, and the Indian way of making arts and crafts can be sold for money, then Indian art should be taught here too."

"Okay, but nobody's gonna get rich making Indian art."

Her dark eyes flashed. "Are you saying that when a fine artist like Lone Star Dietz turns that into a painting"—she motioned to the chalk drawing on the board of the warrior riding a horse—"he won't sell it for a decent sum?"

Realizing his misstep, Matt wasn't about to tell her he couldn't think of one Indian artist who was like Picasso and those French guys when it came to selling paintings for millions. He studied Lone Star's chalkboard drawing, hoping to regain his footing. The Indian on the horse was equipped for battle and painted for war. The horse was painted too, with several handprints on its flank. "Before I go all fortune-teller on you," he said, putting on a pensive look, "I have a question." He gestured to the horse's hind end. "Why does the horse have handprints on it?"

"You're obviously not from a tribe on the plains," she replied with a haughty look.

"No." He remembered the tribe Alfred had assigned him. "I'm a Mandan."

Her mouth quirked. "I see." She returned her attention to the chalk drawing of the warrior on a horse. "It's an Indian tradition among many tribes. Before going into battle, a warrior paints handprints on his body and his horse to fend off arrows and bullets."

Matt jogged his head in approval. "Cool. Do women do it too?"

She stifled a laugh. "I don't think so."

"But don't you think women deserve equal protection under the . . . handprint?"

She shot him a quizzical look. "You talk in the strangest ways."

Matt knew he should take her look and words as a warning, but he was too pumped by their flirtation, too eager to break through her wall of reserve. "I'm just saying that if I were a warrior"—he tossed a hand at the chalk drawing—"like the guy with the horse, and I wanted to protect you from danger, would I put handprints on you?"

Tawny's face froze and began to flush. She turned and hurried out of the art studio.

Watching her hasty exit, Matt kicked himself. His line-throwing skill to a 1907 girl was even more miserable than his fat-football-throwing skill.

Tawny's bustling exit didn't escape Miss De Cora. She addressed the other students. "What happened?"

Lone Star, within earshot of Matt, hitched a thumb at him. "Wrong-Way Pants just became Wrong-Way Mouth."

"Mr. Grinnell," Miss De Cora said sternly, "see me after class."

As they resumed their seats in the circle, Matt muttered to Lone Star. "You're a lot of help."

He slid Matt a conspiratorial smile. "I plan to be."

After the last student had left the studio, Miss De Cora sat next to Matt. "What did you do to make Miss Owl flee?"

Matt went with the truth for two reasons: one, he wanted to know if all the women at Carlisle—buttoned up in their high-necked dresses—were as priggish as Tawny; and two, it might help with the new playbook he had started in his head, *Girls 1907*. "I asked her if I was a warrior, and I wanted to protect her from danger" he explained, "would I put handprints on her."

De Cora's reaction made Matt realize that the stereotype of the stone-faced Indian wasn't totally false.

"Mr. Grinnell," she began, "I believe in preserving the old ways through art, but not necessarily through action. The days of dropping your blanket outside the family teepee of the girl you like and waiting for the girl to sneak out and crawl under your blanket are over."

"It's not like I was waving a blanket at her," he said. "I was just trying—"

She cut him off. "I know what you were trying and look how it worked out. Which brings me to a larger point. You have been sent here for the same reason every Indian has been sent here."

He chuckled at how far off the mark she was. "I don't think so."

"I *do* think so," she insisted. "You've come from a different time and place."

Her words stunned him. There could be only one explanation. "Are you a Jongler?" he asked. "I mean, is De Cora your married name?"

"Certainly not. What I'm saying is that *every* Carlisle student is from another time and place."

The idea that everyone there was a time traveler only deepened his shock. "You—you're kidding, right?"

"No, I'm serious. Today, every Indian is out of sync, teetering between the way of the buffalo and the way of the reservation.

Our hearts cling to the past while our minds and bodies are being pushed down the white road."

Matt breathed a sigh of relief. She wasn't being literal; she was going all metaphorical on him.

"But that doesn't mean our hearts are wrong," she added. "We must cling to what we can of the past. That's why I thought you wanted to be in my class: to reclaim some of your culture. But if your only ambition is to put handprints on Miss Owl, you don't belong here." She held him with hard eyes. "Think about what you want to do. If you wish to touch your past, come to class tomorrow. That's all, Mr. Grinnell."

Matt wasn't off the building's stone stoop before a voice pulled him around. "Sounds like your first day in Drawing was as successful as your first day on the field." It was Lone Star, leaning against the stonework.

"You heard all that?" Matt asked.

Lone Star smiled. "I love the sound of her voice."

Matt smirked. "I bet you like whips and chains, too."

Lone Star ignored the racy rejoinder. "The fact is, you don't know the first thing about girls."

"I can hold my own."

Lone Star pointed at Matt's crotch. "Which is what you'll be doing the rest of your life if you don't learn the basics of courtship."

"Courtship?" Matt laughed. "I don't wanna marry her, I just wanna have some fun."

"Listen and learn." Lone Star turned back into the studio.

Matt stopped him. "What are you doing?"

"Courting Angel De Cora."

"Hello, she's a *teacher*!"

Lone Star broke into a beguiling smile. "Yes. And a woman."

Matt hung by the door and eavesdropped as Lone Star and Miss De Cora talked about their plans to include more Indian designs and artwork in the school's newspaper. When she tried to bring up the student she had just reprimanded, Lone Star gently interrupted and told her that he wanted to hear about *her*. At one point, there was a long silence and Matt could have sworn he heard kissing. A moment later, Lone Star strode out the door.

As Lone Star jauntily moved off the stoop, Matt followed. "Did you just kiss her?"

"Yes," Lone Star admitted. "That's what you do when you're courting."

Matt had heard about "teachers with benefits," but he'd never known an actual recipient. "Can't you get kicked out of school for that?"

"You can get thrown out of school for ruining a girl, but you can't get expelled for treating her right."

"But why her?"

"We have a lot in common: art, music, and perfectly matched lips. To advance yourself in the society of the other sex," Lone Star counseled, "namely Miss Owl, it's usually wise to begin with what you have in common."

Matt frowned. "Like we have anything in common."

"Maybe not. But if you would stop plunging your foot in your mouth and let Miss Owl talk about herself, you might discover something."

Matt fell silent. Lone Star, despite all his fancy language, had a point. Matt had spent so many years calling the plays, especially with girls, that he wasn't much of a listener. He made a new entry in *Girls 1907*: *Shut up and listen.*

9.

DAMAGE CONTROL

In Belleplain, Matt's disappearance had cranked up the rumor mill. The speculation ran the gamut. Matt had gotten so trashed at Arky's house the night of the semifinal that he was in an alcohol-induced coma in the BU Hospital, but Gunner was keeping it a secret to protect Matt's college prospects. Matt was so upset about being dumped by Kelly—because of his stupid prank with the topless video—that his remorse and heartbreak had made him jump off a bridge into the river. And Arky's favorite: Matt was so freaked about playing in the state championship final that he had run away and joined the Marines.

Meanwhile, Arky and Iris had begun their punishment of being grounded for a week. On Sunday, when Danny came by and wanted Arky to join him on one of the search crews scouring the fields and woods around Belleplain for any signs of Matt, Arky had to say no. Danny thought his excuse of being grounded "totally sucked" and accused him of being a "shitty friend." Arky resisted the urge to tell Danny that one more searcher combing the countryside wouldn't matter if Matt had been relocated to a different bubble in the spacetime loaf. After Danny left, Arky spent the morning doing homework. Iris spent it in her room, reading the rest of their mother's journal.

In the early afternoon, their father left to join one of the search crews. Besides being a good citizen, Howard, also being a city councilman, was expected to take part.

After heating up a can of chili, Arky went down to the basement den and took a break from the insanity of the last thirty-six hours. He turned on an NFL game. His respite didn't last long.

Iris came down the stairs. She carried the leather-bound journal. "I've got to read you something."

Arky, stretched out on the couch, didn't budge. "If Matt's gone over the 'horizon' and we won't be seeing him for a while, can't it wait?"

"No." She picked up the remote and muted the game. "Did you read the part about the paradox of time travel?"

He conceded the TV-muting but pushed back. "Time travel is an *endless* paradox. It's the infinite loop of loopiness."

Ignoring his commentary, Iris read the part where Octavia considered a conundrum about time travelers. "'If, as the legend has it, time travel to the past is possible, and has been going on for the four centuries the JCA has been in existence—'" She glanced up. "'JCA,' that's short for Jongler cor anglais."

"I know."

She continued: "'. . . why don't time travelers who make a voyage to the past and return to their present speak of their extraordinary travels?'"

"I read it," Arky pointed out. "Mom proposed that in past centuries, returning time travelers who talked about it got pitched into asylums, and that modern time travelers may end up confusing time travel with past lives."

"Right. Do you know what she wrote next?"

Arky drummed his fingers on his chest and watched the silent game on TV. "Even if I did know, I'm sure you're gonna tell me anyway."

Iris resumed reading.

If this is the case, that modern time voyagers confuse time travel and past lives, then maybe memory of time travel is somehow *repressed* when the voyager returns to the present. Perhaps it's similar to how post-trau-matic stress disorder can push harrowing experiences into the darkness of the subconscious. Or, maybe the power of repressing memories of time travel lies in the cor anglais itself.

She glanced up. "Did you think about what that means?"

Arky had not. When he had read the first part of the entry he had experienced such a panic attack about the scenario of Matt returning, accusing Iris of a crime, and the Jongler-Jinks family becoming a freak show, he had not focused on what Octavia had written next. Hearing it now put a knot in his stomach. "You tell me, what does it mean?"

She sat on the arm of the couch. "If the cor anglais is good at triggering visions, like with me and Mom, maybe it also does the *opposite*. Maybe it somehow *hides* the visions and memories of going to the past."

"Like amnesia," he suggested.

"Or," Iris continued, "maybe the cor anglais pushes the memories into the subconscious, like all the stuff we experience when we're babies but don't remember when we grow up."

Arky swung up to a sitting position. "Why are you suddenly obsessed about Matt coming back and blabbing about time travel? You were the one who wanted to tell Dad everything."

She fixed on her brother. "If Matt comes back and goes public, and the cor anglais gets taken away from us, we're gonna lose the one thing that's gonna help us find Mom. That's why we need a plan for damage control."

Arky met her gaze. "Okay, for once we agree. How about asking the cor anglais? Maybe it'll show you a plan."

"I already tried," she told him. "I got nothing. We have to figure it out ourselves." Iris tapped the journal. "I think Mom was onto something when she wondered if the cor anglais could hide a time traveler's memories."

"You mean by playing it?"

Iris nodded. "Yeah."

"Okay, if that's true," he reflected, "and Matt appears out of the blue, then we have to be EMTs."

"EMTs?"

"Emergency musical technicians."

She shot him a scolding look. "Arky, I'm serious."

"So am I," he insisted. "We need an emergency alert system, and we need to get to Matt ASAP with the cor anglais. The alert system's easy; we always have our cell phones. We only text, no calls, and we text in code."

"Why code?"

"For secrecy," he explained. "When it comes to Matt's disappearance we're probably persons of interest. The police could be monitoring us."

"Okay, what if our text code is 'MB'?" she suggested. "For 'Matt's back'?"

"That's good," he agreed. "If and when we go 'MB' we do two things. You get the cor anglais, which you should keep as close by as possible, and whoever gets to Matt first gets him to a prearranged place with no witnesses, like our house."

"That'll be coded too?"

"Gotta be. Text 'one' for our house, 'two' for the obstacle course in the woods behind the school . . ."

Iris jumped in. "'Three' for the lightning shelter in City Park."

"Okay." He glanced up at her. "So we get Matt to one of those places with the cor anglais. Then what?"

"I play and we hope for the best."

After a moment he said, "There's one other possibility we haven't considered."

"What?"

"Mom comes back first."

Iris smiled. "Nothing would be better."

10.

PENN STATE

In Carlisle, Matt was pondering two mysteries. One was off the field. How could Lone Star Dietz dating a teacher be okay, but asking Tawny Owl an innocent question about handprints was practically sexual harassment? The other was on the field. During the Hotshots practice, Jim and the players who had beat up Matt the night before acted like it had never happened. They even went out of their way to give Matt advice on blocking, tackling and the finer points of playing guard.

Matt still got pushed around in the scrimmage, but because of his size, and because he was beginning to get the basics, he was doing better. After a good tackle, Newashe threw him a compliment. "Keep that up, Grinnell, and you might make the Varsity bench."

At dinner Matt sat at a table with a bunch of Hotshots. He only opened his mouth to shovel in food. It was the thing he was practicing off the field: listening.

His ears gathered one piece of intel that gave him a jolt. At another table he heard the name "Theodore Owl." He knew the player, a second-string halfback on the Varsity, but he had never heard his last name. He went all paranoid. *The minute he finds out I hit on his sister he's gonna go savage and scalp me!*

After being dismissed from dinner, Matt joined Lone Star on the way to their quarters and asked the pressing questions. "Is Theodore Owl Tawny's brother?"

Lone Star looked amused. "There are lots of Owls in the Cherokee Nation. Don't worry, Romeo, your Juliet doesn't have any brothers here."

His answer cued another question. "Does Tawny have a boyfriend?"

"Not that I know of."

"She should," Matt added, trying to hide his relief. "She's one of the prettiest girls here."

"She's more than that," Lone Star added. "She's pretty *and* smart. Most of the boys are intimidated by her. She comes at you with both barrels." His face brightened. "Just like Angel de Cora."

As Matt split off to his own dorm, he was pleased with his info gathering: no brothers, no boyfriend. If he could get out of his own way, 1907 might not be so bad after all.

Friday, the day before the Varsity game against Penn State, turned out to be a high-low day. The low came when Matt showed up for Drawing class. Tawny was absent. He learned she had transferred to a different class.

The high came after practice when Jim and Matt got pulled aside by Newashe in the Cage. He told them they weren't playing in the Hotshots' Saturday game; they would be taking the train with the Varsity to Williamsport where they would be on the bench for the Penn State game. Jim was so excited he leaped on Matt's back and started yelling about how he was going to ride his pony all the way to Penn State and across their football field. Matt didn't mind. It would make a great story to tell his grandkids someday: he had given the greatest athlete in the world, Jim Thorpe, a piggyback ride.

The high got better when Matt learned that the band was going to the game on the same train. That night, in his room, he tried to write the perfect note to slip to Tawny if he got the chance.

Caleb watched the growing pile of crumpled paper on Matt's bed and took a break from his Latin studies. "Are you writing her a note or planning to light that pile on fire and send her smoke signals?"

"Every time I think of something to say," Matt lamented, "I write it down and it looks totally stupid."

"You're like a halfback who's so jacked up he forgets to follow his blockers," Caleb scolded. "Forget clever, forget stupid, and do what you have to do first. Say you're sorry and that you hope to make it up to her."

Matt was amazed by the simple beauty of it. "You're a genius."

"No, I'm just not in love."

Matt scoffed. "I'm hardly in love."

"Right." Caleb went back to his Latin. "And I'm not the smartest water boy to ever walk the sideline."

Matt had to chuckle. It was weird how Caleb sometimes reminded him of Arky.

Before the bugle played taps, signaling lights-out, Caleb went down the hall to use the bathroom. Matt pulled the piece of chalk from under his mattress and chalked a crosshatch across the four marks on the wall. It had been five days. It reminded him how bizarre and unbelievable it all still felt. It also made him realize that back in Belleplain, the state championship game between the Cyclones and the Rockford Wolverines was being played with the second-string QB, Gary Allen, leading the Cyclones.

Matt's insides surged with a pang of regret. He indulged in it for a moment, then pushed it away. *As crazy as this is,* he mused, *there's one positive. My dad must be shitting a brick.*

Early Saturday, the Carlisle eleven, the second-string, along with the reserves handling the equipment, piled into horse-drawn buses for the short ride to downtown Carlisle.

Matt noted the irony. He was stuck in a caravan of horse-drawn buses while in Belleplain the Cyclones were riding atop convertible Mustangs provided by Gunner Ford in either a parade of victory or consolation. Matt buoyed himself with what he most looked forward to: passing his note to Tawny.

When they reached High Street, the band and a large group of students were boarding the train that would begin their hundred-mile journey to Williamsport. Matt was glad to see Tawny climb aboard. They weren't riding in the same car, but that was easily overcome.

After switching to another train in Harrisburg, Matt walked through the band car with a couple of other players to check out the scenery from the viewing platform at the back of the train. A few minutes later, Matt headed back to his car and passed the seat where Tawny was sitting. He pretended to spot something on the floor in the aisle, faked picking it up, and handed Tawny the note he had written. "You must've dropped this," he said nonchalantly.

She slid him a quick glance. "How do you know it's mine?" she asked curtly.

He showed her the writing on the outside of the folded note. "It's got your name on it."

Realizing Matt's subterfuge, Tawny's seatmate grabbed the note and dismissed him with a "Thank you, sir."

As Matt moved down the aisle toward the next car, he noticed Alfred sitting in a rear-facing seat, watching him. Matt responded with bravado. "Hey, Mr. Jongler. In the battle of the bands today, I hope Carlisle kicks brass!"

Gliding out of the car on a wave of laughter, Matt didn't regret his indulgence in future-speak. It was an old band joke he had heard from Arky once, and maybe it had just gotten a lot older. *Whatever,* he thought, *if it got a smile from Tawny, it was worth it.*

Seeing the football field at Penn State gave Matt a chuckle. Its 500-seat bleachers were like Little League bleachers compared to the college stadiums he was used to seeing on TV that rocked with 100,000 screaming fans.

Even though the Nittany Lions fans were a fraction of what they would be in a century, they were just as passionate. In fact, when Matt saw what greeted the Redmen as they jogged onto the field, he was sure a riot was going to break out. Several Penn State students had dressed up as cowboys and Indians and were conducting a mock battle in the middle of the field. It ended when the cowboys drew knives and "scalped" the Indians.

As Matt gawked at the vicious display, he turned to the player next to him, a lanky guard over six feet tall with one of the weirder Indian names Matt had heard: Afraid of a Bear. "Aren't you guys gonna do something about that?"

"We do what we come to do," Afraid of a Bear answered. "Beat tar out of 'em."

Matt spent the first half on the bench next to Jim. The game stayed so tight they knew they wouldn't see any action unless someone got hurt. That was fine with Matt. For the first time he was looking at an opposing team with major weight on the front line. He wasn't thrilled with the idea of going head-to-head against one of the big Penn State linemen, much less getting pulverized in the line-bucks and cross-buck plunges they kept running inside.

Jim and Matt watched the battle between brain and brawn trade blows. By the end of the first half it was the Indians' smart game, 10, the Lions' ground-and-pound game, 5.

While Jim wasn't getting playing time, he filled it with scheming time. Determined to get the Lions back for their scalping stunt before the game, Jim devised a plan and recruited Matt to help. At halftime they put the scheme into play. Jim gave a friend in the stands a few bucks to buy some items at a sporting goods store in town. Meanwhile, Jim and Matt used spare uniforms and padding to construct a human dummy dressed in a Nittany Lions jersey they had found in the visitors' dressing room.

At the start of the second half, they put their improvised Nittany Lion in a wheelchair and rolled him to the Carlisle sideline. Then they used what Jim's friend had bought at the sporting goods store to let the Penn State fans know exactly how many points the Indians had. Using a bow, Jim fired ten arrows into the dummy.

After that, as both teams struggled to score another touchdown, Jim and Matt waited. Hauser finally kicked a field goal, putting Carlisle ahead 14-5. It gave the Redmen on the sideline the chance to impale their "Nittany Lion" with four more arrows.

Matt let Jim and the others shoot the arrows. They had a score to settle; he didn't. Besides, he had another distraction: grabbing glimpses of Tawny in the stands. He wanted to see if his note had had an effect. At one point she pulled out a small sketchpad. Matt wondered if she was going to write him a note back. Even though it looked like she was drawing in it, his insides jumped at a realization. He had discovered something they had in common: they both carried blank pads and made entries in them. As for something in common, it wasn't much more than both having hands and feet, but it was a start.

Hauser booted another goal from the field and the bench-riding Indians pulled more darts from their quiver. When the last whistle blew, the wheelchair-bound Nittany Lion bristled with arrows. The Redmen had triumphed 18-5.

11.

CROQUET

Matt's first Sunday at Carlisle yielded new surprises. The first was not sleeping in. Reveille sounded like every other morning, except a bit later than 5:30. The second surprise greeted him when he returned from the bathroom down the hall. Caleb had taken a scroll of cloth covered with photos of Carlisle football teams since 1894 and hung it over the tally of days Matt had been chalking on the wall beside his bed.

"What'd you do that for?" Matt asked.

"It's against the rules to draw on the walls," Caleb explained. "If an orderly saw it during inspection, he'd make you wash it off and wash every wall on the floor."

Matt pushed aside the hanging scroll. His chalk tally of six days was still there. "So you're covering for me?"

Caleb flashed his snaggletooth grin. "Isn't that what room-mates do?"

The surprises kept coming: Matt learned that every student had to spend Sunday morning in church.

As Caleb and Matt walked with the mass of other boys toward the assembly hall for the service, Caleb turned to Matt. "I've been meaning to ask, whose idea was it to shoot a Nittany Lion full of arrows? Yours or Jim's?"

"Jim's," Matt replied. "I'm not that clever."

"Well, it's not original," Caleb added, stifling a cough. "It's been done before."

"Really?"

"In '05 against Dickenson. They did the same stunt with the

cowboy and Indian scalping, and we answered with arrows in a dummy for every point."

Matt shrugged. "Okay, it's not original, but the players and the Carlisle fans ate it up." He shot Caleb a curious look. "Why are you telling me this?"

"I'm just saying, don't let Jim pull the wool over your eyes. Sure, he's a big track star and he's going to be a big football star, but he can be wilder *off* the field than on. He can be a bad egg that'll take you to rotten places."

Matt was tempted to spill some of the crazy stuff he and Danny Bender had gotten away with. Wild in the next century made 1907 look like Boy Scout camp. "Don't worry," he assured Caleb. "I'm not gonna go jackass on ya."

Making trouble would have been easy after Matt saw the seating in church. All the boys were on one side of the aisle, the girls on the other. During the sermon, Matt had fantasies of running up the aisle, taking over the pulpit and telling everyone how their great-grandchildren would be sitting in sex education class, looking at pictures of penises and vaginas and learning about STDs. He didn't, of course, for a couple of reasons. One, it would make Tawny think he had gone from dumb jock to demon. And two, it would violate one of the rules he had set for himself: *What happens in the future stays in the future.*

After lunch, the football team almost had the day off. The one thing Pop ordered his players to do was to take a hike in the fields and woods surrounding the campus. It would keep the circulation pumping and minimize the pooling of blood from bruises and sprains.

Matt enjoyed the walk because the guys and girls, if they could escape the eyes of the chaperones, got a chance to intermingle. As he kept a lookout for Tawny, his head-craning didn't escape Jim. When Jim asked him which "Kickapoo maiden" he was looking for, Matt hesitated as he remembered Caleb's warning. Then he thought, *Screw it. My game plan with Tawny has hit a wall. I need fresh eyes.*

Matt's confession of having a thing for Tawny didn't surprise Jim. While he didn't have any advice, he approved of Matt's taste. "How can you not like a girl named Owl?" Jim quipped. "Especially when you hear her hoot."

When they got back to the quad, they saw why Tawny had not been in the woods. She and her friends were playing croquet in the croquet yard near the Girls' Quarters. A minute later Jim had hatched a plan. It involved crossing over to the girls-only turf where Jim had extracted Matt a few days earlier. When Matt pointed this out, Jim gave him a skewed look. "Do you like the girl or not?"

Matt nodded. "Done deal."

"And did you not scare her out of art class with your vile mouth?" Jim asked, laying on the scorn.

Matt grunted. "Done deal."

"Then, my friend"—he clapped a hand on Matt's shoulder—"action speaks louder than words. Let Jim help you be the hero."

Jim and Matt lingered at the base of an elm until the matron sitting on the first-floor porch, who was monitoring the girls playing croquet, put her knitting down and went inside.

Jim and Matt advanced on the girls as Jim fired up his charm. Not only did he persuade them to continue their game, he convinced them to let Jim and Matt join them, with the handicap of having to start at the beginning of the croquet course when the girls were already halfway through. Matt was encouraged when Tawny didn't drop her racquet and leave.

As the game resumed, Jim was less committed to driving his ball through the proper wickets than in pursuing the leader in the game. When Jim's ball struck the leader's ball, rather than take his extra shot for hitting her, Jim sent her ball the length of the course, far from her next wicket. While the girl was mortified by his mean behavior, the other girls were thrilled at the chance to take the lead. It also gave Matt a chance, after making his way through several wickets, to draw closer to Tawny.

She surprised him by speaking first. "May I ask you a question, Mr. Grinnell?"

"Why not, Miss Owl? Wait a minute," he corrected with a serious expression, "'why not?' is a question. And you asked first. What's your question?" He threw up his hands in mock frustration. "Oops, that's another question."

She seemed amused by his playful bumbling. "In yesterday's game, whose idea was it to wheel out that dummy and shoot it full of arrows?"

Her question threw him, especially since Caleb had asked him the same thing that morning. "It was Jim's," Matt said before he had to take a turn. He hit his ball through a wicket and noticed Jim lining up his shot to go after Tawny's ball.

"You're next, Miss Owl," Jim taunted. "Jim's going to send you to the woods where you belong." Jim's shot missed her ball and rolled a ways past.

It gave Matt a chance to finish answering Tawny's question. "I know it's not the first time the arrows-in-the-dummy thing has been done. It was done in the 1905 Carlisle-Dickenson game."

"Is that so?" Tawny asked. Their conversation distracted her from noticing Jim stalking her again.

When Matt's turn came, he hit Jim's ball.

Jim acted like it was the end of the world. "Oh, Big Bad Jim almost had that Tawny Owl."

"Now Big Bad Jim is going to pay," Matt announced. With a big mallet swing he sent Jim's ball almost to the flagpole in the middle of the quad.

Jim chased after it in the throes of tragic woe as all the girls but Tawny applauded Matt's valor.

Tawny granted him a tight smile. "Thank you, Mr. Grinnell. While the arrows-in-a-dummy trick has been done twice, the saving-a-damsel trick is as old as chivalry itself." Her smile released a bit. "That doesn't mean I don't appreciate it."

Before Matt could feign innocence and protest it wasn't a trick, the shouts of a matron assaulted the croquet field. She hustled toward them with her knitting needles held in front of her like a beefy Joan of Arc charging with a double lance.

"Run!" Jim shouted as he dropped his croquet mallet. "Run for your life!"

Matt took off, with the condemnations of the matron driving him on.

As soon as they got across the quad and behind the Small Boys' Quarters, Jim and Matt tumbled on the grass and rolled with laughter.

12.

TRICK PLAYS

On Monday, Matt returned to the routine of classes, the Printery and football practice.

As the week's *Arrow* came off the press, he looked for the sports article covering the Penn State game. It included how two scrubs devised "a Nittany Lion that got perforated with 18 feathered projectiles." Matt also checked *From the Ball Bin* on the back page. As usual, it was short and to the point.

> Turning an opposing "player" into an arrow porcupine is not a first. The stunt was first performed in the '05 Carlisle-Dickenson game when a Red Devil bristled with 36 arrows. — Pigskin

Matt was struck by the coincidence: he had heard the same footnote from both Caleb and Tawny, and now Pigskin was writing about it. Before jumping to any conclusions, Matt reminded himself that the Carlisle-Dickenson game had been played only two years earlier. There were still lots of people at the school who would remember it. *But who is Pigskin?* he wondered. *Caleb? Tawny?* He chuckled at the last possibility. *What girl—especially one as pretty as Tawny—would call herself Pigskin?*

Later, as the Hotshots suited up for practice, Matt learned that Jim would be practicing with the Varsity all week.

With the Hotshots, Matt and the lineman spent some time drilling shoulder blocks. Then they hit the charging sled to strengthen leg drive while the coach rode the sled and screamed, "Get down! I wanna see some worm-kissin'!"

By the time the lineman joined the other Hotshots, Matt's legs were rubber. In the scrimmage that followed, Newashe chewed him out for half blocking one guy, then going for another defender. "I don't wanna see you looking for man number two till you've got man number one flat as a pancake!"

Matt was beginning to think he would never make it as a lineman when Newashe pulled him and Caleb aside at the end of practice. Newashe told them that Pop wanted Thorpe and Grinnell on the bench again for the next Varsity game on Saturday. He told Caleb to find Jim and get them "suited up for the game against Syracuse." While Matt was intrigued by getting to see another powerhouse college team, he was baffled by the coach's order. As he and Caleb walked to the Cage, Matt aired his confusion. "Why are we 'suiting up' now, five days before the game?"

"You'll see." Caleb grinned. "After you've showered and dressed."

Caleb, Matt and Jim took the trolley into town and went to a clothing store named M. Blumenthal & Co. Besides racks of suits, coats and everything a man needed to be nattily attired, the walls were crammed with Carlisle pennants, flyers of game schedules and announcements and pictures of various teams and star players. It was a regular clubhouse for Carlisle football, baseball, basketball and track.

After Caleb explained to Mr. Blumenthal that Jim and Matt were now on the travel team and needed to be decked out for the trip to Syracuse, Blumenthal treated them like the most important players on the squad. As he outfitted them with three-piece suits and all the accessories, he told them to call him "Mose," and explained Pop's policy of providing fifty dollars a player to turn them into "knobby dressers." Pop believed in first impressions. When the Indians showed up at a school, he wanted to debunk the heathen image. These Indians were upstanding gentlemen who were as civilized as their white opponents.

While Matt tried on a suit jacket, he noticed a football jersey on the wall framed in a glass case. It was crimson and gold with a big C on it. When he asked about it, Mose declared, "You're not a true Redmen until two things happen. You wear one of my suits, and you know the greatest trick play of all time."

Matt couldn't resist. "What's that?"

Mose moved him to an array of full-length mirrors. As he used a sliver of soap to mark up the suit for tailoring, Mose regaled Matt with the story.

"It was the Carlisle-Harvard game of '03. Pop gave me a Redmen jersey belonging to a lineman named Charlie Dillon. Pop asked me to sew a band of elastic into the bottom of the jersey. Dillon was a big fellow who never ran the ball, and he had that jersey on when Harvard kicked off to begin the second half. As the ball soared through the air, the team all ran to Jimmie Johnson, who caught the ball. The players formed a wall hiding Johnson, Exendine and Dillon. Then Ex lifted the back of Dillon's jersey and Jimmie stuffed the football up under the elastic hem. Jimmie yelled 'Go' and the Indians scattered like a spilled sack of marbles. They all hunched over, pretending to have the ball, except for Dillon. He chugged down the field with his arms swinging like he was looking to block someone. The Harvard men ran after several Indians who were pretending to carry the ball but soon realized they were empty-handed. Meanwhile, the crowd, having spotted the bulge in the back of Dillon's jersey, screamed at the last Harvard player between Dillon and the goal to make the tackle. Dillon raised his arms to block and the player jumped aside, letting Dillon go. By the time the Harvard eleven realized where the ball was, it was too late. Dillon crossed the goal line; Johnson was right behind him to pull the ball out and touch it down for the score."

The story was so outrageous Matt wondered if it was their version of an urban legend. "It had to be illegal, right?"

"There was no rule against it," Mose said proudly as he double-checked his marks on the suit. "But even Pop has regrets about that one. He says it's best that Harvard won that day. Pop didn't want the Redmen to finally beat Harvard because of a band of elastic."

After Matt and Jim were fitted with overcoats, Mose told them to take the overcoats with them and that their suits would be ready for pickup on Wednesday.

Back out on the street, Jim claimed that a trip to town would be wasted without a trip to the Chocolate Shop. As they walked, Jim shot Matt a grin. "You'll get that suit in the nick of time. Come Wednesday night you can strut into the social looking like a man about town." He added with a wink, "And catch the eye of Tawny Owl."

"What's a social?" Matt asked.

Caleb shook his head in disbelief. "You really are a heathen, aren't you?"

"One hundred percent," Matt conceded.

Jim threw an arm around Matt. "A social is the one time they let boys and girls get together and do what we're supposed to do: touch each other."

"It's called dancing," Caleb interjected. "Wednesday night, the Mercer Literary Society is having a dance."

Matt frowned. "I can't dance."

"Well, you'll have to learn," Caleb said, "if you want to do more than steal a word or two with Tawny during a raid on a croquet game."

Matt gave him a quick look. "You heard about that?"

"I hear everything."

Resisting the urge to say *And so does Pigskin*, Matt stuck to the subject. "Are you guys going to the dance?"

Caleb nodded. "I'm planning on it."

Jim broke into his trickster grin. "Jim doesn't have to go to a dance to touch girls."

Matt's curiosity about what Jim meant was cut short as Jim led them into the Chocolate Shop. On one side of the narrow shop was a chocolate and sweets counter and an old-time soda fountain with stools. Along the other wall was a row of booths. It also had something in common with Blumenthal's: the walls were covered with Carlisle sports memorabilia.

It made Matt flash back on the equivalent in Belleplain. The Belleplain Diner was stuffed with Cyclones sports memorabilia. Matt wondered if a new picture had been put on the wall: the State Champion Cyclones, with Gary Allen holding the championship ball. *No way,* he told himself. *The Cyclones probably got blown away.*

"Matt!"

He broke from his rumination and saw Caleb and Jim straddling stools at the counter. "Do you want an egg cream or not?" Caleb asked.

Matt had no idea what an egg cream was. "Sure."

After ordering three egg creams from the soda jerk, Caleb spun around and spotted Pop Warner in the back corner booth. "Hi, Coach."

Pop didn't look up from the forest of salt-and-pepper cellars he had on the table in front of him. "Hello, boys."

At first, Matt thought Pop was playing checkers with them. Then he realized he was using them to design a play.

"Mr. Blumenthal just introduced Grinnell to your famous hidden ball trick," Caleb continued.

Pop moved a salt cellar. "Is he still awarding all credit for the play to his elastic?"

Caleb chuckled. "Yep. He's still *stretching* the truth."

Pop grunted a laugh and moved a couple more cellars.

"Any new tricks worked up for the Syracuse game?" Caleb asked.

Pop looked up. His blue eyes twinkled. "It's the opposite of the hidden-ball trick. It's the many-balls trick."

"Really? Can you tell us?"

Pop went back to his salt-and-pepper players. "If I told you, it wouldn't be a trick, would it?"

13.

THE SOCIAL

When the evening of the social arrived, Caleb had such a bad headache he retreated to bed. Matt recruited another wingman to protect him from doing something idiotic at the social, like introducing beer pong a century early.

Before leaving the room, Matt paused at the door and tossed back to Caleb, "Hey, I heard a rumor that you're Pigskin. Anything to that?"

Caleb's laugh was cut short by a bolt of head pain. "What makes anyone think that?"

Matt shrugged. "You're the water boy. If you *were* Pigskin and wrote something bad about the team, you'd be in deep shit."

Caleb settled back in his pillow. "Interesting theory, but Caleb Phillips doesn't go by any other name."

After leaving, Matt pondered Caleb's answer. Either his speedy denial pointed to guilt, or his headache was making him keep things short.

Matt met Lone Star in his room for inspection. Between the attachable collar, the shirt studs and the glassy shine on his black leather shoes, Matt felt like he was going to prom. After a few tweaks, he passed muster. But Matt's biggest worry wasn't his outfit. He hadn't had the time to pick up a dancing lesson from someone, much less learn what the hot dance was in 1907.

As he and Lone Star left the dorm room, Lone Star filled Matt in on the etiquette of "dance cards." At the beginning of the event, the gentlemen were allowed to approach each girl they wanted to dance with and ask for a dance. The girl could say no, or have a gentleman sign her dance card. The dance card hanging from her wrist would have a list of all the musical pieces the orchestra was going to play, and a gentleman would sign his name next to the piece the girl granted him for a dance.

It left Matt perplexed. "Boy, you guys know how to complicate things."

Lone Star gave him an arched look. "Don't blame the Indian for the white man's road."

Outside, a light rain was falling as the sun set. Matt and Lone Star joined the irregular stream of boys, all in their finest suits or uniforms, as they headed to the gymnasium. Matrons armed with umbrellas herded a column of girls in pretty dresses to a separate entrance of the gym.

Intermixed with the patter of rain on the big elms, and the banter of boys nervously anticipating the chance to mix with the girls, was another sound that caught Matt's ear. It was vaguely familiar and put him on edge. As Matt and Lone Star got closer to the bandstand, the sound grew louder. Recognition dawned. It was the murky sound of a cor anglais playing a wistful melody. Matt also recognized the figure in the bandstand playing the long woodwind: Alfred Jongler.

Matt's gut reaction was to ignore the sight and the beckoning sound. As soon as he did, his mind rebelled. *What am I doing? If Alfred and the cor anglais are ready to send me back, I gotta get back, even if I missed State.*

Matt stopped in his tracks.

Lone Star turned back. "Don't tell me you're getting cold feet."

"No, no," Matt reassured him. "I forgot something in my room. I'll be there in a minute."

"Okay"—Lone Star held up a warning finger—"but if you don't show your mug in five minutes, I'll come and force-march you to the dance."

Matt answered with a laugh and waited for Lone Star to

join another student on the way to the social. He turned to the haunting music. With his insides tightening, Matt moved to the bandstand and its shelter from the drizzling rain.

Alfred acknowledged him and continued playing. Matt anxiously glanced toward the gymnasium. The last of the boys disappeared inside. With no one else in sight, Alfred finished a phrase and stopped playing the cor anglais with the spider carved on its bell.

"What are you stopping for?" Matt asked. "Isn't it time?"

Alfred blinked. "I don't know, is it?"

"How should I know?"

"How should *I* know?" Alfred echoed. "Like I said before"— he lifted the instrument—"the cor anglais is in my hands, yet out of my hands."

Matt bristled at his word games. "If it's not time, what are you doing out here playing in the rain?"

"All fine instruments made of wood, from cellos to woodwinds, need to be played to keep life in the wood."

Matt felt a weird sensation of being caught on the fence between frustration and relief. "So it's a false alarm."

"Seems to be," Alfred concurred. "Not a bad thing, since I've been led to believe you are looking forward to the social."

Matt stiffened at the thought of Alfred spying on him. "How would you know?"

Alfred rippled his fingers on the cor anglais. "I have my sources."

Having heard enough, Matt moved back down the steps into the drizzle. "I'm outta here."

"See you inside," Alfred said.

Matt turned back. "What are you doing there?"

Alfred answered with a gentle smile. "Someone has to conduct the orchestra."

Matt headed for the gymnasium. It was like walking away

from a man with a gun. It felt like a trick. He waited for the music to start up again, for it to go weird, for mists to slither after him. But all he heard was the *swoosh* of his dress shoes cutting through the grass.

The Mercer Literary Society had decorated the gymnasium in autumnal colors; Carlisle's red and gold hung from the ceiling. A small orchestra was playing. A student was conducting until Mr. Jongler arrived and took over.

Matt found Lone Star at the punch bowl. After being handed a glass of red punch, Matt took a big gulp, hoping it was laced with vodka, rum or anything alcoholic.

His gulp and taut expression didn't escape Lone Star. "Sorry, chief. Just because it's red doesn't make it firewater. Besides, given your first attempt to impress Miss Owl, it's not tongue-loosening you need." "Don't worry," Matt retorted. "I'm gonna keep my handprints to myself."

As Lone Star chuckled, Matt scanned the girls in their formal dresses. He didn't see Tawny, but was intrigued by the dance cards dangling from their wrists, secured by fancy ties of ribbons and froufrou. "All the girls look like quarterbacks with arm play holders."

Lone Star laughed at the bizarre notion. "If Mounty put our plays on a dance card, the other team would rip it off and use them against us."

"Yeah, dumb idea," Matt acknowledged, glad to be off the hook from future-speak slippage.

Lone Star spotted someone and pulled Matt along. "Come on, I'll show you how it works."

They approached Angel De Cora, wearing a pretty dress with lots of Indian necklaces draped around her neck.

Matt still couldn't get over Lone Star having a thing for a teacher. "You're going to dance with her?" he whispered a little too loudly.

"Mr. Grinnell," Angel said with a disarming smile, "it won't be the first time."

"Miss De Cora," Lone Star said impeccably, "may I have the honor of a dance or two with you?"

"Certainly, Mr. Dietz," she answered, offering the dance card at her wrist. "I prefer the odd ones."

Matt watched bug-eyed as Lone Star began signing all the odd numbers on Angel's dance card. "You can do that?"

"I'd sign them all . . . ," Lone Star said, still signing as Angel gamely finished his thought. "But we wouldn't want to raise suspicions." They both shared a laugh.

Matt left them to their flirtation and looked for Tawny. If he could find her before anyone else, there was no telling how many dances he might be able to sign up for. Soon he did find her and, while her dress wasn't as fancy as the other girls', she was still the most radiant girl in the room.

"Miss Owl," he said, parroting Lone Star, "may I have the honor of a dance or two with you?"

She gave him a skewed look. "Mr. Grinnell, I'm sure you said hello first, but you must have spoken so softly the orchestra drowned it out."

"Right," Matt said, silently cursing Lone Star for setting him up for another stumble. "Hello, Miss Owl, how are you and who won the croquet game?"

She smiled at the memory. "No one. We were all sent to our rooms for fraternizing with boys."

"The matron threw the flag." He threw an invisible penalty flag. "Ten yards, illegal boy-time."

She gave him a curious look. "What's the flag?"

Matt kicked himself for another future-speak. Having seen several games, he'd learned penalty flags hadn't been invented yet. He told himself to stop being nervous. After all, she was just another pretty girl. He could handle pretty girls as easily as he could handle a football. Okay, a modern-day football. "Ah," he fumbled for an alibi, "I thought that's what the matron was knitting—a flag."

Tawny chuckled. "Whoever heard of knitting a flag? Really, Mr. Grinnell, you are a strange one."

"That's me." He made an oogie-boogie face. "The *stranger*."

She laughed at his goofy face as Matt saw one of the football players, Afraid of a Bear, coming toward them.

He had to get back on track. He stiffened and said in his most courtly voice, "Hello, Miss Owl. May I have the honor of a dance with you?"

"Yes," she answered, offering her dance card.

Good news: she said yes. Bad news: her dance card was all signed except for one dance two-thirds of the way through the evening. Worse news: it was a waltz. Matt knew as much about waltzing as he knew about knitting. Nonetheless, he signed her card as Afraid of a Bear joined them.

"Tough luck," Matt said to the player. "I just nailed the last dance."

Afraid of a Bear broke into a smile. "I 'nailed' first one."

As other couples moved onto the dance floor, Matt headed for the sidelines. He noticed Alfred, now standing in front of the orchestra with a baton. Matt's relief over Alfred no longer holding the cor anglais was short-lived. A new worry bubbled up. His *Girls 1907* playbook was open to a totally blank page: waltzing.

14.

WALTZ

When the first dance ended, Matt pulled Lone Star away from Miss De Cora, who had another partner for the second dance. Matt explained his predicament; he didn't know squat about waltzing. Lone Star grabbed his arm and pulled him outside.

The rain had stopped and the sky had cleared.

Lone Star raised his hands. "I'll show you the man's part first, then we'll switch and I'll be the girl."

"Whoa," Matt protested, "I don't wanna dance with you. I just want you to show me the steps."

Lone Star gave him a put-upon look. "It's no different than when we face off on the line, except instead of trying to hurt each other, we're going to try *not* to hurt each other. I only have so much time before my next dance, so if you want to learn how not to hurt Miss Owl, you better step up and let me lead."

Matt heaved a sigh and caved.

Lone Star kept it simple and showed him the basics: the stationary box step, the rotating box step and the ladies underarm turn. Twirling under Lone Star's arm, Matt cracked up laughing.

His teacher stayed on task. "That's what she'll do if you don't get this right. Now you."

"Now me what?"

"Now you lead."

Matt waved a hand. "That's okay, I got the idea."

Lone Star persisted. "There's offense and defense. You can't play the game until you go both ways."

Matt accepted his fate. He put up his hands and waltzed Lone Star in a box and a rotation. As Matt was leading him into an underarm turn, Jim emerged from the darkness into the light spilling from the gymnasium.

Matt spotted him and jumped away from Lone Star. "He's teaching me how to waltz."

Jim kept his deadpan stare. "Now Jim knows why he never goes to socials. They teach funny things."

Lone Star flicked a hand at him. "Go back to your hound-dogging, Thorpe. I'm sure that's why you're prowling around in the dark."

Jim backed into the shadows, muttering, "Linemen. Jim never understand 'em."

Matt burned with the embarrassment of being caught dancing with a guy, even if it was only practice. But the moment contained another first: it was the first time he was glad to be in 1907. What happened in 1907 stayed in 1907. The consolation allowed him to recover and ask his dancing partner, "What do you mean, 'hound-dogging'?"

Lone Star didn't answer as his focus shifted to the music coming from inside. "My next dance is coming up."

Back in the gym, Matt hung out with some football players on the boys' side of the room, sipped punch and waited for his dance with Tawny. There was no talking to her between dances because the chaperones made sure, except for the opening mixer, that the dance floor was the only field for mingling.

During an earlier waltz, before his fateful one, Matt discreetly took tiny steps, practicing his moves. As they began to feel comfortable, he realized that the rhythm wasn't much different from the three-step move he made after an under-center snap before a quick-release pass. As soon as he imagined the waltz being just another way for a QB to move in the pocket, it became second nature. He was going to be a waltzing fool.

When his dance came up, Matt met Tawny on the floor. The music started, he offered his hand and they began. He settled into the rhythm, reveling in how much better Tawny's hand and waist felt compared to his last partner's.

After moving smoothly into their first rotating box, Matt had the confidence to go for the next level: dance *and* talk. "I have two apologies to make," he began. "One, for my dancing, and two, for what I said in art class."

"I'll accept the second but not the first," she replied.

He pulled back and caught her eye. "Am I doing something wrong?"

"The fact that you can apologize and waltz at the same time," she said with a slight smile, "means you don't have to apologize."

He moved her into a rotating box again and kept up his three-beat mantra: *Step-step-plant, step-step-plant.* They were styling!

She spoke again. "About those handprints, I was thinking about them."

He almost lost his rhythm—"You were?"—and retreated to a stationary box step.

"If anyone should wear handprints to ward off harm, it should be you fellows on the football field."

"Really?" He risked an underarm turn. He wasn't sure if she was joking or not.

"Really," she echoed, completing the turn. "There are so many injuries and it's so dangerous. Handprints could be a protection only the team would know about."

He assumed she was serious and went with it. It was straight out of his *Girls 1907* playbook: *Don't act, react.* "So besides getting taped up we'd get handprinted up?"

She nodded. "Exactly."

He thought about the awkwardness of who'd be doing the handprinting on players' bodies. *Caleb? Pop?* Matt wondered. *No way am I proposing the idea, especially after being caught dancing with Lone Star.* "Make you a deal," he offered Tawny.

"The day I make the starting eleven, I'll propose the handprint idea."

She flashed a smile. "Deal."

"Now I have a question for you, Miss Owl."

She moved her head closer and whispered, "When no one's listening you can call me Tawny."

The small victory made Matt feel like a conqueror. He smiled at the absurdity of it: he never imagined calling a girl by her first name would make him feel like a stud. "Okay, Tawny." He moved her into another twirl. "Here's my question." She turned back. "Is your name also Pigskin?"

She laughed. "That's ridiculous."

"Why?"

"It's a boy's game, written about by men," she replied. "Why would I waste my time being a reporter when I'm training to be a nurse?"

He didn't back off. "Because you seem to be totally into football. You love talking about it, thinking about it, and that makes you want to share whatever you know about the Carlisle Indians with the world."

She shook her head dismissively. "That doesn't make me a reporter. It only makes me another rooter in the stands."

The music stopped and Matt swayed her to a standstill without letting go. "Your passion for football makes me wanna share everything I know about it with you."

She stepped back, removing her hand from his. "Then keep sharing it, Matt Grinnell." She turned toward the next gentleman coming for his dance.

As Matt left the dance floor, he knew he had touched something inside her. He still didn't know if she was Pigskin or not, but he had done something better. He had laid a handprint on her heart.

15.

SYRACUSE

Because of Matt's improving skills as a lineman, he was moved up to practice and scrimmage with the Varsity before the Syracuse game. Even though Carlisle's starting eleven were faster, smarter and worked like a well-oiled machine, Matt's size allowed him to hold his own. In one scrimmage, he almost sacked Mounty a couple of times before Pop whistled him off to prevent damage to their star QB.

What Pop couldn't whistle off, and Matt couldn't ignore, was the strange feeling that had begun to overtake him while playing on the line. He felt good there. Something about it felt right.

When practice ended, Wallace Denny, the trainer, ordered Matt, the low scrub on the totem pole, to police the field and make sure nothing had been left.

At the far end, Matt found a football that one of the kickers had forgotten in the grass. He grabbed it and felt its bulbous shape. He hadn't touched a ball since his disastrous attempt to prove he was a quarterback. His curiosity kicked in. As he returned the ball, he tossed and chased it down the empty field. Each throw got a little better. Then, as he moved his hand back to the narrow end of the ball, he launched a 30-yard pass with a good spiral.

"Hey!" Denny yelled. "Stop dawdling and get that leather in here."

Matt scooped up the ball and ran it in. He had found more than a stray football; he had found the key to throwing the watermelon ball.

The Friday before the game, the team boarded a train headed to Buffalo, New York, where the game against Syracuse would be played. They needed the large football stadium at Olympic Park because over 10,000 fans were expected.

As the train wound through the Appalachians, Matt's only disappointment was that the band wasn't with them. A trip for that many students was too expensive for the school so early in the season.

Caleb had let the rest of the travel squad know that Pop had a new trick up his sleeve. They pestered Pop all the way to Buffalo to try to get the trick play out of him, but Pop only gave them a cryptic hint: "What can football players learn from butterflies?" By the time the train arrived at Union Station in Buffalo, the players were convinced Pop had designed a uniform with a set of wings so they could fly over the enemy line.

Saturday, when the players entered the dressing room at Olympic Park, Pop's scheming was on display. He had altered the running backs' jerseys. On the belly of each one, a leather patch the shape and color of a football had been sewn on. "Boys," he explained, "just like a butterfly deceives its predators with big eyespots on its wings, our running backs are going to deceive the predators of the gridiron with football spots."

When the Carlisle Redmen ran onto the field, they were greeted with a thunderous roar. Not only was the stadium overflowing with 12,000 fans, many were Indians. Buffalo was surrounded by reservations of the Iroquois League. The thousands of long-haired Indians who had made the trip, dressed in traditional buckskin clothes and wrapped in blankets, greeted them with wild whoops.

Matt was unnerved by the celebrating Indians. He had to pinch himself to make sure he hadn't traveled farther back in time and was about to be flung into a bloody massacre. Once over the shock, he was awed by the eye-popping spectacle of the teeming Iroquois braves.

The team joked that half the Indians were Mounty's cousins since their star quarterback had been born and raised on the nearby Tuscarora Reservation.

Before the game started, the coach of the Syracuse Orangemen protested against the football patches on the jerseys of the Indian backfield. But the referee agreed with Pop. "There is no rule against it."

From the opening kickoff, Matt wondered if the Syracuse players had felt the same bolt of fear that had raised the hackles on Matt's neck upon entering the stadium; the Orangemen played like threatened animals. They slugged and tripped and piled on after every play. But the Indians were up to the beating. Hauser kicked a 20-yard field goal to put the Redmen on the board first, 4-0.

Besides their stunt with uniforms, the Indians pulled off a trick play that Syracuse and none of the fans had seen before. Mounty set up to punt, started his motion, then pulled up and passed to Gardner for a huge gain. The fake punt had been invented. The Indians in the crowd, seeing a local Iroquois outwit the palefaces, whooped and hollered like they were at a moose hunt. A few moments later, from five yards out, Hauser plunged over the line for the touchdown. His conversion kick made it 10-0.

After that, one of the toughest Orangemen, Stimson, tried to take his growing frustration out on Hauser by tackling him as hard as he could. Stimson only succeeded in knocking himself out and getting carried off the field. While Stimson was still seeing stars, the Syracuse quarterback saw daylight and ran the ball forty-five yards for a TD, chopping the deficit to 10-5.

It was too little too late. Hauser booted another field goal, making the final tally 14-5, Carlisle. As soon as the whistle blew, the crush of Indians surrounding the field flooded across it, howling loud enough to raise the dead.

When the players made it back to the dressing room, Matt saw that many of their faces, covered in dirt, sweat and blood, were streaked with tears. When he asked Caleb if they had ever played in front of so many Indians, Caleb, with a transfixed expression, shook his head.

Watching the players celebrate, Matt realized what had triggered their tears. They now understood they were more than a football team. Every time they took the field, they were playing for their race. They had the power to lift the crushed spirit of a people and let it soar again.

Pop quieted the room and spoke. "Boys, today you rattled more than the bones of the Orangemen, you rattled the bones of every red man, living and dead. Today you showed what an Indian can do."

The team took the train back home late that afternoon. By the time they got to Carlisle, it was late at night. Nonetheless, they were greeted at the station on High Street by several hundred cheering students who waved pennants and jabbed burning torches in the air as the band blasted a victory song. The victory rally even included a "uniform": they were all dressed in their nightshirts.

Matt stared out the train window at the jubilant crowd. "How do they know we won?" he asked Caleb.

"For the big games we set up a telegraph link at Indian Field," Caleb explained. "As the telegraph reports on the game come in, the action gets drawn on a chalkboard, and one of the rooters reports the game as if he was there."

Matt shook his head in awe. He wondered what it would be like to have modern-day fans so crazed by football that hundreds of them gathered around one guy with a smart phone as he turned tweets into nail-biting play-by-play.

The rooters led the team in a snake dance through town. As the band played Indian songs, Carlisle residents came out on their porches and waved at the victory parade.

Matt wanted to get to Tawny and tell her all about what he had seen at the game. But the crowd was laced with matrons running interference against boys trying to infiltrate groups of girls, including the girls in the band. Filling Tawny in on the game would have to wait.

16.

SCRIMMAGE

On Sunday, after church and lunch, Pop sent the team out for their usual walk in the countryside.

Matt and Lone Star were following a trail in the woods when they heard a strange bird call. After it sounded a few times, Matt asked, "What is that?"

"I'm not sure," Lone Star said with a knowing smile. "But if I were you, I'd try to find it."

Matt took the hint and followed the bird call. After moving through the trees for fifty yards, he came around a huge boulder. His heart jumped as he saw who stood behind it. "You made that sound?"

Tawny raised a shushing finger and spoke softly. "Some owls do more than hoot."

He laughed as she leaned back against the boulder, finding a patch of sunlight coming through the treetops. "I read about the game in the newspapers this morning," she said. "But I'm sure they didn't cover all the details. Please, tell me about it."

Matt leaned back too and launched into everything he had seen and heard, from Pop's hint on the train about his new trick to the thousands of Indians pouring onto the field after the game. Tawny listened with the kind of rapt attention the pastor in church that morning would have sold his soul for. Matt was describing the victory celebration in the dressing room when they heard a matron calling Tawny's name.

Tawny pushed off the boulder and put a finger to Matt's lips. "I'll go first," she whispered. "Wait, then you." She gave him a warm smile. "Thank you." She disappeared around the rock and called to the matron with an excuse about looking for a four-leaf clover.

Matt leaned his head back, shut his eyes, and felt the sun along with the thrumming memory of her finger on his lips. He knew he was crushing out; this girl was throwing his timing off. Back in Belleplain, any girl who had put her finger on his lips would not have escaped without giving up a kiss, or more. But Tawny had something that knocked him off his game.

On Monday, Matt hoped that Tawny, having forgiven him, might return to Drawing class. She didn't. During his afternoon in the Printery, he scoured the submissions to the next edition of *The Arrow* to see if any of the details he had revealed to her about the Syracuse game came in under Pigskin's byline. By Tuesday afternoon, Pigskin, whoever he or she was, had still submitted nothing.

Later, as the scrubs gathered for practice on Indian Field, Coach Johnson told them they were going to scrimmage against the Varsity eleven and give them the kind of game their next opponent played. Jimmie would be coaching them "U Penn style."

Matt was assigned to left guard, where he would go up against the starting right guard, Little Boy. He was called Little Boy because he had such a baby face. The rest of him defied the name. Little Boy weighed 190 and was low and broad, like an ATV on steroids.

For its backfield, the "U Penn" side had all the second-string backs: Thorpe, Bill Winnie, Theodore Owl and the backup QB, Louis Island. Matt had to squash a laugh when the pint-sized Island barked out the first play in the scrimmage. Island was five foot five and weighed no more than 140. During the play, Matt paid for the distraction. Little Boy flattened him and tackled Jim for a loss.

Because the University of Pennsylvania's style was up-the-middle line plunges with an occasional end run, Matt spent the scrimmage battling it out on the inside with Little Boy. Matt made some good blocks and a few tackles. When it was over, Little Boy slapped him on the back and said, "Wrong Way begin like feather, end like grit and sand."

Matt felt a surge of pride. Minutes later, he got a second dose of jump juice when Coach Johnson informed him that Pop liked what he saw and there was a chance Matt might see his first Varsity action against U Penn.

It wasn't until after Matt had showered and dressed that his swelling head was deflated by a disturbing thought. Before the dinner bell rang, he hurried across the quad through a shower of autumn leaves. Reaching the Academic Building, he headed for the music rooms.

Sitting at his desk in his office, Alfred looked up with a startled expression as Matt barged in. "Is there something wrong?" Alfred asked.

"Maybe yes, maybe no," Matt said. "I don't know how this works."

Alfred opened his hands. "I work better with specifics."

"I might go into the game against U Penn."

Alfred smiled. "That's good."

"No, it's not," Matt protested. "What if I do something that, you know—"

"Changes history?"

"Yeah."

Alfred leaned back in his chair. "I've been thinking about that too."

"I can't throw history out of whack. That would be bad, right?"

Alfred adjusted his glasses. "So you think you might get in the game, recover a fumble, run it in for a touchdown and change the outcome of the Carlisle–U Penn game of 1907?"

"Ye-ah."

Alfred studied his voyager. "It's good we're thinking about such things. Have you also considered the outcome you might affect if you fall for an Indian girl and alter her life in ways that can't be reversed?"

Matt covered his surprise with a scoff. "We're just friends," he lied. He instantly felt his face begin to flush. "Besides, she's a girl. This is about football, about the record book."

"Life has a record book too, the story of people's lives. You're worried about changing a football record but you're not afraid of changing a girl's future?"

Matt knew he had a point but he wasn't about to admit it. "Okay, fine. If I'm such a threat, why not just whip out the oboe and send me back?"

Alfred gazed at him over his glasses. "First of all, if you want it to do your bidding, you might start by using its proper name: cor anglais. Secondly, you know it's not a matter of 'whipping it out.'"

"Yeah, yeah," Matt grumbled, "it's out of your hands. But maybe you should carry it around all the time and play it every time you see me."

Alfred ignored the absurd picture this painted. "I play it more often than you think. It's shown me a thing or two."

"Like what?"

"To be patient. To wait for a sign."

The clang of the dinner bell sounded outside.

Alfred's eyebrows arched. "That's not the sign I'm waiting for. But your stomach might want to heed it."

Matt didn't move. He was sick of looking at the little man's sphinxlike expression but he wasn't leaving without an answer. "Should I play in the U Penn game or not?"

"I don't see why not. After all, it's only a game."

After Matt left, Alfred's façade of inscrutable composure

collapsed. He pulled out his cigarettes and lit one. He wished his brother was still alive to assure him that the cor anglais, and the Jongler possessing it, always got it right in the end.

As Matt headed to dinner, he couldn't escape a vexing thought. He had always known chasing a girl could have unintended consequences, especially a . . . His mind jammed on a word he couldn't remember. It was one of his labels from Girls 101. *Funny,* he thought, *I can't remember the terms.* As much as his forgetfulness bugged him, he was entangled by a bigger worry: chasing a girl in 1907 had so many consequences it made his head spin.

17.

SINGLE WING

The next day in the Printery, Matt found the submission to *The Arrow* he had been waiting for: Pigskin's *From the Ball Bin* entry on the Syracuse game.

> Football patches on jerseys: above or below the belt?
> Whichever, they herald things to come. As Romulus
> and Remus founded Rome, Deception and Cunning
> will found the modern science of football. — Pigskin

Even though it didn't solve the mystery of Pigskin's identity, Matt was leaning toward Caleb. The Romulus and Remus reference seemed out of Caleb's playbook, not Tawny's.

There was one other clue pointing toward Caleb. Pigskin's submission might have been slow to come in because Caleb had been fighting a cold since returning from Syracuse. Between a bad cough and fatigue, he barely had the energy for classes and practice. When Caleb went to the hospital to see Dr. Shoemaker, the doctor confined him to his room and only allowed trips to the dining hall.

At the beginning of Wednesday's practice, Pop gathered the Varsity and reminded them of a formation they had practiced earlier in the season. He told them they were going to work on it the rest of the week and unleash it against their archrival, the U Penn Quakers. Matt didn't know what formation he was talking about until Pop used its name: "the single wing."

Matt knew the term as the old name for what would eventually be called the wildcat. It was named the single wing because, unlike the T or I formations, with their symmetry in the backfield, the single wing swept a curve of backs behind one side of the line. This "wing" started with the tailback and fullback flanked behind the center, with the quarterback to the right of them, and the "wingback" at the tip of the wing outside of the right end. The unique formation put *three* backs in a position to receive the snap from the center. From there anything could happen: run, pass, quick kicks and combinations that turned the single wing's kaleidoscope of options into a racing wildfire that scattered defenders like panicked animals.

Matt was put on the defensive line against the first string as they reviewed the formation. It gave him the perfect view of Pop putting his starters through their paces, especially when each play began as walkthroughs of the assignments. Matt quickly realized the single wing wasn't something Pop had borrowed from someone else; he was *inventing* it. Matt was witnessing the birth of a formation that would revolutionize football. It gave him the chills.

Matt had never seen so many gadget plays from the same formation. But the biggest surprise was something Pop did with Mounty. As quarterback, Mounty still called the plays and mostly lined up behind one of the guards. But in the up-the-middle running plays in which he wasn't hiked the ball, it was Mounty, the quarterback, who led the blocking through the line. Pop called him his "blocking back." For Matt, a *blocking* QB was as unnatural as a green sun.

After running a dozen single-wing plays, Coach Johnson came up to Pop and jogged his head toward the stands. A lone figure in a newsboy cap stood in the shadow of the bleachers, watching them practice.

Pop's eyes narrowed. He turned and gave the scrub with the least seniority an order. "Grinnell, run up there and get rid of that kid. We don't need any spies selling our plays to the Quakers."

Matt trotted off the field toward the stands. As soon as the kid saw him coming, he took off. Matt sprinted after him. The kid was no match in a footrace, although Matt was surprised how fast he ran.

Reaching him, Matt grabbed the kid's arm and spun him around. The flushed face, filled with fear, was all too familiar. It was Tawny, dressed as a boy, with her long hair hidden under her cap.

"Holy shit," Matt exhaled as he let go of her arm.

She backed away, not saying a word. She didn't have to; her pleading eyes said it all: *Let me go.* She turned and ran.

Staring after her, Matt uttered softly, "You *are* Pigskin."

When he jogged back to the field, Johnson asked who it was. Matt told the coach it was one of the little boys from the school; he had been spying in hopes of learning a trick play or two to use on the small boys' football team.

The next day, it was as if Tawny had radar for him. Every time Matt tried to get close to her between classes, she scurried away or escaped into a herd of girls. It's not like he could run her down when she was wearing a dress; everyone would think he was a pervert.

Later, in the Printery, Matt was startled to find a second submission from Pigskin for that week's *Arrow*.

Already famous for trick plays, against Penn our braves will become famous for a trick offense. Yes, the "Quakers" will earn their name when Franklin Field becomes the epicenter of an earthquake that will shake gridirons from coast to coast. — Pigskin

Matt beamed at the final proof. Caleb wasn't at practice when they had started working on the single wing, and the team had been sworn to secrecy. Pigskin was Tawny.

After dinner that evening, another incident sealed it for Matt beyond the shadow of a doubt.

Jim snuck a football out of the Cage and persuaded Matt to go with him to the lower field. In the dying light, they threw the ball back and forth. Jim wanted to work on his passing because several of the single-wing plays involved a running back throwing a pass. Even though he was second-string, Jim wanted to be ready in case he went into the Penn game. Matt jumped at the chance to get his hands on the fat ball and work on his own throw. As the two of them kept stretching the distance between them, Matt was pleased to match Jim's spirals out to about thirty yards.

When it was almost impossible to see the ball, Matt spotted a girl watching them from the rise between the lower field and Indian Field. She was silhouetted against the glow of the school's lights. He threw one last pass to Jim and jogged toward her.

Mistaking it for a pattern, Jim yelled, "Grinnell goes long!" He heaved a pass.

Matt instinctively turned to try and find the ball in the gloaming. At the last second, he saw the ball drop out of the sky and he caught it. When he turned back to the rise, the girl was gone. There was no doubt in his mind it was Tawny. What other girl had the spunk to leave the girls' ground and go to the lower field in near darkness? What other girl but Pigskin?

18.

ART OF THE DEAL

The next morning, the train that left Carlisle for the trip to Philadelphia was a circus train of excitement. One car was filled with the football team, while five others carried the band, 200 students, and a dozen chaperones and matrons to oversee them. Besides the game, they were going to see the sights, be treated to a night in Hotel Normandie and have lunch at the famous Gimbels department store, all before the game Saturday.

Nobody was more thrilled than Caleb. He had bounced back from his cold and convinced Dr. Shoemaker that he was healthy enough to travel. While the sights of Philly were a bonus, the only prize that mattered was being on the sideline for his team as they took on their archrivals, the fourth-ranked team in the nation.

Later that afternoon, as the team and the students visited the Museum of Science and Art, Matt meandered through the halls with the other players checking out the displays, paintings and sculptures. With his eye out for Tawny, he finally spotted her with another girl, standing in front of a painting.

He broke off from the guys, stood behind the two girls, and looked over their heads at the painting. It showed a man and a woman riding some kind of zip-line over crashing surf and rocks. The man was holding the woman's limp body, and her blowing scarf covered the man's face. You could feel the wind, sea spray and danger.

Noticing Matt's looming presence, Tawny looked for skulking matrons while her friend tittered nervously. Not seeing any matrons, Tawny whispered to her friend. The girl took her cue and bustled off.

Matt stepped next to Tawny but kept his eyes on the painting. "Some painting, huh?" It wasn't his most brilliant open, but it wasn't foot-in-mouth.

"It's called 'The Life Line,'" she said. "It's by Winslow Homer."

Hearing the name "Homer" triggered a play he wanted to run. "What do you think is happening in the picture?"

"It's obvious," she answered. "It's a man rescuing a woman from a shipwreck."

"I'm not so sure," he said pensively. "We've been reading *The Iliad* in Literature class, the part where Paris kidnaps Helen and steals her off to Troy."

She turned from the painting with an incredulous expression. "You think it's an allegory?"

"I'm not sure what an 'allegory' is, I just know that sometimes things aren't what they seem. Maybe it's not a rescue, maybe it's a, uh . . ." His words trailed off as he realized his play was about to crash and burn.

"Is the word you're looking for 'abduction'?" she asked. "Or even 'rape'?"

Matt's cheeks prickled with heat. It felt so wrong that he was the one who was embarrassed by the word when she was the one from an uptight century. "No," he backpedaled, "maybe it's a robbery."

Her hand smothered a laugh. "A robbery at sea?"

"It's not that lame," he said, pointing at the painting. "I mean, the guy *is* wearing a mask. He could be a bandit."

"That's her windblown scarf covering his face."

"Okay," he conceded, "it's a scarf. But why did the painter put it over his face?"

Tawny studied the picture. "Maybe Mr. Homer didn't

want us to look at the man. Maybe he wanted us to look at the woman."

Having barely recovered from the r-word, Matt had to fend off the instinct that now she was blatantly flirting. He struggled to keep his mouth in 1907. "All I'm saying, Miss Owl, is that you shouldn't judge a painting at first glance, or judge a guy by the first doofus words out of his mouth, or assume that this Homer is the only one in the museum hiding a face to trick us into looking somewhere else."

Tawny eyed him curiously. "Oh really? What other artist is practicing misdirection?"

"It's not an artist. It's someone named Pigskin."

Her eyes narrowed and she gave her head a little shake. "What are you saying, Mr. Grinnell?"

He looked right at her. "I think Pigskin is a great writer and shouldn't hide behind a made-up name."

She chuckled. "You should know. You know all about hiding things. Like that you can throw a football."

Her verbal pivot caught him off guard. "You've been doing your homework."

"Yes, I have. I also know you're not from the Mandan tribe, you've never had an Indian name, and there's not a drop of Indian blood in you."

Matt refused to panic. "I think you're bluffing."

She turned to him, her face set. "First of all, when you didn't know about handprints on warriors and horses, and said you *weren't* a Plains Indian, but then claimed to be Mandan, I knew you were lying."

Matt grimaced. "Mandans are from the Plains?"

"North Dakota. And to be certain you weren't a Mandan who had been raised under a rock, I wrote the council on the Mandan reservation. They've never heard of Matthew Grinnell. Nor have they heard of the name you have in your student record: Hakuna Matata. What kind of Indian name is that?"

He strained to keep a straight face. "It means no worries."

"Well, you *should* be worried," she said with foreboding eyes. "If Pigskin were to drop all that in the *Ball Bin*, you'd be investigated and expelled in a week."

He studied her. "Is that what you want? For me to leave?"

Her face softened. "No. But if everyone finds out who Pigskin is, they might kick *me* out of school."

"Or stop listening to you 'cause you're a girl?"

She nodded sharply.

"I don't want that to happen," he assured her, adding a smile. "I'm happy to be blackmailed by you."

She frowned. "I wouldn't call it that. It's an understanding that sometimes secrets make us stronger. And these secrets will be something we hold in common."

"Miss Owl!" a voice scolded as a matron swept in. "You've stared at that painting long enough!"

"But it's so dramatic," Tawny exclaimed as the matron whisked her away. "I can't decide if it's a rescue or an abduction!"

The cry of "Miss Owl!" reverberated as Matt watched them disappear around a corner. He beamed. His play had done what all great plays do: exceed expectations.

19.

MATT CHANGES HISTORY

Saturday afternoon, 22,000 fans pushed through the turnstiles at Franklin Field. Nine out of ten were rooting for the Pennsylvania Quakers.

Pop had saved the surprise of the single wing for their first big Ivy League matchup of the season for a reason. In the six times Carlisle had played U Penn, the Indians had never won. There were two victory game balls the Redmen still didn't have in their trophy case: U Penn and Harvard. If they were going to beat the mighty Quakers, they needed a new and deadly weapon.

The Indians started with the single wing from the get-go. Mounty took the snap, spun and handed off to Hauser. Hauser scooted to his right and released a beautiful spiral, arcing over the field. Many in the crowd had never seen a football thrown so far. The ball came down in the arms of Gardner, turning into a 40-yard gain.

The stands went eerily quiet. They were stunned by the aired out pass. The only style of football they had ever seen was a game of pile-to-pile combat. The Quaker players looked to the sideline at their coach, baffled as to what to do against this kind of play.

While they were trying to figure out how to defend against the ball being snapped to one of three backs, all triple threats—runner, passer, kicker—Mounty booted a field goal, putting the Redmen on the board 4-0.

Flushed with confidence, and wanting the ball back to employ their trick formation again, the Indians smothered the Penn offense and forced a punt.

Not long into the first half, Albert Payne limped off the field and Pop yelled, "Thorpe, in for Payne!"

Jim burst off the bench and onto the field.

The first time he got pitched the ball, Jim was so juiced he raced past his blockers and got buried by tacklers. Pop waved his arms, screamed and turned beet red. Matt thought he was going to bust a vein.

On the next play, Jim settled down. He followed his interference and shot past Penn players like their feet were nailed to the ground. Seventy-five yards later, he sprinted over the goal line, thrust the ball in the air and touched it down for his first Varsity touchdown.

From the bench, Matt cheered Jim's triumph.

For the Redmen, everything was clicking. Mounty would drop back for a fake punt, then throw a 50-yard pass. When the Quakers thought the Indians were about to pass, they ran; when they thought the Redmen were going to run, they passed. Penn didn't look undefeated, they looked unglued. They were ranked number four in the country all right, for discombobulation. Over 20,000 Penn fans were benumbed by the sight of their Quaker boys being humiliated.

Late in the second half, Penn began to play dirty. Little Boy got slugged so hard at the bottom of the pile he had to be helped off the field.

"Grinnell, in for Little Boy!" Pop yelled.

Matt jumped off the bench. Jogging onto the field, his insides churned. He yearned to prove himself; he didn't want to make a fool of himself or let the team down. But now his guts twisted with a new fear. He wasn't sure how hard to play. Every time he had ever stepped onto a football field, he had wanted to *make* history. Now he was scared of changing it. Which set up his biggest quandary: he wanted to play well enough to impress Tawny.

As Matt faced off against the Penn guard he needed to block on his first play, all his churning worries and hopes vanished with the snap of the ball. He easily drove the guard to the inside. After a decent gain on an off-tackle run, Matt jogged to the new line of scrimmage feeling fifty pounds lighter. The Penn players were beaten, going through the motions, wanting the game to end. Pop sent in more subs, including Mike Balenti at QB. The scrubs were in to do what scrubs do: mop up. Matt noticed the stunned crowd beginning to head for the exits.

Unbeknownst to Matt, his contribution to the game was not over. Several plays later, Little Boy, who had recovered, came back in for Matt. Little Boy wanted to be on the field when the last whistle blew.

Trotting to the sideline, Matt found Tawny in the stands and caught her beaming smile. He wanted to give her a shout-out— *Hakuna Matata!*—but thought better of it.

He got a pat from Pop and a compliment from Jim who announced loudly to the team, "Wrong Way play right!"

As the last minute counted down, Matt stood with the other players as Caleb wove through them, offering ladles of water from the water bucket. Matt noticed Caleb's face was pale and he struggled with the bucket. When Caleb got to him, Matt offered to help with the bucket. Caleb looked up just long enough to take his eyes off the ground, strewn with discarded headgear and shin guards. Caleb stumbled on a guard and lunged forward with the bucket. Matt grabbed the back of Caleb's jacket and saved him from doing a face-plant, but the body-catch didn't stop the bucket from flying out of his hand. It hit the ground and launched a small wave that soaked Pop's leg.

"Goddamnit!" Pop shouted at the shock of cold water. His eyes shot from the spilled bucket to Caleb, still dangling from Matt's arm. The players went as quiet as the fans exiting the stands. "What the hell do you think you're doing?" Pop thundered.

Caleb scrambled to his feet. "I'm sorry, sir." His face was as white as paper, which is a lot to say for an Indian. "It was—"

Cutting him off, Matt called the quickest audible of his life. "It's our way of saying you're covered with the same blood, sweat and mud as the rest of us. It's our way of saying you're an Indian."

Pop's face eased from anger to delight. He started to laugh. The players laughed and howled along with him. A moment later, Jim and Lone Star moved in, holding the water barrel between them, and dumped its contents on Pop's head. The laughing and howling spilled into the stands.

Matt shook his head and chuckled.

Caleb stared at him, still pale as a ghost. "Thanks."

"Just coverin' for ya."

20.

TRAIN HOME

When the last whistle blew and the Indians raised their soggy coach on their shoulders, the final score, 26-6, didn't tell the full story. Two stats proved the thumping the Indians had delivered. Carlisle gained 402 yards to Penn's 76; the Redmen had twenty-two first downs to the Quakers' three. The Indians had also set a new benchmark since the forward pass had been legalized in 1906: they had risked sixteen forward passes and completed eight.

After the team, their jubilant fans, the band and the weary chaperones boarded the train back to Carlisle, Matt settled into a seat at the end of the team car along with Caleb. Caleb was now more than pale; he was getting chills. Matt got a blanket and tucked it around his roommate.

Five minutes out of Philly, a distinguished gentleman with a big salt-and-pepper moustache entered the other end of the car. Matt watched as the man moved to Coach Warner in the middle of the car and shook Pop's hand.

Caleb spotted the man and sat bolt upright. "That's Walter Camp!"

Matt looked clueless. "Who's Walter Camp?"

Caleb frowned at his friend's woeful ignorance. "The father of today's football. He played for Yale thirty years ago. He invented the line of scrimmage, the snap from the center to the quarterback, and the rule that you have three plays to gain a certain number of yards or you have to surrender the ball." Caleb's excitement was flushing his cheeks with color. "If it weren't for him, we'd still be playing rugby!"

Matt nodded, impressed. "Okay, Camp is cool."

They watched Camp sit in the empty seat next to Antonio Lubo. "Shhh," Caleb ordered as the Carlisle eleven crowded around the celebrity in their midst.

"Boys, I'm trying to understand your new style of play," Camp announced. "It's lightning fast. When Mount Pleasant throws a pass, it's no puny thing; it's a lordly throw that goes farther than most kicks. And your ends, they're as light on their feet as dancers."

The players teased Gardner and Ex with dancing poses and catcalls.

"I mean it," Camp continued. "Your ends pirouetted in and out till you shot the ball to them like a bullet. Penn was so flummoxed, all they could do was run in circles and emit pathetic *yawps.*"

The Indians burst into a chorus of "Yawp! Yawp! Yawp!"

Pop beamed at his warriors.

Camp stood and addressed the team. "In the past, with your trick plays, you Indians were a novelty act, a plucky team playing over your heads. Now you're a powerful, undefeated machine that made one of the best teams in the country look slow and stupid. If I'm right, and I'm rarely wrong, your wide-open style of play is going to change the game forever."

Pop nodded. "These boys do take to it. And we'll be taking our revolution to Princeton and Harvard next."

Camp turned to Pop. "What do you call it, Coach? The Carlisle formation?"

Pop answered. "We call it the single wing."

Camp tipped his hat. "You boys have a lot to be proud of. As well as changing football, you may be changing history."

The weight of his words left the team silent as Camp moved down the aisle and disappeared into the next car.

Captain Lubo stood up. "Did you hear that, fellas? Last

century, history changed us. This century, we're going to change *it.*"

As the team burst into a whooping, back-pounding celebration, Matt added a shout to the cacophony. Then he sat down next to Caleb, who had resumed shivering under his blanket. But no chill could wipe the smile off his face.

Taking in the euphoric players, Matt felt the tug of two feelings: awe and regret. He admired these scrappy guys for changing the game, but was struck by the fact they would never play in the NFL for big money. The NFL didn't exist yet. As quickly as these currents swirled inside him, they were overtaken by another feeling: envy. The dream he had always chased—Division 1, the NFL, *gaining* so much from the game—felt small next to what these guys were *giving* the game. He made a mental note: *If I ever get home and make it in the NFL, I'm gonna campaign to make October 26th Native American Football Day, the day the modern game was invented.*

His thoughts were interrupted by the train car door opening at his end. Jim entered and took in the boisterous scene. He plopped on the seat across the aisle from Matt and Caleb. Caleb's head rested against the window. His forehead was beaded with sweat.

"You just missed Walter Camp," Matt reported.

Jim winked. "Walter Camp just missed Jim."

Matt laughed and wagged his head toward the rowdiness. "Aren't you gonna join the fun?"

"Nah, had my fun on the field. The playing's better than the celebrating."

His diffident remark roused Matt's curiosity. "So, what's your favorite sport?"

"You'll never guess."

"It's got to be track or football."

Jim shook his head. "Nope. Hunting and fishing."

Matt decided not to mention that was two sports. "Why?"

"Hunting and fishing are nothing but doing," he replied. "That's Jim's big secret. He likes doing."

A dangerous thought popped into Matt's head. Even though he might have changed history by introducing the water cooler douse of a coach a little early, it seemed harmless; now he had the chance to change Jim's history for the good. "Since we're trading secrets," he told Jim, "I've got one for you."

"Not sure I want a secret from a fella named Wrong Way," Jim said with a dubious look.

"Like you said, sometimes Wrong Way is right."

Jim tossed a shrug. "All right, I'm all ears."

"You're on your way to being a great athlete," Matt began cautiously, "maybe the greatest in the world. But I wanna give you some advice. A lot of guys go off and play semipro baseball in the summer. Don't do it."

Jim's face lit up. "Hey, you just give Jim great idea."

Matt blanched at the thought that he might have just triggered the tragedy of Jim Thorpe. "No! I didn't! Did I?"

Jim gave Matt a teasing whack. "Nah, been thinking about it for a while."

Matt relaxed. "Well, you gotta trust me on this. Don't do it."

Jim eyed him curiously. "Why not?"

Matt tried to construct a better answer than the truth: *When you win Olympic gold, they're gonna take it all away 'cause playing semipro ball made you a professional.* "Because," Matt said, "a baseball moves a lot faster and is a lot harder than a football. You get hit in the head with a fastball, it can kill you."

Jim laughed. "A lot more players get killed in football than baseball. Besides"—he tapped his noggin—"Jim has hard head."

Matt smiled. There was no use changing Jim's fate. "Yeah, in more ways than one."

Jim stood up and dug in the pocket of his jacket. "Oh,

almost forgot." He pulled out a folded slip of paper. "Someone wanted me to give you this." He handed it to Matt with a sly wink and headed up the aisle.

Matt opened the note and read it: *Meet me behind the Chocolate Shop. — T/P.*

21.

THE PLAY

In Carlisle, the train was greeted by several hundred students in their nightshirts, wielding torches, banners and no shortage of school spirit.

Matt had concerns other than the celebration. In the last hour of the train ride, Caleb had started sweating profusely. Wallace Denny had come to check on him and taken his temperature: 102. Pop had telegraphed ahead from Harrisburg and when they arrived at Carlisle, his motorcar met them so he could drive Caleb straight to the hospital. Matt carried Caleb to the car; Pop drove away with Caleb and Denny.

Afterwards, Matt made his way to the back of the Chocolate Shop. Tawny was waiting in the dark shadows near the back door.

"Hey," he said. "What are we gonna do, break in and make an egg cream?"

"No." She pointed to the top of the door frame. "There's a key up there. I've seen the owner use it."

Matt raised his arm and slid his fingers along the top of the frame until he felt a key. He pulled it down and opened the door. "So we *are* gonna make an egg cream?"

Tawny chortled. "I want to show you something."

Inside the shop, the spill of the gas streetlights gave them enough light not to trip over each other. Tawny produced a candle and struck a match. She stopped at the back-corner booth, dripped some wax on a napkin and planted the candle on the paper candleholder. She slid into the bench seat nearest the rows of salt-and-pepper cellars.

Matt didn't follow. "You're sitting in Coach Warner's booth."

"I know." She started moving the salt shakers into a football formation.

"Do you think you should do that?"

"I'll put them back. Sit down," she practically ordered, "and set up a basic seven-two-two box defense."

Matt smiled at her football expertise. He grabbed the pepper shakers and began setting up the defense.

When they were done placing all twenty-two shakers, she waved a hand over the salt shakers. "Recognize that?"

"Yeah," he nodded. "It's Pop's single-wing offense, and it just made Penn dizzy."

She looked up. "The 'single wing,' I like that." She moved a couple of salt shakers in the backfield. "Have you ever seen a nesting killdeer pretend to have a broken wing to pull a predator away from its eggs?"

Matt chuckled at her random comment. "Never have."

She threw him a smile. "You should spend more time observing nature."

He returned her gaze. "You're nature enough for me."

Tawny's eyes dropped back to the table. "I'm pretending you didn't say that."

He enjoyed the color rising in her cheeks. "I'll do the same."

Taking the salt shaker representing the left guard, she pulled it back off the offense's line.

Matt watched quizzically. "What is that?"

"It's a play I designed."

"You came up with a play?"

"Yes. I'm calling it the guard-back broken wing."

He studied the arrangement of shakers. He pointed at the two wingbacks, set back and outside the right tackle. "There's the broken wing." He pointed at the left guard set back and leaving a gaping hole in the line. "And that's the guard back. Is it a pass play or run?"

"Pass."

He laughed. "Why would a guard be set back in a pass play? He needs to be on the line to block and protect the passer."

"That's the killdeer part, the deception part," she explained as she lifted the shaker representing the center, unscrewed the top, and placed the top back in the center spot. She poured a trail of salt on the table to show the movement of the ball. "The snap goes to the quarterback, the fullback rushes into the hole left by the guard"—she dropped another salt trail showing the fullback's move into the line, taking the guard's block—"and as the guard pivots and moves right, he gets the ball from the quarterback." She sprinkled another salt trail showing the guard moving past the quarterback and rolling right.

Matt stared. "The *guard* gets the ball?"

"Right." She ignored his disbelief. "The defense has no idea what they're looking at, and the guard passes to either the quarterback who has slipped over to the left, or one of the wingbacks who have run deep right."

He wagged his head, pretending to go along. "They're running clear-out routes."

"Something like that, yes."

"It's a screen pass."

Her eyes flashed in the candlelight. "No, it's a guard-back broken-wing pass. That's my name for it."

"I've seen backs and ends throw a pass, but never a guard. Tawny, it's insane."

"Not if no one's ever seen it and you have a guard who can throw the ball. It's total deception."

Matt held on her for a moment, then let out a breath. "You are something."

"So are you." She leaned forward. "I've seen you throw the ball with Jim. You could pull this off."

Her eyes blazed with excitement. He wanted to fall into them. "Can I kiss you?" he whispered.

"No." Her mouth bent with a smile. "But you can kiss Pigskin."

He leaned forward and met her lips.

Their kiss had only begun when a loud rattle threw them back in their seats. Someone was trying the front door. It was locked. The din of celebrating students was drawing closer.

Matt blew out the candle. They slid low out of the booth and scooted out the back door of the shop.

From the alley near the Chocolate Shop, Tawny darted back into the slipstream of jubilant students; Matt followed a minute later. As fleeting as it had been, they both carried the ballooning thrill of a first kiss.

With Caleb in the hospital, Matt had their room to himself. He pushed aside the hanging scroll hiding his tally of days and chalked another mark on the wall. He didn't have to count to know it was his twenty-seventh day at Carlisle.

He killed the light and got into bed. Staring into the darkness he wondered if crushing out on Tawny was turning into something bigger. He wondered if he was being crazy. Crazy enough to . . . He cut the thought short. He wanted to replay his kiss with Tawny over and over, right into sleep.

22.

SUNDAY

After lunch in the Football Dorm, the Sunday walk was canceled because it was raining. Matt grabbed the chance to go into the dorm's reading room, which was supplied with newspapers reporting on the big upset of Carlisle over U Penn. He wanted to check the media's take on the game so he could report to Caleb when he visited him in the hospital. He also wanted to see if he "got ink" for his first playing time. The account in *The Philadelphia Press* caught him by surprise.

> With racial savagery and ferocity the Carlisle Indian eleven grabbed Penn's football scalp and dragged their victim up and down Franklin Field, not relinquishing their grip until the seventy minutes of the time allotted to the process was up and the figures 26 to 6 told the tale.

"Whoa," he mumbled, "talk about a racist shout-out." He read the full article. While he was relieved that none of the second-stringers who played late in the game got a mention, he was also a little let down.

When Matt went to the hospital, he learned Tawny wasn't on the Sunday shift. Regardless, he was still walking on air from their Chocolate Shop encounter. The mystery of Pigskin had been solved, but an even greater mystery had unfolded before him: Tawny Owl.

Caleb was laid up in a ward and looking better, though he

still had a fever. Matt told him about the racially-tinged article in *The Philadelphia Press*.

Caleb responded with a half smile. "When the white man has to tip his hat to the red man, his hat gets bent out of shape."

Dr. Shoemaker cut Matt's visit short so Caleb could rest. On the way out, the doctor asked a favor. Someone needed to go into town and pick up some medicine for Caleb at the drugstore. Matt was happy to take the trolley into town.

After knocking on the door to the pharmacist's apartment above the drugstore and collecting the medicine, Matt headed back to the trolley stop. On the way he was surprised to see a light on in the Chocolate Shop. On Sundays Carlisle was usually a ghost town. Hoping to score something from the soda fountain, Matt crossed over to the Chocolate Shop and tried the door. It swung open. No one was behind the counter and the glass cases were empty. Then he noticed someone in the back booth. Moving closer, he recognized the broad backside of Pop's head.

"I thought the shop was closed," Matt said as he scanned the salt-and-pepper shakers opposite Pop. The arrangement had not been moved since Matt and Tawny had left it the night before. Matt's apprehension was lessened when he noticed that the salt trails had been scattered, probably from when he had blown out the candle.

Pop looked up from the sprawl of newspapers in front of him. "The shop may be closed but not my office." He gave Matt a wary look. "You're not here to throw more water on me, are you?"

"No, sir," Matt said. "That only happens when the game's in the bag."

Pop eyed his player. "I've seen a lot of strange Indian customs, but that's a first."

"It probably won't be the last."

237

"I hope it was." Pop harrumphed. "Otherwise, a coach's reward for a winning season will be pneumonia." He swept a hand over the newspapers on the table. "I'm beginning to think the single wing won't last. Listen to what they're saying about us." He poked one of the papers. "This fella says the passing game is turning football into basketball: 'footballers into roundballers,' he says." He thumped another paper. "This one says it's going to queer the game. He calls it 'whiff whaff.' And this chucklehead claims that Pop Warner's new version of football is 'effeminate' and is going to 'emasculate' the game." Pop looked up in disgust. "Hell! Who wants to be the father of the passing game if it turns you into a dame?"

Pop's doubts caught Matt off guard. "That's not what Walter Camp said on the train last night."

"He's only one voice," Pop grumbled.

"I just don't think you should give up on it, Coach."

"Why not?"

Matt cleared his throat and made the case for the future of football. "I can think of three reasons. One, the passing game beat the crap out of the Quakers. Two, girls are gonna love it."

Pop's head recoiled. "What the Sam Hill do girls have to do with it?"

"It's like what Mr. Camp said: it's more like dance. The passing game opens up the field, turns it into a bigger stage, makes it more dramatic. It lets football players be everything from bulldozers to ballet dancers."

Pop's eyes narrowed. "That might be true, but the day they start belly dancing, I'll quit the game."

Matt flashed on all the crazy end-zone dances he had seen. "You never know what they'll start doing in the end zone."

"The what?"

Remembering there was no "end zone" yet, just a goal line, Matt backpedaled. "You know, like when a team celebrates a touchdown."

"Right," Pop huffed, "like those damn Harvard boys who do handstands after they score."

Matt was happy to know end-zone dancing went so far back. "Exactly."

Pop raised an eyebrow. "So what's the third reason?"

"If girls like the more open-style game, that's twice as many fans. Twice the fans means more butts in the seats, and more butts in the seats means a lot more money." He shut up before he added the invention of television and the billions of dollars it would deliver to the game.

For the first time, Pop's expression brightened. "You're smarter than I thought."

"Thank you, sir. I'm not just a dumb lineman."

Pop's face soured. "There's no such thing as a dumb lineman. *I* was a lineman!"

Matt was at a loss for words.

Pop filled the awkward silence. "If you're so smart, I've got a mystery for you."

"I'll give it a go, sir."

"Why am I sitting here feeling like Papa Bear in *Goldilocks*?"

Matt drew a blank.

Pop pointed at the shakers arrayed on the table. "Someone's been messing with my salt-and-pepper cellars."

Feeling a surge of panic, Matt wondered if Pop was the one who had tried the door the night before. But Pop couldn't have taken Caleb to the hospital and gotten back in time to catch them. Matt played dumb. "Did someone mess with a play you'd set up?"

"I don't remember what I'd laid out, if anything," Pop replied, his eyes riveted on the shakers. "But there's something here that's got my brain in a bind."

Matt took in the "guard-back broken wing" formation Tawny had arranged with salt shakers. In the light of day, it looked even more bizarre. He had to choose his words carefully and not propose Tawny's crazy scheme of a guard throwing a pass. He pointed to the gap in the line in front of the set-back guard. "Is that a guard back, or has the left side of the line shifted outside for a back?"

"Could be either," Pop muttered as he pointed to the two wingbacks set outside of the right tackle. "But why the hell would you want *two* wingbacks on one side? It looks like they're about to run a three-legged race."

Matt was relieved it wasn't making sense to Pop. "If you ask me, sir, there's no mystery about it. Either someone accidentally moved some shakers or this place has mice." Matt reached for the shakers. "I'll just—"

Pop raised a hand. "What are you doing?"

Matt's hand froze. "Ah, moving the guard back to where he belongs."

"Leave him right there," Pop ordered. His eyes dropped to the shakers. "I'm not done letting this ruin my Sunday." He heaved a breath. "I see the deception—the guard back—but not the misdirection. You see, a trick play has to have two things: first deception, then misdirection. Deception confuses, misdirection conquers. Combine them like nitro and glycerin and you have an explosive play."

As tempting as it was, Matt didn't want to show Pop how the deception of Tawny's play set up the misdirection. He had struggled too hard to build up what little football cred he had with Pop. He wasn't about to blow it by showing him how the guard could throw a screen pass. Instead, he reported that he had to get some medicine to Caleb.

23.

A PLAY IS BORN

Monday brought the routine of morning classes, an afternoon in the Printery, and football practice. The college they were playing the next Saturday, Princeton, was one of the big four, and they lived up to the name. Their players were meat on the hoof. For that reason, Pop was working several more open and fast-moving plays into the Redmen's single-wing offense. Matt was relieved to see that none of them involved a guard back or two wingbacks on the right side. In fact, he wondered if Pop had forgotten about the mystery play laid out in his booth. During practice the coach never said a word to Matt, much less looked at him. Matt was back to being an invisible scrub.

By Wednesday, Matt was frustrated by not being able to speak with Tawny. His yearning was heightened when, in the Printery, he read one of the lines Pigskin had submitted in the upcoming edition of *The Arrow*: "Matt Grinnell sees first action and makes a splash!"

He liked its double meaning. "Splash" could be referring to the water-bucket dump on Pop or their too-short kiss in the Chocolate Shop.

After football practice and showering, Matt was heading out of the Cage when Jim grabbed him and pulled him toward the football field. He had a football under his arm.

"It's kinda late for a throw," Matt pointed out.

Jim kept pulling him along. "That's the best part. Nobody will catch us."

A few moments later, they were tossing the ball back and

forth. Matt was getting better at throwing the watermelon ball. He wasn't ready to air out a 60-yard bomb, but he could float a 35-yard spiral and fire a decent 20-yard bullet.

"I heard you'll be getting your first ink in *The Arrow* for playing time last week," Jim said. "Maybe you'll get more time against the Tigers." He threw the ball.

Matt caught it and gripped it near the end. "Right now, the only tiger I'd like to tangle with"—he threw a nice spiral—"is Tawny."

"That's a tall order"—Jim caught the ball and spun it—"when the only thing you've done is swap notes."

"True," Matt conceded with a lie. He hadn't told Jim about the Chocolate Shop episode for good reason. If Jim knew she was designing football plays, he might suspect she was Pigskin, and that could end badly for her. Matt knew it wasn't right that a woman couldn't be as obsessed with sports as a man, but it's not like he was going to tell everyone how girls would one day have as much right to play sports as guys. Hell, as he had learned in his Civics class at Carlisle, women couldn't even vote yet.

"Trading notes is fine and good"—Jim cocked his arm—"as long as it leads to something more." He arced a spiral through the dying light. "Jim might help you with that."

As they returned the ball to the Cage, Matt pressed Jim about what he meant by "help." Jim evaded answering and went on about how the twilight reminded him of when he was a kid and hunted all night with only his dogs for company.

Thursday, after work in the Printery, Matt checked in on Caleb at the hospital. Not only had the medicine almost eliminated his fever, Dr. Shoemaker wanted him to go outside and get some fresh air.

As Caleb and Matt walked in the quad, Matt learned that the doctor, concerned about a relapse, wasn't allowing Caleb to travel with the team on Saturday to New York City for the Princeton game. Caleb was crushed about missing the trip because the game was going to be played at the Polo Grounds, where the New York Giants played baseball and so many famous players had taken the field.

Friday was a light, short practice because the next morning the team would be boarding the train to New York City.

With the sun dropping toward the mountains, Matt headed toward the hospital to see if Caleb needed anything from their room before the team left early Saturday. He didn't get far.

Jim and some other Hotshots raced around a corner of the Cage, grabbed Matt, and hustled him toward the lower field. Matt's protests fell on deaf ears as they told him they were going to play "Throw Them Off Their Horses."

"You're not an Indian unless you play Throw Them Off Their Horses once a year!" Theodore declared.

Matt had no choice but to go along.

When they hit the field, the lighter guys jumped on the shoulders of the bigger guys. Jim spun Matt around and leaped on his shoulders as he yelled, "C'mon, pony! Jim ready to ride!"

Matt didn't resist. The game was immediately recognizable. All kids played a version of it, and the goal was universal: throw the other shoulder-riders off. The last pair standing wins. Matt charged Jim into battle.

After Jim wrestled a third victim off his "horse," the sound of girls' voices wheeled the boys around. Jim seized the distraction to pull another rider down. As Matt jostled underneath, he recognized who was leading the girls onto the field. It was Tawny, carrying a football.

Jim leaped off Matt's shoulders. "Off Their Horses trumped by Girl Ball every time!"

Matt turned to Jim, grinning at the rush of girls in their

white dresses like a man on a deserted isle seeing a ship sailing toward him. "Did you set this up?" Matt asked.

Jim looked helpless. "Jim has no control over them. They are heap free modern women."

Tawny marched up to the guys. Her game face couldn't hide the delight in her eyes. "Has anyone explained the rules"—she looked at Matt as she shovel-passed the ball to Jim—"to the new kid?"

Jim and the guys pushed Matt to the middle of the field, laying down the rules on the go. The girls played football rules: they could run and pass the ball. The boys played soccer rules: all they could do was kick the ball to advance it.

"And no holding!" one of the girls cautioned, as if she had been victim of some errant holding in a previous game.

"What about blocking and tackling?" Matt asked as Jim prepared to punt the ball.

"Without blocking and tackling," Jim declared, "Girl Ball wouldn't be fun." He booted the ball to the waiting phalanx of girls.

The girls formed a flying wedge and ran it to midfield before the boys broke up the wedge. One grabbed the ball carrier around the waist and lifted her in the air.

The girls ran a flurry of running plays with Tawny leading the team and calling the signals. Just as when Matt had seen her with the parasol drill team, she was the most focused and the least interested in all the free-spirited contact. He couldn't figure out how the girls ran so well in their long dresses until he noticed they were barefoot.

The boys took over the ball and kicked it wildly around the field until the girls recovered it. When the girls' next running play ended with a shrieking, giggling tackle, a girl grabbed her knee, limped toward the sideline and yelled, "Substitution!"

Matt looked around. There were no subs.

"Grinnell in for Spotted Horse," Jim decreed.

Matt gave him a befuddled look.

"When a girl goes out, we give 'em a player." Jim shook a finger at Matt. "But you have to play like a girl."

Over the laughter, another player yelled, "Easy for Wrong Way!"

As the guys cracked up, Tawny gathered her troops, along with their new player, and called a play. "Guard-back broken wing."

Matt scanned the other girls. Surprisingly, they seemed to know what she meant.

Tawny shot him a smile. "You're the guard back."

As Matt took his position, the girls lined up in the formation Tawny had laid out on the table in the Chocolate Shop. The center side-snapped to Tawny. Matt turned and took her handoff.

When the guys, tussling with the girls and in no rush to break through the line, saw Matt with the ball, Jim yelled, "Get the big girl!"

Matt rolled right as the line of guys surged toward him. He looked left; Tawny had drifted out in perfect position. He lobbed the ball before the rushing boys buried him in a pile-on.

By the time he escaped and could look downfield, he saw Tawny racing down the field behind a wall of white dresses.

A whistle pierced the air. Everyone whipped around to see Pop Warner striding toward them. He didn't look happy.

"What in hell are you doing?" He charged up to Jim, knowing he was always the instigator. "Playing with girls the day before a game! Have you lost your mind? What if you got injured?" Remembering his manners, he thrust an arm at the girls coming back up the field. "What if one of them got hurt?" He took a step back. "All of you, back to your quarters before I go to the major and have you suspended!" Without a peep, the boys and girls jogged off the field. "Double time!" Pop roared.

Matt broke into a lope when he heard, "Grinnell! About-face!" He spun around.

Pop pointed to the ground in front of him like he was summoning a dog. "Get your butt over here!"

Matt trotted back to Pop, wondering why he was being singled out.

The coach's eyes narrowed. "Did you just run the guard-back play you saw on my table?"

Matt's insides relaxed; maybe he wasn't going to get ripped a new one. "Actually, sir, Miss Owl ran it."

Pop's expression melted from anger to excitement. "Did you see how that line of boys was so eager to get to you they took themselves out of the play?"

"Yes, sir," Matt nodded. "The girls kinda released 'em to come through."

"That's the deception," Pop declared, "then came the misdirection: you passed back to the girl and she had her whole line, a wall of interference, to lead her downfield!"

Matt bit his tongue before he called it what it was.

"Where did you learn to throw the ball?" Pop demanded.

"I've been practicing, sir."

"Well, not a word about this to anyone. Now go on. I'm through with you for now."

Once he turned away, Matt couldn't hold back a grin. Of course he was going to talk to someone about it. He was going to tell Tawny that she and a bunch of Indian kids had just invented the screen pass.

24.

PRINCETON

Before sunrise, the team boarded the train for the trip to New York City. Because of the distance and the expense, the band stayed in Carlisle.

When the sun's first rays pierced the train windows, they crowned the players with golden laurels. The Carlisle Indians were seven games into an undefeated season. They were armed with their full quiver of arrows: a swift running game, deadly passing and a bevy of trick plays that would leave the heavy and slow Princeton Tigers dumbfounded. The press had drummed up national excitement about the Indians' new open style of play; thousands of fans had paid exorbitant prices for the privilege of packing into the Polo Grounds and seeing the contest.

Halfway to New York the sun disappeared behind a canopy of gunmetal clouds. By the time they pulled into Penn Station, it had been raining in the city for eight hours. When the Redmen took the field, the sky continued to dump so much water the field was a sodden mess.

Despite the rain, expectations for the game were hardly dampened. The Polo Grounds' double tier of grandstands held 30,000 cheering fans and almost as many umbrellas. New York society had showed up in their finest suits, dresses and fancy hats. Young belles were bedecked in ribbons and feathers.

Matt sat on the bench minus his usual bench buddy. Jim was starting his first Varsity game at halfback. The game began slowly on the soaked field and got slower as the sod became a mud pit. There was no footing for the Redmen to run their thrilling end-arounds and reverses. The ball was so slippery and soggy it was almost impossible for Mounty or Hauser to throw. Even if they did launch a pass, the curtains of rain made it difficult to see. The Tigers, with their burly, slow-footed players, outweighed and out-pushed the Indians in what turned into a mud-wrestling match.

At the half, the mud-caked Indians headed into the dressing room for a ten-minute break from the rain. No roof could protect them from Pop's deluge of scorn. He lambasted them for their listless play. Then he tried to rally their downtrodden spirits.

"Listen, boys, we've been here before. Eight years ago, when Carlisle played the University of California, they made us play on a field of sand with an oversized, weighted ball. But we slogged through the sand and carried that rock to victory. Now it's Mother Nature who's making us play on a field of slop. But we can pick ourselves out of the mud and carry the ball to victory. We can do it again!"

During the pause that followed, Little Boy muttered something under his breath.

"What was that?" Pop demanded.

Little Boy raised his voice. "Football no good fun in mud."

"Well, let me do you a favor," Pop fired back. "You're *outta* the mud!" His fierce blue eyes shot around and found Matt sitting in the back. "Grinnell, you're in for Little Boy. Go in and show him some 'good fun.'"

Pop turned to the team. "Are you going to let a little rain wash away what no Carlisle team has ever accomplished? You're on the path to an undefeated season. This team can make history. Don't leave your spirits bogged in the mire. Remember all the Indian bones buried in that mud. Rise up! Stomp those white Tigers into the muck and reconquer a field that once belonged to your ancestors!"

The team jumped to their feet with a roar and clattered out of the dressing room.

Matt stood for a second, still stunned by Pop calling his number. Little Boy lingered too, glaring at Matt.

Jim, almost unrecognizable in his crown-to-cleats sheath of mud, wheeled back from the team. "C'mon! Little Boy have good fun watching Wrong Way drown in mud!"

Which is almost what Matt did as he thrashed it out with a big Princeton guard named Cooney. Matt held his own as he and Cooney took turns driving each other's faces into the muck. Despite Pop's appeal to his Indians to reclaim Manhattan, they failed to rise from the mire and tame the Tigers. They were shut out 16-0.

The Indians' thrilling new game of flashy runs and soaring passes had met an opponent they couldn't beat: the weather.

Early that evening on the train home, Pop subjected the team to his brand of tough love. He speculated that their loss was meant to be, and that if he had been reading the signs he would have seen it coming. What else could Caleb Phillips throwing a bucket of water on him portend but having to play the next game in a monsoon? What else could his players indulging in Girl Ball foretell but the team being emasculated, stripped of the manliness needed to play in bad weather?

Then he got to the point. "Because these ill omens and foolish mistakes cannot be blamed on anyone but us, there will be consequences. Starting tomorrow, except for church, classes and practice, you're confined to quarters. For the next seven days you'll do nothing but eat, drink, breathe and fart football."

The team was so dejected no one had the spirit to laugh.

Pop reached into a gym bag and pulled up a football he had retrieved from the game. It was encrusted in mud. "This is more than a mud-covered ball," he declared. "It's the bitter pill of disillusionment. For those of you who haven't learned the word 'disillusionment,' I will give you a definition. When all of your tribes suffered defeat at the hands of the white man, your great warriors sank into disillusionment. Your grandfathers and fathers feared for the future of their tribe and the proud path of the Indian. But they didn't abandon hope. They didn't crawl into the hole of their reservations and die. They sent their sons and daughters out of the reservation to Indian schools like Carlisle and Haskell. They sent them to rise above defeat and disillusionment. They sent you to become the next generation of great warriors in a white world."

Pop paused and let his words sink in. As all the players stared at him, the only sounds were the rush of the train and the *clackety-clack* of wheels on iron.

He continued. "Many Carlisle men have come before you and become, once again, proud warriors. But none of your gridiron brothers have ever defeated Harvard. It's the last ball missing from our trophy case. For the first time I'm looking at a team that's good enough to beat 'em. In seven days, this ball is going to Harvard." He turned slowly, displaying the ball to everyone. "We're going to strip it of mud and disillusionment. We're going to beat the Crimson Tide and carry this ball back to our trophy case. We're going to make history."

Matt twitched with the urge to leap up and answer Pop's speech with a yell. But he didn't dare go first. Instead, he watched Pop put the ball back in the bag and sit down amidst the pressing silence. Matt looked around. The players were either stone-faced, staring straight ahead, or hanging their heads. He wanted to ask Lone Star, sitting next to him, what it meant. But he didn't violate the silence. Only one thing seemed certain: Pop's words had struck every one of them like an arrow through the heart.

25.

OUTING AND INNING

On the long ride home, the heavy silence that followed Pop's stirring speech wasn't the only surprise. Despite the loss, when they arrived in Carlisle, they were greeted by a contingent of rooters cheering and waving torches and banners as the band added a fight song.

Stepping off the train, Matt was mystified. "Did someone forget to tell 'em we lost?" he asked Lone Star.

"They followed the game via the telegraph hookup. They just—" Lone Star didn't finish, but instead waved to someone.

Matt saw Miss De Cora at the back of the crowd, waving. As Lone Star plunged into the throng, Matt looked for Tawny in the band. Before finding her, a little boy tugged on the sleeve of his jacket and handed him a note. Matt opened it. It read: *I need to know all about it. Someone will be your scout. — T/P.*

Matt lay in bed wide awake. Even if he wanted to share his insomnia with someone, there was no one to talk to. Caleb, despite being on the mend, was still in the hospital. Matt's mind flip-flopped between two movies. One was the game and his battle in the mud with the Princeton linemen; the other was imagined and close encounters with Tawny.

Reality intervened with a *creak* as the door pushed open. The figure that slipped inside whispered, "Psst, Grinnell, wake up."

Matt recognized Jim's voice and wasn't surprised that he was Tawny's scout. "I'm awake."

"Good." Jim stood over the end of the bed. "Might as well

enjoy our last hours before we're tossed in football jail and Pop throws away the key."

Matt rolled out of bed, still clothed. "Where we going?"

Jim's teeth gleamed in the darkness. "Where Jim's favorite outing is good for an inning."

"To the baseball field?"

Jim snickered. "You still have mud on the brain."

In the light of a nearly full moon, the two of them moved along the quad toward the Girls' Quarters. When Matt, keeping his voice low, asked how they were going to get into the quarters and past the matrons, Jim whispered back, "For once in your life, be an Indian and shut up."

Reaching the far end of the dorm with its tiers of long porches, Jim cupped his hands over his mouth and sounded a soft hoot. A few moments later, a long cord made from sheets lowered from the second-floor balustrade.

Jim flashed Matt a smile. "My girl's around the corner. And don't fall asleep. They'll send you both back to the reservation faster than Jim can say 'shotgun wedding.'" He disappeared around the corner of the dorm.

Matt looked up. A girl's head poked over the railing. It was Tawny. She motioned for him to come up. He stared at the corded sheets and grinned at the craziness of it.

Climbing the improvised rope, he wondered how tight she had tied it and if he might go crashing to the ground. Reaching the second floor, he saw the sheet was well secured to a post. He swung over the railing.

Tawny's face brimmed with excitement. She pointed to his shoes and motioned for him to remove them.

As he fumbled with his shoes, one of his fantasies had already come true. While the students always greeted the train in their nightshirts, the band members were always in uniform.

He was finally seeing Tawny in her nightshirt. His eyes and imagination weren't disappointed.

After setting his shoes down, she took his hand and led him silently along the portico. She stopped at a door and they pushed inside.

The room was dark, but enough moonlight spilled in for Matt to see it was a small meeting room or lounge. Tawny led him to a couch and they sat. She started unbuttoning his shirt. He didn't resist but was thrown by her boldness. This was the girl who had raced out of the art studio when he had mentioned putting handprints on her. "What are you doing?" he asked.

"I heard you played the second half."

He watched her hands continue to unbutton. "Yeah, so?"

She pulled his shirt off his shoulders. "I'm going to rub away all your aches and pains. I'm your rubber."

He resisted the urge to say something racy and stupid. "Okay," was all he managed as she removed his shirt.

"For every ache and pain I rub away," she explained, "you have to tell me something about the game."

"You know how it turned out."

"Yes, but I wasn't at the Polo Grounds." She pushed him facedown on the couch. "You have to take me there."

Matt went through the game series-by-series as she rubbed his back, chest and legs, giving special attention to each tight or tender spot. When he was done with the game, he wanted to pull her to him, to answer every touch with his own. But something stopped him. His account didn't feel complete without including the trip home and Pop's muddy-ball speech. So he told her about it: how every student had been sent to Carlisle to overcome disillusionment and to become the next generation of warriors. For some reason he stopped short of telling her how the team had responded with silence, how some had hung their heads in shame as if they had disappointed their fathers and grandfathers.

As their own silence filled the dark room, Matt sat up. The space suddenly collapsed between them. Her mouth found his. He answered her passion. Hands broke free, racing over skin, clothes, curves. Then as quickly as it began, they stopped.

Matt felt her warm hands on his face. He opened his eyes. A glint of moonlight shone in each of her black eyes, tiny beacons inviting him in.

She lay back on the couch. Her white nightshirt seemed to glow in the faint spill of light. Her hands slid slowly down like two dark birds gliding down a white cliff. They gathered a bit of white and slowly lifted her gown, revealing shins, knees, the beginning of her thighs.

Matt gazed down at her. He had never wanted a girl so much. At the same moment, another feeling held him still; his lust hesitated. In his flicker of doubt, he realized why he had felt compelled to tell her about Pop's speech. He wanted all of her— Tawny and Pigskin—to know *everything*. She wasn't just another girl. She was the girl he loved.

After a long moment, he cupped her hand in one of his. "Tawny, as much as I want to, I can't."

Her eyes flickered with surprise and disappointment. "Is it because I'm so dark?"

He shook his head with a smile. "Not at all. It's because you're so beautiful. You deserve better than a paleface like me."

"You're not a paleface. You're a Mandan warrior."

"You did your homework. You know I'm not Mandan."

She didn't move, her eyes locked on him. "Who are you then?"

His chest swelled and he let out a breath. "I think I was sent here to find out." He raised her hand, kissed it, and set it back on her thigh. "Don't ever forget how beautiful you are."

Matt walked across the dewy grass and hoped Tawny would

remember to pull up the cord of sheets. *Of course she will,* he told himself. *She's a girl who knows how to keep secrets.*

As he approached the bandstand, a cloud scudded across the moon, casting the quad in darkness. Matt didn't notice a dark figure, sitting motionless under its roof.

The man's head followed Matt as he moved silently toward his quarters. The man returned his gaze to the Girls' Quarters. The cloud slid past the moon, bathing the grassy expanse in new light. He watched the white-clad figure of a girl gather up a cord of sheets hanging from the balustrade.

Moonlight dripped off the bandstand's eave and splashed on the man's wire-rimmed glasses. Alfred Jongler wore a troubled expression. He didn't know what had happened between Matt and Tawny. He didn't know if they had performed an act that might change Tawny's future in irreversible ways. His only comfort was the note his brother had left in the cor anglais case, which Alfred had found after James had died: *When in doubt, play the cor anglais. It will show you things.* While it had not shown Alfred how to recognize the moment when it was time for a voyager to go home, the cor anglais had shown Alfred how to ask for a sign.

He lifted the cor anglais from the bench and began to play. He kept the melody low and soft, so as not to wake anyone. As he played, he felt an odd sensation: his fingers grew light, as if they were feathers. The sensation grew more intense and exciting: he felt the keys *pushing* his fingertips. The pressing keys transitioned the tune to a jumble of ill-fitting phrases. Alfred's thrill over the cor anglais coming to life was overcome by the shock of his hands being possessed by a style of music he detested: modern. He yanked the reed from his mouth, silencing the chaotic music.

Recovering from the shock, Alfred's face relaxed, then creased into a smile. The cor anglais had awoken and delivered a message.

In his dark room, dimly lit by moonlight, Matt lay in bed. His exhaustion from the long day was no match for his urge to relive the day and night. The memories of the Princeton game were branded in him. But his most burning image was of Tawny's beautiful face shining in the darkness.

Trying to evade his crosscurrents of desire and regret, Matt rolled toward the wall. It was covered by the hanging scroll with the crinkled photos of old Carlisle football teams. He pulled the scroll aside and hooked it on the metal bedstead. He could make out the crosshatched "fences" chalked on the wall: his tally of days. He pulled the piece of chalk from under his mattress, but hesitated before scoring another mark on the wall. Chalking off the day would put an end to it. He didn't want the day, this day of days, to end. He rolled on his back.

Without looking at them, Matt knew the number of marks on the wall: thirty-three, soon to be thirty-four. For thirty-four days he had lived and played and loved in 1907. He wondered if the days would keep rolling along, taking him with them. He wondered if he would only see the last of 1907 when it became 1908. He wondered if he had reached a point of no return. Of all the ifs spinning in his head, there was one more captivating than the others. He wondered if Tawny Owl, with her hand on his heart, could become his future. *If so,* he told himself, *next time there won't be a choice. She will be mine to have and protect . . . forever.*

26.

TWIN DISCOVERIES

In Belleplain, time had slowed to the pace of dread. The undeniable truth of Matt's disappearance pressed on the town. The hopeful optimism of the first few days had bled out and congealed to despair. All was lost, including the likelihood of the Cyclones winning the state championship. In the days since he had vanished, the backup quarterback, Gary Allen, had repeatedly faltered on his way to becoming QB1. It was Thursday night, the eve of the championship, and the gloom in Belleplain was palpable.

While the town's fog of malaise had crept into corners of the Jongler-Jinks' house, it had not suffocated the candle of hope still burning there. Iris and Arky were determined to consult the cor anglais one more time before the big game.

After their father left to teach his adult ed class on the Civil War, the twins, with the cor anglais in hand, trudged up the narrow stairs to the attic office. Once there, Iris began to play Poulenc's "Sonata for Oboe and Piano."

Arky listened for a while before he could no longer hold his tongue. "Why are you playing like someone died? It sounds like a dirge."

Ignoring his commentary, she continued to play, slowly, softly, with haunting beauty.

After listening another minute, Arky tossed his hands. "I don't know if you're making me sleepy or suicidal but I've heard enough." He moved to the door.

Iris stopped playing and inhaled sharply. "I saw him."

Arky turned back. "Don't mess with me."

"I saw Matt."

Her absorbed expression pulled Arky back to the chair. "What did you see?"

She spoke just above a whisper, not wanting to dispel the vision. "He was lying in bed with his head on a pillow. He was awake, staring at the ceiling. He was so close all I could see was his head, his shoulders and part of his chest."

Arky winced. "Don't tell me you were in bed with him."

Iris slid him a disparaging look. "It was a vision, not a nightmare." She returned to the vision wavering in her mind. "There was something between us, like a screen."

"What kind of screen?"

"It was like a net, but not a net."

"A mosquito net?" Arky asked.

"No."

His eyes cut to the opposite wall of the office, with its display of galaxies and supernovas caught in a spiderweb of silky fibers. "Was it a spiderweb?"

Isis shook her head. "It was more like a field of white marks with crosshatches."

Arky's face tightened. "Did anything happen?"

"Yeah," she murmured. "His face turned to me, towards the screen of marks. He lifted a piece of chalk off his chest. He was about to add a mark to the others but he stopped. His face became so peaceful and serene he looked like someone else. Then he dropped the chalk and opened his hand. At first I thought he was waving to me, but then he pressed his hand against the screen and wiped the marks away. When the last marks disappeared, so did Matt."

Arky waited a beat. "That was it?"

"Yes. That's when I stopped playing."

His face bunched as he fixated on a detail. "The crosshatches, were they like he was marking off days?"

"Yeah."

"How many marks were there?"

"Lots."

"More than six?"

"More like dozens," she replied.

Arky's heart was already racing. "If they were days, we're talking Einstein 101."

Iris cocked her head. "What do you mean?"

"Time is relative." His voice kept pace with his heart. "While a week ticked away here, weeks or months might have ticked away for Matt. Time might unfold at different rates in different bubbles in the spacetime loaf."

Iris was half listening. She was obsessed with something else. "Mom talked about having a last vision of a time traveler before they went 'solo,' before they disappeared to a Jongler's consciousness. She called it an 'horizon event.' Maybe what I saw was another kind of horizon event. Maybe it's a sign Matt's coming back."

Arky reined in his excitement. "Or, when you saw him wipe away the marks, maybe your first instinct was right. He *was* waving. Maybe it's a sign he's *not* coming back."

27.

NIGHT MUSIC

Darkness shrouded Matt's room. He slept soundly, lying on his side and facing the wall. The hanging scroll had been moved back into place, covering the chalky cloud that had once been his tally of days.

The door to the room creaked open and a silhouette appeared. The figure held a curved instrument. Alfred quietly shut the door. He moistened the reed of the cor anglais. The moment a distant bugle began to sound reveille, he inhaled and played a low, barely audible note.

Matt woke with a start and cursed reveille for sounding even on Sunday. Then he heard the cor anglais. He rolled over and saw Alfred playing.

The moment Alfred had begun to play he felt the same sensations that had overtaken him in the bandstand. His fingers surrendered to the pressure of the keys. While the keys carried the tune to atonal and chaotic, a new sense possessed him. The cor anglais was sucking air out of him; he could barely feed it fast enough.

Matt shouted. "No!"

The door suddenly flew open, striking the cor anglais. The blow ripped the reed from Alfred's mouth, ending the music with a cry of pain.

Whoever had thrown open the door darted inside and punched on the light. Jim looked like he had dressed in a hurry. He gaped at Mr. Jongler, the cor anglais still in his hands. Blood trickled from Alfred's lacerated lip.

Jim's mouth was as fast as his feet. "Funny time for a music lesson." He turned to Matt. "I wanted to make sure"—he paused, concocting a story—"you didn't go drown yourself over the Princeton loss." His eyes cut to Alfred. "Looks like you didn't." Jim turned and ran down the hall, hoping to get back to the Football Dorm before his absence was discovered.

Matt and Alfred stared at each other, still stunned by the tumble of events.

Matt swung out of bed and jumped to his feet. "Great! Jim's gonna think he walked in on some weird gay thing!"

Alfred produced a handkerchief and pressed it to his bleeding lip. His insides roiled with emotions. He was elated by the cor anglais possessing him but mortified by his disastrous attempt at sending his voyager home. He heaved a breath to calm himself. "What Jim thinks doesn't matter. Your time here is done."

"Maybe by your clock, but not mine." Matt jabbed a finger at his intruder. "Blow it again and I'll break it in two!"

Alfred studied his belligerent voyager. "If you did, you could never go home. Your fate would be abandoning the future to live in the past. And you would always know it. Is that what you want?"

The convoluted words sucked Matt into an undertow of confusion. He answered with a contradiction. "I don't know what I want. I just want some time."

Alfred managed a bloody smile. "Jim helped you with that." He lifted the cor anglais. "This is hard enough to play with a full set of lips. One and a half won't do."

"I wanna wait till after the Harvard game," Matt clarified.

Alfred's brow knitted. "That's a week from now."

"So? What's the big deal?"

Alfred had no idea what might unfold if a voyager overstayed his welcome to Tempi Passati. "Look," he said, trying to sound assertive, "all I know is that something happened last night. I don't know what it was but I know what it means. Your voyage to the past is over. However, thanks to Mr. Thorpe, I won't be able to send you home"—he pointed at his bloody lips—"until these work again."

Matt returned Alfred's gaze. He realized he was looking at a man, bloodied and dejected, who was as much a victim in all of this as he was. "Mr. Jongler, you're right. I've learned how to play a different kind of game. I've learned how to block and tackle and get down in the mud and duke it out till you've got nothing left, and then keep going. It's football like I've always wanted to play it. And I wanna play it here, one more time. I want to play in the Harvard game."

Alfred raised an eyebrow. "Is that all you want?"

Matt felt he had confessed enough. He didn't need to tell him about Tawny, or his hope of being part of the guard-back screen-pass play Tawny and Pop had invented. "Yes," he said. "That's all I want."

Alfred studied Matt, then lifted the cor anglais as if giving it a moment to weigh in. "Who knows, Matthew. Maybe you're not ready to go home after all." He moved to the door. "Maybe Mr. Thorpe bursting in was more than fortuitous." He disappeared into the hall.

Matt didn't know what "fortuitous" meant; he didn't have to. He knew his escape from the cor anglais had been too easy. *Maybe he can still play the thing with a cut lip,* he thought. *Maybe he's faking it to get me to lower my guard so he can pop around a corner and blow me away.*

Whatever the case, Matt made a vow: until the Harvard game, he would avoid being alone; he would stick to people like glue. There was safety in numbers. Alfred would never blow him away in front of witnesses.

Matt rushed through his Sunday-morning cleaning chores, then went to Lone Star's room and waited for him to finish his chores before they went to breakfast.

When they walked into the football dining room, Matt was shocked by the cheerful mood of the team. If it weren't for all the newspapers in the reading room with stories faulting the Indians for their poor play in the rain and mud, you might have thought the loss to Princeton was just a bad dream. But the players seemed to have shaken it off overnight. They weren't talking about Princeton anymore; their focus was on Harvard.

After a huge breakfast of pancakes, bacon and sausage, Matt was never so glad to go to church in the assembly hall, especially when he saw Alfred conducting the small orchestra, a bandage covering his lip.

In the afternoon walk with the team, Matt tried to find Lone Star to walk with, but he was nowhere in sight. He didn't have to wait long for company.

Jim ran up and cut to the chase. "How'd you make out with Tawny? And what was Mr. Jongler doing in your room?"

Matt shrugged. "We decided to be friends."

Jim gave him a cockeyed look. "Tawny or Jongler?"

"Tawny, of course."

"Friends with a girl?" Jim frowned. "If you don't grab a girl when you get a chance, you might want to check into the hospital with Caleb."

Wanting to snuff any suspicions Jim might have about Alfred being in his room that morning, Matt voiced the excuse he had concocted in church. "I used to play the oboe a little and I borrowed one from Mr. Jongler to see if I could still play. He needed it back and came to get it."

"At five-thirty in the morning?" Jim asked dubiously.

"He needed it right away 'cause the oboe player in the orchestra for church broke his and I had the only spare."

Jim looked like he was half buying it. "So why was Jongler playing it?"

"He was testing it to make sure I hadn't broken it."

Jim mulled it over for a second. "Okay, but if Jim was you, he wouldn't be wasting time planting lips on some music stick when he could be planting 'em on a girl stick, especially one with the curves and knobs of Miss Owl."

Matt thanked him for the advice and changed the subject to the Harvard eleven.

28.

SCREENS

Matt went to the hospital to visit Caleb. While checking in with the head nurse, Miss Rose, Matt learned Caleb had been moved to the second-floor ward. Caleb had taken a turn for the worse, and had finally been diagnosed with typhoid fever. But he was in the early stages. There was every reason to believe he would recover in a week or two.

As Matt climbed the stairs to the upper floor, he saw Tawny coming down in her nurse's uniform. He was glad she was on duty. "Hi," he said.

She kept moving without a word.

"Tawny," he tried again. She disappeared around the switch-back of stairs. He was taken aback. He had known a few girls who wouldn't look at him after a night of wild fun because they wanted to pretend nothing had happened. But with Tawny, he didn't know if she was ignoring him for what *little* they had done or for the thing they *hadn't* done. He fought the urge to follow her, and continued up the stairs.

Caleb's symptoms included a bad cough, stomach cramps and a mild fever. Newspapers were scattered across his bed. Being sick wasn't going to stop him from devouring accounts of the Princeton game.

Matt pulled up a chair and told Caleb everything the newspapers hadn't covered. Matt detailed his battle with Cooney in the second half and Pop's muddy-ball speech on the train, from the Indians' "bitter pill of disillusionment" to how the Redmen were going to go on and finally beat the Ivy swells of Harvard.

When he'd finished, Caleb stared at the ceiling. Then he asked, "Have you ever read *The Time Machine* by H. G. Wells?"

It was so out of left field Matt wondered if the drugs Caleb was taking were making him loopy. "Uh, no."

"That's what the gridiron is," Caleb said. "Our time machine."

Matt's face squinched. "How's that?"

"That's what the Harvard game is: our chance to travel back in time." Caleb didn't take his eyes off the ceiling. "The fathers and grandfathers of those Harvard boys stole our land, ordered the extermination of the buffalo, and threw us on reservations. Our people were left staring into the twin barrels of disease and starvation and facing extinction. But something happened. A few of us escaped the reservation, went to school, reforged ourselves as gridiron warriors, and now we're about to travel to Harvard, step onto the time machine of Soldiers Field and refight the war we lost. In the name of our fathers and grandfathers we're going to defeat the sons and grandsons of our white enemies." His eyes unlocked from the ceiling. He turned and gave Matt a weak smile. "On Saturday, we will rattle the bones of the living and the dead."

Matt started to speak but Caleb was wracked by a coughing fit. Matt offered the glass of water on the bedside table. Caleb waved it away and shut his eyes. His trance-like reverie seemed to have drained him.

Matt left him to sleep and went back downstairs to reception. He asked Miss Rose if Miss Owl was still on duty. The nurse told him Tawny had left because she wasn't feeling well and had returned to her dorm. When he learned that one of Tawny's duties during the nightshift would have been to keep an eye on Caleb, Matt offered to fill in for her, at least the watching Caleb part. Miss Rose's reluctance faltered when he explained that football players looked after each other and Caleb was part of the team. Miss Rose voiced her concern about Matt getting enough sleep to get through his next day of school, work and practice. He assured her he could use the empty bed next to Caleb's for a few "power naps." When she raised an eyebrow and wanted to know what power naps were, Matt explained that power naps, a practice of his tribe, allowed an Indian to go for days with next to no sleep.

Returning to his room to fetch his nightshirt, Matt congratulated himself for killing two birds with one stone. He could spend more time with Caleb, and he had just made it harder for Alfred to get to him. Of course, there was another reason he wanted to stay in the hospital for the night, or several nights, despite the risk of catching typhoid fever himself. It raised the odds of seeing Tawny, and figuring out what terrible guy-on-girl crime he had committed to deserve death by cold shoulder.

Monday afternoon, football practice was full of surprises. After warm-ups and separate drills for the linemen and backs, Pop called the team together.

"Boys," he said, "we know how our single wing soared against Penn and how its feathers got tarred in the Princeton game. As long as we have decent weather against Harvard, it can soar again. But to make sure the single wing can fly in all sorts of weather, we're going to add a new play to our arsenal. It's a short pass called the guard-back screen pass."

Matt fought a smile. He wished Tawny were sitting in the stands to hear Pop announce the introduction of her play to the Carlisle Indians.

Pop started positioning players with Little Boy in the left guard-back slot and the flanking wingbacks off the right tackle. Matt, as a second-stringer, was put on defense facing off against the right guard.

After Pop got everyone in position and explained all the assignments, they moved through the play at a quarter speed, then half speed without the final screen pass from Little Boy to Mounty. Then they ran it full speed with the pass Little Boy was supposed to lob to Mounty out to the left. Each time, Little Boy's pass looked like a water balloon wobbling through the air.

Pop finally threw up his hands. "Grinnell, switch spots with Little Boy. Let's see if you can game it."

As Matt swapped with Little Boy, the look he got from the starting guard made him glad Little Boy didn't have a knife.

Knowing Matt was familiar with the play, Pop ran it full speed right off. Matt took the handoff from Mounty, rolled right, turned back toward the onrush of released defensive linemen, and lobbed a nice spiral back to Mounty behind his screen of blockers.

Before the players had finished shouting their approval, Pop blew his whistle. "All right, that's enough on it today. We'll hit it again later in the week."

It was one thing Matt admired about Pop: he knew how to manage his players, especially their emotions. There was no way Pop wanted Little Boy leaving practice wanting to kill Matt, or the guard who had pulled off the surprise of throwing a perfect pass getting a big head.

29.

PROPHECY

After practice, Matt went to the hospital before dinner hoping to see Tawny. His hopes were dashed when Miss Rose told him that Miss Owl had swapped with another girl and had done her shift earlier in the day.

He still looked forward to telling Caleb about what had happened at practice. When Matt entered the second-floor ward, Caleb seemed to be muttering about something. Getting closer to his bed, he realized Caleb was actually talking in his sleep in either his Lakota language or gibberish. He tried to wake Caleb, but he only kept murmuring nonsense.

Back downstairs, Matt asked Miss Rose about it. She explained that Caleb's "muttering delirium" was typical of someone with typhoid fever. The good news was his fever had stopped rising and, while it didn't look it, Caleb was on the mend. Thinking that Matt's presence overnight might have been helpful, Miss Rose encouraged him to continue staying in the hospital.

Tuesday's practice delivered no surprises except for some extra hard hits from Little Boy during a tackling drill. Matt was glad tackling practice came before they spent five minutes running the guard-back screen pass with Matt lobbing passes to Mounty. Each time Pop congratulated Matt on his throws, Little Boy looked more like Big Killer.

After dinner, Matt went to the hospital and had more luck. Miss Rose informed him that Caleb had recovered from his muttering delirium and Tawny was back on the evening shift. Matt found her watching over a sleeping Caleb.

With two days to prepare, he had perfected his opening line. "So, I get the feeling Tawny Owl wants nothing more to do with me," he said quietly, so as not to wake Caleb. "But I can still be friends with Pigskin."

She shot him an icy look. "Please don't call me that."

"Okay, I won't." He sat on the edge of the bed he had been using. "On one condition: you talk to me."

She set her jaw. "What do you want to talk about?"

"Two things. I want you to know we're practicing your play to use in the Harvard game."

Her face softened and she looked over with thawing eyes. "Really? The guard-back broken wing?"

"Pop saw you run it when we were playing Girl Ball. But he calls it the guard-back screen pass."

She looked back to her patient with a slight smile. "'What's in a name? That which we call a rose by any other name would smell as sweet.'"

A dim memory fired in Matt. "I've heard that before."

"It's Shakespeare. Have you heard of him?"

"Does he play for Harvard?"

She clamped down on a laugh. "What's the other thing you wanted to talk about?"

He checked out Caleb, who looked pale and sick. His face had begun to look gaunt. "Is Caleb gonna make it?"

Tawny touched the blanket covering Caleb's arm. "We're all praying for him."

Matt wanted to say he was too, but he wasn't the praying kind. And he wasn't going to lie about it because of a vow he had made. Even though he couldn't tell Tawny the whole truth, he had vowed to at least not lie to her.

Tawny started to go and turned back. "Miss Rose tells me you've taken over some of my duties on the late shift."

He nodded. "Yeah."

"Thank you."

Watching her go, Matt listened to the rustle of her skirt. His insides churned with regret.

The next afternoon in the Printery, Matt checked the composition of the upcoming *Arrow*. He was surprised to see that Pigskin's weekly entry was a lot more than the usual few lines found in *From the Ball Bin*. It was a poem.

DREAM

Off to Manhattan our Redmen did romp,
To catch a Tiger in a Polo swamp.
Yet all they did bag was one muddy ball,
And a speech from Pop on Carlisle's fall.
That night they did dream with sore fitful sighs,
Of tackles they missed and elusive thighs.
But come the sunup they rose with no shame,
And set their bright eyes on Saturday's game.
To Harvard they're off, a victory they seek,
With a whoop of war, "Remember last week!"
And in their quiver, a play never seen,
A trick this poet has seen in a dream.
It starts with a guard who steps out of line,
He's covered in dirt but oh can he shine.
With pigskin in hand he looks like an ox,
Yet behind his eyes, cunning as a fox.
The rooters will shout, "He floats out a pass!
'Tis so high and sweet he throws like a lass!"
The ball will drop where no one had thought it,
To the same Redman who had first caught it.
Wide open he'll be with blockers galore,
A wall to the goal for a touchdown score!

Over the cheers the rooters will sing,
"That was guard back, with a broken wing!"
And after it's done—the Crimson Tide fall—
Our men will bring back the game-winning ball.

— Pigskin

Matt's first reaction was panic. She had spelled out the play in such detail she'd practically diagrammed it for Harvard. He had to remind himself there wasn't an Internet yet; no one could e-mail it to them. On top of that, it was on the back page of *The Arrow*, not exactly a paper the white world read on a regular basis.

Reassured that Tawny hadn't blown the Indians' newest trick play, Matt read the poem again to make sure he hadn't missed any of her references to things only the two of them knew. He smiled at her subtle digs: "elusive thighs" and saying he threw like a girl. It made him wish her "Dream" would come true. It also made him yearn for one more kiss.

30.

GHOST SHIRT

On Thursday, as Matt moved between classes, meals and the Printery, he searched groups of girls for Tawny. She was mysteriously missing. His worry was that some adult had seen Pigskin's poem before it came out in the paper on Friday, considered it scandalous, and Tawny had been grounded, or worse, suspended. Then there was the possibility that Pop had seen it and had it put under lock and key, along with Tawny, for revealing too much. His fears continued through practice, which was light and short because the team would be boarding the train Friday afternoon for the trip to Boston.

After practice, a quick check at the hospital yielded a double dose of bad news. Miss Rose informed Matt it was Tawny's day off, and Caleb had worsened. His fever had spiked so high his muttering delirium had returned and escalated to full-blown delusion. Matt witnessed Caleb's confusion when he read the copy of Pigskin's poem he had snuck out of the Printery. Caleb thought it was a newspaper account *after* the game, and that Carlisle had finally beaten Harvard. When Caleb tried to get out of bed to go see the coveted game ball that had finally been added to the school's trophy case, Matt had to restrain him and call for Miss Rose's help. She gave Caleb a shot to calm him down.

"What did you give him?" Matt asked as Caleb slipped into unconsciousness.

"Morphine."

Matt searched the nurse's eyes for confirmation of his worst fears. Her expression gave away nothing. Even if he asked, he knew she wouldn't tell him the truth.

After dinner, Matt was walking across the quad to his quarters when he passed near the bandstand and almost dropped dead from fright.

Standing in the bandstand, staring at him, was Alfred, with his hands clasped behind his back.

Matt slowed his pace, waiting for Alfred to reveal what he might be holding. If it was the cor anglais, Matt was ready to leap on the bandstand, grab the oboe and snap off the reed before Alfred could blow a note. Nothing was going to stop him from seeing Tawny one more time.

Alfred didn't move. He stood there, still as a gargoyle staring down from a cathedral. The wound on his lip had healed from a scab to pink flesh.

Matt's skin crawled and he hurried away.

Alfred swung an arm into view and raised a lit cigarette. His mouth cornered into a smile. Despite the possibility that he was the Jongler who had drawn the most confounding time voyager yet, he had a plan. He drew on his cigarette. Everything was in place for him to play the cor anglais so the cor anglais could play him.

Back in his room, Matt stripped off his military uniform, put on his suit and stuffed the minimum of clothes he would need for Boston into a leather satchel. He was in and out of the room in less than three minutes.

Heading to the hospital, he saw that Alfred had left the bandstand. But for all he knew, he was hiding around the next corner or lurking in the shadows of the hospital, ready to pounce.

By the time Matt reached the hospital steps, he was sweating and out of breath. At first he was petrified that he had caught typhoid fever from Caleb. Then he realized he was having a panic attack. It might be a matter of minutes or seconds before Alfred blew him out of Carlisle and back to his hometime. With his panic came the overwhelming urge to tell someone the truth before it was too late. He wanted someone to be able to tell Tawny, and give her a choice. She could believe he was just another Indian who had run away from school and was never heard from again. Or she could believe, as crazy as it sounded, that Matt Grinnell had blown in from the future, and the force that transported time travelers had taken him away.

Inside the hospital, the first person he saw was Miss Rose at the nurse's station.

She eyed him with concern. "Are you okay?"

Matt sleeve-wiped his face. "Just fine. Light workout today and I have a sweat quota. If I don't sweat enough in practice I still gotta sweat it out later."

He moved to the stairs leading to the second floor. Miss Rose was definitely not the one to hear his time-travel confession; she probably knew where the straitjackets were.

In the ward, Matt yanked off his suit jacket and slid into the chair next to Caleb's bed.

Caleb blinked awake. He took Matt in with surprisingly clear eyes. "Hello, Wrong Way."

Matt was startled by the clarity of his voice. Even though his friend still looked gaunt, his pallor was gone; he looked almost healthy. "Good to see you, buddy. There's something I gotta tell you."

"I'm listening."

Matt cleared his throat. "You know how you were telling me that Soldiers Field was a time machine?"

Caleb nodded. "Yes, and then you tried to bamboozle me into thinking we had already played the Harvard game and had won it." He gave Matt a wry smile. "I know that's not so. It's only Thursday night and the game is Saturday."

Matt was so pleased over Caleb's return to lucidity he didn't mind getting blamed for the confusion. "Wow. You really are feeling better."

"Yes, I am. How do I look?"

"You look . . ." As Matt searched for the right word, he heard the sound of gentle rain outside. "Alive."

Caleb smiled. "If I didn't look alive I wouldn't be asking. I'm asking"—he passed a hand over his chest—"how do I look in my ghost shirt?"

Matt blinked. "Ghost shirt?"

"Yes, a ghost shirt. They can be difficult to see. It's one of the reasons they're called ghost shirts."

Caleb's weird claim slammed the brakes on Matt's relief over his friend's recovery. "Okay," he said, playing along. "What's a ghost shirt?"

Caleb splayed a hand on his chest. "It takes more than a single handprint on a warrior's chest to fend off harm; it takes the handprints of all Indians of every tribe woven into a cloth from which ghosts shirts are made. The warrior who wears a ghost shirt not only fends off death, he conquers it."

The only thing Matt could think of that conquered death was a vampire or a zombie. "How can you conquer death?"

Caleb seemed to stare through him. "I'll give you an example. What was the last Indian massacre?"

Matt shrugged.

"Wounded Knee," Caleb filled in, "only seventeen years ago. Why were we massacred there? Because at Wounded Knee we unveiled the ghost shirt. And by doing so, we revealed our mastery over death."

Matt was so focused on trying to follow Caleb, a future-speak slipped out. "So a ghost shirt's like a bulletproof vest?"

The term didn't throw Caleb at all. "More than that, it's a death-proof vest."

"What makes it death-proof?"

"Because the Indian who wears it becomes a time traveler."

Matt jerked back. His mind raced with possibilities: Caleb was a mind reader, or a medicine man in training with mystical powers, or he was even more delusional than the day before. "Time traveler?" he echoed. "How does a ghost shirt make you a time traveler?"

Caleb's shining eyes locked on Matt. "An Indian never dies, he just dries up and blows away. Why? He is from the land, he is of the soil, and dust never goes away. It shifts and moves with the wind. The white man thought he could wipe the earth clean of the red man, but he might as well try to sweep away the earth itself. The Indian *is* the earth. He is the dust under our feet."

Riveted by whether Caleb was making sense or had gone stark raving mad, Matt didn't hear the rustle of a skirt outside the door to the ward.

Caleb took a raspy breath and turned to the ceiling. "That's what the ghost shirt does. It wraps a warrior in the knowledge that death is illusion. It tells him he will soon dry up, blow away, and that his spirit, swirling in the dust, will rise again in the body of another warrior."

"Okay." Matt nodded. "You're talking reincarnation."

"No, endless incarnation," Caleb corrected, "for as long as the earth and its dust turns through space. That's how we time travel." His gaze returned to Matt. "The Redmen taking the battle to Harvard are more than you think. You are the same warriors who have fought the white man since the first white man stepped on the sand of the Sand Tribes, and began their march across the dust of the Dust Tribes."

Matt couldn't dismiss Caleb's delusional thoughts; they

shared too much with what he wanted to confess. "So you believe in time travel?"

Caleb coughed and turned back to the ceiling. "Anyone who doesn't is a fool. Time is only a curtain that hangs between us and the past. Time travel is as easy as parting the curtain."

"That's what I wanted to tell you," Matt offered. "I've parted the curtain. I've traveled through time."

Caleb shut his eyes. "I know. You are a warrior who blew in with the dust."

"Caleb, I'm not a warrior from the past. I'm a warrior from the future."

Caleb's face pinched, with pain or confusion Matt wasn't sure. Caleb replied with closed eyes. "Who is to say what the dust contains? A warrior from the past or a warrior from the future. Only the warrior would know."

"Exactly," Matt said. "And I'm from the future."

Drawing strength from somewhere within, Caleb's eyelids opened. He stared at Matt. "When are you from?"

"From the next century."

"Have you come to stay?"

Matt shook his head. "No."

"When will you leave?"

"After the Harvard game. I believe I was sent here to fight in that battle."

Caleb did a slow blink. "So, I may not see you again."

Matt squeezed his friend's arm. "I need to leave but you don't. You need to stay here. You don't need that ghost shirt yet. It's not your time to dry up and blow away. I'm the one who's going to dry up and blow away, not you."

"How can you be so sure?" Caleb whispered.

Matt leaned in close. "Because you are my warrior brother, and one of us has to stay and fight for the present. Your brothers are going to fight and win the battle on Soldiers Field, but *you*

278

need to fight and win even bigger battles for your brothers and sisters."

Caleb's eyes closed as he managed a faint smile. "I hear you, Wrong Way. I have taken off my ghost shirt. I will stay and fight our battles."

Matt didn't move as he watched Caleb's shallow breathing barely lift his open nightshirt. He had never been happier to see a sign of life. It filled him with an impulse. Rising a little too suddenly, the chair scraped on the floorboards.

It didn't rouse Caleb, but out in the hall Tawny heard it. She scurried across the hallway and disappeared through an open door.

Matt came out in the hall and went downstairs.

Tawny emerged from her hiding place, checked on the sleeping Caleb, and noticed the leather satchel on the bed next to his. Knowing Matt had been staying in the hospital, she knew he would return soon. She slipped back out into the hall, went in the opposite room, and waited.

A few minutes later she heard Matt's solid footfalls on the stairs. She waited for him to go back into the ward before taking up her position outside the door.

Matt's white shirt was speckled with rain. He stood over Caleb. With his left hand, he spread Caleb's open nightshirt wider. Matt lifted his right hand, splayed it open and laid it on Caleb's chest. When he took it away, it left a handprint of red clay.

31.

LAST LOOKS

In the darkened ward, Matt slept under the covers. The rain, falling harder now, muffled the byplay of Matt's rhythmic breathing and Caleb's labored breath.

Matt woke with a start. A figure sat on the edge of the bed. Fearing it was Alfred, he struggled to get his arm from under the covers to stop what was coming. When a hand fell on his arm, he realized who it was. Tawny.

"What are you doing here?" he whispered.

"Boys aren't the only ones who can sneak out and go prowling in the night," she said with a slight smile.

"Aren't you worried about getting caught?"

"Aren't you worried about not saying goodbye?"

Matt silently conceded the point, although he knew she was referring to a goodbye before the team headed to Boston. "I'm so glad to see you." He tried to sit up.

She gently pushed him back down. "We've come full circle. This is where we first talked."

"But you were sitting in a chair, not on the bed."

She nodded. "Yes, it was a long time ago."

"It sure was."

"I came to say goodbye and give you a gift." Tawny gestured to the satchel at the foot of the bed. "I put it in there. But you can't open it until the morning of the game."

"Will it help me not throw like a girl?" he asked.

"Maybe. But there's another gift I'll give you now. A new name."

"Uh-oh. What did I do to deserve it?"

She ignored the playfulness in his voice. "It's what you didn't do. You are no longer Wrong Way. You are Right Way."

He was pretty sure what she was referring to, but he didn't feel like he deserved it. "Okay, but every time you call me Right Way, I'm going to call you Pigskin."

A rueful smile visited her lips. "'What's in a name?'"

The same bittersweet feeling tugged at his mouth. "'That which we call a rose by any other name would smell as sweet.'" He watched her dark eyes pool with moisture. "Will I see you tomorrow?"

She didn't blink. "I've heard it said that time is a curtain."

His heart thudded as two possibilities careened through him: either she had overheard his conversation with Caleb or she was so smart she had figured it all out.

"True or not," she whispered, "the curtain of time never hangs in the heart." She raised his hand and pressed it over her heart. "I will see you here, always."

Taking her other hand, he placed it on his own chest. "Always." He felt the tremulous thrill of Tawny holding his heart in her hand.

She eased down for a kiss. He felt the wet of her mouth and the hot splash of tears on his cheeks.

After a kiss long enough to savor a lifetime, she opened the space between them. She rose from the bed and started away.

"Goodbye, Tawny Owl," he said.

She paused at Caleb's bedstead. "Goodbye, Matt Grinnell."

Friday, after lunch, the horse-drawn buses took the football team into Carlisle and to the train that would carry them to Boston. There was the usual contingent of cheering students to send them off, and the band played rousing Sousa marches and school fight songs.

Matt couldn't see over the crowd to find Tawny in the band;

he boarded the train for a better view. Finding a window seat on the side facing the band, he stowed his satchel on the overhead rack. As he sat and searched for Tawny, he sensed someone standing beside him. Lone Star leaned over him, pushed a hand through the opening at the top of the window and waved.

Matt looked out and saw Angel De Cora answer Lone Star's wave with windmill-like sweeps. As Lone Star laughed and plunked down in the seat, Matt asked, "So, how's the student-on-teacher romance going?"

Lone Star beamed. "We're getting married next year." Before Matt had the chance to offer congratulations, Lone Star threw the spotlight back on him. "How about yourself? Have you gotten any better at talking to girls?"

"Yeah, a little." Whatever pride Matt felt for being able to answer honestly was vaporized by the sight of someone entering the car at the other end.

Alfred lifted his bag to the overhead rack.

"What's Mr. Jongler doing on the train?" Matt asked. "The band's not going to Boston."

"With Caleb down, Mr. Denny needs help on the training side," Lone Star explained. "Jongler offered to fill in."

The train suddenly jerked and began to move.

Matt's eyes snapped to the window, found the band and zeroed in on Tawny playing her flute.

Matt jumped up and tried to lower the window; it was stuck. All he could do was repeat Lone Star's move: stick his hand out the opening at the top of the window. As he waved, he watched Tawny lower her flute and raise her arm. However, because she was unable to see past the shimmer of reflections in the train windows, she couldn't find Matt.

He thrashed his hand back and forth. She kept waving at another car with a brave smile. She slipped out of sight. Matt jumped over Lone Star, ran down the aisle and out between the cars, and hung from the handrail. Their last look couldn't be hidden by a veil of glass.

But his view of the retreating throng of students, and Tawny, was blocked by a banner hanging over High Street, saluting the Carlisle Indians. By the time the band emerged from behind the banner they were a blur in the distance.

Matt pulled back between the cars and slumped against the woodwork. The last vision of her—looking for him, not finding him, waving blindly to someone who would never return— shook him to the core. His face twisted. His sob was silenced by the wail of a train whistle.

32.

FRIDAY NIGHT

Matt stuck close to other players for the rest of the train trip and steered clear of Alfred. His safety-in-numbers strategy was easy sitting next to Lone Star. Players kept stopping by to congratulate and tease him about his plan to "desert the ranks of bachelordom."

Pop even came by and shook Lone Star's hand. After the coach wished him luck, Pop turned to Matt. "Ready for some playing time against those Harvard boys?"

"Yes, sir," Matt answered, game face on.

Pop nodded. "Good, you're my guard back."

As Pop moved on, Matt didn't miss the evil eye he got from Little Boy a few seats up.

After arriving in Boston, Matt was relieved to get Jim as a roommate when they checked into the Copley Square Hotel. He figured Alfred would never try blowing the cor anglais anywhere close to Jim. If there was a screwup and Jim Thorpe got sent to the next century, Alfred would be knee-deep in trouble with whatever rules committee made sure time travel didn't unravel history as we know it.

Matt's only worry about Jim running interference for him was Jim's nonstop cutting up. One of his stunts was going up to the hotel desk and trying to check in under the name "Chief Jim." When the clerk asked him if he had a reservation, he said, "Yes, sir, but it's back in Oklahoma." If Jim went any further with his practical jokes, Matt feared Pop might put him on a train back to Carlisle, which would make Matt a sitting duck.

The team had dinner in one of the hotel's banquet rooms; it was a feast. Jim limited his cracking wise to standing up, raising a raw oyster high and declaring, "In Jim's book, the bravest man in the world was the first one to stick an oyster in his mouth." Then he slurped it down.

When everyone had polished off a dessert or two, Pop rose from the head of the starters' table to address the team. His speeches at Syracuse and after Princeton were warm-ups to this one. As Matt listened, he wondered if Pop had hired Caleb as a speechwriter.

"Boys," he began, "tomorrow you face the sons and grandsons of the men who conquered your people. They are the descendants of the white men who ordered the ruination of your tribes." He looked at Al Exendine and named his tribe. "The Delaware." His eyes shifted to Bill Gardner—"The Chippewa"—then to Pete Hauser and his brother Wauseka—"the Cheyenne." He continued around the starters' table, acknowledging each player and naming his tribe: "The Oneida, the Apache, the Caddo, the Umatilla, the Seneca, the Osage"—until his eyes found the players seated next to him, Mount Pleasant and Captain Lubo— "the Iroquois and the Cahuilla. And now, the sons and grandsons of your conquerors want their turn to fight the tribe that has risen against them: the Carlisle Indians." Pop's voice began building to a crescendo. "But this time, unlike the wars of the past, the contest between red men and white will be waged on equal terms. This time, the playing field is level and you're going to beat 'em at their own game! This war is yours to win!"

The room erupted in cheers and war whoops. An oyster or two sailed through the air.

When the room quieted, Captain Lubo rose and addressed the team. "Tonight, as we sleep, it is my wish that each of us dream of our ancestors. If our fathers and grandfathers appear, tell them that when the dust settles on Soldiers Field, the buffalo soldiers will be scattered and beaten. The ground that has been soaked with our blood and tears, the earth that has become the burial ground of our dreams, has been retaken. And our peoples, the tribes of the Indian nation, have risen again in triumph."

The pandemonium that followed was so loud the hotel's security personnel burst in the room thinking a riot had broken out. Discovering that the only assault was on their ears, the security detail retreated before the Indians mistook them for Harvard boys and began the battle early.

Later that night, Matt had a dream of his own.

He was in the game for Little Boy at left guard. Mounty called for the guard-back screen pass. They ran the play. Matt took the handoff from Mounty, rolled right and threw over the rushing Harvard linemen to Mounty, who ran for a sizable gain behind his blockers. It worked perfectly.

The dream jumped to later in the game. Mounty called the play again. Matt set back off the line. The Harvard players started yelling; they knew what was coming. Then, as Mounty shouted signals, another shift happened. The Harvard players transformed into Rockford Wolverines in modern football uniforms. The Carlisle players turned into Belleplain Cyclones—all but two: Matt and a small player lined up at left end. They were the only ones still wearing the old Carlisle uniforms and leather headgear.

The ball was snapped to Mounty. Matt started right for the handoff, but Mounty kept the ball and reversed left. Matt looked back in confusion as Mounty handed off to the small player in the old uniform pulling off the end, starting an end-run to the right. Matt recognized the ball carrier—Caleb—and he instantly understood his assignment: to lead the blocking for Caleb around the right side. Matt leveled the Wolverines' defensive end with a low block. The end landed on top of Matt, smashing his head into the turf. He opened his eyes. Crawling over the grass toward him was a large black spider.

Matt snapped awake with a gasp. His eyes shot around the darkened room. There was no figure standing over his bed. No dreaded cor anglais. No spider.

There was only Jim, snoring softly in the other bed.

33.

TROLLEY RIDE

The team took breakfast again in the banquet room.

After eating, Pop pushed himself to his feet and took them in. "Early this morning I received a telegram from Carlisle. Caleb Phillips died last night."

Shock hit the room like a concussive blast. No one moved. Time had stopped. After a long moment, time resumed to the sound of murmured prayers, quiet sobs and the silent tumble of tears.

Captain Lubo stood and began to speak about Caleb.

Matt didn't listen. All he heard were Caleb's last words: "I have taken off my ghost shirt. I will stay and fight our battles." All he saw was Caleb in his dream: the ball tucked under his arm, his intense face framed by the headgear, his small body running for dear life.

Matt was pulled from the dream by the sound of singing. The players were quietly giving voice to a hymn Matt had heard once before, when he had first arrived at Carlisle: the hymn that had carried Albert Jackson in his little black coffin to his grave.

Still reeling from the shock, Matt and Jim returned to their room to pack their bags. They would be returning to Carlisle after the game.

While Jim was in the bathroom, Matt pulled Tawny's gift, still wrapped, from his satchel. It was surprisingly heavy; he thought it might be a book. He opened the envelope tucked under the ribbon and pulled out a note: *For My Warriors. From Pigskin.* At the bottom, she added, *P.S. I have one of you;*

you should have one of me. An arrow pointed to the edge of the paper.

Matt turned it over. On the other side was a pencil drawing, beautifully rendered, of Tawny, her long hair down, wearing her nightshirt. Unlike his last glimpse of her as the train had pulled away, her self-portrait gazed out at him. He answered her look with welling eyes.

He shook off the tears and opened the present. It was a thick rectangle of red clay: Carlisle clay. He remembered the handprint he had put on Caleb's chest and how it had failed to protect him. The lump in his throat rose again.

As Jim came out of the bathroom, Matt sucked it up and stuffed the drawing and the clay in his jacket pockets.

Two trolleys, one in front of the other, waited to take the team, their equipment and their luggage to Soldiers Field.

Matt boarded the front trolley, which held most of the players, and took one of the last empty seats on the back bench next to Lone Star. Adding to the usual pregame mood of subdued intensity was the pall of Caleb's death. What few words were spoken were hushed whispers. Even Jim's mischief was silenced.

Matt watched Alfred move past the front trolley toward the second one. There was no mistaking the wooden case in his hand. He was carrying the cor anglais. He boarded the second trolley, which held Denny, the trainers, a few players, their luggage and the duffle bags of equipment.

The last player to climb on the front trolley was Little Boy. After spotting no empty seats, he saw Matt on the back bench. He started down the aisle.

As Matt watched Little Boy coming, he pulled the wrapped slab of clay from his pocket and turned to Lone Star. "Do you remember the handprint on the warrior and his horse?"

Lone Star nodded. "You wanted to put one on Tawny."

"She gave this to me." Matt handed him the wrapped clay. "It's for the team."

Lone Star gave him a puzzled look. "Where are you going?"

Little Boy arrived in front of Matt and stood menacingly. He jabbed a finger toward the trolley behind them. "Scrubs ride on next one."

Matt turned to Lone Star with a flicker of a smile and answered his question. "Where I belong."

When Matt got up and slid past Little Boy, Lone Star called after him. "See you there."

Matt turned, gave him a thumbs-up, not caring if such a gesture existed yet, and moved down the aisle.

Boarding the second trolley, Matt moved past Alfred and several scrubs in the front seats. Continuing past the seats filled with luggage, he found the last empty bench seat. Behind it were two small mountains of duffel bags filled with uniforms, pads, shoes and headgear.

The trolleys started, beginning the trip that would take them over the river to Cambridge and Soldiers Field.

After a few minutes, Alfred stood and moved down the aisle toward Matt. Alfred carried the wooden music case.

Matt noticed the case no longer had the leather straps that usually encircled it. He knew what was coming but he had a plan to buy some time: as soon as Alfred opened the case and started putting the woodwind together, Matt was going to jump out the window and run to Soldiers Field. Even if he wasn't able to suit up, and had to watch from the stands, he had to see the game.

Alfred sat next to Matt on the bench seat and set the music case across his knees.

"Can't it wait till after the game?" Matt asked.

"I don't think so," Alfred answered gently.

Between the divide of luggage in front of them and the buffer of street noise, Matt wasn't worried about the players upfront overhearing them. "What's a few more hours?" he implored. "What if they need me, even for one play?"

Alfred gave him a smile. "You've played well, on and off the field. You've played your way home."

Matt gestured to the players up front. "What about them? What are they going to think when I disappear?"

Alfred considered the question as a rising noise pulled his attention to the road ahead.

The two trolleys stopped at an intersection clogged with Harvard boosters and rooters. They were part of a parade of vehicles and raucous Crimson Tide fans, sounding their support with blaring horns and noisemakers. The slow-moving cacophony was making its way to Soldiers Field.

Alfred answered Matt's concern. "Maybe the team will think you're no different than Twoguns: you heard a fire wagon and went chasing after it. Or maybe they will think you're one of those phantom students who suddenly appear at Carlisle and just as swiftly disappear."

As if emphasizing the point, Alfred suddenly stood and placed the music case on the seat beside Matt. Then Alfred squeezed between the two piles of duffle bags behind them and disappeared in the back of the trolley.

His actions mystified Matt. It's not like there was a bathroom at the very back of the trolley. *And why would Alfred leave the music case? Matt wondered. Is this some test to see if I throw the cor anglais out the window?*

Before he could solve the mystery, the Crimson Tide parade hit a new decibel level. A chorus of motor horns blared. When they stopped, the parade noise scaled back to a thunderous din; but Matt heard a new sound added to the mix. A murky note emerged from the rear of the trolley and broke into a melody. Matt threw open the music case. It was empty . . . except for the leather fold of Matt's wallet.

Realizing Alfred's trick—presetting the cor anglais in the back—Matt grabbed his wallet and leaped up. He tried to throw open the window but it was stuck fast. His eyes flew to the front of the trolley; the scrubs had gotten out of their seats to get a better look at the loud parade. They were blocking the aisle and door. As the cor anglais music, barely audible over the ruckus on the street, began making its shift from melodic to jarring, Matt realized his only option.

He turned and bulled through the tight opening between the mountains of duffle bags. As soon as he saw Alfred in a cavity of space at the rear of the trolley, playing the curved cor anglais like a man possessed, Matt regretted his move. The space was already a snake pit of writhing mists. Before he could scream, a band of mist shot forward and encircled his throat; others ensnared his legs and torso.

Alfred, with his hands and lungs in the grip of the cor anglais, stared in wild wonder at the serpentine mists encircling Matt in a cocoon of white. As the cor anglais emitted an unearthly trill, the enveloping cocoon pulsed into a rapid vibration. The trill reached a dizzying pitch. For a moment, Matt's dissipating figure loomed from within. Then the cocoon exploded in a burst of radiance. The blast blinded Albert and knocked the reed from his mouth. The sound of rowdy fans and horns rushed in, filling the void.

Albert's eyes blinked open. He gaped at the empty space where Matt had been. Drained by the instrument's possession, Alfred slid down the back wall of the trolley. His mask of stupefied awe was tinged with pride. He had done what Jonglers do. He had sent his time voyager home.

PART III

ENSEMBLE

1.

HOMETIME HIGH

Slabs of sunlight pierced the windows of a jostling bus. Matt was sprawled on a bench seat in the back. His legs hung into the aisle next to a door announcing EMERGENCY EXIT.

He came to with a start. His face pruned against the harsh light. Sitting up with a grunt, his surroundings sharpened into focus.

He was in the back of a moving school bus. In the front of the bus, small heads jostled above seatbacks. The bus turned in front of a school. Matt recognized it as the grade school he had gone to. His mind grappled for traction. *Is this a dream? Am I in 1907 and dreaming of Belleplain? Or was 1907 a mega-dream after I went on a bender?* But he wasn't buying that. *If I'd been on a bender, where's the hangover?*

A sensation pulled his eyes down. The discovery startled him: he was wearing a three-piece black suit; it vaporized his mega-dream theory. His last moments in 1907 scrolled: Boston, the trolley, on the way to the Harvard game. He patted his jacket pocket. His wallet was where he had jammed it before trying to stop Alfred. A question bolted to mind. *Who won?*

The bus stopped. The tableau in front of him gave him pause. Rows of tiny faces peered over the backs of seats like prairie dogs eyeing an intruder. He realized they were kindergartners being delivered to their afternoon session.

The bus driver, wearing a North High Cyclones hat and a bewildered look, uttered a question. "Matt Grinnell?"

While the sight of a man riding their bus and wearing a funny-looking suit was puzzling, the sight of the star quarterback of the Cyclones wearing a funny-looking suit was too funny. The kindergartners erupted in giggles.

Matt yanked the lever on the emergency door, threw it open and jumped.

He ran around the grade school and up the small hill toward North High. Getting closer, he heard the sounds of a pep rally in the gym. He figured it was for a basketball game. He had been gone for over a month. But leaves still clung to the trees; there was no snow on the ground.

He ran past the main building toward a wing attached to the big high school. He threw open the glass doors to the library media center. Inside, he rushed to a bank of computers and googled HARVARD VS CARLISLE 1907. He clicked on the Wikipedia entry that came up.

His entrance hadn't been missed by a smattering of students who preferred study sessions to pep rallies. They stared at the guy in the three-piece suit with the overly neat hair and tried to place him. He looked familiar.

Also taking in the well-dressed young man wearing a shirt with an attached collar was the librarian. She hadn't seen an attached collar since she had helped a student with a paper called *Arrow Shirt Man: Fashion Superhero.*

Matt scanned the Wikipedia article. "C'mon. Where's the game?"

The librarian appeared on the other side of the computer table. "Can I help you?"

When Matt looked up, she recognized him and swallowed a gasp. If Matt Grinnell had reappeared with his flowing locks, cargo shorts and flip-flops, the librarian might have shouted for joy and welcomed him back with a hug. But the fact that his hair was shorn and he was wearing a strange outfit triggered her training in dealing with students who might have suffered a trauma. She reminded herself to remain calm, not bring attention to the student's unusual behavior and, if necessary, call 911.

"Yeah," Matt blurted. "I gotta know who won the game!"

The librarian peered over her glasses. "It hasn't been played. It's tonight."

He blinked in confusion. "What?"

She fought her growing concern. "The state championship, Matt. *Your* state championship."

His mind reeled, trying to comprehend. *I was in 1907 for almost six weeks but I've only been gone seven days?* As shocking as that was, it didn't shake his rabid desire to know. "Not *that* game, the Carlisle-Harvard game!"

A ripple of laughter sounded from the study geeks. They too had recognized Matt, and were witnessing the biggest jock at North High losing what little mind he had.

"The Carlisle-Harvard game?" the librarian echoed.

"Yeah, in 1907."

More laughter ensued from the study geeks.

Ignoring them like stadium noise, Matt threw the librarian another clue. "Jim Thorpe played in it."

"Carlisle-Harvard, 1907, Jim Thorpe," she reiterated. "Now *that* we can process." She waved for Matt to follow. "Come with me. I know just the book for you."

Running a gauntlet of incredulous stares, Matt followed the librarian into the stacks.

One of the students pulled out her phone.

Iris Jongler-Jinks liked to sit out pep rallies in the band room. She usually had it to herself and it gave her extra time to rehearse her audition piece for the summer programs at Julliard and Oberlin. She was playing a section of the Poulenc sonata when her phone sounded with a text alert.

She stopped playing, dug out her phone and read the

text: *Guess who's short-haired, dressed retro and going weird in the library? Makeover Matt Grinnell.*

Iris gasped, dropped her oboe in its case and dashed out of the band room as she fired up a new text.

In the gym, Arky Jongler-Jinks sat in the bleachers along with his cross-country buddies. Because the Cyclones' true QB1 was not seated on the gym floor with the rest of the team, the pep rally was more subdued than usual. Given the dim prospect of QB2, Gary Allen, carrying the Cyclones to the state title, there was watered-down joy in Belleplain.

A vibration in Arky's pocket signaled a text. He pulled out his phone and read it: *MB. Library.* At first it didn't compute. Then he saw it was from Iris.

He sprang to his feet and bounded down the bleachers, hitting the gaps between kids and ignoring their protests.

In the library's biography aisle, the librarian pulled a book off the shelf and handed it to Matt. "I think you may find Thorpe's account of the Harvard game in here." The book was titled *Jim Thorpe: Original All-American.*

Matt stared at the photo on the cover. It was a black-and-white shot of Jim in his practice uniform, cradling a football. His wide mouth held a faint smile; each dimpled corner of his mouth held a bottomless well of mischief. The fact that Matt had just been hanging out with the guy was almost too bizarre to fathom.

Matt flipped through the book, looking for Jim's account of the Harvard game.

The librarian reappeared at his side with another book. "This one tells about the game beginning on page one hundred and fifty-eight."

"Thanks," he said, eagerly taking the book.

As she left, Matt looked at the cover of the second book. It showed a picture of Carlisle players, in formation, ready to start a play. The halfback on the right was Jim. Matt scanned the title, *Carlisle vs. Army: Jim Thorpe, Dwight Eisenhower, Pop Warner . . .* He gave up; it was too long. He flipped to page 158.

2.

INTERVENTION

The account of the 1907 Carlisle-Harvard game began early in the second half with Mount Pleasant running back a punt, and breaking one tackle by flipping a Harvard player over his back. Mounty then ran the ball across the goal line as many of the 30,000 Harvard fans cheered his dazzling 85-yard run. The score was now 18-10 with Carlisle leading on a perfect autumn day, on a fast and dry field.

A few minutes later, a big Harvard lineman named Waldo Pierce lost it and decked Bill Gardner with a left hook right in front of the ref. Even though Pierce was tossed from the game, the incident rallied the Harvard side. A couple of plays later, a Harvard player hit Pete Hauser with such a brutal tackle, Hauser fumbled the ball and the Crimson recovered. Minutes later Harvard scored a touchdown and the game tightened to 18-15.

With about seven minutes left, the Redmen took possession on their own 10-yard line. Mounty urged his team, "We've got to score again!" In a quick series of runs and short passes that made Mounty look like a master of ceremonies, he moved the Redmen toward Crimson territory. Having advanced to their own 35, Mounty went for a long pass and threw to Bill Winnie, running down the left sideline. Winnie made the catch and ran it another thirty yards to the 4-yard line. Hauser pounded it over the goal line. When the final whistle blew, Carlisle had beat Harvard for the first time ever, 23 to 15.

Matt let out a whoop of joy and almost threw the book in the air.

He ignored the laughter from the study geeks but he

couldn't ignore the librarian when she appeared at the end of the stack. "Is everything all right?" she asked.

"Fantastic!"

He stuck his head back in the book and scanned the next paragraphs. After the Indians' triumph, they took the train back to Carlisle. They were met by a huge victory parade. Matt felt a stab of regret. *It would have been so cool to be there with Tawny.*

The thought stirred a memory. He reached into his jacket pocket and pulled out a piece of paper: Tawny's note. He turned it over and gazed at the drawing she had made for him. Taking in her beautiful face, he felt a lump in his throat. *Not the time or place,* he told himself. He tucked the note back in his pocket with a comforting thought. *I'll have her picture forever.*

Returning to the game account, Matt was struck by what wasn't there. There was no mention of a Carlisle player going missing before the game, or whether the Redmen had run the guard-back screen pass, or whether the Indians had played with clay handprints on their chests. There wasn't even a mention of Caleb Phillips's death.

Before he reopened the first book to see if Jim's biography recalled any of these things, Matt's eyes fell on the sentence beginning the last paragraph:

Thorpe had watched the entire Harvard game from the bench, but he knew his time was coming.

Iris was crossing the schoolyard and had almost reached the library media center when she heard her name. "Iris!" She turned to see Arky dashing toward her.

He caught up with her in front of the library's glass doors. "What are you doing here?"

"I wanna talk to Matt."

Arky tried not to shout. "Iris, we have a plan. Your job is to get the cor anglais. Where is it?"

"In the car in the parking lot."

"Then get it. I'll get Matt out of the library."

She didn't move. "It might be too late. He's in there wearing a retro suit and acting weird."

"I don't care if he's wearing a toga!" Arky's eyes darted around the schoolyard just as a muffled roar sounded from the gym. "Get the thing and bring it to the boys' locker room. We'll do it there."

"What if it doesn't work?"

"Then we're totally screwed. Now go!"

She didn't budge. "You gotta ask him about Mom, if he learned anything or saw her."

"I will. Now go!"

Arky bolted into the library. He slowed down and tried to look casual as he checked the stacks. Passing the biography aisle, he dismissed the guy in the dark suit, standing in the aisle with his face in a book. Arky moved to the next aisle before recognition dawned. He jumped back and stared at Matt. "Holy shit."

Matt looked up. "Ark, you're not gonna—"

"C'mon, QB One," Arky cut in as he plucked the book from Matt's hands, tossed it on the shelf and pulled him away. "You're in the wrong place, wrong time."

"No, I'm not," Matt protested as Arky hustled him through the study tables. "I wanna check those books out."

Arky pushed him toward the glass doors. "Plenty of time for that later. You're late for the pep rally."

The study geeks watched them go. The girl who had texted Iris weighed in. "Go bookworms!"

Moving Matt across the empty schoolyard, Arky grabbed the chance to fire questions. "Why'd you cut your hair?"

"I didn't do it." Matt chuckled at the memory. "A barber did, with help from some Indians."

"India Indians or American?"

"American." His voice rose with excitement. "Ark, you're not gonna believe where I went!"

"No, I believe it," Arky conceded. "You would *never* cut your hair, and you would never wear such a dorky suit."

Matt splayed his hands, showing off his threads. "I think it's cool."

"The point is—as impossible as it should be—Iris blew you to another bubble in the spacetime loaf."

"I don't know about a 'spacetime loaf,'" Matt said with a huge grin, "but I went to Carlisle, Pennsylvania, in 1907!"

Arky squashed the urge to ask a thousand questions and kept to the basics. "Did somebody named Jongler blow you back?"

"Yeah, Alfred Jongler, he's a music—" Matt's own curiosity kicked in. "How'd you know that?"

Arky noted the full name and moved on. "Not important. Did you see my mother?"

The random question made Matt stop. "No. Why would I see your mother?" His eyes widened with an epiphany. "You mean, she might've gone to the past too?"

"Doesn't matter," Arky snapped as he got Matt going again. "Now's not the time for trading intel. What nobody gets here is why Matt Grinnell isn't in the gym with the rest of the Cyclones. You gotta get your ass in there, but you can't go dressed like that."

"Why not?"

"You're QB One, not some freak from, what did you say, 1907?"

"Yeah, I played football for the Carlisle Indians."

A question exploded in Arky's head that he couldn't shut up. "How long were you there?"

Matt didn't hesitate. "Forty-one days."

"No shit?" Arky flashed on Iris's vision of the crosshatched marks Matt had been chalking on a wall.

"But it seemed like a lifetime," Matt added before flashing a smile. "I even got a nickname: Wrong Way."

Arky shook off the million other questions flying through his head and got back to job one. "Wrong way, right way, sideways, it doesn't matter now. You're QB One, you've got a team to war up, a game to win and a full-boat scholarship to nail to a Div One school. And you're not gonna do it looking like you're going to prom."

Matt laughed at another memory. "I went to a social. I'm a waltzing fool!" He tried to spin Arky in a turn but Arky fought it off and guided his giddy friend down the stairs leading to the locker room under the gym.

"Forget dancing," Arky ordered. "We've got scrambling to do!"

As much as Arky wanted to throw Matt in a car, drive to a safe house, and hear his entire story, Arky knew it would open a Pandora's box that could destroy the future he had mapped out for himself. He had to execute the damage-control plan he and Iris had concocted, and hopefully bury Matt's memory of time travel. If not, the skeleton of the Jongler cor anglais would be out of the closet, and the Jongler name would be "freak."

3.

COVER-UPS

In the locker room, Matt traded his suit and shirt for his football jersey and sweatpants while Arky grilled him about who else had seen him, besides everyone in the library, after he had gotten back.

As Matt dropped his black leather shoes in his locker and extracted his sneakers, he remembered that Tawny's note was still in the suit jacket. He couldn't leave it there; he needed it for good luck. But he felt weirdly self-conscious about the drawing on the back of the note; he didn't want Arky to see it. It was his secret.

Matt spotted the squeeze ball in his locker that he used to strengthen his throwing hand during long game-film meetings. He "accidentally" knocked the ball off the shelf. As it bounced and rolled away, Arky went to grab it. Matt pulled Tawny's note from the jacket pocket and slipped it in the thigh pocket of his sweats. Arky was none the wiser.

As Matt sat on the bench and put on his sneakers, he told Arky how one second he'd been in the back of a Boston trolley, the next he was in the back of a school bus.

Unbeknownst to them, Iris stood just inside the locker room door, out of sight. She held the Jongler cor anglais, fully assembled. She wasn't going to play it until she had heard as much of Matt's story as possible. She longed for every detail.

A roar from the pep rally in the gym overhead lifted Matt's eyes to the ceiling. "I still can't believe it's only been a week here and forty-one days there."

Again, Arky battled his curiosity. Anyone with half of

Einstein's brain would be an idiot not to debrief Matt on his journey. But this time something more powerful censored Arky. It wasn't his fear of the Jongler family being outed. It was an instinct as old as his Jongler bloodline. He fixed on Matt. "What happened to you in 1907 could have taken weeks or the blink of an eye. It doesn't matter. It was your training for *now*. Don't look back. Clear your head and play the game you were meant to play."

Matt stood up. "But that's the thing, Ark. I learned so much about playing football at Carlisle, I can't wait to share it with the team. That's what I'm gonna do up there."

Arky silently cursed Iris for not getting there yet with the cor anglais. His only option was to stall. "Matt, you gotta trust me on this. If you go up there and start blabbering about time travel, they're not going to put you in the game tonight, they're gonna put you in the nuthouse."

"Who cares?" Matt proclaimed. "We're not talking game changer, we're talking reality changer!"

Iris couldn't wait any longer. She lifted the curved cor anglais and began to play. Within seconds a familiar sensation stirred in her fingers. Her fingertips felt as light as down wafting on a breeze. The keys quickened with their own life.

Hearing the music confused Matt. At first he thought it was an audio flashback. Then he realized the tune was too sentient and clear to be in his head. It was coming from the other end of the locker room.

By the time he emerged from the row of lockers and saw Iris playing the old cor anglais, the melody had shifted to the racing staccato of a tune unfamiliar to human voice or hand, a tune belonging to the Jongler cor anglais alone. Strands of mist trailed from its bell and coiled across the floor.

Matt froze, confused and shocked. "I just got back!" he shouted as the first misty rope wound up his leg. It stilled him, locking him in its entwining grip.

Arky stood nearby, frozen in disbelief. He tried to shake away what he feared was his first episode of synesthesia. But snaking mists kept pouring from the cor anglais. Arky's faith in the solid sphere of science was unraveling before him as sure as the white strands swaddling his friend in a sphere of music.

As Matt disappeared inside the rippling cocoon, and the cor anglais segued to a playful variation of "Great Big Indian Chief Loved a Kickapoo Maiden," the cocoon's surface flickered and pulsed with erratic images: a shiny old jalopy motoring along, old-fashioned football players colliding at the line, an Indian girl in a long white dress spinning a parasol, Jim Thorpe grinning, salt-and-pepper shakers guarding a table, a man in a bandstand playing a cor anglais, Matt's hand opening and pressing on the chest of a bedridden Indian boy. The last scene sank in the mist, ending the picture show mesmerizing Iris and Arky.

As the cor anglais pulled a long last note from Iris, the misty cocoon contracted slightly and grew still. Then, with the note's dying vibration, the cocoon exploded in a radiating blast. The shock made Arky and Iris recoil.

When they straightened and opened their eyes, the twins were relieved to see Matt still standing there in his Cyclones jersey. His expression teetered between befuddled and blank, like someone who walks into a room and has forgotten what brought them there.

Arky and Iris didn't speak. They were holding their breath, waiting to see if the cor anglais had spun the magic they were hoping for.

A burst of cheers from the gym pulled Matt's eyes upwards. They darted back down to Iris. He stared at the curved wind instrument in her hands, then blinked into a sly smile. "Lemme guess, Iris. You took a wrong turn on the way to the band room?"

Iris cut a look to Arky and stopped herself from shouting, *Mom was right, it buried his memory!* Instead, she feigned an embarrassed laugh. "Right! What was I thinking?" She turned and exited with the cor anglais.

Still thunderstruck by what he'd seen, Arky gaped at his friend, unsure whether Matt's memory of 1907 was totally gone.

"You alright, Ark?" Matt asked. "You look like you've seen a ghost."

"No, no, I'm fine," Arky assured him as he collected his wits. "It's just my sister, she's such a loser."

Matt led the way to the door. "You should cut her some slack, Ark. She's not such a bad egg."

Hearing the expression fired Arky's worry. "Bad egg? Where'd you pick that up?"

"Dunno." Matt shrugged. "Probably from my granddad."

After the boys went up to the gym, Iris slipped back into the locker room. Finding the locker with Matt's name on it, she opened it and pulled out the clothes he had brought with him from the past. Feeling a weight in his jacket pocket, she reached in and pulled out his wallet. She quickly checked it—no evidence from the past—and put it on his locker shelf. Taking the clothes and shoes, she left.

4.

DÉJÀ VU

Matt's appearance at the pep rally whipped the students into a frenzy and dashed all rumors of their QB's fate. It also prodded Coach Watson to text Gunner Grinnell, informing him of his prodigal son's return.

After the rally, the coach escorted Matt to the principal's office where his father lay in wait. Gunner Grinnell ripped his son a new one for almost blowing everything they had worked toward for so many years. After venting his wrath, he finally got around to demanding to know where Matt had been for a week.

Matt explained what he knew. He had gone to the victory party at Arky's house the Friday before. He remembered leaving after he had ticked off his girlfriend, who had left him without a ride. He had begun to walk home . . . at this point Matt's scrambling ability kicked in. "I ran into a bunch of frats from BU who were on a road trip to drink their way around the state. 'Cause I was so miserable about Kelly dumping me, I took off with the frats and then one thing led to . . ." His voice trailed off.

Gunner's eyes hardened. "Led to what?"

Matt hung his head. "Bullshit."

"What are you talking about?" his father barked.

Matt looked up. "I don't know what happened. I remember leaving Arky's house . . . The next thing I remember was this afternoon, in the locker room, just before the pep rally."

"I'm not buying this crap!" Gunner exploded.

"Matt," the principal said, trying to infuse some calm. "The first time you were spotted this afternoon was on a school bus. You were wearing an old-fashioned suit."

Matt looked confused. "Really?"

"You don't even know what you were wearing?" Gunner sniped.

The principal kept his focus on Matt. "What was the suit about?"

"God, I dunno," Matt said, tossing his hands. "Maybe I ended up in a scavenger hunt and borrowed an old suit."

"Christ!" Gunner bristled. "When I was your age, I could lie better than that."

Matt shook his head with a wan smile.

His father didn't miss it and got in his face. "What's so funny?"

Matt met his father's blazing eyes. "You win, Dad. You're top dog."

Before Gunner could respond, the principal stood. "Mr. Grinnell, enough for now. I'm ready to render my decision."

Gunner jerked back in his chair.

The principal sat down. He turned to Matt. "While your absence from classes for a week is a problem, I believe we have mitigating circumstances. In fact, there's nothing in our Student-Athlete Code of Conduct listing amnesia as a reason to disqualify you from participating in a game. For that reason, I'm allowing you to play in the game tonight on two conditions. One, we get you to the hospital for a complete workup to make sure you haven't suffered a brain trauma." He leaned forward and lowered his voice. "Two, if anything like this happens again, Matt, in the spring, you will not be on the baseball team, and your high school diploma will be in jeopardy. Do you understand?"

Matt nodded. "Yes, sir." Despite feeling like he had just dodged a major bullet, something inside him flinched when he heard "sir" pop out of his mouth. He never said "sir." *Where did that come from?* he wondered.

On the way to the parking lot, Matt listened to his father lecture him about how lucky he was and how thankful he should be for having been born in a country that believed in second chances.

In the lot, Matt was about to get into Gunner's Expedition when the librarian flagged him down. She was carrying two books. "If I'm not mistaken," she said as she reached Matt, "I think you wanted to check these out." She handed him the books.

He took them and stared at one of the covers. It showed the photo of a young Jim Thorpe, in a simple uniform, holding a football. A recollection stirred. Matt had seen it somewhere before but he couldn't think of where. His eyes lifted to the librarian. "I don't remember wanting 'em . . . but I'll take 'em just the same. Thanks."

As Matt got into the SUV, Gunner glimpsed at the books in his hand. "What's with the interest in Thorpe?" he asked, the rancor still in his voice. "Something else you picked up on your 'scavenger hunt'?"

Matt studied the photo of Thorpe, still mystified by his sense of déjà vu. "Nah. They just look interesting."

"Wherever the hell you went," Gunner said as he started the car, "at least someone gave you a haircut."

Matt tugged at his short hair. It was the first time he'd noticed it had been cut. Oddly, even though it probably made him look like his father, the cut didn't bother him.

Gunner turned to him, his eyes seeming to glisten, and said quietly, "Don't ever scare me like that again."

Matt tweaked a smile. "Don't worry, Dad. It was a one-time thing."

At the BU Hospital, Matt was subjected to a battery of tests, including a CAT scan to determine if his amnesia had been caused by a brain trauma. While the tests showed residual evidence of some minor head bruises, there was nothing serious. He was found fit to play football.

Back at his house, Matt had a half hour before an early pregame dinner. He went to his room and stretched out on his bed, hoping to catch a power nap. Needing something to put him to sleep, he picked up one of the books the librarian had given him: *Carlisle vs. Army*. On the cover, an old black-and-white photograph showed Indian football players in position and ready to hike a bulbous football. Matt flipped through the book, stopping at a dog-eared page. It was something about the aftermath of a Harvard game in 1907. His eyes fell on a paragraph.

Thorpe had watched the entire Harvard game from the bench, but he knew his time was coming. Carlisle was becoming more dominant by the day, and as Thorpe joined his teammates in their victory march through town, he couldn't wait to become a starter and really give this town something to celebrate: a national championship.

Matt laid the open book on his chest and thought about it. In some ways he felt like Jim Thorpe. Even though Matt had always been a hotshot starter on every football team he'd ever played on, he felt like there was a piece of him still riding the bench, like the best football player he could be had yet to step on the field. But now, like Thorpe, Matt felt like "his time was coming."

He lifted the book back up to resume reading. As he raised his knees for a book rest, he felt something against his thigh. He reached into the side pocket of his sweats and pulled out a folded note of stiff paper. In black ink and flowing cursive someone had written, *For My Warriors. From Pigskin. P.S. I have one of you; you should have one of me.* An arrow pointed to the edge of the paper.

Matt was consumed by a sense of déjà vu, but he had no idea who "Pigskin" might be. Nor could he recall how the note had ended up in his pocket. He turned it over.

On the other side was a pencil drawing of a pretty girl with Indian features. Her long black hair fell over her shoulders onto a white shirt of some kind. Most striking about the drawing were the girl's eyes. They stared out with haunting intensity. Matt didn't know who she was, but as his insides ballooned with a strange warmth, he wished he could meet her and get to know her.

He dismissed his dreamy ruminations as the first hints of sleep. He tucked the note in the book and set it aside. It felt right. A note about warriors, with a picture of a pretty Indian girl, was a good bookmark for a book about Jim Thorpe and an Indian football team.

A few moments later, Matt was asleep.

After eating the five-egg omelet with a four-leaf clover his mother had made, Matt drove to North High, suited up with his fellow Cyclones, and boarded the bus that would take them to Belleplain University's stadium.

On the bus, Danny Bender sat next to Matt. Convinced that his amnesia story was a cover, Danny peppered Matt with questions about where he'd *really* been the last week.

Matt shut him down. "Danno, if I was making it up, you'd be the first to know. Now do me a favor. Shut up and get your inner cyclone spooled up so I can go over my three-play sets." He tapped the arm play holder on his left wrist. "One thing's for sure, I haven't looked at these in a week."

After Danny went quiet, Matt scanned the sets on his arm play holder. He was surprised how easily he remembered them; he could see each play unfold in his mind.

When he finished, Matt gazed out the window. They were

driving through downtown Belleplain as the descending dusk brightened the lights of storefronts. The passing scene and the reflection created by the dim lighting inside the bus comingled on the window. Matt stared at the mosh of light and movement, letting it become a disjointed movie. He recognized a familiar sensation; he was going into his pregame numb-out. He focused on his breath and let his mind go free-range. He let the wash of movement and blurring lights on the window become his mental screen. An image flashed. It was the book cover: Indian football players in old uniforms, set up over a fat ball.

Usually in his pregame numb, Matt just acknowledged the image and let it go, but this time the image of Indian football players did more than linger, it moved. It wheeled around and pivoted so Matt was looking down on it. The players shifted and the lineman playing left guard jumped back, leaving a hole in the line in front of him. The center hiked the ball to the quarterback, who handed off to the set-back guard as the guard dropped back to the pass. As much as Matt wanted to ignore the craziness of the play and keep free-ranging on the window, he couldn't. He was mesmerized. The guard with the ball pumped a fake downfield, then turned left and threw a screen pass to the player who had drifted out left: the quarterback.

Matt blinked, trying to get back to the random tumble of images. But the vision on the window reset. The all-Indian team was back in the same position with the left guard, set back, ready to run another play. Hypnotized by his daydream, he watched the play unfold.

"Grinnell!"

Matt broke from his reverie. "Huh?" He found Danny Bender, in his football uniform, standing in the aisle. Matt glanced around. The last players were getting off the bus. They were at the BU stadium.

"Are you gonna sit there and space," Danny demanded, "or get your head in the game?"

Matt wanted to ask Danny if he believed in the thing about sleeping with a book and absorbing what was in it, because that's what he was sure he had just seen: some plays out of the Carlisle playbook. He didn't ask, of course. He had to be QB1, not QB Flake.

5.

THE GAME

Forty thousand fans jammed into the stadium for the state championship between the Belleplain Cyclones and the Rockford Wolverines.

Usually Arky sat with his cross-country buddies, but he had decided against it because of the "tagalong" who had insisted on sitting with him. Iris was attending her first Cyclones football game ever.

Matt's mom and dad were seated at the 50-yard line, a few rows back for a good view of the field and for Gunner to keep an eye on the recruiters from Division 1 schools who had come to the game. Gunner was not only an ex-QB who knew how to read defenses, he was a salesman who could read people, even if all he could see was the back of their heads.

The game started fierce enough with twenty-two hopped-up players looking for a dogfight. The first quarter went scoreless as the Cyclones and the Wolverines probed each other's line with bruising runs and tested each other's secondary with a flock of passes. But neither side could put together a drive that got them into the red zone or within field-goal range.

In the second quarter, Matt followed Coach Watson's game plan laid out on his arm play holder. One of the major hurdles to sustaining a scoring drive was the Wolverines' linebacker, Jim Warpinski. He kept blitzing through the left side and chasing Matt out of the pocket or nailing him for a lose. Every time Matt got sacked, he heard Gunner yelling at him for not using his feet.

Late in the first half, the Wolverines drew first blood on a long pass for a touchdown. The roar of their fans was quickly muted when the Cyclones returned the kickoff for their own touchdown. The only thing spoiling the counterpunch was the extra point. The Cyclones booter had an excellent toe, but a six foot seven Wolverine on the D-line had better hands. He blocked the extra point. The first half ended with the Wolverines leading 7-6.

Halftime in the Cyclones locker room started with the line coach chewing out his O-line for letting Warpinski treat them like turnstiles. Danny, who was having a good game shutting down the Wolverines' number one receiver, claimed he had enough energy to go both ways, and would be happy to subject Warpinski to what Danny called his "rib-relocation program." Coach Watson hit the team with his usual platitudes about determination, gutting it out, and how the game was theirs to win. Matt kept his mind focused on the game plan and was relieved that his father hadn't made one of his locker-room appearances to inspire the team with a story about his glory days in the Big Ten.

Instead, Gunner lay in wait when the Cyclones came through the tunnel leading back to the field. Over the crowd noise, Gunner shouted dos and don'ts at Matt. Half hearing them came easy to Matt because of the cloud of fatigue enveloping him. While he was still clueless as to where he had been for the last week, one thing was certain: in the chemical warfare being waged in his body between adrenalin and drag-ass juice, drag-ass was winning.

The third quarter continued as a tight game dominated by defense. Then Matt aired out a long bomb to Tripp Olson that got the Cyclones inside the 2-yard line. Two plays later, the front line stepped up and Matt sneaked in behind key blocks. The Cyclones led for the first time, 12-7.

It must have fired up the Wolverines' windmill of a lineman because, once again, the giant got his mitts in the air and blocked the extra point.

The Cyclones' lead lasted deep into the fourth quarter until their halfback, Miguel Guzman, got stripped of the ball and a Wolverine recovered the fumble on the Cyclones' 30-yard line. A few plays later, they ran a sweep around the right side for a touchdown. When the extra point split the uprights, the Wolverines were back in front, 14-12, with fifty-eight seconds left on the clock.

The deflation on the Cyclones' side of the stadium was like a giant fist knocking the wind out of the fans and the team. Adding to their misery, the Cyclones were out of timeouts.

Miguel took the kickoff in the end zone, followed Coach Watson's orders, and took a knee for the touchback, stopping the clock.

Matt ran onto the field and gathered his team in a tight huddle. He spoke calmly. "This is clock management, guys. The coaches are out of it. It's our best eleven against their best eleven, and whoever makes the clock their twelfth man wins the game."

Tripp Olson gave voice to the baffled looks in the huddle. "'Best eleven'?"

Matt didn't know where he'd picked up the term but it didn't matter. "Shush and listen. Warpinski has been blitzing all night and he's not gonna stop. So we're gonna tempt him and shut him down with a QB sucker screen."

Miguel squinted. "That's not in the playbook."

"I know. It's in the playbook of Matt." He tugged his center closer and started to finger-draw the play on his jersey. "I want the entire left line to shift out one player."

Tripp butted in. "That'll give Warpinski a free pass."

"Exactly," Matt shot back as he pointed to his fullback. "But Tim's gonna fill the hole and we're gonna run a wildcat screen."

"Wildcat?" Miguel exclaimed. "We don't do wildcat."

"We do now," Matt ordered. After finger-drawing the rest of the play, he scanned his players' anxious eyes. "Everyone got it?"

"Yeah!" they boomed back.

Matt turned to Miguel. "Remember, time management. *Do not* get tackled inbounds. On set two."

They broke from the huddle and lined up in a formation the Carlisle Indians would have instantly recognized. Matt was set left of center in the guard-back position, with a huge hole in the line to sucker the blitz.

On the sidelines, Watson stared in disbelief.

In the stands, Gunner was equally stunned. He knew the Cyclones' playbook inside out; the old single wing wasn't part of it.

On Matt's "Set, set!" the ball shot back to Miguel lined up at tailback, set right of the center. Matt spun toward him, took the handoff and rolled right. Behind him, he heard the pop and crunch of Tim plowing into the left guard-back hole, taking out the Wolverines' rushing guard. Surprisingly, Warpinski resisted the blitz, following Matt right and covering the flat. Looking downfield, Matt spotted his end and right flanker pulling the secondary deep right. He pumped once, pulling the play further right, then glanced left and saw the Wolverines' line release toward him, including Warpinski. Matt turned left, set and delivered a bullet to Miguel near the left sideline.

Matt got hit after his release, but the pain of being slam-sandwiched between beef and turf was blown away by the explosion of sound from the Cyclones' side of the field. He struggled to his feet and saw Miguel dart out-of-bounds just short of the 50-yard line. The play had only eaten eight seconds off the clock.

In the stands, Arky and Iris had rocketed to their feet along with everyone else. Iris was jumping up and down, trying to see over the bellowing fans in front of them. "What happened?" she shouted.

Arky's celebration was infused with shock. "They ran a wildcat! They've *never* run a wildcat!"

Iris stopped craning to see and gaped at her brother. "What did you call it?"

"The wildcat!"

As lightning leaps from cloud to ground, "wildcat" bolted through Iris, illuminating something she had seen on her computer that afternoon.

Down on the field the Cyclones huddled up. Matt noticed some of his players checking out the sideline, trying to get a read on Coach Watson, who seemed torn between pumping his fists and throwing his hands in furious incomprehension.

"Forget the sidelines," Matt ordered. "Coach said this is ours to win and that's what we're doin'. They're thinking short pass to get us in kicking range; we're going long. Same wildcat formation but this time we make Warpinski see red." Matt tugged his center closer, finger-drew the play and issued assignments. "Everyone got it?"

"Got it!" the Cyclones echoed.

"On 'split.'"

Matt set behind center and shouted a gibberish audible as Warpinski danced behind his guard barely able to hold back before blitzing the hole in the left-guard gap. To really set his head on fire, Matt went in motion by the hole as he yelled another audible. "Omaha, red-red, peek-a-boo-pinski!"

In the stands, Gunner looked apoplectic over the double insanity: a QB in *motion* while shouting a gibberish audible. His dream of getting Matt to the NFL was going up in smoke. The recruiters exchanged baffled looks.

On the sideline, Coach Watson was speechless.

Matt reversed motion and headed for the gap between his two backs. A moment before he got there he shouted "Hut, hut, split!" The center rifled the ball at Matt. He took it on the move and rolled right. In his peripheral he saw Warpinski and the Wolverine guard disappear behind the bulldozer blade formed by Miguel and Tim filling the gap.

As Matt stepped back to plant he saw Chase covered deep right, but Tripp had gotten jets and beaten his man. Matt stuck his back heel and launched a bomb.

The stadium went quiet as the ball arced through the blaze of lights.

Tripp turned to find the ball and bring it in. But in that moment where the glory of what you're about to do fogs your vision, he took his focus off of finishing the catch. He turned toward the end zone a nanosecond too soon. The ball slipped through his hands.

The reaction from the Cyclones' side was a howl of disappointment; the Wolverines' side exploded with delight.

The only person in the stadium who hadn't seen the bobble was the cornerback, who, having almost caught up with Tripp, had left his feet in a desperate dive to make the tackle. He hit Tripp and they both landed hard.

6.

MISDIRECTION

Matt shook off his disappointment and checked the clock, which had been stopped by the incomplete pass. He looked downfield. Tripp Olson wasn't getting up. Matt's mind raced on double tracks: concern for Tripp and the realization that Olson was his go-to guy on the next play.

The trainers ran across the field as Tripp gripped his knee and writhed in pain.

"Matt!" he heard Watson shout. He turned to the sideline as the coach threw a gesture. "Get over here!"

In the stands everyone was still on their feet. Seeing Matt jog toward the sideline, Arky turned to fill Iris in on what was happening. He stared at the empty space next to him, shaking his head. *Leave it to Iris to come to her first game and leave at the climax.*

Matt reached the sideline and told Watson, "I need Bender in for Olson."

Watson shouted an order, "Bender in!" then returned to Matt. "What the hell are you doing out there?"

"Trying to win the game," Matt answered.

"I mean the plays, what's with the wildcat?"

"We set 'em up with deception, now we hit 'em with misdirection." After the words popped out of his mouth, Matt was almost as startled as Watson. Matt wasn't sure where the words had come from, but it didn't matter. They felt as right as anything he had ever said.

Their standoff was interrupted by the buzz of a phone. Watson dug in his pocket. Matt's eyes flew to the stands, to

Gunner, cell phone in hand, glaring at him. Watson pulled his phone out and checked the text.

"Is that my dad with a play?" Matt demanded.

The coach nodded. "Yeah."

"I bet he wants a play that makes me shine for the recruiters."

Watson nodded again. "Something like that."

"I bet the Wolverines are thinking the same."

"Most likely."

Matt stripped off his arm play holder and tossed it on the ground. "Tell 'im I've got one of my own."

As Matt turned and headed back on the field, the coach's face twitched into a smile. "Hey, Grinnell." Matt turned back; Watson added a thumbs-up. "It's yours to win."

Heading to the huddle, Matt saw the trainers helping Tripp off the field. Matt knew his receiver's agonized expression was a mash-up of physical pain and misery over dropping the pass. Matt called out to him. "Hey, Tripp, no worries. This one's for you."

Matt reached the huddle, with Danny replacing Tripp at left end. Matt called the play: "QB sucker reverse." Using his center as a whiteboard, Matt began finger-tracing the second wildcat option he had seen in the bus window.

In the stands, Arky stood along with every Cyclones fan, craning to see if Matt could pull off the impossible.

In the huddle, Matt finished with, "Remember, time management. Get the ball OB. On first 'set.'"

The Cyclones lined up with twenty seconds on the clock. Again, Matt set behind the open left-guard slot, the "QB sucker" position. As he called a fake audible he could see the doubt in Warpinski's face; after his previous blitz had been stuffed, he was caught on the fence. On "Set!" the ball shot back to Miguel, Tim crossed to fill the guard hole, and Miguel moved left.

Matt eye-locked on Warpinski, still trying to read the play

and make his move. In his peripheral, Matt saw Miguel hand off to Danny peeling off the left end for the sweep to the right side. Warpinski had missed his chance.

Matt took off right and spotted the Wolverines' defensive end shift out to stop Danny from clearing the corner. Matt went full out, lowered his shoulder and leg-drove into the D-end with such force he took the player off his feet like he was a stuntman in a pull harness.

Danny shot around the corner and headed downfield. He only made one mistake. When the cornerback came up on him, Danny juked a move inside before going for the sideline, misjudged the cornerback's quickness, and got tackled inbounds on the 24-yard line.

Matt's eyes flew to the clock: ten seconds and clicking. He screamed at his team to get to the line as the Cyclones kicker ran onto the field.

The left side of the Cyclones line, confused by the super hurry-up, set up as they had for the last three plays, with the empty guard hole gaping wide, giving the Wolverines' giant a clear shot at smothering the field-goal kick. There was no time to shift. Matt jumped in the hole.

As the clock ticked down to one, the ball flew back to the holder.

Matt drove off his legs low and hard at the big man's midsection as he uncoiled to block the kick. Matt hit him so hard he folded like a flip phone.

The ball sailed over them clear and away.

Pinned under the big man and a Wolverine pile, unable to see the kick, Matt realized every lineman had something that the glory boys who ran and caught the ball rarely experienced: they *heard* before they saw. What Matt heard was a human bomb go off, detonated by Cyclones fans.

The field goal was good, making it 15-14.

The Cyclones had won the state championship.

In the insane rush of fans pouring onto the field, Coach Watson found Matt and shouted over the pandemonium. "Where the hell did that end-run set-up play come from?"

Matt wanted to tell him the truth—*From a bus window*—but he didn't want Coach thinking he was totally insane. Instead, he shouted back, "I just figured the last thing they expected was a blocking quarterback."

After the celebration on the field funneled into the locker room, Gunner finally got to his son.

Matt could read the dos and don'ts in his father's eyes. Before he could say a word, Matt intervened. "Dad, you've always taught me winning is everything. Can we just leave it at that?"

Gunner read the resolve in his son's face, and moved on to other matters: the praise the recruiters had heaped on Matt for how he'd led his team, particularly in the last series as he marched the Cyclones to victory. In fact, several of them were waiting in a luxury box to meet him.

Matt listened, then told his father that he wanted to go celebrate with his team before he started pressing the flesh with the recruiters.

Gunner let him go with two caveats. "No going AWOL, and no getting suckered into a scavenger hunt, okay?"

Matt smiled. "Been there, done that."

As Matt turned to leave, Gunner gave him a pat on the shoulders. "Great game, son."

7.

PARTY

Since Arky and Iris had served their week of being grounded, and because their father was as excited as anyone about the Cyclones winning State, Howard allowed, with his supervision, an after-game party to be held at the Jongler-Jinks house.

After school and before the game, Iris had grilled Arky and learned that Matt had gone to Carlisle, PA, in 1907, and played football at an Indian school. While she was disappointed that Matt had learned nothing about their mother, Iris was thrilled to hear it was their great-great-grandfather, Alfred Jongler, who possessed the cor anglais at the time and had sent Matt back. In her follow-up research online, Iris confirmed that Matt had gone to the Carlisle Indian Industrial School, which had fielded an excellent football team. She also verified that the clothes she had taken from his locker matched the styles of 1907.

It was this follow-up research, which included a reference to the "wildcat," that had made Iris bolt from the game and race home to learn more about Carlisle football. It confirmed what she had suspected. Matt running plays from the wildcat wasn't something he had made up. *He'd brought it with him from the past.* However, as much as Iris was fascinated by how football in the past had changed Matt's game *on* the field, she was more intrigued by how the past might have changed his game *off* the field.

As tempted as Iris was to stay at home and observe Matt at the party, she decided against it. Of course she wanted to ask him endless questions, but she didn't want to raise suspicions. And she certainly didn't want to come across as some fawning football groupie because he had won State. As the party ramped up, Iris was in her room, preparing to leave and spend the night at a friend's.

Despite Howard's presence, the cheerleaders had smuggled several cases of beer into the basement. The victory juice was being disguised in plastic cups.

Matt's girlfriend, Kelly, had accepted his apology for his prank with the topless video and had forgiven him. The two of them sat on the couch in the crowded living room as Matt nursed a beer. He was back to his jock uniform of cargo shorts and flip-flops. The new item was a black t-shirt that boasted STATE CHAMPS in gold.

As much as Matt liked having Kelly back and being the object of her adulation, his uncertainty had not gone away. But his doubts were no longer about how she was a great Horizontal who might never make the leap to a Vertizontal. In fact, he wondered if the whole Vertical-Horizontal-Vertizontal thing was stupid and "caveman" like Arky had said. It was more compli-cated than that. He took a swig of beer and tried to stop himself from thinking about it. He was supposed to be celebrating. But he couldn't escape a thought. *The two things we have in common, sex and popularity, don't exactly add up to real conversation.* Which triggered another thought. *Something's missing.*

Matt half listened to Kelly chatter to her friend, Becca, who occupied the other half of the couch along with Tripp, his knee encased in a leg brace and packed with ice. Matt scanned the crowd of bodies jamming the room. They reminded him of buoys bobbing in a crowded harbor. A gap opened between two human buoys; Matt's gaze moved through it. On the far side of the room he saw the statue he had visited so many times. *Oh my God,* he mouthed as he stared at the Egyptian figure with its touchdown arms rising from the top of its head. In the hours before the game, he had totally forgotten about Dr. TD. He couldn't believe they had won State without his traditional visit. Matt raised his cup, offering a toast. "You da god."

Kelly's face swung in front of him. "I'm not a god, I'm a goddess."

Matt bobble-headed. "No doubt."

She crooned "Hel-lo" in her signature way of turning the word into a call for attention. His forced smile made her draw back. "Is something wrong?"

He shook his head. "Nah"—and flashed a genuine smile— "it's all good."

"Then you better start acting like it, buster, or you might miss out"—she pushed her chest into him—"on two more *touchdowns.*"

As Kelly bit his neck and growled, Matt spotted Iris squeezing through the crowd in the kitchen. She had her backpack on; a black music case protruded from the top.

When Iris reached the door leading to the garage, she turned. Through the gauntlet of kids, she was startled to see Matt on the couch, looking at her. She faltered—his eyes were an invitation—but she checked herself. *All the questions,* she told herself, *have to wait.*

Matt watched Iris open the door to the garage.

When Kelly pulled back, he stood up.

"Where are you going?" she asked.

He held up his cup. "Grabbin' a refill."

8.

GARAGE BANTER

In the garage, Iris opened the rear door of the Subaru. She stopped when she saw Matt come through the kitchen door. She smothered her surprise. "Ah, the party's behind you."

"I know," he acknowledged. "I just wanted to ask you something. Actually a couple things."

She swung her backpack into the backseat. "Ask away."

"I get why you're leaving." He hooked a thumb at the music and noise behind him. "A bunch of loud jocks and their crew swilling beer. I especially get it after the last party here."

Iris shut the car door. As much as she was dying to know what he remembered from their encounter in her bedroom before he was blown away, she played the dead hand. "You said you had a question."

He motioned toward her backpack in the backseat. "It's Friday night. Why are you taking your oboe with you?"

The question stoked her curiosity. Even though it was her oboe and not the Jongler cor anglais, his query begged another. *After a time traveler returns, do they fixate on wind instruments like dogs on sticks? See one and they have to chase it?* "I'm going to a friend's house for the night," she explained. "We have rehearsal tomorrow and a recital in a week."

He nodded. "That's cool."

She ignored his newfound appreciation of music and kept fishing. "So you remember I play the oboe."

"Actually," he said sheepishly, "you played it for me once. Remember?"

"Oh, right," she said, playing along, "in my room."

He shifted uncomfortably. "Iris, I don't remember every-thing that happened—"

"It was only a week ago," she interjected.

"Right. Although, it seems a lot longer."

She studied him for a hint of irony. He looked more embar-rassed than anything. She continued her inquiry. "So what do you remember about that night?"

"I remember going to your room and asking for a juggling lesson, and when you said no, I kinda made you play the oboe for me." Heat rushed to his cheeks.

"And after that?" she asked. "What do you remember?"

"Nuthin. Not for days. I'm just hoping I don't pop up on Face-book doing crazy stuff. It could screw up my shot at a scholarship."

She resisted telling him not to worry; they didn't have Face-book in 1907. "No," she clarified, "what I meant is, what do you remember right after I played for you? Do you remember what happened next?"

Matt's face got redder. "No. Nuthin else happened, right? I mean, we didn't—"

She saved him the agony. "Nothing else happened. You were pretty tipsy. You left and went on your bender."

"I owe you an apology for being such an asshole."

"Matt, I really appreciate that—you know, thought that counts and all—but nobody should have to apologize the night they're state champs and the game's MVP."

"Yeah, that's most valuable prick." He banged himself on the head. "That didn't come out right."

Iris laughed. "I guess not. So take your foot out of your mouth and go enjoy your victory bash before my dad shuts it down when he discovers the beer."

Matt was grateful she was letting him off the hook. But he didn't want to end it there. "Okay, I'll go, but would it be okay if I came to your recital?"

She stared at him, not sure if he was sincere, putting a move on her, or really being the dog after a stick. "Why would you do something like that?"

"To hear you play again."

"That's funny," she said. "I finally saw *you* play tonight."

"You did?"

"Yeah. I was at the game. It was fun except for the part where every guy tries to kill the other guy."

"That's what you see at first, but there's more to it than that," he explained with a hint of excitement.

"Really?"

"Yeah, you have to look at football like ballet with collisions." Again, the weird words coming out of his mouth surprised him. But it was nice; they made Iris smile.

"Never heard that one," she said.

"Neither have I, till now."

"What's more fun? The dancing or the collisions?"

He grinned. "I'm a quarterback; I'm a dancer."

She laughed at his unjock-like claim. "Quarterback, dancer, I'm sure you've got all sorts of hidden talents."

"Yeah, except one." Matt dug in his cargo pockets and pulled out a Hacky Sack ball, the ball from his locker and an apple. "I still don't know how to juggle."

Iris blinked in disbelief. "You're kidding, right?"

His face set with mock gravity. "I never kid about the nerd sport. Please, just gimme the first move I need to work on."

"Okay," she conceded. "But then I gotta go."

"Deal."

"First off, put the apple away. We don't need it." He did. She motioned him over. "Gimme."

He came around the front of the car and handed over the Hacky Sack and the ball. She held them in her right hand and tossed them in the air one at a time, catching and throwing with only one hand. "Once you can do this with each hand, you add a third ball, and you're juggling."

"It's that easy?"

"Pretty much." She flipped him the Hacky Sack and the ball. "Try it."

He tossed and caught them a couple of times before fumbling and dropping them. They both bent down to retrieve the Hacky Sack and the runaway ball at the same time.

The door to the kitchen opened and Arky entered the garage just as Matt and Iris stood up, rising into view from behind the car. Arky stopped short, imagining the worst. "You gotta be kidding."

Matt's hand shot up with the ball. "She's teaching me how to juggle."

Arky flailed his hands. "That's how it all begins! And the last time you two got together . . ." his voice trailed off. He gestured toward the party. "They're calling your number, MVP."

Matt took the Hacky Sack from Iris and shot her a grin. "Thanks for the lesson." He started for the door and turned back. "See you at the thing next week."

Arky waited for Matt to disappear, then turned back to his sister. "'The thing next week'? What's that about?"

She shrugged. "He's coming to my recital. He seems to have a new fascination with oboes."

He glared at her. "Iris, don't even think about going there again."

"But, bro," she teased as she opened the driver's door, "one lesson does not make a juggler."

"I'm not talking about that, I'm talking about the cor anglais!"

"Oh right," she deadpanned. "We need to talk about that, too." She slid behind the wheel.

"There's nothing to talk—" Arky was cut off by the car door shutting.

9.

FINAL TUNE

Late Saturday morning, Iris returned from her rehearsal to find Arky cleaning up the house from the party. She went to their mother's attic office and made several preparations. Then she waited for their father to leave.

After he did, Iris looked for her brother. His door was shut and she could hear the shower running. She wrote a note and slipped it under his door: *Meet me upstairs. I have something amazing to show you.* She went back to the attic.

When Arky opened the door of the attic office, a quick scan of the room told him something was up. Iris was sitting in their mother's practice chair. On the bookshelf were some items he had hoped to ignore for a while. The Jongler cor anglais rested on the folded suit and shirt Matt had been wearing when he had returned. Arky recognized their mother's journal, *The Book of Twins: Sphere of Music.* Next to it was a photo album.

"I have five minutes," he announced. "What's up?"

Iris motioned for him to sit opposite her in the chair at the desk.

He exhaled a sigh. "Really?"

"Really." She waited for him to sit. "I did some research on the Carlisle Indian School. Everything Matt told you about the place is true."

He shrugged indifferently. "Okay."

She waved at the computer behind him. "Click the mouse."

He did, and the screen filled with an old black-and-white photo of a circular bandstand.

"That's the bandstand in the middle of the Carlisle quad," she explained.

He turned back to her. "So?"

She handed him the old photo album. "This is Mom's Jongler family album."

He opened it to a bookmarked page. He stared down at an old photo of what looked like the same bandstand. Standing on the top step was a slight man in a band uniform. He bore a surprising resemblance to Arky.

"That's Alfred Jongler, our great-great-grandfather," she announced, unable to hide her excitement. "He taught music at Carlisle in 1907."

"And he most likely had the old cor anglais. We know that." Arky closed the album and handed it back. "So what's the amazing thing you wanna show me?" He tapped his watch. "The Cyclones' victory parade starts at noon."

She stared at him, puzzled by his apathy. "Arky, don't you get it? If Matt was sent to a time and place where there was a Jongler to send him back home when he was ready, then the same is true for Mom. She's back in time, but things haven't worked out for a Jongler to send her back."

"Okay," he conceded without matching her intensity. "But Matt was gone a week; Mom's been gone more than a year. Why did Matt get the express and Mom's stuck on the local?"

"Because Matt *changed*!"

"Changed?"

"You know he has," she insisted.

"He might've picked up a few quirks from 1907," he admitted. "But it's not like his time-warp road trip mutated him into a superhero and he's going to start saving the planet on a daily basis."

She swallowed her frustration. "That's not the point."

"What is the point?"

"There was a bunch of stuff—the way Matt treated people, the way his dad treated him, his doubts about playing football—messing with his destiny. You said it yourself in the locker room. You told him, 'Play the game you were meant to play.' You were talking about his destiny."

Arky admitted it was a weird moment, especially after watching Matt lead the Cyclones to victory using the wildcat. "I said it to get him up to the pep rally."

"You were doing more than that and you know it," she insisted. "You were being a Jongler. Why can't you accept that? Why can't you accept that somehow the cor anglais knows when a person's destiny is out of whack, and it can help them by sending them to the past?"

Arky sat back with a resigned look. "Okay, I knew this was coming, so let's do it. Lemme tell you what I accept. There's decent proof that Matt went back in time." He waved at the suit. "He came back with evidence, and what he told me was fairly convincing. And lucky for us, the cor anglais did what Mom thought it might: repress his memory of what happened to him. I accept that some things happened that can't be explained by science. But, and it's a big but, the laws of nature are tested by *repeated* experiments. If the same experiment yields the same outcome, the law is confirmed. That's how science works."

"Exactly," Iris interjected. "And the other 'experiment' is Mom. She's stuck in the past too."

"We can't prove that."

"What do you call the note she left me?" She snatched the journal off the shelf. "What do you call her writing about time travel?"

"That's *circumstantial* evidence." He tossed a hand at the cor anglais. "The only thing we have is that."

"But—"

"Lemme finish," Arky entreated. "I admit"—he pointed at

the cor anglais—"that thing scares the crap out of me. It's rocked my world. But I'm not ready to *change* my world for it, not yet. If I was, I'd drop out of school and devout my life to understanding what makes the cor anglais tick. Which is exactly what Mom was doing and look what happened to her. The point is, we haven't found her other research on the cor anglais, *The Book of Twins: Sphere of Science.* All we've got"—he gestured to the leather-bound journal—"is her *Sphere of Music* and the spider crook. We're missing the third leg of the stool. And until we find it, I'm gonna keep my marbles"—he tapped his head—"in the sphere of science. I'm gonna learn everything I can about quantum physics, astrophysics, the block universe theory and the possibility of spacetime travel."

"But, Arky," Iris finally said, "we *know* it's possible. That's why we have to try to find Mom now."

"How are we gonna do that?"

She rested a hand on the cor anglais. "By sending one of us back."

Arky let out a laugh. "Right now?"

"I've got a feeling the time is right."

He stood up. "And I've got a feeling I'm going to miss the victory parade if I don't get out of here."

She looked up at him. "Arky, if you're right, that it was a one-time freak accident with Matt, then there's no harm in trying. If you don't wanna do it for me, do it for Dad."

He returned his sister's gaze. "If I sit down, and I'm still here when you're done playing, will you please, please, please let me go back to normal, at least for a while."

Iris smiled and gave him a nod. "Sure."

He sat. Even though he was risking a statistically invalid possibility, he wasn't going to let her see him sweat. "Go ahead, sis, blow me away."

Iris wetted the reed and began to play. She played a section from the Poulenc sonata. She played beautifully. But the keys didn't lighten in her fingers. They didn't press back. Not a wisp of mist emerged from the bell.

As she finished, her eyes brimmed with tears. She had never played so well. The music had soared like wind from her soul. But she had merely played an old and curved cor anglais adorned with a spiderweb inlay and a spider on the bell. She had not played well enough.

"Impressive," Arky said quietly, "it really was. But if the spider crook only comes to life when someone's destiny is out of whack, then our destinies must be humming along. We're where we're supposed to be: here and now." He stood up. "And we've both got a life to live."

"So does Mom," Iris said as she placed the instrument across her knees. "I'm going to keep trying to find her, no matter where she is."

At the door, Arky turned back with a gentle smile. "If you play your oboe like that for your auditions in February, you're gonna nail 'em."

10.

VICTORY PARADE

Before the Cyclones began their parade along Main Street, a large crowd, decked out in black and gold, had gathered at the town center. On a stage erected for the occasion was the football team, with a huge STATE CHAMPIONS banner riffling in the breeze behind them. After praising the team for their triumph, Coach Watson presented the game ball to the MVP, Matt Grinnell.

To great cheers and applause, Matt accepted the football. He stared at what was painted on it: STATE CHAMPS: BELLEPLAIN 15 – ROCKFORD 14. Holding the ball triggered a sensation; it felt oddly small in his hands, like it was youth sized. The feeling rendered him oblivious to the quieting crowd waiting for him to speak.

Danny broke the growing silence with a wisecrack. "Hey, Grinnell, you're not gonna cry, are ya?"

An explosion of laughter yanked Matt back to the crowd and the waiting microphone. "No," he said, "I was thinking how this ball feels small compared to the huge contribution everyone made in last night's game, and every game that led up to the Cyclones taking State."

His proclamation produced a deafening cheer.

He waited for the throng to quiet. "Next year, us seniors will be gone, and the team will be different. But the sophomores and juniors will step up to fill our cleats and pads and deliver their own brand of smack."

He grinned as he got a laugh. "And the year after that, another batch of seniors will move on." He paused, not having a clue where he was going with the thought. The crowd went silent as he groped for another sentence. Thought failed him. Nonetheless, words welled up and poured out. "What I wanna say is that we're all Cyclones. And no matter where being a Cyclone spins us, or where being a Cyclone sets us down, I just want everyone to remember"—he held up the game ball—"it's not about a ball. It's about the game that's played around it, on the field, off the field, and in every direction in space and time."

The breathless silence that followed surprised Matt as much as his words. It wasn't like calling an audible—reacting to what's in front of you—it felt like someone else had spoken for him. And as quickly as the voice had possessed him, he was back to tongue-tied Matt, grappling for a final word. He thrust the ball in the air and shouted, "I love you all! Thanks!"

As the crowd exploded with cheers, Arky stood at the back, studying his friend. Arky had hoped that coming to the victory parade would thrust him back into the world of normal, and that, just as the cor anglais had hidden Matt's memory of 1907, the celebration would tamp down Arky's memory of the last week. But Matt's sentimental speech had done the opposite. It made Arky face an agonizing truth: his sister was right. Matt had done more than change, he had transformed. He now possessed qualities more life-changing than skills on a football field. Even if the cor anglais had tucked away his memory of the past, those qualities were now woven into the fabric of Matt. They were coded in his DNA.

The insight pushed Arky into new and foreign realms. *If Matt can reset his inner compass by a forty-day immersion in the past,* he ruminated, *why would it take Mom so long to do the same? How could she have wandered so far off course that such a long journey to the past was necessary? What did she do? Was it so unspeakable that she's been sent to the past for life?*

Or, he continued to muse, *is Einstein 101 at play? Relativity. Is the span of a year in our present the span of a day in Mom's past?*

The blast of the band launching into the Cyclones' fight song yanked Arky's tether and brought him back to earth. "C'mon, dude," he muttered. "You got a parade to march in."

In the attic office, Iris was still sitting, silent, motionless. She broke from her reverie and looked down at the cor anglais resting on her legs. An urge stirred. She reached out and put her fingers on the black spider carved in high-relief on the instrument's bell. As she stared at her hand and wondered where the impulse had come from, her fingertips seemed to rise and fall.

She blinked. Was it a twitch? Or had her fingers been moved by a ripple in the wood?

Despite the fear that the spider might be coming to life, Iris's mind churned. *The cor anglais comes to life when someone's destiny is threatened. It came to life for Mom. It came to life for Matt. Did it just ripple under my fingers because* my *destiny is in danger?*

Iris didn't know the answer. She only knew what all Jonglers know. *Tempus omnia revelat.*

Time reveals all things.

APPENDIX:

1907 FACT AND FICTION

Pop Warner and the Native Americans at the Carlisle Indian School were really there in 1907; they are presented true to character and the historical record. The fictional exceptions are Alfred Jongler, Caleb Phillips and Tawny Owl. Caleb and Tawny could have easily been students at Carlisle. "Pigskin" did write squibs about football in *The Arrow*, but Pigskin's true identity remains unknown.

All the Carlisle football games, scores and game accounts happened as depicted. Pop Warner's trick plays are not a trick of fiction; they all happened, too.

For a nonfiction look at how Pop Warner and the Carlisle Indians revolutionized football in the early 1900s, see Sally Jenkins's fantastic book, *The Real All Americans*.

The original meaning of "cor anglais" was indeed "horn of angels." The woodwind instrument was invented in the 1720s in Silesia, now part of southeastern Poland. However, a cor anglais decorated with a spider motif and the powers of time travel has yet to be crafted ... that we know of.

The Cumberland County Historical Society, Carlisle, PA

Part of the Carlisle Indian School Quad. The Girls' Quarters building is on the right, with the bandstand beyond it. Girls, in their white dresses, can be seen on the Girls' Ground.

The Cumberland County Historical Society, Carlisle, PA

The Starting 11 for the 1907 Carlisle Indians:
Back row (L-R): Hauser, Exendine, Afraid of a Bear, Gardner
Middle row (L-R): Payne, Aiken, Lubo (Captain), Little Boy, Wauseka
Front row (L-R): Hendricks, Mount Pleasant

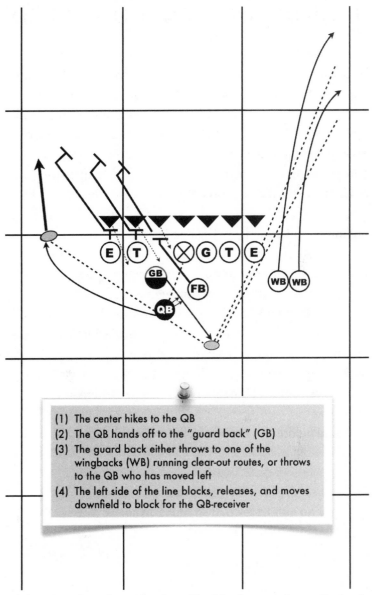

(1) The center hikes to the QB
(2) The QB hands off to the "guard back" (GB)
(3) The guard back either throws to one of the wingbacks (WB) running clear-out routes, or throws to the QB who has moved left
(4) The left side of the line blocks, releases, and moves downfield to block for the QB-receiver

While Tawny showed Matt her "guard-back broken wing" using Pop's salt-and-pepper shakers, this is how a coach might draw it up.

BLOWBACK TRILOGY CONTINUED

In *Blowback '63*, Iris and Arky continue their search for their mother, Dr. Octavia Jongler. Their rescue mission is blown off course when Iris and the cor anglais perform a shocking double blowback: Arky and his friend, Danny Bender, are launched back to 1863 and the Civil War. As the Union and Confederate armies camped on opposite sides of a river ramp up to the Battle of Chancellorsville, the boys find themselves on a "battlefield" forgotten by history: in the spring of '63, "baseball fever" broke out in the Yankee and rebel camps.

Meanwhile, back in Belleplain, Iris plays a dangerous game with Matt as she tries to unlock his memory of time travel to help her retrieve Arky, Danny and her mother.

After being pressed into the Union Army, Danny, a pitching ace, is recruited into a series of games that climax in a secret matchup between the Yankees' "best nine" and the rebels' best nine. It's up to Arky to find a Jongler with the cor anglais and get them back to their hometime before a boy's game turns into a man's war.

And before Iris and Matt fall head over heels.

ACKNOWLEDGMENTS

This story would not have been possible without the critical eye of my go-to editor Gerri Brioso and our countless trips to the "woodshed." Gerri continues to patiently escort me there as I continue the *Blowback Trilogy*. I also thank other "feedbarkers" who have lent their hearts and minds during the story's evolution: Nathanial DeMelis, Pierre Ford, Sara Crowe and Frank Taylor.

A tip of the hat to my cowboy friend, Vern Smith, for telling me about *The Real All Americans*, by Sally Jenkins, which mines the vein of the Carlisle Indian School and football, and was the inspiration for my story. Besides Ms. Jenkins's fascinating account, I am thankful to Tom Benjey and Lars Anderson for their masterful and deep histories on Carlisle football. It is the writers of history that prove "truth is stranger than fiction." A note of gratitude must also be sounded for the wonderful oboist, Lauren Williams, who spent a musical afternoon introducing me to the modern cor anglais.

Last but not least, an arms-around thanks to my Three Muses: Cindy, Holly and Kendall Meehl. Their truth beats my fiction every day.

ABOUT THE AUTHOR

Brian Meehl has published four novels with Random House: *Out of Patience, Suck It Up, Suck It Up and Die,* and *You Don't Know About Me.* The first was a Junior Library Guild Selection, the last won a Blue Ribbon from the Bulletin for the Center for Children's Books, while two of them garnered starred reviews in *Publishers Weekly.*

In a former incarnation, Meehl was a puppeteer on *Sesame Street* and in Jim Henson films, including *The Dark Crystal.* His transition from puppets to pen included writing for television shows such as *The Magic School Bus* and *Between the Lions,* for which he won three Emmys.

Meehl lives in Connecticut and is writing his next two books: *Blowback '63* and *Blowback '94.*

For more, visit blowbacktrilogy.com and brianmeehl.com.